# ANNIHILATED

## Samson McCune

*To my feet, who supported me far more than my knees, but far less than my family.*

# CONTENTS

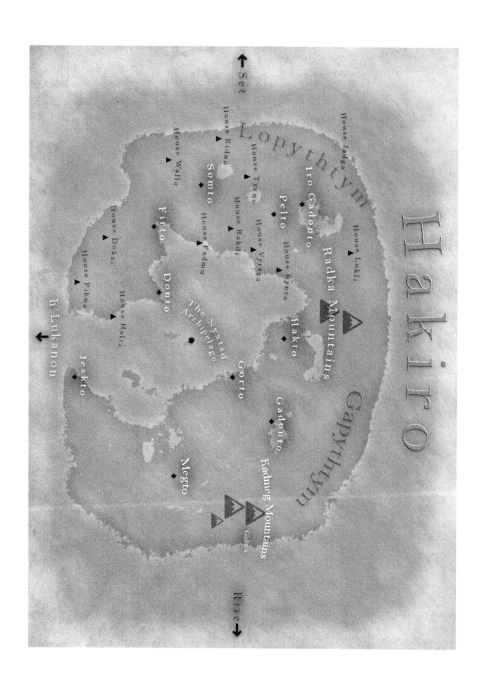

# A GUIDE TO DOK: THE LANGUAGE OF HAKIRO

I would like to begin by explaining that I am not fluent in Dok; no one is, that I know of. It's a dead language. In this sense, there are a lot of things that we don't know about it. The grammatical structure and the alphabet used for writing are easy enough to decipher; it's the speaking that is difficult. Mostly because no one who was fluent in it is still alive. There seems to have been a cataclysmic event that ended their culture, but some remnants of it still survive to this day.

Dok means "word" from what I've been able to tell. This isn't much of a surprise, as it was a very primitive language. Some historians believe that it was the first language to be used throughout all of Hakiro, meaning "land of two." Due to the simplicity of the vocabulary, I am going to make some assumptions about the speaking system based on the written language.

I am going to claim that it is a phonetic language. This is mostly for ease of pronunciation among the older Dok names that we still use today. Some people, highly educated scholars included, disagree on how Dok places are pronounced, so I hope to put these concerns to bed. The term *phonetic* mostly just applies to the way the vowel sounds are used within the language. The "h" is not silent, the "g" sounds like a hard g, and so forth. "Th" is one of the only consonant combinations, and it sounds just like the beginning of the word *thistle*. The consonants have no special characteristics. The "y" is being counted as a vowel, always. The "a" makes an *ah* sound, like an exhale. The "e" makes an *eh* sound, like in egg. The "i" makes an *ee* sound. "Y" sounds like *ih*, "o" sounds like *oh*, and "u" sounds like *oo*. Some examples of a few Dok words pronounced would be as follows: "Gaz" is *gahz*, and "fir" sounds the same as the common word *fear*.

Below are the most basic roots for Dok that I have found. This list also includes word modifiers and verb modifiers.

Roots
- Sky: pyth
- Land: hak
- World/All: gaz
- Fire: hel
- Air: tir
- Water: sig
- Metal: lyf
- Stone: meg
- Magic: nyx
- Pain: kad
- Book: fot
- Tree: pel
- Word: dok
- Gem: fir
- Ocean: don
- Field: gor
- Cliff: som

General Vocabulary
- Sword: jesk
- One: gro
- Two: iro

- Three: hid
- Four: pact
- Five: jod
- Six: kaf
- Seven: tyd
- Eight: len
- Nine: fir
- Ten: sot
- Eleven: wyr
- Spear: hrithak
- Shield: grathyk
- Monster: fryd

Verb Modifiers

- Basic verb modifier: ta
- Past tense: tak
- Future tense: tag

Word Modifiers

- Negative/Dark: ga
- Anti: do
- Positive/Light: lo
- Hot: ki
- Cold: ra
- Commander: kav
- Lieutenant: ri
- King: lok
- Queen: lyk
- Kingdom: tym
- Person who: tad
- People of: tan
- God of: rad
- Power: ka
- Lord of: ti
- City of: to

Miscellaneous

- First-person pronoun: rom
- First-person possessive: ram

- Second-person pronoun: dyr
- Second-person possessive: dir
- Male third-person pronoun: dar
- Female third-person pronoun: dal
- Third-person possessive: dab

This list gives a general idea of the most commonly used words or word types in the archives we have that are written in Dok. It does not, however, list how one would be able to construct a new word. With this list, it is possible to write the word *Sun*, even though the word is actively absent. From what I can tell, those who spoke this language had few words to choose from and became creative with descriptors. They would say "lopyth" instead of Sun. This works because the word modifier *lo* makes something positive, and *pyth* means sky. In their minds, the positive sky was the Sun, or *lopyth*.

Now, the rules around word modification are strange. There is some leniency, but consistency exists across texts. For example, word modifiers that use two letters and are abstract descriptors go before the main root. This would include *ga* through *ra* on the list above. All of the others on the list would go after. Unfortunately, Dok is a language of feeling. It makes sense to those who can write in it, but being able to explain all of the rules is difficult. Exposure is important for understanding those rules.

The verb modifiers all go after the word, which is helpful. The problem is how basic the basic verb modifier is. *Ta* applies the idea "to" to the root that it is written behind, but most of the roots are nouns, so this allows for a lot of interpretation. "Megta" could mean *to mine*, which is what it was commonly used for, or it could also mean *to stone*, as in: to stone someone to death. The possessives and pronouns are always by themselves; they are their own words. Dok is so heavily reliant upon culture to bring its words meaning. This is why no one still speaks it today; the people of Hakiro have lost their connection to the words and ideas backed up by it.

I hope this short guide can help you in your search for what is right and wrong.

-    Avyl

# PROLOGUE

*Some people spend their lives fighting. Others spend their lives being led as if they were cattle. The people who rise, the people who become great, aren't remarkable. Sometimes there will be a particularly strong warrior or a brilliant scholar. However, the characteristic that sets the greatest heroes of history apart from the common folk is intuition—the ability to know when to fight and when to be fought for.*

- *The Freer of Fools*

Rykar sprinted through the woods, his heart in his throat. His sister ran close behind him, but she wasn't as fast as he was, so he had to slow down to allow her to catch her breath.

He was nearly hyperventilating and unaware if it was because of panic or exhaustion. The nearest village, Tirano, was only a little bit farther away. They could make it there and back before the Sun set, he knew it.

Still running, he leaped over a small creek, carrying enough speed to continue seamlessly. At the last second, he decided to turn around and check on his sister to make sure she could keep up.

She wasn't too far behind, but it was apparent that this pace was taking a toll on her eight-year-old body. She looked as if she was going to faint any second. Her usually well-kept, brown hair was in shambles, and her bright face had gone pale. She wasn't going to be able to keep this up for much longer.

His body was far fitter, as he was beginning to set, so his father had said. He was turning into a man. Plus, he was eleven, so he had an advantage over his sister in age.

"Nyr, we gotta go," he pleaded, almost in tears.

"I . . . can't . . . keep . . . going . . ." she gasped.

"C'mon. Only a little farther, you can do it," he said, trying to encourage her.

They kept going, except this time it was at a much slower pace. Much to Rykar's dismay, their bodies had limits, and the initial boost of adrenaline had faded long ago. His legs felt like they were being dragged in mud, and they grew heavier with each step.

He felt a sob rise in his throat as he fell and began crawling. They had done a horrible job planning the pace for the journey, but they had no other choice. Their parents needed them.

Slowly rising, he realized something. His motions became reenergized and frantic. Where the Hel was Nyral?

"NYR!" he screamed. "PLEASE, WHERE ARE YOU?"

He ran out of breath quickly and stopped to listen. The forest was silent. Not so much as a leaf moved. There were no gusts of wind or noises that sounded like animals. At that moment, the forest felt completely and utterly dead.

Suddenly he heard an ear-splitting scream followed by a roar. His heart nearly stopped. Every Instinct in his body was telling him to get away—to run, to find safety. He was not ready to be mauled by a beast, whatever it was.

He ignored his Instincts and summoned what energy he had left to sprint straight toward the noise. His sister would not be killed on his watch.

After a few moments of running, he slowed at a clearing only to find a grizzly bear on its hind legs, a few strides in front of Nyral. She was hugging her legs in the fetal position, and her face was hidden in between her knees. From the sound of it, she appeared to be crying.

The beast was huge, over twice as tall as he was. The primal power it exuded seemed unreal. It roared, shaking Rykar to his core. Its bloodlust seemed endless, and it was targeting Nyral.

He took a second to try to figure out what had happened. It was unusual for bears to attack unprovoked, and Nyral was an incredibly gentle girl. Rykar couldn't imagine a universe in which she would attempt to attack, or even harm, anything.

Then he realized that the bear was a mom. A few cubs huddled behind her, and it all made sense. Nyral was known to be attracted to small, cute creatures. She had probably seen one of the cubs and tried to pet it, which antagonized the mother. The bear's stance helped him confirm the gender.

Suddenly the bear got back down on all fours and began rushing toward Nyr. It seemed like it was planning an attack. For a second, Rykar found this funny. A huge bear seemed to think that his tiny sister was a threat and was choosing to kill her.

Then reality sank in. *That bear . . . is trying to kill . . . my sister.* Rykar panicked. In no time at all, his amusement transformed into horror. How would he save her? If she were killed, what would he tell his parents?

Like a snap, his fear turned into anger and motivation. He would NOT let her die here. She didn't deserve this.

He was too far away to do anything. His emotions were cycling incredibly quickly, shifting from hope to hopelessness in a matter of moments, constantly.

He closed his eyes and wished he knew what to do.

Suddenly he heard a loud noise to the side.

*Another bear?* he thought in a panic. He certainly couldn't deal with a second, and he was far enough away that he was confident the mother bear couldn't run to him first.

He opened his eyes and looked around. His sister was sitting less than two steps to one side, and the bear—the only bear—was the same distance to his other side.

"How did I get here?" he whispered to himself.

He turned to the bear, who was now charging, and felt his body fill with power. He couldn't explain it. It was almost like he was a sail filled by the wind when the air was stagnant before.

Time slowed. The bear was in slow motion, galloping toward him and his sister. Nyral was peeking out above one of her arms, and a look of awe seemed to form on her face as she noticed Rykar for the first time.

After a moment, the bear got within arm's reach of Rykar. He stepped to the side, and to his surprise, even though time appeared to have been slowed, he could still move normally.

He walked up to the bear's eye, and with as much force as he could muster, he punched it.

Rykar seriously underestimated his strength. He felt his fist collide with the bear's skull and pulverize it. The bone shattered on impact, blowing the creature's head off at the same time.

This should have surprised him. He wasn't powerful enough to do this. He didn't think anyone was. Unfortunately for the corpse of the bear and the logical side of his mind, he was in a trance. One where he would stop at nothing to save his sister.

He kicked the dead bear in the ribs, feeling a similar sensation of shattering. The broken ribs fell under his foot, scratching his shin. He pulled out one of his legs to see that it was, in fact, cut, but he was unsure whose blood was whose. He moved on to the bear's thighs, crushing them with his feet while he screamed bloody murder.

He did this for a little while longer, moving around, systematically breaking the body of an already-dead creature. After not too long, it was looking less like a bear and more like a mess of blood and bone.

In the midst of his hyper-focused rage, something tapped his shoulder. He whipped around, backhanding whatever it was.

Time stopped. He stared at Nyral with a look of horror on his face. He felt her back snap as his hand connected. Her face was still innocent, still childish. Still pure.

His understanding of time sped back up, and she immediately collapsed. He rushed to help her.

"Please," he heard her whisper.

"Nyr," he sobbed. "Are you ok?" He knew she wasn't. He knew that he had broken her, that she would probably die. At best she would never walk again.

"Please, go away," she whispered as she passed out.

Her fear of him broke Rykar's heart.

He didn't know how to carry someone with a broken back. Not knowing what to do, he grabbed the inside of her knee as well as one of her wrists. He easily hefted her over his head onto his back to carry her.

Panicking again, he sprinted back the way they came. His sails were still full, and he made great time. It felt good to be able to move like that.

He got home in a matter of moments. What had taken him almost a full day before took him a fraction of the time now.

Standing on his front porch, reality crashed down on him. His parents needed the medicine that only the other village had. He had broken Nyral's back, and she would probably die as a result. He was about to set her down on the porch and sprint to the other village when he felt the energy dissipate. The wind had left his sails.

With dread filling his chest, he opened the door to their

small but comfortable home. He took one step inside, and his worst fears were realized.

His parents were lying in their bed, faces pale, not breathing. Their heads were turned toward each other, as if to say to the world that even in their last moments they were happy just to be together. He was too late.

Still on his back, Nyral stirred.

"GET OUT!" she screamed. "GO AWAY! I HATE YOU! WHO EVEN ARE YOU? YOU KILLED MOM! YOU KILLED DAD!"

Rykar set her down on the bed and stared at her. He couldn't process this. He wasn't made for it. He wasn't strong enough. He didn't know how.

Not thinking, he turned and sprinted out the front door, the familiar power helping him along. He ran across the countryside until long into the night, thinking about how he had failed, and how he was truly an awful person.

As his mind disconnected from the present, the one thing that kept echoing through his mind was a single, distant thought: *you killed Mom and Dad,* almost as if he could still hear Nyral's pained screams.

# START OF PART I

# THE HUNT

*Hope: the bulwark that protects the hearts of men from the depths of despair. I only wonder what place it has in the mind of a general.*
-    Drydnar Vyrtra

**7 Years Later**

The wind howled through the trees behind Rykar. He pulled his black robe close to his body. The sheer cold of winter in the mountains—at night, to make matters worse—was a difficult burden to bear. Unlike most of the people in Gidura, his woodland village, he loved the cold. Unfortunately for this preference, he also liked avoiding frostbite, and the world was becoming dangerously chilly. The snow was up to his ankles, and his feet were freezing.

Waist-high icicles sprouting from the ground guided him through the tundra. The monster of pure ice, Fryd, was the source. He gave off a powerful aura of frost that made tracking him easy. For a hunter, this was convenient. Rykar always knew where his target was, which was the hardest part of the hunt for him. Since he was someone who thrived on curiosity, however, Fryd was irritatingly mysterious.

Even though he was hired to hunt the beast, he had little to no information concerning Fryd. He had found a letter on his front porch a few mornings prior. All it said was:

*Hunter,*

*I have been told that you are skilled in both stealth and combat. I would like to hire you to claim the life of a beast known as the Gasigfryd. It is an elemental being, made from ice and water, and is going to cause untold damage. If you accept and are successful, I will pay you with something more valuable than all the gold in Hakiro or even on Gaz. The Gasigfryd drops off spikes that are easy to track. There should be some outside of Gidura, for reference. Good luck.*

He wished he could have been given more information in the letter. Rykar hated the fact that he didn't know who his client was. Mysteries were always difficult for him to stomach, but he wouldn't be able to do anything about that one, so he did his best to forget about it.

The other thing that he didn't like was the Gasigfryd. When the client named it, Rykar felt like he had a connection to him and immediately thought of the beast as a living creature instead of a target. That annoyed him. Plus, Rykar wanted to know about the source of Fryd's power. The nobility had access to nyxka—the powers of the gods—but Rykar had never heard of an animal with similar abilities.

Without warning, the forest ended, and he stepped into a field. The night sky was beautiful beyond comparison. In front of him, the stars shone brightly in his blue eyes. Rykar walked farther through the snow into the clearing and took a moment to see what the rest of the heavens looked like.

Behind him, he could see the light of the Moon appear over the peaks of the Kadmeg Mountains. Hakirons, like himself, believed that the Moon was a goddess of pure destruction. She knew how to break rocks to create valleys for rivers in the same way that the Sun could create land. They went by the names Gapythrad, for the Moon, and Lopythrad, for the Sun, when they were prayed to. Rykar didn't worship either, but he believed in them. How could he not? They could be seen in the sky each day and night. They certainly existed.

He smiled and turned around, following the upside-down icicle path again. They were sharp enough to impale him if he fell on them, so Rykar made an effort to be careful.

The more he moved through the field, the less comfortable he felt. The world was blank and empty. The only things that stood out were him, the ice spikes, and the forest behind. Rykar hated standing out like he was. His whole life, he had naturally avoided intense attention. The darkness of night shrouded by the forest was where he felt comfortable. His dark hair and average size allowed him to be stealthy. Surrounded by the whiteness of snow while he wore a black robe, though, Rykar was extremely easy to spot. He hadn't planned on walking in a snowfield.

Then, when his eyes were turned away from the sky, something caught his attention. It almost looked like a star had fallen out of the sky, but Rykar couldn't tell. *Focus,* he thought. There was a battle ahead of him. Whether it be with the debilitating cold of winter or Fryd, Rykar didn't yet know. He just had to keep moving, do his best to keep out distractions.

Except, there the light returned. On the horizon, it bounded through Rykar's vision. Confusion flooded through his mind. *What the Hel is that?* The light circled Rykar from a distance, keeping to the edge of the world. Its hue mimicked that of a star, but it was something else. Something far, far stranger.

Rykar turned as it passed farther and farther behind him. After a moment, it jumped up to the top of the Kadmeg Mountains and stopped there, hidden by the Moonlight. Rykar knew that he had to continue, to keep moving to avoid hypo-thermia, but something about the light was fascinating, so he waited to see if anything more would happen. He hoped to learn more about the magical light before he caught Fryd and had to return to a simpler life in Gidura. No longer able to see the light, Rykar looked down, away from the top of the mountain.

*RUMBLE*

The ground shook underneath Rykar's feet. The trees at the base of the mountains started to shake, and snow fell from their branches. Moment by moment, the rumbling grew louder.

Snow broke through the trees with a momentous crash. The forest splintered, shattering under the weight of the ice. Rykar looked up to see the side of the Kadmeg Mountains falling, and he realized that an avalanche was upon him.

"What the Hel!" Rykar screamed as he turned and sprinted away from the coming wave of destruction.

The deafening noise of the avalanche was overpowering. It rocked Rykar to his core. Each thump beat itself into his chest. The white noise took over Rykar's mind, drowning out any semblance of thought. Able to understand the true danger of what was behind him, Rykar turned away and took off into a sprint as a familiar power surged through his body.

The snow slowed him down just enough that he couldn't break away from the speed of the icefall. If it hadn't been there, Rykar was sure that he would have been able to escape, but alas, luck was not on his side.

Each step brought doom one step closer to colliding with Rykar. The roar of death grew louder as Rykar's breath quickened. Fatigue set in, and he found that he couldn't keep running. He stopped to try to catch his breath, but at the last moment, he realized that this was a mistake. A wall of snow hurtled toward him, shattering the icicles Fryd had created. After what felt like forever, it hit him, and everything went black.

---

Rykar felt a dark presence watching him. He tried to run from it, but it only grew stronger. He frantically searched around himself, looking for a place to hide from the desolation it brought with it.

Suddenly the whole world began to fade to black as a dark mist swirled through his vision. All of his Instincts told him that he had to flee, to find a safe place free from the darkness. Everywhere he looked was full of what he could only describe as despair.

He felt his heartbeat racing, his breath becoming more shallow and quick as hyperventilation found its way into his chest. *It can't kill you,* he thought, attempting to reassure himself. *It's only the darkness. The Sun will rise, and you will be free of this torture.*

All at once, the black wave hit him. His life was agony, every breath, every thought, bringing him more and more pain. Moments turned into an eternity, and it started to feel like the night would last forever. The Sun felt like a distant memory. One of love and life. One that he would never be able to return to.

He noticed a gradient forming on the horizon. Slowly, an orange-yellow light made its way into the black skyscape. Rykar felt a wave of relief. He was finally going to be saved, to be free from the destructive nature of the darkness.

The light approached. Rykar felt its warmth and life as it got within an arm's length of him. It seemed to reach out to him, offering its help. No matter how much he wanted to or how much he willed himself to do so, he physically could not reach back. He didn't know how to reciprocate the touch.

Hope seemed disappointed and began to back away. It left much more quickly than it arrived and only took a few moments to completely fade into black.

Rykar had no response. No feeling. He just sat there with

wide eyes, questioning what he was supposed to do, how he was supposed to respond, what he could have done differently. He wished, more than anything, that he could go back and fix it.

He fell to his knees, the hopelessness sinking in. The light would never return. He needed to be free of this prison, but if that symbol of hope couldn't save him, then nothing could. Rykar looked straight up, facing the sky and the center of the dark mists. He screamed as hard as he could, but no sound came.

Feeling defeated, he held his head in his hands and only sobs followed.

---

The avalanche felt as rough as it looked. Rykar tumbled through it, being thrown around like a small toy. He felt weak, insignificant, and at that moment, he learned how strong nature was.

Having difficulty breathing, Rykar decided that he would need to get his head above the snow to survive. He would have to worry about freezing to death later; breathing was his priority.

Something hit him in the shoulder. It hurt like Hel, and Rykar was pretty sure he felt a pop when it happened. He tried to move the arm but found that the movement was restricted. Something was wrong with it; he just didn't know what.

With effort, he tried to swim toward the surface of the wave of ice. It was hard to tell if he was making a difference by doing so, but there was nothing else he could do. As he swam, he was pelted by various pieces of debris from within the avalanche, which bruised and scratched him.

Finally, his head broke through the surface, and he could breathe again. He tried to continue rising so he could get out of the area completely, but the snow started to settle. An insane amount of snow and ice was compressing itself, creating a compact material that was as tough as some stone. He was able to breathe, so that was good, but he didn't have a way to get out. The pressure of the remnants of the avalanche was keeping his body restrained.

Rykar was becoming claustrophobic due to his lack of mobility. Panicking, he found a strength inside of him that allowed him to move a little bit. He capitalized on the space to generate speed and increase his momentum. He was aggressively wiggling to freedom.

To his luck, wiggling worked, and soon he had enough room to climb out of the hole he had created. He brushed himself off and looked to see how much the avalanche had altered the world.

Trees lay uprooted among the debris left behind. Rocks, chunks of ice, and various other broken pieces of the land were scattered throughout the area. Rykar couldn't believe how powerful a simple icefall was.

His mind broke away from the avalanche as he remembered why he was out there in the first place. Finding the Kadmeg Mountains, Rykar reoriented himself and tried to locate the icicle path once more.

He took a step and realized that his body was not ok. His ankle had practically yelled at him when he put weight on it. One of his shoulders felt off, but not broken. He didn't have full mobility in a lot of his joints, but he didn't feel any severe injuries.

After a moment of limping through the corpse of a once-lively landscape, Rykar jumped down from the snow pile only to find what he was looking for. Fryd's ice spikes continued just to the edge of the leftovers of the avalanche.

Rykar followed them, noticing something unnerving as he went. It appeared as if red drops of liquid were now going where Fryd went. As a hunter, Rykar knew that this could mean a few things. For one, a predator could be tracking Fryd and was impaled by a spike, but it still wished to continue hunting. The second and more likely option, in Rykar's opinion, was that Fryd was bleeding. He had probably been affected by the power of the avalanche.

Rykar followed the trail a bit farther and, sure enough, there was his prey. Unlike the description Rykar had been given, Fryd did not appear to be made of ice or snow. He was a yak—an animal that lived in the Kadmeg Mountains—that also had special powers.

Fryd's breath was ragged. His majestic, white coat was getting infected by the redness inside him, and even though Rykar was supposed to hunt him, he felt sadness as Fryd's beauty began to fade. He limped up to Fryd and, for some reason, began to stroke his head. He didn't know why he did it. Maybe he was trying to comfort Fryd as he experienced this incredibly painful death. Regardless of the reason, it just felt right.

Rykar looked down at his face, and, as he saw him suffer, he knew what must be done. He pulled a knife out of his sack, then reached down and slit Fryd's throat. Rykar closed Fryd's eyes with his good hand and then proceeded to close his own.

He remembered a time when he had felt like he was almost fully grown, like the world would soon make sense. All of that felt foreign to him now as he held Fryd's powerful head in his lap. The fragility of life humbled him, and he realized that no matter how old he was, a part of him would always be a confused child.

"Not only do I take your horns as mine, but I also take your life, your legacy. Never have I seen such majesty and grace within a wild animal. As you travel up to the stars to meet with the Pythrad, I shall do my best to share your power with the world so that you will never be forgotten," Rykar said. Even though the words were improvised, they came out of his mouth as if they had been recited a thousand times, for they felt right.

Finally opening his eyes, he looked back down at Fryd and began sawing off one of his horns with the knife he still held. Destroying his body felt disrespectful, but Rykar figured the only way to confirm the kill was with a piece of him.

Right as he was placing the horn in his bag, he noticed something out of his peripheral vision. There was the light again, except this time it appeared to be moving toward him. Rykar pulled out another knife, preparing himself for the worst, hoping that it meant him no harm.

As it got closer, he could tell that it was a man holding a torch that gave off a silverish-blue light. The man was moving inhumanly fast, much quicker than anything Rykar had ever seen before. Soon he arrived, and Rykar finally got a good look at him. The stranger was wearing a loose-fitting, gray robe. His white hair and eyes were certainly a mystery, but Rykar doubted that he would learn anything about them. And his eyes weren't totally white. They had the normal white part on the outside and a black outline where most people's color started, but instead of brown or blue on the inside, they were white again. Even so, the most peculiar thing about him was perhaps his presence. The man was barely any taller than Rykar, but he felt much larger, like his existence was one of power, and he wanted Rykar to know it.

"Who are you?" Rykar asked.

"You have been recognized as worthy by Pythti. Simply say the words 'I accept your offer of divinity,' and you will be granted great power and a role in the Warrior Division of the Nyxtad Collective," the peculiar man answered.

Just as Rykar was about to ask another question, in an attempt to fight back some of his curiosity, the man leaped away. Rykar looked around, hoping he would return, but deep down he knew that he wouldn't.

"What on Gaz are you talking about!?" he muttered to himself after a moment of confusion.

# ASCENDANCE

*To create. To destroy. All mortal beings reside on one side of this duality. To prove otherwise is to prove yourself divine.*
- *Pythti*

Sunbeam hit Ghar in one of his golden eyes, awakening him from his slumber. He briefly forgot where he was, but the feel of the wooden desk against his face and the sound of his tutor lecturing quickly reminded him.

It wasn't uncommon for him to fall asleep in class. It was becoming more and more frequent for him to grow bored with the content and drift away in his mind. He soon realized it wasn't because he hated to learn. He spent most of his free time pushing his mind to gain new information. The class was just . . . dull.

He looked around, trying to reorient himself and figure out what Wyndel was teaching him and his brother that day. Brushing his golden hair from his eyes, he tried his best to look like he had always been mentally present in class.

Unlike Ghar, Nadren was incredibly attentive. He could always be seen studying, answering questions, and being a model for nobility. He was a considerably better student than Ghar, usually catching on to new material far faster and being able to recite more of it. Ghar, however, didn't think that made him smarter. *He just cares more*, Ghar always thought to himself.

Right as Ghar felt his mind drift off again, this time into the nuances of his nyxka, Wyndel interrupted him.

"Master Rakdi, I believe I asked you a question," she admonished.

Ghar shot a glance at his brother, hoping that she was talking to him. He had no such luck. Silently panicking, he searched his mind for any memories of questions she had asked him. Unfortunately, nothing came up.

"Do you mind repeating the question?" Ghar asked, hopeful.

Wyndel looked almost angry, but Ghar knew how she felt. He was used to being a disappointment, to people knowing he would fail. To most people, he was a small, funny second son. Nadren was the golden boy, the heir to the house, and who many believed to be the next Sun King. Living in his shadow was almost unbearable.

"Please list the twelve major noble houses of Lopythtym," she repeated, although he was still unsure of whether or not she had asked the question in the first place.

Like clockwork, Ghar recalled and recited the answer.

"Vyrtra, Rakdi, Pikna, Halti, Tyrno, Dokzi, Wafla, Fadmu, Kidno, Jadga, Lokli, and finally Rynta. Although the Vyrtra are the only ones we need to pay attention to," he intoned.

Nadren gave him a look of approval, seemingly proud that he knew twelve basic family names. Small gestures like this always rubbed Ghar the wrong way, but he contained his frustration and returned his attention to Wyndel.

"While it may be true that your attention should be

focused on the structure of the Vyrtra as of right now, it is important to be extremely familiar with all twelve. You never know who may ascend to the throne in the event of the death of our dear Lopythlok Vyrtra," she explained, although Ghar already knew this.

Their lesson went on a bit longer, mostly covering succession rights, as well as some of the main purposes of the noble houses. Most people found that part dull, but Ghar always thought it was important.

For what seemed like the thousandth time, Wyndel explained that the passing of the throne was not by physical blood, but rather by divine blood. The person who held the blood of the Lopythlok could summon the strongest Sun Avatar and therefore ascend to the throne.

That part always interested Ghar no matter how many times it was repeated. Each time, he felt as if he could feel the position given to him as it was being explained, and each time, he imagined his ascension.

In his mind's eye, he saw the crowd cheering as he entered Pelto, their capital. The grand heights of the Pelrad grew into the heavens, and he could feel the Sun beating down on his face as he accepted his place as the leader of the people.

Eventually, Wyndel indicated that class was over, and Ghar left the small room, beginning to feel invigorated. One of his favorite things, besides studying nyxka, was imagining Pelto and its reception for him.

As he was about to wander the halls of the mansion, keeping the mental image of him as king in mind, Ghar was stopped just outside of the classroom by Wyndel.

"I know how much you think you're in the shadow of your brother," she began. This hit Ghar full in the face as he was unaware that he was that transparent. He stared at her in shock as she continued.

"I know how it feels. To see someone better than you at what you love, being revered by the people you need love from. It sucks, I know. But Hel, man, try not to fall asleep in class.

Those moments are what people hear about and see, and they are why Nadren would be a better king than you," she finished, quickly walking away from Ghar in the opposite direction that he was going.

Suddenly, imagining himself as king felt less like reality and more like a dream. He knew, in his heart of hearts, that Nadren was smarter, faster, stronger, more charismatic, and mostly better than he was at everything.

While this was frustrating to think about, he tried to keep in mind that the ascension to the Sun Throne was not based on tests of personal merit of all kinds—just one. There were not always great kings, but there had always been powerful ones. The Lopythlok was picked based on nyxka mastery.

Truly, the emotional process he experienced in those few minutes was amazing. He quickly went from elation to despair to a type of hope in the form of ambition and Knowledge.

He figured that with a few more months of training, he would be able to summon a much more powerful Sun Avatar than Nadren. He knew that he had a book full of exercises and a training plan, with the idea that Frakt Vyrtra, the Lopythlok, wouldn't die for a little while yet.

Unfortunately for him, Nadren was incredibly talented with his own nyxka as well as everything else he did. Even more unfortunate for Ghar was the group of men in gray robes running through the courtyard, announcing the death of the king.

---

Ghar followed his father down the hall toward the holy chambers of the mansion. The men in gray robes, who remained a mystery to Ghar, seemed to float down the hallway behind Ghar. Nadren was standing beside him with a few of their other "siblings" who were chosen by their father.

None of them were related by blood except for Ghar and

Nadren. The rest were found in villages or settlements around the world and happened to have a nyxka. Ghar thought that his father did this to increase the chances of Rakdi ascension, but he denied it. In the past, there had been wars, known as the Nyxka Wars, where noble houses had fought over ownership of villages to increase their chances of getting children with nyxka. Drydnar's descendant, Ryvnel Vyrtra, had fixed the problem by defining borders for noble houses so their territories no longer overlapped.

Eventually, they arrived in the room of worship, of power. Even just stepping into the room always made Ghar feel stronger, safer, and revitalized. Strangely, it did not seem to have a similar effect on his peers.

Smiling, Ghar looked upon the beautiful, stained glass depiction of the Hakiron religion. In the middle was the Pythrad. A gray being, completely detached from the morals of humanity, the Pythrad was said to be the one who saw people after death. To his side was the bright Lopythrad. The Sun God was thought to have been made by the Pythrad. He had been crafted from pure creation. On the Pythrad's other side stood the Gapythrad, the goddess of the Moon. Also created by the Pythrad, she was a destroyer through and through.

Ghar smiled. The use of color was beautiful; the artist who made it had a good vision when he built it. A perfect gradient from black to white traversed the glass, with cool colors on one side, grayness in the middle, and warm colors on the other side.

Ghar shifted his attention away from the artwork to the situation at hand. He was excited but nervous to get a chance to ascend to the position of Lopythlok. As everyone filtered into the room, Ghar's father stepped in front of them to deliver what he assumed would be a heavily recited speech. His father was nothing if not loquacious.

"You stand here before me on the precipice of greatness," his father began. "You will leave this room as a king, a nobleman, or a failure. It is up to you to decide which. Long has the Vyrtra dynasty reigned, taking the power and trust in the Rakdi name.

"Long have we waited, planning for this, knowing that one day we will rise from the grave that was dug for our glory and prevail. Only we can lead this world into the future with the grace of a dancer and the power of the Gods. Only we can hold the throne for Lopythtym to be called a true paradise."

Ghar's father always had a way of moving Ghar. The way he emphasized certain parts, the speech patterns, his unusually large stature—all of it came together to make an incredibly charismatic leader. Ghar felt his arms, noting that not for the first time, his father had given him goosebumps.

"Which one of you will rise?" his father continued, yelling this time. "Which one of you will ASCEND? WHICH ONE OF YOU WILL PROVE YOUR WORTH AND WANDER INTO REALMS ONLY KNOWN TO GODS?" Ghar's father looked down theatrically, then looked up a tiny bit, meeting the eyes of a few of the children.

"Show me," he whispered with a smile after a moment of silence.

After a brief tick of a nearby clock, the whole room broke out into applause. The fire they felt in their hearts, the one that pushed people to great things, seemed to have been handed up from the depths of Hel itself, for its power and heat could not be extinguished.

One of the men in gray robes walked toward the front of the room and began to speak. Listening to a boring orator after an exhilarating one was like eating gourmet food and then licking dirt. It just felt wrong, like you were disgracing the legacy of the former.

"The first one to be examined will be Thrax," the man said in a very monotonous voice.

One of Ghar's adoptive siblings walked up to the man. He was quite young, almost at his rising—the change from a boy to a man. His nyxka was quite underdeveloped, so Ghar was confident that he would have little to no success in summoning a Sun Avatar at all.

Just as Ghar suspected, Thrax could not complete the task. He strained and forced, seemingly trying to push the Sun Avatar out of him, but to no avail. He just didn't know how to do it.

A few of the other children tried as well and had similar results. Ghar was surprised to see how weak they were, but he also realized that he didn't know all of his siblings. His father had been busy while Ghar was stuck studying.

"Uhhh, the next one will be Ghar," the man grunted.

Ghar walked over, trying to hide his nerves beneath a blanket of confidence. Slowly, he closed his eyes and began allowing energy to gather inside of his body. He drew it in from all around. The room, the planet, and the sky itself all lent him some power for the next technique.

After he felt he had enough, he released it in one quick breath. All of the tension, fear, jealousy, it all faded in that one moment. He opened his eyes only to see the brilliant, yellow light of the Sun inside the very room.

This did not come as a surprise to him. He knew that he could summon a Sun Avatar. It wasn't uncommon for there to be many noblemen who could summon one. That was presumably why the men in the gray robes came to measure the size and power of each one.

"Size, 18 rays, power, 24 rays," the man announced. It was said that the day Drydnar Vyrtra awoke to begin the Vyrtra dynasty, a ray of Sunlight hit him in the face. That was the history behind their choice of distance measurement, although this had always confused Ghar.

He was about 10 rays tall, being well below average for men who had finished their rising. Nadren was 11 rays tall, which was a little bit above average. Their father was nearly 12.

Ghar also didn't know why size and power had the same units, but a power-to-size ratio of 24 to 18 was incredibly rare, so Ghar was pleased with his score.

He walked back to where he was standing, and the man called Nadren to the front. Being the last person to go besides their father, all Ghar had to do was score better than Nadren, and then he would be the person they would send in for the spot of the king. Both hope and fear found their way into his heart and mind.

Nadren approached his spot to perform, appearing extremely confident. He wasted no time beginning, summoning his Sun Avatar almost immediately.

"Size, 16 rays, power, 14 rays," the man said.

Ghar felt a tense breath leave his body, incredibly relieved that he had won.

"Oh wait, this is new," the man muttered.

Ghar looked over to Nadren. His Sun Avatar appeared to be growing and getting more powerful.

"Wait! What's happening?" Ghar yelled. "I won, right? Mine was bigger after the count!"

After a few more moments of growth, Nadren's Sun Avatar was done. It was full-sized and much larger than anything or anyone Ghar had ever seen.

"New size, 42 rays, new power, 60 rays," the man muttered.

Ghar felt his heart drop. His hopes, his dreams, and his future seemed to shatter before him. He held his head in his hands, and everything went silent. At that moment between moments, he was truly and utterly lost.

Only later did Ghar hear that this was the most intensely powerful Sun Avatar ever, excluding Drydnar Vyrtra's ascension exam.

His father ran to Nadren and held him in a deep embrace. The adopted children half-heartedly cheered, knowing that he would become king. Even the men in gray robes, who at first glance appeared to be emotionless, seemed impressed and even happy.

Ghar slowly walked out of the room with a blank expression on his face. He felt disconnected from his body, almost as if at that moment the seal that held his mind to his body was breaking. He imagined that that was a lot like how dying felt —the mind slipping away from the body with numbness being all that remained.

As he wandered around the mansion, he thought about almost nothing. His mind remained empty except for random sparks of anger or sadness. He truly had no idea what to do or where to go.

More mindless wandering and he found himself at the entrance to the library. He didn't know what brought him there or why he bothered, but he entered and began browsing the collection.

He walked over to his favorite section almost by Instinct. Realizing it probably couldn't hurt to try to take his mind off of things, he picked up his favorite volume and began reading.

*In the Words of a God* by Theodar Vyrtra was always an interesting read for Ghar. The biography of Drydnar Vyrtra's life with a focus on him after his ascension had reshaped Ghar's worldview multiple times over.

He flipped the cover of the book over and saw the famous quote that had pulled him into the book the very first time.

"The only difference between the man who succeeds and the man who fails is one of them forgets to keep moving forward," he read aloud.

He felt tears streaming down his face as he forced his eyes to run over the quote, again and again, drilling it into his mind. At that moment, he hated himself. He hated his weakness, his laziness, but most of all, he hated his ineptitude. Deep down he always thought that the Sun would smile on him, granting him the role of king.

Never would he have guessed that Nadren would be rewarded for his hard work.

He slammed the book shut and ran back to his room with it under his arm.

Standing on the balcony, the Sun shone right into his

eyes, but he didn't even care. He deserved the pain for his shortsightedness; he had to learn to accept it.

"WHY AM I EVEN HERE?" he screamed. "I'M NOBODY! NO GOOD! WORTHLESS! THEY THINK I CAN'T DO ANYTHING RIGHT! EVERYONE KNOWS I'M A JOKE!"

Slowly, the screams of self-loathing turned into sobs, and he collapsed, whispering to himself, "Will I ever be accepted . . . ?"

# TAKEN

*The greatest generals aren't always brilliant tacticians or strong men. They are the people who can inspire their soldiers to walk up to death with smiles on their faces, to fight when nothing could be more certain than their demise.*
-    *Grax Rakdi*

The trek back to Gidura was much easier than it had been when he was following Fryd. Even with his injuries, it took him less time to return to his village because he could map a straight path. Often the trail that Fryd left would go in circles or even cross back over itself. Needless to say, the efficiency of a planned route was definitely on Rykar's side.

After almost a day and a half of straight walking, he saw Gidura at last. It was just approaching Sunset, and Rykar was glad to finally have a bed for the night. He was not surprised when no one came out to greet him as he walked through the dim streets of the wooden village. Most of the hunters were largely ignored; they killed the pests so that people could go about living their lives normally. Why make a big deal of it?

Maybe it was just his fatigue and pain, but during this particular return, Rykar's reception frustrated him. It felt like none of his people cared about him or what he offered to the community. They didn't understand what it was like to survive an avalanche just to get a step closer to the kill.

At that moment, limping through the barely lit streets of a small port city, he felt completely alone. Of course, he would never let anyone know he felt that way. Rykar's posture indicated supreme confidence and will—as if nothing could ever faze him, let alone hurt him.

Out of the corner of his eye, he saw a dark pool flowing through the cracks of the smooth cobble a few steps ahead of him. Rounding the corner, he noticed that the liquid pool was blood, and its origin was a middle-aged man lying unconscious on the ground in the alleyway.

Rykar reached down to check the man's pulse, trying to determine whether or not he had been murdered. Luckily, the man was still faintly breathing. Rykar dragged him into the street so that he could properly examine him with a little bit more light. He noticed that there were a few cuts and bruises along his bare chest, and his mouth was dripping blood. It seemed like a street fight where the aggressor pummeled the man's ribs and then went for his face when it was exposed.

Rykar grabbed the unconscious man's wrist and inner thigh to lift him onto his back for a carry. He wasn't any kind of doctor, but he assumed that being inside would be preferable to sleeping in the middle of the street.

Finally, after a few minutes of carrying the medium-sized man, he arrived at his home. As usual, Gyl sat on the patio, sipping from a mug with a shadow of a smile on his face. Rykar's mentor didn't make any mention of the wounded man on his shoulders; he simply stepped to the side to give Rykar the space needed to enter their house.

Rykar scooted his way in and immediately headed to the

nearest empty room to set the man down. Luckily, it wasn't too far; he just had to make his way through the kitchen to the hallway that led to their rooms and the guest room.

He lowered the man down into the empty bed that greeted him as he walked in. Fortunately, he had been able to relocate his shoulder before the trek back to Gidura, and carrying the man had not strained it that much. On the other hand, Rykar's ankle was still bothering him, but he figured that that would soon fade away, the same as all physical pain.

Rykar exited the room to find his master lounging in the kitchen. The wooden chair and table did not seem particularly soft, but Gyl always found a way to look comfortable, no matter how uncomfortable the situation seemed. In this particular case, the lanky man had his feet on the table while he leaned back in his chair. Gyl's long, blond hair partially covered his eyes, but the smile was still there, uninhibited by his luscious locks.

"How'd the hunt go?" Gyl asked as he sipped from his mug.

"It was fine. You know how these things go," Rykar replied as he sat down across from his mentor. "The beast was large, likely almost as tall as me, so I only took a horn for proof. Hopefully, that's enough for the client."

"That should be fine," Gyl said. He suddenly leaned forward as his smile morphed into a look of eagerness. "What was he like? The beast I mean. I heard he was so dangerous that he killed five men without any problem. How did you kill him? Can I see the horn?"

The questions kept coming, but Rykar was used to this. Hunting always made Gyl excited, and in his experience, the only way to deal with his mentor was to wait until he was calm. As much as the energy annoyed Rykar, it made him feel good to know that someone would listen to him.

"It was pretty simple, really," Rykar began. "He was easy to track because, as I'm sure you know, he gives off waist-high ice spikes everywhere he goes. An avalanche threatened my life, but I survived. Luckily for me, that was what finished him off."

"Ah," Gyl responded. "The old 'kill two birds with one stone' situation." His face changed from amused to confused in an instant. "But tell me this, how the Hel did you survive an avalanche?"

Rykar opened his mouth, ready to respond, until he realized he had no idea what the answer to this question was. The devastating crash of ice and rock had uprooted the strongest trees. It even killed Fryd, a creature that had surely seen and survived many of these disasters in the past.

"I honestly have no idea. I guess it was just luck," Rykar answered. This did not seem like it was a satisfactory response in Gyl's eyes, but that wasn't very important to Rykar at the moment. He had other more pressing things on his mind.

"There is something I would like to talk to you about," he said. "After I took the horn off of Fryd, I was approached by a man." Rykar could sense that he was losing Gyl's interest, but he hoped that the man would listen long enough for him to finish the story. "He was really weird. I don't know much about him, except for the fact that he wore grayish robes, and his hair and eyes were both white."

"Why are you telling me this?" Gyl asked. Rykar knew he wasn't trying to sound uninterested, but Gyl only cared about hunting and fun hunting stories.

"He told me that Pythti chose me," Rykar replied, trying not to show his frustration with the older man. "He mentioned that if I said some phrase that I would have a role in something called the Warrior Division. Oh, he also said something about great power. I think he meant that I would be given a nyxka."

Gyl sat back in his chair with a wide-eyed expression. He was surprised by what Rykar had just said, but he couldn't quite keep the look of skepticism from creeping onto his face.

Gyl shook his head. "This was probably some crazy old man you happened to stumble upon."

"No, that's the thing!" Rykar shouted, more forcefully

than he had intended. Gyl gave him a look of disapproval, and he knew that he had almost crossed a line. "Sorry," he said, quieting down. "It's just that he wasn't old. I've also seen my share of crazy people and would be surprised if this guy happened to be insane. I don't think he was lying. He at least thought he was telling me the truth," Rykar finished.

"Ryk, I think you're reading too far into this," Gyl responded, clearly feeling exasperated. "Crazy people can have lucid moments, and the white hair and eyes could just be dyed, or a trick of the light." Gyl paused, giving Rykar a strange look. "There is one way to tell if he was telling the truth, though."

Rykar perked up at this. He loved being able to confirm various suspicions or theories. To him, investigating was as fun as hunting was to Gyl. Rykar figured that he could probably spend the rest of his life trying to solve mysteries and would never get tired of the feeling of finding out more.

"You simply say the phrase that the man told you to say," Gyl finished. "That is if you can remember it. When did you last see him?"

"I remember it, it was only a day or so ago," Rykar answered. "Alright, fine. I'll say it, just make sure nothing goes wrong."

Gyl laughed. "Kid, what could happen?"

"I don't know. Just be prepared," Rykar said. For some reason, as he was about to say the words, he felt his heart beating in his chest. He was nervous when he knew he had no reason to be. He closed his eyes and took a deep breath. "Ok, the phrase was 'I accept your offer of divinity.'"

He felt a gust of wind against his hair and face. It suddenly smelled salty. Rykar opened his eyes and saw where he was. There were various cylindrical columns of rock poking out of the huge body of water in front of him. Bridges connected most of the islands, and on top of most of them, he saw rocky towers. Directly in front of him was a particularly massive tower. It had a beauty to it, with light poking out of a multitude of windows that riddled its surface.

Too shocked to even process what had just happened, he stumbled across the sandy beaches toward a staircase leading to one of the islands. Maybe if he were lucid, he would have thought about the distant thumping coming from the largest tower.

---

Rykar looked down the staircase he had just climbed. He had no memory of going from the beach to where he was now —on an island in an archipelago. He had no idea how he even got to the sea in the first place. His last memory was of him in his kitchen, talking to Gyl about the hunt.

*This is just a very lucid dream,* he thought. *No need to worry. I probably passed out from exhaustion mixed with the pain of my injuries.* He tried to calm himself down as he walked underneath an arch, which was presumably the entrance to wherever he was going.

With the ocean spraying into his face, he was beginning to have trouble believing it was just a dream. Everything felt so real, from the lamps curved atop the cobblestone path he was on to the smell of the sea. The trail that led to one of the rope bridges he had seen earlier in conjunction with the ocean to either side of him reinforced the fact that it wasn't a figment of his imagination.

Once he neared the end of the bridge, he saw yet another arch. This one was much grander than the last, with a few purple and blue gemstones embedded in the top. The first arch had no gemstones and was just made of stone. He passed through the second arch, and to his side, the mist coalesced into a man.

Rykar wasn't usually very jumpy. He could face wild animals and the misty darkness of the forest with a sense of comfort. However, this scared him. The unknown and its depths, always trying to stay hidden—there was a reason that Rykar felt the need to reveal the mysteries of the world.

His fear manifested itself in his actions. He jumped up a bit, obviously feeling alarmed, and then ran up to the man and punched him as hard as his adrenaline-filled body could, right in the stomach. The man clutched his stomach, and to Rykar's surprise, he only coughed quietly.

"I suppose I should begin to expect this kind of treatment from people like you," the man said as he began to chuckle. He stepped out from the corner where he had formed and into an area lit by one of the lamps. The improved lighting allowed Rykar to see that it was the same man who had approached him on the mountain.

"Who are you? What's going on? What do you mean by people like me?" Rykar asked as he felt all of his questions pouring out onto this stranger. He realized that the man probably felt like he did when he spoke to Gyl about hunting missions.

"My name is Tim. I am a member of the Research Division of the Nyxtad Collective, the organization that has gifted divinity to the worthy," Tim began. "As to what's going on, I feel like it's perfectly clear. You accepted our lord's offer, and you have found your way to his home in the Nyxtad Archipelago. Finally, by people like you, I mean our Warriors. They usually think of using their fists before their wits."

Rykar felt his head spinning. "How the Hel did I get all the way from Gidura to these islands?" he demanded.

"As I said before, you found your way here on your own," Tim calmly answered. "Your methods are your own, and I am not privy to them."

It took Rykar a second to realize that Tim had started walking toward the looming tower that stood in front of them. He was hesitant to follow but realized that he must if he was to get more answers.

"What does it mean to be a part of the Warrior Division?" Rykar asked.

"I'm sure many of its members disagree upon the general philosophy," Tim said as he chuckled again. "Basically, we Researchers need a shield and spear for our studies, otherwise it gets . . . messy. The Warrior Division offers this."

"Ah," Rykar breathed. "How can I be sure that the Collective is worthy of my protection?"

Tim slowed to a stop as they approached the entrance to the large tower. "That is the million ray question. I guess you'll just have to wait and find out," he finished with a smile as he opened the wooden doors and gestured inside.

Rykar peeked into the room. After he decided that it was, in fact, safe to enter, he shuffled in as he looked around, trying to absorb every detail. The room was much brighter than the night sky, and it took a few moments for his eyes to properly adjust to this new environment.

What he saw was impressive. From the inside, it looked like the tower was just one huge dome. Rykar's eyes scanned up the wall, and he noticed balconies spaced out evenly by height, presumably indicating where new floors began. Each balcony got smaller in area until it reached the top, where there was a room with glass flooring, allowing anyone to see into it.

Lights were spaced out along the railings of each balcony. On one side of the building, there were all of the warmer colors—red, orange, and yellow. On the other side were all of the colder colors, such as blue and purple. The very middle of the warmer side had a white light, whereas the other side had a completely black light.

"Is there any reason that the Collective chooses to use these specific colors?" Rykar asked.

"Those oranges and yellows are usually associated with the Sun, and therefore creation. The darker colors, like blue and purple, represent the Moon and destruction. We employ both because our lord is the father of both," Tim recited, almost as if he had given this very explanation hundreds of times before.

Rykar was, of course, familiar with the Hakiron religion. The skeptical part of him was still trying to prove that Tim was not who he said he was, that this was all an elaborate trick or a deep dream. The hopeful part of him saw the consistency and wanted for it all to be real.

As they walked through the center of the tower, Rykar noticed that Tim was leading him toward a door on the dark side of the building. He kept glancing around, trying to take in the new sights, but he was also trying to stay focused on Tim and where he was being taken. He would not be killed all because of a simple distraction.

Getting closer to the wooden door, Rykar noticed something odd. It looked almost exactly like the one he had gone through entering the building. Even certain knots in the wood seemed to match up perfectly in his mind. *Don't get caught off guard,* he thought. *A few oddities won't be the cause of your death. Pay attention to Tim and whatever he brings with him.*

The room on the other side was very dark, much darker than the night sky. Other than a few odd purplish or bluish lights, it was completely black. Rykar waited a few seconds for his eyes to adjust, hoping that he would soon be able to see better, but nothing seemed to change.

"This is the Room of Destruction," Tim whispered into Rykar's ear. "It will judge you under the power of the Gapythrad. May the children of our divine smile upon you."

"Judge me how?" Rykar asked skeptically.

"It will tell you whether you are worthy of death or power," Tim answered, fading into the blackness of the room, leaving Rykar all alone once more.

Rykar began to turn around, hoping to understand the room better. As he searched, he noticed that the lights he had seen earlier were moving. More specifically, they were slowly floating toward him. He ran to the side, but they seemed to be able to track him, to follow him. They weren't very large, approximately the size of his thumb, nor were they bright.

One of the lights briefly touched his arm, and a flash of pain ran through it. He decided that it probably wasn't a good idea to touch any of these dangerous orbs for very long. Rykar sprinted away from them, determined not to get hit. *If this is some kind of test for whatever Tim is doing, then hopefully the goal is to stay away from those things,* he thought.

He dodged the lights for what felt like an eternity. After a while, he lost all track of time, and his body began to move on its own. He stopped thinking about anything but not getting hit. Random flips and jumps felt easy to him at first, but he was beginning to feel the fatigue. Rykar's movement slowed for one second, causing him to get hit square in the chest by a purple light.

The pain was so unbearable that he thought he was going to die. He let out a huge scream on contact, but this only took away more of his breath. He fell to the ground panting. Slowly, all of the other lights gathered around him, and Rykar felt his eyes drooping. The few things he could discern were the burning pains he felt everywhere and the distant screams that he could only assume were his own.

# THE VISITOR

*Most people fit into categories or stereotypes, the absolute average of society and what it wants. Those who fall to the outside of this curve by Instinct are those who are remembered, for they are remarkable.*

- *Hadrian*

T he next few days were all very boring. Most of the time, Ghar just sat on his balcony, watching the world he was supposed to rule. The longer he did this, the more he realized that he wasn't ready to accept the fact that he wouldn't be king.

The part of him that hoped to be the Lopythlok seemed to be his only defining characteristic for his entire life. He couldn't remember a time when he didn't want to rule over the entirety of the set half of Hakiro.

Deciding not to accept defeat, Ghar found himself back at the mansion's library to learn more about the politics and history of Lopythtym. He figured if a loophole were anywhere, it would be found there.

He started where he had first found *In the Words of a God.* The political section always fascinated him. The philosophy behind government and economics seemed incredibly simple at first glance, but a deeper dive into it revealed a much less satisfying truth: very few people fully understood politics.

As he browsed, he came across a few volumes that spoke to him. *Leviathan* by a mysterious author, TH, seemed to describe a social contract. Ghar wasn't entirely sure of the origins of the book, as some of the phrasings felt off, maybe even translated.

Another book that appeared to be important was *A Record of the Rakdi Dynasty* by an unknown author. It was like a distant family tree, but more importantly, it described the world under Rakdi rule.

Finally, he picked up *Lopythtym and Light.* The document was supposedly written by the Lopythrad himself and highlighted the important parts of their religion and culture. It explained how these influenced the current government. In his mind, it was crucial that he understood that specific book.

Holding those three books, he journeyed to the more distant and unknown parts of the library. After quite a bit of random searching and wandering later, he decided to settle down in a section about a mysterious art known as "engineering."

Most of the books he picked up were only partially translated, as there were parts that had strange symbols. He wasn't quite sure what they were or what they meant, but he was intrigued, nonetheless. Perhaps if he could understand engineering, he could get an edge on Nadren and be one step closer to becoming the king.

A little bit of digging revealed something called "electricity." It seemed as if it was a mysterious force that could power almost anything. As it turned out, lightning was made of electricity, so Ghar figured it was pretty powerful.

Unfortunately for his curiosity, that was all he could

comprehend from the various books he read. A few of them mentioned things like "internal combustion engines" and "turbines," but none of it made sense to him, so he stuck with the political and philosophical books.

A few hours of research later and he still did not know much more about the structure of Lopythtym's government. From what he could tell, it would be classified as an absolute monarchy, although there were instances in which the king could be overridden by a unanimous vote from the twelve noble houses.

The noble houses themselves could not make laws; all they could do was show the will of the people in disagreeing with poor decisions from the Lopythlok. The Lopythlok could overrule a veto, so the veto was only used as a wake-up call for the Lopythlok when he was doing something wrong.

Ghar already knew some of this, and even though he now had some more info, he wasn't entirely sure if it would help him achieve his goal. Thinking he had reached a dead end, he set down *Lopythtym and Light* and moved on to *Leviathan*.

There were some things he didn't exactly understand, especially since the language was so dense. A lot of things appeared to be lost in translation or time.

The things he did learn, however, seemed to be incredibly important. People subscribed to a ruler or government via a social contract in which they agreed to be ruled to gain certain things. In the case of Lopythtym, people agreed on who the king was, and the king would maintain order in the kingdom.

This was where Ghar became confused. If the culture and tradition disagreed with what most people agreed, what would happen? Did the common people truly believe in the rule of the Lopythlok, or had his power become a tradition? If someone were to try to rule without the title of Lopythlok, what would happen?

These questions were what led to his plans to gain the throne. He figured if he could get everyone to think of him as a king or ruler, then it would be difficult for Nadren to do his duties, and the throne would be Ghar's.

With a satisfied smile on his face, he began planning. It seemed to him that the most important part of gaining the trust of the people would be fixing his reputation. It would be a long and arduous process, but he had to show that he was no longer a lazy goof-off.

Another thing that seemed important to him was his image and attachment to the culture of the people. If he was disconnected from them, it would be difficult for them to relate to him, thus deterring them from believing in him.

He decided that it would be a good idea to publicly worship the Sun and show that he was sticking closely to the teachings in *Lopythtym and Light.* In his mind, this would appeal to the people as most were incredibly religious, primarily agreeing with the teachings of the Lopythrad. Migrants from Gapythtym would most likely not find him appealing in this case, seeing as they agreed with the philosophies of the Gapythrad, so he had to find another way to attract their attention.

He quickly jotted down some notes and ideas as to how he was going to achieve his goals, then hid them away. He knew that what he was doing was technically considered treason, so he had to be careful not to be caught by his brother. It was unlikely that he would be executed due to his blood relation, but the punishment would certainly be severe.

He walked out onto his balcony and sat down to watch the set. A part of him had always wondered what was beyond the edge of the map, hidden by the fire and life of the Sun as it fell, bringing darkness.

Perhaps there was a civilization where things made sense. Where children could be happy, not worrying about achieving goals and competing at an early age. Where people could live life to the fullest, not being distracted by artificial constructions.

Just as his mind was about to wander down this path, he

heard a knock at his door and a voice—presumably a butler—saying something.

"Master," it said. "You have a visitor."

---

Kalia Vyrtra, the new head of the Vyrtra family, sat before him in his sitting room. Unlike most of the nobility, she did not have bright-blonde hair. Hers was more of a blood red. She was probably about the same height as him, 10 rays, but carried herself as if she were the largest in the room. She was thin, but not in a weak way. She seemed agile and dangerous.

After a moment, Ghar realized they had been eyeing each other in silence long enough for it to be awkward. He decided that it would make sense for him to speak first, although he was preoccupied with his plans, so he would try not to waste time with her.

"I'm assuming you have no idea why I'm here," she began.

Ghar blinked in surprise. "That would be a safe assumption to make, I believe," he responded. The nobility always spoke in a grandiloquent manner, which he chose to ignore. That is until he realized how important image was, so he decided it might be a good idea to alter this trend.

"Why don't you make a guess," she said, almost as if she were tired of talking to him already. "Why would I, the head of the Vyrtra family, which happens to have just lost a six-hundred-year dynasty, talk to the brother of the current king?"

"You want my help in overthrowing Nadren."

"You misunderstand. I want to overthrow nothing. I would like to reclaim the throne, rebuild my family's legacy, and prevent the government from being infected by those who are not worthy."

Ghar searched carefully for his next words. Being diplomatic and stern was difficult, but he had to get better. This was good practice, regardless of whether or not it led to anything.

"What were your Sun Avatar's dimensions?" he asked, measuring each word with care.

At this, her face fell. Ghar could tell that she was disappointed with her performance, as was he. She saw the throne as hereditary and was prepared to become the queen simply because of her family name. She probably hadn't been ready for the exam or the death of her father.

"I was unable to summon one," she said calmly, attempting to maintain her air of confidence at the same time.

Ghar couldn't contain his laughter. The politics of a conversation were unfamiliar to him, but he knew well-timed laughter could give someone an incredible amount of power in the discussion.

"And I thought I was pathetic for losing to my brother," he practically yelled. "You truly redefine the word."

He was being harsh, but not without reason. It was rare for the nobility past their rising to be unable to summon an Avatar. He also wanted to experiment with the direction of the conversation, trying to see where this choice would take him.

Not surprisingly, anger flashed across Kalia's face. Losing her composure, she stood up looking like she wanted to punch him.

"So I've been told," she said, calming herself with what appeared to be a practiced breathing exercise. This indicated that she had at least a mild anger issue. *Interesting,* Ghar thought.

"Mine was 18 rays for size and 24 for power," he explained. "I am unsure of how familiar you are with the history of the examinations, but these numbers have only come in second one time before. Your ancestor was truly something amazing."

He hoped that inserting a compliment like this would make him appear empathetic, Knowledgeable, and noble. The more he spoke, the more conversation fascinated him. He would have to practice more.

"He truly was," she whispered, then straightened up and

put her confident face back on. "It may surprise you that I did not come here planning to get shamed. I have a proposal, which I think you will find quite interesting."

Ghar was growing bored with the direction of the discourse and was beginning to think that he wouldn't be able to extract much more practice from it. Kalia wasn't nearly as composed as most of the nobility, plus her red hair threw him off. She didn't feel like royalty at all. Perhaps that was why the Lopythrad chose Nadren instead of her.

Still, she continued speaking.

"I want you to help me regain the throne. In return, I will give you a say in certain parts of kingdom politics. Essentially, you would be my second-in-command."

"Why would I do that when I could take the throne for myself?"

"I have the name recognition," she responded. "If you go around asking the peasants who the royal family is, almost everyone will say Vyrtra. It is a staple of our culture at this point. In truth, I would be a far easier ruler than Nadren simply because of my family name."

Ghar couldn't argue with that. People liked consistency. Change was often met with a decent amount of resistance, and big, groundbreaking things like he was planning would hardly be accepted with open arms. Continuity was important.

This gave him pause as he realized that his plans needed to be amended. He had no intention of conceding power to Kalia, although it might make sense to let her think that while they worked together. He would certainly have to deal with the influx of information after the meeting concluded.

"So, will you help me?" she inquired eagerly.

"Perhaps, although we must amend the deal for it to be more appealing to me," he said as he turned and walked toward the balcony. The set was almost fully complete, with a dark shadow working its way down the sky.

"You may stay in the guest quarters while we plan," Ghar said calmly. "This is a temporary arrangement. We will meet tomorrow during the rise in front of the library. The butler will show you out," he commanded, waving dismissively. It felt good to exert authority over someone else. To not be pushed around, but to be the force pushing. That kind of power was why he needed to be king.

The tactic of ending the meeting both demonstrated his power and gave him time to plan. He was going to need time to think about his options. Most importantly, Kalia highlighted an enormous problem that he was going to have to deal with.

For people to think of him as a king, they needed to see him performing kingly duties. That would be easier for a Vyrtra, as they had the name recognition, but a Rakdi would need to create that.

Another thing to think about was whether or not he should accept the deal with Kalia. Frankly, it would be easier to work with her because he could watch her moves. If he didn't have a way to surveil her, she would simply become another point of conflict.

In the end, he decided it would be a good idea to make daily appearances at various villages around the kingdom while working with Kalia. This would allow him to limit the moving pieces he would have to deal with while also gaining the favor of the common people.

He sat down at his desk and began preparing individual parts of his plan.

The first thing he would have to determine was a reasonable time limit to achieve his goal. Either he could wait out his brother, succeeding him after death, or he could wait before his brother's reign was truly cemented and steal the position at the last second.

As much as he was jealous of Nadren for being the Lopythlok, he still loved him. The first option was not one that he was patient enough for either. He would just have to take on the role without his brother's consent. Plus, tricking and manipulating people sounded like a really difficult challenge, so it could end up being fun.

He stayed up most of the night arranging the specifics of his plans. Strangely, he couldn't recall a time when he needed more than a few short hours of sleep. It was rare for him to even feel tired. He found that at times like these it was best to follow the flow of energy and where it was taking you. Falling into habits like resting could be detrimental.

The more he worked, the more he understood what was going on. Contingencies were born. He had everything determined down to the smallest detail. Now it was time to kick everything off. All he had to do was lie to an entire kingdom.

# THE NYXTAD COLLECTIVE

*Of course, I wonder about the condemnation of conquerors. We unite, we save, we bring order to a chaotic world. We are the closest things to gods that mortal men will see.*

-     *Drydnar Vyrtra*

R ykar awoke feeling refreshed. He began to stretch out his arms as he tried to understand where he was. He was sitting on a wooden bench in a room with a bright-white ceiling and dark-black flooring. It was strangely both light and dark at the same time.

Not far to his right, on the same bench, sat a man. He had darker skin than Rykar but not by much. His hair was black, and he didn't appear to be muscular, though his clothing could be hiding it. Slouched over, he wore a robe that appeared to be cloaked in light. A naked blade resided across his lap, its sheath noticeably absent. It just lay there, homeless on the lap of the man cloaked in light.

At the front of the room stood a man on a pedestal. He looked nearly identical to Tim, except for the fact that he was a little bit more muscular. His loose-fitting, gray robes looked odd when worn tight, with his muscles bulging and taking out the normal amount of slack.

"Rejoice, for your lives have been given to you by Pythti," the man began. "You have been given a new purpose, a new name, and most of all, a new family. You are children of the Pythrad, siblings of the Gapythrad and the Lopythrad, and protectors of order. With this rebirth comes responsibility and power. However, this power is not your own. It is a small fraction of the Pythrad that you have been granted so that you may carry out his will."

Rykar listened to the man explain power and divinity and felt himself becoming excited. He had always been jealous of the nobility because of their nyxka. No more, for now he had one all to himself.

"You will begin at the lowest rank of the Warrior Division, which is the fifth class. After you have been sent to the member of the Pactri who currently resides at HQ, you will be in his hands, and your service will begin." With that, it seemed as if the announcer was done, and he stepped down from the pedestal and walked off the stage toward the doors behind Rykar.

*He didn't fade into mist,* Rykar thought. *Nyxka must have some sort of uniqueness to them, or Tim is more advanced than this man. Either way, there is something behind this power that they're neglecting to share.*

Lost in thought, Rykar almost didn't notice the Warrior falling toward the pedestal where the announcer had been standing. The shockwave from the impact was nothing like he had ever felt. He was thrown against the back of his chair with an overpowering force. The man who was now standing on stage did not seem to be similar to Tim or the newer announcer. He wore no shirt, perceptibly having nothing against flaunting his extremely fit frame. The things that stood out most to Rykar were the four vertical lines tattooed on his chest as well as his medium-length, brown hair. Most people either had blond or black; brown was rare.

"I am your commander," the man said. Then, without any warning, he walked off stage, leaving the same way the original announcer did.

"I expect you to follow," he said without turning.

"Yes, Commander."

Rykar turned to the man in the light robes, surprised. He had seemed quiet, timid even. The confidence he displayed in responding did not match up with Rykar's idea of who he was.

"Yes, Commander," Rykar quickly added as he began to follow the light man and their commander.

The two of them followed him for a while. They wound through many hallways and stairwells, so many that Rykar almost lost track of where he was.

After a few minutes, they stopped in what appeared to be a training hall. The room was empty except for a few wooden practice dummies and weaponry along the walls. Their commander stood with his hands crossed in front of him, appearing to disapprove of Rykar and the other man.

"My name is Leopold, and as I said, I am your commander. More specifically, I am a member of the Pactri," Leopold began. Rykar immediately felt himself asking a question, but he had to suppress this urge. Now was the time for listening, not talking.

"You are here today to receive your divine names and to discover your nyxka. In my experience, the best way to realize your true power is to put yourself in a life or death situation," Leopold continued. "You will fight me, and when we are done, I will give you a divine name, and you will know your power." He looked back and forth between Rykar and the other man.

"Now then, who's first?" Leopold asked.

Rykar looked at the swordsman, hoping that he would

volunteer. The man stood as still as a statue, unfazed by the situation. Rykar sighed and stepped forward.

"I guess I'll go fir—" he stuttered as Leopold grabbed the back of his neck and rammed his knee into his gut, interrupting him.

"Always act with certainty," Leopold whispered to Rykar. "If your team knows that you're guessing, they will lose faith, and you will lose power." Leopold let go of his neck and was suddenly halfway across the room. It looked like he had instantly traveled that length.

"How on Gaz did you do that?" Rykar asked with fascination. "Is that your nyxka? Teleportation? That's aweso—" he stopped again as Leopold's elbow collided with his jaw.

Rykar looked up, massaging his jaw from the blow. The pain was unbearable, but strangely he felt something. Something he assumed most people would never feel when facing a man like Leopold. He felt excited.

He looked up, and through his spotted vision, he could make out one expression on Leopold's face. A grin. He was enjoying it as well.

Suddenly Leopold's smile vanished, and he went with it. Rykar frantically searched around the room, knowing full well that a surprise attack was coming. His eyes provided him with no extra information, so, to avoid distractions, Rykar closed them and focused on calming himself.

He began to feel something. A presence. It wasn't necessarily physical, nor was it entirely in his head. It was more of a feeling than it was a being. It felt like pressure, like strength, like power.

Accompanying this presence was another, this one much darker. It felt like guilt, hatred, and most of all, pain. He quickly reopened his eyes, afraid of what the dark presence would do to him, angry at what it had already done.

Unfortunately for him, a distraction was the last thing he needed. He realized this all too late as he saw the hint of a fist fly into the right side of his vision, and with it came blackness.

---

Rykar opened his eyes, feeling as if history had just repeated itself. He was sitting in the same room where Leopold had first introduced himself. It felt eerily similar to that experience, except this time the swordsman was standing and Leopold was already on stage.

He felt his head and stomach, checking to see how bad his injuries were from the fight against his commander. Strangely, he felt no pain, even when he touched directly where he had been struck. It was almost as if he had been healed in the short time between him being knocked out and when he had awoken.

It took him a moment to realize that Leopold was speaking.

"First, you were cleansed by the powers of either destruction or creation," he was saying. "Second, you were broken down by me, stripped away of your pain and happiness only to be built up again by our cause. Now, this process of being rebuilt begins. You will be given a divine name, and I will tell you what your nyxka is."

Rykar perked up at the sound of this. He was, by nature, a very curious person. When it came to new experiences or subjects, he often had to do a good job filtering his questions to not come off as annoying or overeager. In situations that he was familiar with, he sometimes became bored and didn't care to learn, because he frequently lost interest.

"I will begin with the swordsman," Leopold continued. "You displayed incredible prowess during our battle, being able to maintain consciousness for one of the blows I delivered. You even managed to touch me with your sword. All of these would be impressive for anyone up through the third class. I am proud to offer you the name Ahren. As for your nyxka, Pythti offers you the gift of the sword so that you will be able to protect all you deem worthy."

Rykar looked toward the newly named Ahren, trying to understand what this meant to him. He figured he should try to get a feel for him at some point, so why not start as soon as possible?

To his surprise, Ahren had tears in his eyes. Something about what Leopold had said resonated with him, but what?

*Maybe he is just thankful for the praise from such a high-ranking individual,* Rykar thought. *He did seem to understand more about the Warrior Division than I did when we first met Leopold. He could also be happy for the ability to protect people, thankful for the nyxka, or just relieved that he passed whatever trials were given to him.* Rykar continued to speculate, but one thing was for certain: those tears were an important part of who Ahren was.

"Now we come to the hunter," Leopold began, staring at Rykar. "The only person in history to take a blow from me and smile. The only man, woman, or child to look me in the eye after one of my elbows. The true resilience that I sense from you is astounding. You are worthy of an honor far higher than just the fifth class, but you will find duty and responsibility within all of the ranks of our Division."

"Your new, divine name is Frederick," Leopold announced. "Pythti has also given you the nyxka of—"

"Umm sorry, sir, permission to stop you there?" Rykar interrupted, wincing. "I would prefer to keep my old name, for personal reasons." He wasn't sure why he made the request. It was just a name, after all. It didn't define him. Except, he did feel like it was an important part of who he was. He wasn't Frederick, he was Rykar.

The look that Leopold gave him was very strange. It seemed to be a mixture of anger at the interruption and fascination at the request.

"Unfortunately, no. Officially, your new name will be Frederick," Leopold responded firmly. "We will keep no records of your past within our libraries or archives, although you may share your preferences with your squad."

"Now, back to what I was saying," he continued. "Pythti has determined that your nyxka is the same as mine. You have been granted the gift of teleportation."

*There are a finite amount of nyxka, then. If not, then the chances of me getting the same one as Leopold are nearly zero,* Rykar began to speculate. *Maybe there are different classifications for nyxka.* He was interested, so he tucked the subject in his back pocket to be studied further.

He was intrigued by the fact that he had the same nyxka as Leopold for more reasons than just the one. As one of the Pactri, Leopold was probably one of the best combatants in the Warrior Division, meaning Rykar had a good source of Knowledge on his abilities.

He stopped daydreaming about nyxka and the future and noticed that Leopold had stopped talking. He looked around, saw Ahren walking out, and decided that he should follow. Ahren seemed to know what he was doing.

He got up, but before he could fall in behind Ahren, Leopold appeared before him, stopping him.

"That was bold." Leopold paused. "But also insubordinate. Never, and I mean NEVER, interrupt me when I'm speaking," he said firmly. "That being said, I'm glad to have someone like you in the Division. It's good to have something to fight for, to defend." His voice grew softer toward the end.

"Sir?" Rykar asked.

"What is it?" he responded.

"Well for one, I'm sorry for interrupting, but do you think you could teach me how to use my nyxka, seeing as we have the same one?"

"Apology accepted," Leopold said. He then turned on his heels and began walking the same way that Ahren had gone.

"Sir?" Rykar yelled. "What about nyxka training?"

"I think you'll find that much is not as it seems," Leopold yelled back as he walked through the wooden door.

Rykar followed him, incredibly confused. *What does he*

*mean by that?* he thought. *Another thing to make sure I remember.* The general ominousness of that statement did not sit well with Rykar, so he decided he would focus on uncovering whatever mysteries he might find at HQ.

He passed through the exit, saw Leopold a little bit ahead in the stone corridor, and ran to catch up. He hated getting lost, especially in an unfamiliar and uncomfortable setting.

After following the corridor for a while, they finally entered a large banquet hall. It was lined with people, all dressed almost identical to Tim. When they stood side by side, it was easy to tell them apart. They had different skin tones, different body types, and different facial features, but they all had the same hair and eyes. There was probably someone in the Nyxtad Collective with a nyxka that allowed people to change their appearance to create a familial feeling.

Rykar awkwardly stood there for a second, unsure of what he was meant to do and where he was supposed to go. He looked over to Leopold, who was nodding his head to the front of the room.

Rykar started up a staircase that led to a stage and uncomfortably stood around the center. Shortly after, Ahren walked up the same way Rykar had gone and stopped to stand next to him. Finally, Leopold made the same journey and stood in front of both of them, presumably about to give a speech.

"Standing before you are the next members of your Warrior Division, our family. These men know horrors most have only imagined. They have gone through Hel to get here, and the future doesn't look much brighter. Their faces have been marred by blood and sweat, and they have kept moving, even when death was certain.

"They have proven their strength in carrying their own lives. Now allow them to carry yours. With men like these on our side, you can feel safe unraveling the secrets of the universe, all for the sake of humanity.

"Now, you two," he said, turning to face them. "Do you accept the risk and reward that comes with this job? It won't be easy. You may even die. Your reward, however, is priceless. You will feel like you are making a difference. You will be able to protect those you love. Most of all, you will be changing the world for the good."

"So, what do you say?" he asked finally.

"I accept the risk, sir!" Ahren shouted immediately.

"As do I," Rykar said, less enthusiastically. "Sir," he added quickly at the end.

A loud cheer broke out, filling the banquet hall. The Collective seemed extremely happy to have them, for some reason. This was easily the warmest initiation or welcome he had ever experienced; it was the first time he had been accepted into any group. When Gyl had trained him to be a hunter, there was no party, no initiation. It just happened.

He stepped off the stage and was immediately met with a swarm of questions and attempts at greetings. People seemed endlessly interested in him and his nyxka. It made sense that these people were scholars—they seemed curious.

Ahren didn't even bother with walking down the stage. He already had a grasp on his nyxka, as he simply jumped on his sword's flat edge and allowed it to carry him away. He stood sideways on it with his knees bent and allowed it to float him out the door. It looked like his nyxka was the ability to move his sword with his mind. Not only that, but he looked like he was quite well-practiced at it already. *Curious*, Rykar thought, making a note to keep an eye on Ahren in the future.

Wading through the crowd of people, Rykar noticed a single gray robe standing off to the side. Naturally drawn to him, Rykar made his way through the crowd and finally found some wiggle room and free space as he approached.

Finding himself out of the mass of bodies, he approached the man. He was short, a little bit shorter than Rykar, and looked to be only a few years his elder. One thing that stood out was his bright-blond hair. He glanced up at Rykar, shot a piercing look with his golden eyes, reached out with an open hand, and leaned against the wall as if he couldn't care less if he were ignored.

Rykar shook the man's hand and decided to introduce himself but was interrupted midway through opening his mouth.

"Your name is Rykar. Or wait, no. Is it Frederick?" the gray robe began. "This whole renaming thing is confusing. Either way, I know you, but you don't know me. So allow ME to introduce myself. My name is Hadrian, I'm one of the Regional Scholars. I'm the same rank as Leopold, except I'm with the Researchers, not the Warriors."

Rykar's eyes turned to slits. "How do you know my name?" he asked.

"Oh, you know. My position revolves around the fact that I know things. When you deal with people like me, you should be asking what I don't know."

"What don't you know, then?" he responded.

Hadrian sighed, dropping his chin to his chest. "Isn't that the million ray question."

Rykar shook his head, confused. Hadrian seemed to be an awfully strange guy. Maybe that's why he was so high up in the ranks of the Collective.

"Well anyways," Hadrian said, kicking off the wall to walk away. "If you have any questions, just look for me, and I'll do my best to answer them. Although, I'll probably know when you need my help." He said this last bit as he walked away, waving with the back of his hand.

While the entire encounter seemed strange to Rykar, he was beginning to become accustomed to strangeness. From Ahren's silent crying to the Research Division fawning over him, he was growing to accept mysterious situations. One thing, however, stood out to him. One thing he couldn't quite shake. *What do they do here?* Rykar thought.

# A SPIDER WEB
# IS WOVEN

*The world needed a savior, someone to unite it against the forces of chaos. So why do you condemn me for conquering it? I offered creation, balance, and you, Pythti, responded with destruction.*
- *Drydnar Vyrtra*

G
har showed up in front of the library right as the Sun peeked above the horizon. Kalia wasn't there yet. He began planning for a situation in which she never showed up. Surprised at how detailed the plan became in a matter of moments, he decided to shift his thought process. He was becoming scarily efficient at planning.

Instead of spending more time thinking about that, he turned his attention to the entrance of the library. In front of him stood a grandiose arch. It held a variety of gemstones with shades that could be found in a fire. On the very top of the arch was the word *Gazdok*, which he was told meant all words. This, of course, was silly, as a library couldn't literally hold *all* words, but he appreciated the symbolism.

It was gilded, most likely wooden underneath the golden shine. It appeared as if it was designed to exemplify the greatness of the Lopythrad, inviting entrance and life while also showing a sort of power with the embedded gemstones.

In the middle of his analysis of the arch, he saw Kalia walking toward him from his side. Her red hair that had been so well kept before was a mess. She had overslept and rushed over when she realized what she had done.

"You did say during the rising," she began, out of breath. "Technically, it is still happening, so I'm not late."

Ghar's head fell. "Kalia. Never do what you just did ever again."

"What? I'm not late!"

"No. If you believe that you did not do anything wrong but it could be seen that you did, leave it alone. Oftentimes, nobody even thinks to be accusatory. You just gave me a reason to say you are late, even though you're right," he finished as he stepped up to the archway and entered the room.

After a bit of walking, they ended up in the politics section. Ghar was comfortable here, as it was where he had spent most of his time. He sat in his favorite chair, which was set diagonally against a corner so he could see the whole room. Kalia picked a similar chair to his side.

"First thing I would like to address," Ghar began, "is that I will not be working for you. I see no reason that this arrangement should make me inferior to you. I have Knowledge, connections, power, and ambition, which are all extremely valuable to you. At a minimum, we will be partners. I would, of course, prefer being the head of all of this, but sacrifices must be made. If you wish to call yourself the leader, I will allow it. Just know you have no real power over me."

"Fair," she said as her lips stretched into a line. It was remarkably easy to read her. "In return, I want to know everything about the plans you have already created. I know you have something up your sleeve, but for this to work, you can't keep anything from me. It all has to be out in the open."

Ghar took a moment to process this. She must have bribed the butler. Otherwise, there was no way she could have known that he was planning something. It was probably a good idea to only take mental notes so that people couldn't see what he was thinking. Unless her nyxka involved mind reading, which he was pretty sure was impossible, he would be safe.

"Agreed, although you don't have to worry about me holding out. I'm truly an awful liar," he lied.

"Good. So, what were your plans, then?" she asked eagerly. Ghar internally laughed at this. Did she think it was going to be easy? She was new to manipulation. Strange that she wished to become a usurper. It seemed so out of character.

"It's important that you become familiar with the philosophy of politics. No one will follow you if you don't give them a reason to. I recommend reading through all of *Lopythtym and Light* every day. Don't worry, it's not that long. It should only take around half a day the first time and even less each time after.

"I also want you to sell me on why you would be a better leader than Nadren. Unless you're planning on killing him, in which case I'm out. You need to prove to the people that you would be such a better choice than him that they should undermine their culture and government to place you in power," he explained.

"Well, those are broad details," she said as if she was disappointed by his answer. "I was hoping you would give me some more specifics for what you had in mind."

"Not yet," he said, shaking his head. "Too early to know what is going to happen."

"I disagree," she said confidently. "We have all of the information we need right now. For example, I plan to get into the court of the king and get them to stop helping him and help me instead. They already know me, so that should be easy.

Then, when the common people see me being treated like royalty and see my name, they will know that I am the Lopythlyk. Except I need you because I need the news of Nadren's ascension to be hidden from the public."

At this, Ghar sighed. He figured she was naive, but not to this extent. It was going to be difficult working with her. For an instant, he wondered whether or not he should even bother. Then he remembered how chaotic and brash she was and determined it would be easier to have her under him.

"Imagine a spiderweb," he began. "Tracing any path should take you to the center, so long as you go in the right direction. Following one path and making a mistake can take you to another destination."

"Where are you going with this?" she said impatiently.

"What I mean is a perfect plan is like a spiderweb. Taking any situation and getting your desired outcome is what every strategist hopes for. Some philosophers refer to this as the Spiderweb Theory for Strategy. It is of great interest to me, no matter how theoretical and impossible it is.

"However, I have formulated what I believe to be the closest thing to a perfect spiderweb ever. The only way it wouldn't work would be if one of the people involved died, and that is highly unlikely. What I mean to say is this: I have prepared for almost every possible outcome of every situation, so you shouldn't even think about that. Just prepare yourself for your role in my plans."

"How can you not keep me, your partner, informed on these matters?" she asked. "You said we would be equal, that I could even call myself the leader, but this feels like the opposite."

He sat forward in the seat, giving her a stern look. "The Lopythlok must create a Sun Avatar each rise to symbolize his connection to the Pelrad, or have you forgotten that? You clearly don't understand the nuance of your plan, let alone one that would work. Without me planning, you would fail immediately. I need your name and your image to be impeccable. In that way, we both need each other and are equal. Does it make sense now?" He said the first part hoping to teach her something, but it turned her expression sour. Perhaps he would try something different next time he was in a similar conversational situation.

She slumped down. It looked like he had somehow defeated her with his words. He stood up and walked over to her. Looking down, he gave her a confused look, although she wouldn't meet his gaze.

"What?" he asked.

"I'm only eighteen, and I already have to deal with stuff like this," she said.

This surprised Ghar. She looked much older, almost like a fully grown woman. Women did rise earlier than men. Certain things began making more sense with this revelation. Her lack of composure and experience, as well as her general moodiness, were not reflections of the rest of the noblewomen or of who she actually was. Kalia was also probably upset that her father had just died. Grief did strange things to people. Before he realized this, she didn't even seem like a human. Just an animated object that he thought of as an obstacle.

Not knowing what to say, he squatted down in an attempt to look her in the eye. She didn't look up or even seem to notice, so he awkwardly moved to speak into her ear.

"Well, I can deal with most of it for you," he said, attempting to sound reassuring. He didn't have much experience with this but hoped he did a decent job with it. "You're not alone."

She looked up with tears in her eyes and hugged him. "Thank you," she whispered.

This made Ghar feel extremely uncomfortable. In front of him was a stranger who thought it was appropriate to not only touch him but also hug him. He tried his best to wait it out, but she didn't show any signs of letting go. He reached up and quickly peeled her arms off of him. As he stood up, he felt relieved, almost as if he had just avoided death. He hated the sensation the hug brought him.

He spun on his heels and began walking out, wishing he could avoid ever speaking to her again. If she wanted them to trust each other, why would she do that? Just as he was about to leave, he heard her asking a question.

"Wait, what happens next?" she called out.

He turned around, hitting his forehead with his palm. Was she this dense?

"We have to wait for the strand of the spiderweb to be chosen, of course," he said, confused as to how she didn't realize that.

---

To Ghar's surprise, peasants were just like the nobility. The only noticeable difference was that they did a worse job composing themselves. He assumed their conversational political structure didn't require that skill as much.

Unlike most people he knew, however, they were incredibly trusting. When he had first flown in, they accepted who he introduced himself as. There didn't seem to be any suspicion among them, and they fulfilled his every request.

Walking through the village gave him a sense of humanity that he thought he had lost. The simplicity of life here was noble in a different way than he was used to. A peasant could find something boring, something tedious, something laborious, and use it as a way to live a long and satisfying life. He felt as if he were here for a different reason: to learn something from them. Unfortunately, circumstances didn't allow for this situation to arise. He was here to be regal. People needed to see him in a leadership position before he could be seen as the Lopythlok.

After a week or so of coming to the village, he was becoming more comfortable with the role. Simply showing his nyxka was enough to prove his identity, which made him wonder why no one else had ever done what he was doing. Probably because impersonating the Lopythlok was treason.

He tried his best to connect to the villagers, but he wasn't practiced enough in their conversational structure. Everything was as they said it was. No tricks, no manipulation. Everything was far simpler.

On this particular trip, he was trying to help a villager whose daughter had run away. From what he could tell, she was in the middle of her rising and refused to listen to her father anymore. It was common for things like that to happen, but Ghar said nothing and decided to use that moment as a time to work miracles. The best way to cement your position as a king was to show power that people associated with royalty.

"So, what does she look like?" Ghar asked. He was using the conversation as a means of stalling while he spread his ka— the essence of nyxka, meaning *power* in Dok—around the area. He would use it to search for the girl.

"Re' small. No' e'en up to me chest yet, Lord Light," the farmer stuttered out. Or was that the way he spoke? Ghar couldn't tell. Some of the villagers spoke like he did while others had a completely different accent entirely. None of that interested Ghar very much, though.

"What about hair color, eye color? More specific descriptions would help," he said as he searched the area his ka was covering. It was almost like he was extending his body to enhance his sense of touch through the ka, except he could sort of see with it too.

"Black 'air, brown eyes, a small scar on 'er 'and from when she tripped as a kid," the man said quickly. "Is that enough, Lord Light?"

"Shh," Ghar said, acting dramatically. "I found her. I sense she is over this way." Rocks swirled up around him and picked him up, allowing him to fly away. This was his nyxka —mental control of rocks. He strangely had an incredible connection with the planet itself.

He flew for a bit—or rather, was carried for a bit—until he found the girl and landed next to her. Covered in dirt, she had specks of brown in her black hair. She looked frightened, angry, and confused. Ghar knew the feeling all too well.

"Lord Light," she said as she saw him, kneeling simultaneously.

"You can stand up, little one," he said calmly. "Why don't you tell me what's troubling you?" He wanted to speak the way the nobility did to assert the fact that he was supposed to be royalty.

"My father. He isn't giving me enough to eat. Any time I ask for more, he gets angry and yells at me. I couldn't deal with it anymore. I had to get away. I'll find my way on my own."

He sat down next to her and patted the ground beside him, indicating he wanted her to join him.

"I wish I had your strength," he began. "You saw a solution to a problem, and you grabbed it, not letting it slip through your fingers. That, my friend, is admirable. Many of the greatest men and women in history would give almost anything to have that.

"Your father only wants what's best for you, though. I spoke to him briefly before I came here. He is giving up his food to allow you to eat. The village itself is starving. He cannot help you any more than he has been."

He looked over, expecting this to be met with anger. He figured she wouldn't understand, that her emotions would get the best of her. To his surprise, she was crying.

"I didn't know," she said softly. "Why would he do that?"

Ghar reached over, realizing this was the appropriate time to hug her. He felt uncomfortable with the gesture, but he figured it would help.

"It's because he loves you," he said simply.

This seemed to confuse her. It was almost as if she hadn't considered the possibility that her father cared for her. Her face looked like she was thinking how that was impossible, how he was a cruel and evil person. That face fell and was replaced by one of shame.

"Can you take me back please, Lord Light?" she asked

with a raspy voice.

"Of course," he said as he pulled away.

The flight back seemed to ease her mind. She was fascinated with the way the world looked from up there. For a moment, Ghar wished he could show her more, could take her to the ocean, to the Pelrad. She deserved to see everything. Then he remembered his plans and grounded his thoughts along with his feet when he landed.

The preteen girl rushed to her father, who held her in an embrace. It was good to see them reunited, but Ghar hadn't solved any problems yet. He had simply patched a hole that would continue to grow, eventually destroying them.

"I will fix your poor harvest and teach you how to become more efficient at farming," he announced. Cheers sounded around him; the people seemed as if they were in desperate need of good news. They were starving.

He searched their fields for excessive amounts of rocks. If they got into the topsoil, they could hinder the spread of nutrients and make the ground less fertile. Not surprisingly, he found a lot of them. They weren't too far down either. He reached in with his nyxka and pulled out all of the rocks, which turned the soil at the same time. This would help the fields.

"Now then, who wants to learn about crop rotation and genetic engineering for agriculture?" he asked loudly.

When no one moved, he wondered if they hadn't heard him. These techniques could help them a lot. About to ask again, he was interrupted by a farmer he hadn't met yet.

"We appreciate the thought, Lord Light, but we have already been educated about these things," she said nervously.

"By whom?" he demanded, trying to sound as formal as possible.

"A man in gray robes," she said.

"Well then, I wish you a grand harvest," he said, addressing all of them. "The Lopythrad smiles on you and gives you his warmth and light."

Alarmed, he jumped and flew away. Ghar realized he

had neglected to ask an extremely important question. He had never even been suspicious of them. Who were the men in the gray robes?

# TRAINING COMMENCES

*Resilience. Oftentimes this is the difference between success and failure. It is a thing of balance, however, as pushing too hard, going too far, can break any will, no matter how strong it might be.*
-   *Aervin Eroborn*

R ykar rubbed his head as he sat up in bed. The party from the night before had been fun, but they had served too many sweets. He would have a headache for a few days.

*Why did I think eating desserts would be a good idea?* Rykar thought. His body had the strength to endure many things, but sugar wasn't one of them. He wasn't sure why that was, but he had no complaints. He found the stuff to be disgusting most of the time.

He vaguely remembered talking to a few people the

night before. Ahren had left immediately. Not knowing anyone else, he was on his own to mingle with a few random scholars. The person who stuck in his head was Hadrian. He seemed like he was a good man to know. Maybe he could give Rykar some answers.

He also remembered talking with Leopold a bit more. It was hazy, but Rykar thought his commander had said something about meeting his squad today. He wasn't sure what to expect, but he planned for two scenarios. If they were terrible, he would stay out of their way and try to get to know Ahren better. He would also try to meet with Hadrian as often as possible to learn more. If the squad was friendly, he would ask them for help and answers. He was getting nervous just thinking about meeting them.

Suddenly his door swung wide open, and two people came barreling into his room. One was massive and must have been a whole head taller than Rykar. Not only that, but he was incredibly muscular as well. His jet-black beard was a strange complement to his entirely bald head. The other, a woman, was almost the opposite. She was slender and short, probably even a little bit shorter than Hadrian. She had bright-blonde hair and no facial hair. It might have been because she was a woman, although Rykar had heard of bearded females before.

"Gooooood MORNING, new recruit!" the man yelled while the woman silently stared at the wall behind Rykar's bed.

"What is happening?" Rykar asked.

"He's Hjalmir. I'm Ada," she replied, appearing to be bored. "Leif sent us to wake you up. We're all waiting down at the training yard, except for Karl and Eydis. They have to go get Ahren."

Rykar wondered how that would go. In his mind's eye, he imagined Hjalmir barging into Ahren's room and getting skewered immediately. He hoped that Karl and Eydis were ok, whoever they were.

"Just get ready quickly and meet us outside of your room," Hjalmir told him. "We'll take you down to the training grounds, and Leopold will give us our next mission. We're all excited to get to meet you guys more. This is one of the best parts of the Division."

Rykar didn't rush to get ready like they wanted. He was incredibly suspicious, hopefully for no reason. He took his time, mentally preparing for the possibility of an attack or something else dangerous. He needed answers soon.

After he was done, Rykar met up with Hjalmir and Ada in the hallway. They led him down a series of corridors with which he was mildly familiar. It would take a bit for him to get used to his new living arrangements.

A few moments later, they arrived at the armory where he had fought Leopold. In the center of the room was a semi-circle with a few people sitting cross-legged. On the other side of the room, entering through the other door, were three people. Ahren had a blank face as he was accompanied by two people, who Rykar assumed to be Karl and Eydis.

Karl was tall and skinny while Eydis was short and chubby. They both had pale-blond hair and looked similar, except for the fact that Karl was thin everywhere she was round.

"Welcome, welcome," the man sitting down said. Next to him sat two young women, who Rykar couldn't help but look twice at. He found them at least a little attractive.

"Leif, we have arrived with the packages you requested," Ada said, unenthusiastically. Leif appeared to be the leader of the squad, and it seemed like he ran it with a sense of humor.

"Goooooooood," Leif responded with a smile on his face. "Come now, join us. We must know who is joining our squad."

Rykar sat down next to Hjalmir, and Eydis joined him on his other side. He figured that Leif did this to build trust. It would help to fight alongside people you joked and had fun with.

"We won't be exposing each other too much here," Leif started. "Just a small introduction, and then Leopold will give us our assignment. Afterward, we can get to training like usual.

"As you have most likely gathered, my name is Leif." He was the oldest of the group, with a few wrinkles creeping across his face and hints of gray in his bright-blond hair. "I am the first-class member of this squad, and I have been in the Division for twenty years."

"Oh right!" he continued. "I nearly forgot. My nyxka is thermal control. I can change the temperature of things my ka touches."

Going around in the circle was sort of uncomfortable, and a part of Rykar dreaded his turn. He wasn't sure what he was supposed to even say as an introduction.

"Hey y'all, I'm Ada," Ada began. "I am of the second class, and I can alter the shape of anything my ka touches."

"My name is Hjalmir," Hjalmir followed. "I am also a second-class member of this squad, and my nyxka is permanence. My body knows how it is right now, and whenever my ka influences it, it reverts me to this form to some degree."

The way Hjalmir and Ada looked at each other made Rykar wonder if they were a couple or just really good friends. The squad seemed close, but romantic relationships were another thing entirely. He would have to pay attention.

"Um, hello," Rykar said, caught off guard as he remembered that it was his turn. "My name is now Frederick, but you can call me Rykar, or Ryk if you want. I'm a new member, which I believe puts me in the fifth class. My nyxka is teleportation, so I think I can move from one place to another instantly. I'm not entirely sure."

He cringed as he said this, hoping his uncertainty didn't make him seem weird. Fortunately, this was met with laughter and even a few pats on the back from Hjalmir. They thought he was funny. That was a relief.

"For some reason, the Collective likes to be cryptic, especially to new members of the Warrior Division," Leif explained. "We have all been in your position before, so we know how confused you are. Don't worry. We can answer your questions after this."

That made Rykar feel better. A part of him thought he was just stupid and that this would make sense to anyone else.

The introductions continued, and Rykar paid attention, but he was most intrigued by his counterpart, Ahren. The man was a mystery. Rykar was curious about who he was and where he came from, but a simple introduction would have to do.

"I'm Eydis. I'm a third-class member, and my nyxka is flight."

"Hello, friends. I'm Karl, also of the third class, by the way, and I can freeze time on objects that my ka affects."

Finally, it was time for Ahren. For some reason, Rykar was excited to hear what he had to say. He seemed quiet and cold, so Rykar had to know more about him.

"I'm Ahren," he started. "Like Ryk, I'm new and in the fifth class. I'm excited to train with you all. My nyxka is swordsmanship, and as far as I can tell, that means that I can fight alongside him," he said as he levitated his blade. "Weird thing is, I could do that before I joined the Warrior Division."

This last bit shocked Rykar. It meant that Leopold or Pythti or someone probably wasn't granting nyxka, or they were and Ahren was a nobleman. Either way, this gave him a lot to think about. It was also sort of unnerving to hear Ahren refer to his blade as "him," almost as if they were friends and not a fighter and a tool.

Next were the two women beside Leif. Neither of them were thin or frail. One of them had blonde hair, and the other had black hair. They looked like they were close to each other but had trouble accepting a lot of other people.

"My name is Mila," the blonde stated. "I'm a fourth-class member, though I really should be in the fifth class."

"Oh hush," Leif interrupted her. "You both deserved that promotion. Don't let anyone tell you any differently."

"Well, ok then," Mila continued. "My nyxka is plant control."

"Hi, I'm Rosa," the brunette said. "I'm also in the fourth class, and my nyxka is the ability to control the winds."

"Excellent!" Leif said as he clapped his hands together and magically rose off the ground to stand up. It looked like he had just flown, which didn't make sense to Rykar with his nyxka being temperature control. "Now, I welcome Leopold, our fearless commander, to announce our next mission!"

Then, almost exactly like during his fight with Rykar, Leopold just appeared. If not for the deafening *Crack* that shortly followed his arrival, it would have been the perfect stealthy appearance.

"Thank you, Leif, for the introduction and allowing the squad to bond a little." His voice boomed through the room and even hurt Rykar's ears a bit; it was that loud. "Your mission is simple. Find a member of the Ruined, Theo this time, and take him out. This operation cannot be a repeat of the last one. We want them to fear us, not walk over us. Dismissed." He disappeared with the same *Crack* as before. Rykar hoped his ability did not do the same thing.

He looked around the room and noticed that the rest of his squad, except for Ahren, was going to the weapons racks on the side of the room. Once Hjalmir had grabbed two swords, Rykar realized that the nyxka and combat training was next. From what he could tell, that was a daily occurrence.

Rykar wasn't sure which weapon he should pick. He was most familiar with a bow and arrow for range and a small hunting knife for practicality. Most of the time, he trapped creatures when he hunted. The times he used a knife to kill, it felt familiar in his hand. He figured that would be his best choice because of muscle memory.

He turned around and realized that everyone had picked a partner to do some basic sparring except for him, Ahren, and Leif. He wandered awkwardly over to Leif with a wicked-looking, curved ring knife in hand.

"Ryk!" Leif said overenthusiastically. "You will be working with Ahren soon, but for these next few sessions, you and I will be working together on some nyxka training. Ahren was going to join us, but he seemed like he already understood his skills fully, so I'm going to let him do some solo practice instead."

Leif led Rykar outside. They navigated what seemed to be overly complex halls and ended up in a courtyard. It was surrounded on three sides by the tower, and the fourth wall looked like it had been broken, the crashing sea revealed by the lack of stone.

"This is where we do most of our nyxka training," Leif explained. "First, we're going to figure out what exactly your ability is. Then you're going to push it to its limits. Sound good?"

"Yeah, let's do this."

"Ok, so let's start with the basics. To use your ability, you have to be in an intensely focused state. It also helps not to think about anything. Let your power carry you to your goal. This is known as 'allowing your Instinct to power you' and is the basis for all nyxka."

Rykar cleared his mind. Right as he did this, he felt the darkness begin to invade. The one that stole him from the light. Its presence was still strong, still overpowering. It scared him more than anything, and he wished he understood it better.

Suddenly he remembered a few moments of power as a child. The sensation was one of freedom and explosivity. He breathed deeply and tried to recreate that feeling.

"Take your time, it won't come immediately," Leif called over. Rykar only just realized that the man had put a decent amount of distance between them, probably for safety.

Rykar felt powerful, but he didn't feel like anything amazing was happening. He figured he would have a moment of thoughtlessness followed by a huge dramatic scene in which his power was realized. This was far less satisfying.

He began walking over to Leif to ask him for help, but he was met with an unfamiliar feeling. He practically leaped across the entire courtyard, leaving cracked stones where he was originally standing. It almost felt like he was a sail that was being fully pushed by the wind. In his mind, he re-membered bones crunching where his blows landed. A snap. Screams. Hatred at himself. He thought he had killed the part of him that was still broken from the encounter.

"Oh, wow," Leif said, sounding stunned. Rykar wasn't exactly sure where he was at first. Leif's original position in the courtyard had seemingly been abandoned. Upon further in-spection, Leif was floating, no, flying above Rykar. So his nyxka *did* allow him to do that.

"Try to imagine yourself using your power!" Leif called down. "If you can move from one place to another instantly, then try to imagine yourself doing that!"

Rykar thought about that for a moment and figured that it made some sense. For some reason, he felt the need to close his eyes when he did this. He imagined himself standing back where he had "stepped" from.

This was met with a substantial amount of pressure in the form of resistance. If he pushed any further, he felt like some massive threshold would burst, revealing untold de-struction. He didn't know how he knew, but he thought it might damage something critical to reality itself.

He tried again, except this time he imagined swapping places with a version of himself made out of air. He pictured that spot with an empty outline of himself while he kept his eyes open.

To his surprise, the world changed. Or rather, his posi-tion did. It worked exactly like he thought it might. He tried it again, except this time he saw himself standing at the top of one of the towers. Strangely, it didn't work.

"Hey, Leif!" he called out.

"What's up?" Leif responded, flying closer.

"Why could I teleport from there to here but not to the top of the tower? Any ideas?"

"Oh, so that's how your power works . . ." Leif said, nodding ponderously. "Everyone has something called ka. It is the conduit for your power, allowing you to interact with the world. Your body naturally leaks it out of you in specific quantities that the Research Division has calculated, but you can control that leak with practice. Since you didn't go to the top of the tower, your ka isn't up there. Essentially, you have to go to all of the places you want to teleport to."

Rykar immediately tried to find a loophole in this rule. What if he stuck his finger through a keyhole? Could he break into rooms without lockpicking? What if he learned to control his ka better? What did that entail? Leif's certainty on the topic did nothing to comfort Rykar. All it did was demonstrate how little he knew about the nuances of nyxka. He took a mental note to talk to Hadrian about ka later.

"Alright, I get it," Rykar announced. "It would probably help me if I could spar now."

At this, Leif flew down and landed next to Rykar. He had a kind smile on his face, but it looked like he was stifling laughter.

"Slow down a bit. Rushing through it won't help you. It took me a little over a month of rigorous training to be able to use my nyxka in a combat situation. You seem like you have some talent, but you must exercise patience and restraint."

"How about this? We spar right here and now, and if you still think I'm not ready for combat after that, then so be it." He proposed this with confidence, knowing that he could handle adrenaline and its side effects. Hunting had conditioned him to *some* things, after all.

At this, Leif laughed out loud. The noise echoed through the courtyard. The older man seemed to think that Rykar was weak and inexperienced. This angered him. He wanted to prove Leif wrong and win. Rykar took a deep breath and felt the wind fill his sails again, pushing him forward.

"Alright, I accept."

Rykar didn't give him time to finish that sentence. Right as he heard Leif give consent, he felt time slow. He hated this power, and he hated himself when he used it, but he had to learn to control it or it would control him. He walked toward

Leif and tapped him on the side of the head, knowing that a punch would shatter his skeleton.

Leif's head slammed to the ground as time sped back up. It hit the stones beneath him with enough force to shatter them. Shrapnel flew up into the air, and Rykar felt some of it hit him in the face.

Rykar almost turned around. He was about to when he noticed Leif brushing himself off and standing up. He silently panicked. He knew he didn't put force into his attack, but it was still enough to break most trees, possibly even stone. Leif was dangerously strong.

"Hot Hel," Leif swore. "That was something else. Leopold was not out of line to praise you so much during your rebirth. Exactly the kind of spunk we applaud here in the Warrior Division. And you didn't even let me finish my sentence. You had all of the information you needed. You won't need much training after all. Your Instinct is astounding."

"However," he said, leaning in to whisper, "you are sorely mistaken if you believe you are even close to the pinnacle of power. I could destroy you on a whim. So, if you make a move like that outside of training, know that you will be lucky to make it out in a hundred pieces."

Leif began to glow, exuding both smoke and frost. Suddenly the air around him seemed to change completely. Part of it combusted into flames and the other froze, dropping icicles. The temperature overwhelmed Rykar's skin, and he realized that burns were forming on certain areas of his body while the other parts were freezing. Looking up, Rykar saw that Leif had created a pillar of heat and cold rising to the clouds themselves.

In the wake of that energy, he felt a wave rush over him: heat, cold, and power. All of it overwhelmed him as he stared at a symbol of power, awestruck. There was a reason Leif was the leader of their squad. Beneath all of his stimulated senses, he noticed a different feeling: relief.

# A SEARCH FOR TRUTH

*There are a few moments that make people into something far greater than just themselves. These are moments of chaos, of destruction. Only in the reconstruction can a person rise above their demons and make their life mean something.*

- *Drydnar Vyrtra*

G har wasn't sure how long he had been researching. He hadn't left the library in days. The library's archives were frustratingly incomplete, but he figured that with enough time and patience, the truth would reveal itself to him. He would soon know the truth about the gray robes.

At first, he thought it would be a good idea to ask his father for answers. His father had worked with them in the past, so he should have been able to provide insight into who they were. Ghar was sorely mistaken.

When he asked his father, all he got were a few evasive answers. He either didn't know the truth behind them or refused to tell Ghar. This infuriated Ghar, as he didn't see a reason to hide that kind of information. What would his father lose by telling him what he knew? He had to know something, anything.

He asked around a bit more, but to no avail. No one in his father's employ would speak, either. Ghar had been initially suspicious of them. They were a mysterious group who didn't fit anywhere that Ghar could see. After his attempts at discovery were met with silence, he was convinced. They were more than just a few religious or cultural helpers.

The library gave him a little bit on them, luckily. Men in gray robes showed up throughout history. The earliest recorded instance of their presence was at Grax Rakdi's ascension to the position of the first Lopythlok. They seemed to be giving him some sort of support, but it wasn't clear how. The book he was reading, *A Record of the Rakdi Dynasty*, speculated that they had given him the power of the Sun Avatar.

Of course, they were also present during one of the most historically significant events ever—Drydnar Vyrtra's ascension. Strangely, they seemed to be friendly at first, but they then became antagonistic after they saw his size and power concentration. *In the Words of a God* described a fight between Drydnar and the men in gray robes. The fight was won by Drydnar, but the account of it claimed that these men had nyxka. They might have been of a secret noble family that no one knew about.

This, however, was where his research came to a dead end. All he knew about the group was that they found themselves in the important political affairs of the Lopythtym, and some of them had nyxka and allegiance to something other than the Lopythlok.

Most of the media they were found in simply emphasized the color gray. A few children's books spoke of gray creatures, such as elephants, who seemed to symbolize the men in gray robes. They were often pillars of wisdom but tried not to interfere with the world directly.

Another book, *The Poet, The Priest, and The Pythti*, stood out to Ghar. It held a lot of information about the world for a so-called children's book. Going over the text once more, it read:

Long ago, there lived a pair of friends. They grew up almost as if they were brothers and spent most of their time together. Even as they realized the world wasn't as simple as they had seen it as children, they remained best friends.

One of them decided to try to explain reality through poetry. He wove his words into beautiful murals of language, creating brilliant works that would pass down through generations. His famous words touched the hearts of many, but they never seemed to satisfy his wonderment. The more he wrote, the more he questioned. Life and reality seemed like a puzzle, and, by writing, he was taking pieces out of it instead of making it more complete.

The other decided to devote his life to worship. He figured if anyone could explain the nuances of the world, it was the Pythrad himself. He spent much of his time praying and teaching about the Pythrad. He even went so far as to sacrifice certain things to appease the Pythrad, all in the name of learning more about the world.

One night, the poet and the priest met up again. It had been a while since they had seen each other. They exchanged ideas and theories but ultimately couldn't agree. The poet saw salvation in his power of creation, convinced that with enough work and profound poetry, he would understand everything. The priest, of course, disagreed. He figured that the only thing that knew of a deeper truth was the Pythrad, the one and only true god. He thought that enough worship and devotion to the sky would bring him the answers he sought.

They each went home their separate ways, refusing to walk with each other. They were frustrated with the other, assuming the other had gone mad or at least become irreversibly stupid. *How could anyone think something so wrong?* they each thought about the other.

A long time later, when they were both old and gray, they found themselves in the same bar they had met up in the last time they had seen each other. The last time they had still called each other friends. The last time they had considered themselves brothers.

They were sitting on opposite ends of the bar, and a man in gray robes sat between them. They planned on ignoring the other as they had both become stubborn, old men, but the stranger waved them both over.

"I sense a disagreement. I sense tension," he said. "Please, help me help you repair your brotherhood."

The poet and the priest looked at each other skeptically. They had no idea how the stranger knew about their history.

"Yes, I know more than I should. Would you like to know how?" the man asked.

The poet and the priest eagerly nodded, hoping to learn more rather than repair their broken friendship.

"One of you believes enlightenment lies in creation. He buries himself in his art and creates works that help many, except it does nothing to help him."

The poet looked down, ashamed.

"The other turns his eyes outward, hoping to find salvation in destruction. He believes that by destroying beauty, he will appease a potentially false god."

The priest glared at the man angrily.

"Neither of you is correct, of course. You both have a part of the answer. You each gravitated to one end of power. One to creation, the other to destruction. Ironically, the answer lies in between both of these. In the middle ground, you will find your answers, but more importantly, you will find your brotherhood."

At that, the man got up and walked out the door. The poet and the priest ran to follow him, to ask him more questions. To their surprise, he wasn't outside of the bar. He had seemingly vanished into thin air.

This time, they walked home together. That night they felt fulfilled in a way that they hadn't in a long time. The poet didn't feel the need to write, and the priest didn't feel the need to pray. They had found the answer in the form of friendship.

Ghar thought that the lesson of the story was stupid. In his mind, enlightenment could only come from Knowledge. He didn't understand how anything else could be true. The story did, however, give Ghar some insight into who the men in gray robes were.

True, it was only a story for children with a focus on friendship, but behind every story was a hint of truth, no matter how small it may be. For instance, everywhere people in gray robes were depicted, they were shown to be opposed to extremes. In *The Poet, The Priest, and The Pythti*, the man in gray robes, presumably the Pythti, preached neutrality and finding the middle ground.

Another important thing he noticed in the story was the name "Pythti." Nowhere else were these men given a name. This seemed important for him to know, so he tucked it away in the depths of his mind. Perhaps he would bring it up to the gray robes in his house to see what reaction they gave.

Finally satisfied with the amount of work he had done, he left the library. It felt good to stand up and stretch his legs for the first time in a long time. He still couldn't tell how long he had closed himself off from the world. At a certain point, time had stopped working correctly for his consciousness, and he drowned himself in his studies.

As he walked out of the dim book room, he put on an act of fatigue and general pain. He put his hand to his head, walked askew, and squinted. If anyone were watching, they would assume he was ready to take a break, but the truth was far different. He felt nothing: no pain, no stress, no fatigue. He felt like he was thirsty in a way that could never be quenched, almost like he was a ship that was stuck in stagnant, windless water.

He felt like he was being watched, that the people in the gray robes would find his research suspicious and wouldn't appreciate what he found. They seemed to be working hard to keep their motives and existence as much of a secret as possible.

Luckily, Ghar had a plan. Like all of his newer plans, he didn't write it down. He found that his mind was extremely efficient at storing information; he rarely forgot anything. This particular plan involved him appearing to retreat to his room and then leaving from the balcony. This was a tactic to figure out if someone was tracking you: follow a very strange path no one would take. If no one followed, then he would go to Pelto to talk to his brother to see what he knew. Either way, he wanted to get the attention of the gray robes.

He slowly walked to his room, hoping to catch their attention before he got there. Out of the corner of his eye, he spotted someone in the courtyard. He shot them a frantic look to see who it was. Luckily, it was just Kalia, whom he had almost entirely ignored for a while. He had explained that he needed her to practice her nyxka to be a good Lopythlyk. That seemed to have placated her for a bit.

A little bit later, he found himself back in his room. He felt strangely exhilarated, like that extended period of studying had never even happened, like he had the wind to his back and was ready to run.

He was about to grab a few books and fly away to Pelto when he noticed something outside of his window. At first, it was just a small, distant noise. Then he sent his ka out in a bubble to try to get a better sense of what the sound was. A part of him hoped it was nothing, but he needed information.

Luck was on his side. He sensed a person floating above the top of his balcony, probably planning to either drop down and apprehend Ghar or just follow closely behind him as he left. Somehow they had an idea of what he was planning.

He gathered up all of the nearby rocks in the area and swirled them around the balcony to confuse the gray robe.

While the man was distracted, Ghar flung the stones up and around him and then began to squeeze. A moment later, a man encased in rocks fell and landed hard on the balcony.

"Well, it appears you've been caught," Ghar said as he looked the man straight into his white eyes.

---

The catch was easy and largely improvised. The more Ghar thought about it, the more he wondered why they had chosen the balcony to stay and keep watch from. He had not indicated that he was planning on leaving from there, yet here the gray robe was.

He controlled the rocks so that they would reshape themselves into the form of a chair. It would probably be easier to interrogate the stranger if he was seated as opposed to lying down. He kept the man's extremities locked down with rocks so that he couldn't leave without Ghar's permission. Before Ghar got the chance to speak, his captive did. That was a pleasant surprise.

"I'm guessing you want to know who we are and what we do. I'll save you the effort. We are just protectors of culture. We help noble men and women who need it."

They most likely had plausible explanations planned in the event that they aroused suspicion. This was going to be difficult, so Ghar prepared another strategy.

"I know you're lying," Ghar said. "I also know what your group does. It's simple. I was surprised to find that you had hidden your work as poorly as you have. Verrrry sloppy, if I do say so myself. If I were your superior, I would expel you on the spot."

He knew he wouldn't be able to ask for any sort of information. The man was prepared for interrogation tactics. The organization seemed strangely intent on keeping its secrets, but Ghar was strangely intent on revealing them. Funny how that worked. He also knew that humans often revealed more with nonverbal signs than intended, so he could capitalize on that.

"You think you know so much," the man responded. "Your ignorance makes you sound sad—silly even. This world is what you see at its surface, everything is as it seems."

This felt too rehearsed, and even if it wasn't, Ghar knew it was wrong. Him simply saying this erased any shadow of a doubt from Ghar's mind, so he pushed the advanced interrogation forward.

"Yeah, you're right," Ghar said casually. "How rude of me to talk about exposing your secrets, which I will do by the way, when I don't even know your name. What is it?"

The man hesitated, then seemed to give in. Ghar smiled as he knew the man would answer, and he realized he had won.

"You can call me Stefan," he said.

This was odd. Ghar had never heard this name before. Most of the names of cities and people were said to be derived from ancient Dok, the mother language of the region. This did not seem to be connected to that at all.

"Say, Stefan, know anything about Pythti?" Ghar asked.

"Oh, Hel," Stefan said as his face grew incredibly pale. "How on Gaz do you know about him?"

Ghar stared at him, confused, although he wouldn't show it. Stefan was scared, and he wasn't faking. His face was one of genuine fear, and Ghar began to question what he had stumbled upon.

"There was nothing in the library that could have given you any new information, I'm sure of it," Stefan continued. "I have to report this, to send an Erinnering to alter your memory. This can be fixed. Just please don't leak what you know."

"No, Stefan. I'll let you go. Just tell your superior to prepare. I would like to negotiate some terms. Perhaps we can be allies. You never know."

He carefully placed two stones on Stefan, one on each side of his upper torso, hidden enough that he wouldn't notice. He also placed a bit of ka on the stones with a command to alert Ghar of everything he did. If Ghar was unhappy with what he was doing, he would simply send the rocks toward each other, ripping through Stefan's heart and killing him.

Ghar watched with a smile as Stefan floated away from his balcony. All of his work was paying off. Mysteries were becoming unraveled, and the true nature of the political structure of the Lopythtym was within his grasp. He was charging at greatness headfirst. He just hoped he didn't trip before he got there.

# THE STARS

*When met with a dead end, push through. When blocked by a wall, push through. Whenever you think you have found an obstacle to your happiness and success, push through. Do it for yourself because no one will do it for you.*

-   *Hadrian*

Rykar was drained. Training with Leif was more taxing than he thought it would be. He had such a long way to go before he mastered his power. The prospect of being able to ooze dominance in the same way Leif did both scared and excited him.

He sat up in his bed and felt the effects of the day before. His ribs creaked under his muscled chest; his hips begged for him to lie back down. Everything hurt. With enough effort and resilience, he could force himself to get up and walk around a bit. Hopefully, a little bit of movement would ease the tightness that sleep brought.

Standing up, he stretched his back and felt a few pops and cracks. The pain felt good, and his movement felt less restricted afterward.

A wardrobe sat across the room, reminding him of the luxuries offered to him there at Headquarters. They had all sorts of products and potions that were supposed to lengthen life and improve its quality: things like soap, something called shampoo, teeth cleaning tools, and lotions that were used to moisturize. The Collective wanted the best for its Warriors and Researchers.

He grabbed his training garb and some of the soaps from where they were stored in his wardrobe and went to the showers. A part of him was nervous; this would be the first time he had cleaned himself like this. Another part of him was excited to see what it was like and how he would turn out. The novelty of the experience was enticing.

A room full of exotic plants and trees stretched before him. It was almost like they were trying to imitate an alien forest where the waterfalls were being repurposed as showers. There were even a few animals present that he had never seen before. The room itself could have kept Rykar occupied for hours. He wanted to know everything about each instance of life. He was incredibly Knowledgeable on a few plants and animals but wished to expand his understanding of the natural world.

Rykar walked over to the waterfall that he would use for a shower this morning. A few other people were in the room with him, but when he stepped close enough to his shower, they all disappeared. He stepped outside the radius and noticed that someone disappeared when they stepped into their shower. There was probably some sort of nyxka being used solely for the purpose of keeping privacy.

Finding a ledge, he used it to place his clothes on. It did feel like paradise. At first, Rykar was uncomfortable as he stripped down to clean himself, but then he reassured himself that no one could see. There was a protective barrier around him. He was alone.

He took a step into the falling water, expecting it to be cold. He tensed to prepare for the chill, but to his surprise, it was quite warm, almost hot even. It felt good on his damaged body, and he let himself relax. For a few minutes, he let the sensation of water running over his body take over, clearing his mind. Then he remembered that he was there to get clean and got to work.

It was amazing how many different types of soaps there were. From the variety of body wash to whatever the Hel conditioner was, he was fascinated. He stood there for a second just running his hands over the bottles, which were made of some weirdly smooth material.

First, the body wash. Its label said something about being for men, and Rykar wanted to smell like a man, whatever that meant. He slathered it all over his body and face and immediately regretted it. For some dumb reason, a sadistic demon had designed body wash to make it burn your eyes.

Rykar ran his eyes under the water for a few minutes to clean them out and ease the pain. He found himself somewhere in between laughing and screaming; laughing because of the novelty and screaming because of the searing pain in his eyes.

Realizing his mistake, he figured the body wash was probably only made for use on the body and maybe not the head. He cleaned off the familiar layer of dirt and grime with the body wash and decided it made sense that shampoo would be used on his head. Rykar also figured that since it would be on his head, it would be ok to possibly go into his eyes. How else was he supposed to clean them?

Wrong again. Moons, this was almost as bad as his first try. The body wash and shampoo demons were in cahoots when designing their potions of pain. He was going to have to get used to this and figure out how not to get the soaps in his eyes.

It was then that he decided that if he was going to truly

clean himself for the first time, he should go all out. He picked up all the body washes and mixed them, then slathered them across his body. The overwhelming scents wafted through the air. He was used to the smell of the hunt, of nature. His ideas of good smells were pine and salt and dirt. Even the occasional hint of fecal matter wasn't too terrible.

This smell was something else entirely. From mountain springs to cooling frost, the man-made scents had nothing on the smell of nature. Not only that, but he would have a harder time blending in if he were to use the soaps before a hunt. Prey could spot odd-smelling things easily.

Suddenly he was reminded that he would probably not be hunting for quite some time. The Warrior Division seemed to be his new life. He felt strangely melancholy at this, thinking it would be easy to let Gyl and some of his other acquaintances go. They had never been particularly close. What made him feel sad, scared, and ultimately alone was the change. Rykar was not known for his ability to deal with change, so he decided to stop cleaning and just stand in the shower for a little while longer. The crashing of the water against his head brushed the bad ideas away and left ripples of satisfaction and relaxation in their wake. Right then and there, he decided that he would shower every day. If not for the cleaning, then for the meditation.

After a while, he was satisfied that he was clean. He dried himself on one of the towels provided near the waterfall and then changed. It felt incredibly good to finally be clean. His joints seemed like they had been lubricated, and he just felt better in general. Strangely, cleanliness brought feelings of freedom.

He took his dirty clothes back to his room and started for the training grounds after. Unaware of where he was supposed to go that morning, this was his best guess. Communication was a problem there. He had no idea what was going on and had no intention of letting that go. Knowledge was important to him. Walking down, he felt a familiar frustration return.

Someone was going to have to explain all of this soon or he was going to leave.

After a moment of mental deliberation, he decided he was going to spend the day doing something other than training. A certain Regional Scholar was going to answer some of his questions before Rykar did anything else to help this potentially evil organization.

---

He wandered around for a bit, unsure of where Hadrian lived. He had mentioned something of knowing when Rykar would need him, but that appeared to be false. Maybe Hadrian had forgotten about him.

He lost track of time. The area was huge. From the multitude of towers to the perplexing hallways that filled them, he was unsure if he would ever be able to navigate it correctly. He didn't even know if he knew where he was right then.

An idea sprang to his mind. It didn't make sense that Hadrian would be able to know what he was thinking—Rykar had never heard of a nyxka that could do that. Maybe Hadrian could hear him? To test this, he yelled out.

"HADRIAN!" he screamed. "I NEED YOUR HELP!"

He put his hands on his knees, panting. That took more out of him than he thought it would, and to his surprise, it worked. Floating down the hallway was the small scholar himself.

"Hey, Ryk. How can I help you?" Hadrian said enthusiastically as he reached out to shake Rykar's hand. Grateful, Rykar returned the gesture.

"I need some answers," Rykar explained. "I have no idea what we do here, why we do it, why I should help, or anything at all. Leif told me he would explain and then didn't, so I figured you could give me some insight."

"Ah, yes. Most people feel that way when they first arrive here. The Nyxtad Collective is secretive by nature, so we often forget that there are people we must share our Knowledge with. I can help you, though, don't worry. Strangely, most people neglect to ask as you did and just spend their time trying to figure it all out on their own.

"The Research Division was founded a few centuries ago by Pythti. Its purpose is simply to gather Knowledge by any means necessary. There isn't much more about the Research Division itself; we're just a school.

"The Warrior Division has a bit of a shorter history. When Pythti realized that some people from faraway lands didn't wish to share their secrets, he formed a group of elite combat nyxtad to steal them. These people became the very first squad of the Warrior Division. Now the Warriors are used whenever the Researchers need protection when trying to learn more. After the formation of the Warrior Division, Pythti decided to rename the organization to the Nyxtad Collective, as we are a collection of all kinds of nyxtad."

Hadrian froze for a second, and Rykar thought he saw something in his eyes. At that moment, Hadrian felt off. He looked . . . wrong somehow. It was almost like he was analyzing the contents of the conversation itself. Rykar tried to ignore his suspicion. Perhaps that was just the way scholars were, trying to learn from everything.

"As to what you, specifically, are doing here, I don't entirely know. I know your next mission is to apprehend a member of the Ruined. They are a terrorist cell that is essentially the largest opposition to the Warrior Division right now. Leopold is Hel-bent on taking them down."

"Can you tell me about Leopold?" Rykar asked.

"He has been a member of the Warrior Division for at least a century," Hadrian began.

Rykar's mind froze. He saw Hadrian's mouth moving, but he didn't register the sound. *A century?!* he thought. How was that even possible? He looked like he was a young man, maybe even just past his rising.

"Although, even with all that information, we still don't

know much about his history," Hadrian continued. "He could be thousands of years old. No one knows, except for maybe Pythti. Some people think Pythti could be a God of Knowledge."

"Wait. Sorry, I didn't hear some of what you said," Rykar revealed. "Could you repeat what you said before you mentioned how little we know and possibly tell me about Leopold's nyxka?"

"Well, that works out, I guess," Hadrian said, chuckling. "You know just as much as I do at this point. According to our records, Leopold is without a nyxka. Even so, it is theorized that he is the strongest combat nyxtad ever."

---

Rykar got some more training in but decided to spend the day by himself. He needed time to think about the news he had just received. If the Warrior Division was used to steal information and secrets, how were they any better than thieves? How could Leopold be the strongest Warrior and not have a nyxka? None of it made sense. Rykar found that Hadrian's answers had only given him more questions that he needed solutions to. Unfortunately, he wasn't sure how to find the answers or who knew how to find them.

He went back to his room and collapsed into his bed. It was far softer than the forest floor or his bed at home with Gyl. Even so, he had a hard time feeling comfortable in it. At first, all of the luxuries and riches that HQ offered were fascinating and amazing, but they were soon becoming unfamiliar and uncomfortable. A large part of him wanted to go back to his old life with his current nyxka, but curiosity stopped him. He had to know more.

As he drifted off to sleep, a dreamscape began mixing itself with reality. Old friends and enemies appeared in his room as well as strange people he had never met. He saw that they were carrying a bear head into the room, which had half-opened eyes, and placed it in front of him, half obliterated.

---

After a while, Rykar decided he had to get up. The dark world wasn't going to do him any favors, and he wasn't going to die just yet. The mists wouldn't leave, but maybe he could find a way out.

Not sure which way was the easiest path to an exit, he picked a random direction and started sprinting. He hoped he could find freedom before too long. A moment later, his legs felt heavy. Running was too difficult, so he decided to walk. A little bit later, walking was too hard, so he had to resort to crawling.

Even crawling was agony. All he wanted to do was lie down and give up. A part of him was ok with the fact that if he gave up, he would likely never find his way out. It wasn't too bad in the darkness.

A larger part of him needed to be free, to see the light again. Hope—the very thing that he had seen before, that had abandoned him. He remembered its warmth and life and swore that he would find it again, no matter the cost. He needed to feel anything but pain and see anything but darkness.

A little bit of rest couldn't hurt. He was going to keep going. After all, he hadn't given up yet. He caught his breath—crawling was becoming a cardio workout—and heard a whisper somewhere close.

At the same time, he noticed that the world was becoming a little bit lighter. The darkness hadn't receded entirely, but it was becoming thinner. This made him feel a tiny bit better. Then he heard the whisper again. It wasn't just his imagination. Someone else was there.

"Help me," it said. "I'm in so much pain. Please help me."

This time it was loud enough for Rykar to locate it. He barely had enough strength to move, let alone crawl, but slowly he made his way over to the other person in agony. At this point, his pain had become so familiar that it hardly even bothered him anymore.

Only when he got close enough did he notice that the person was a young girl. It didn't seem like she could move; otherwise, she would have started crawling toward Rykar.

As he got closer, her whispers turned into screams.

"PLEASE! SOMEONE SAVE ME! PLEASE!" she shrieked at the top of her lungs.

"Hey, hey. Calm down. I'm here to help," he said, but she only got louder. He put a hand on her arm, but she ripped it away. She turned to face him, and Rykar's heart fell. The darkness immediately returned.

"PLEASE, SOMEONE SAVE ME FROM HIM!" Nyral screamed, horror gripping her voice.

---

Rykar woke up, sweat dripping down his face. Sleep was rarely fun for him. His demons always found a way to slip through the cracks of his broken mind and haunt him. He wished he could find a way to stop them, but he didn't think that it was possible.

Getting out of bed, he changed out of his sweaty clothes. Part of him wanted to shower, but one look outside changed his mind. The night was bright, with a full Moon illuminating the cloudless sky. He had to get a better look.

Stars filled the sky, and awe filled his heart. The night sky was something that would never get old. He left his room and walked down to the beach. He wasn't sure why he went but was glad he did. The crashing of the waves, the wind against his face, the Moonlight shining down on him—all of it felt right. It was calming.

He was reminded of the night he arrived and realized he still didn't know how he had been transported. Was it his power or someone else's? He took a mental note to ask Hadrian the next time he saw him. He still wasn't sure how credible the scholar was, but he was the only person who had given him any information. He would have to confirm it through another source in the future, if he could.

Rykar sat down and dug his feet into the sand. The way it wove its way through his toes was satisfying. With nothing to occupy his mind, he thought about his dream. The pain felt so real, so horrible. He didn't understand why sleeping was when he met his demons.

For the first time since he had arrived, he let his walls down. Everything that had bottled itself up came out. All of his hatred, his sadness, and his anger broke through like water rushing through a shattered dam.

In these moments of loneliness, he hated himself the most. He hated his weakness and his inability to move on from his regrets and mistakes. He didn't have the strength to save himself and didn't allow anyone else to help him, not that they would want to. He had been a lost cause ever since the day he killed his parents.

He heard someone walk up behind him and panicked. He couldn't let anyone see him like this. Rykar turned and looked over his shoulder to see Ahren standing a few strides behind him, his sword floating next to his arm.

"We Hakirons have a strange way of thinking about the stars," Ahren began. "No one knows what they are, those bright lights that pierce the darkness and give the Gapythrad company during the dead of night. She isn't alone because of the stars."

At first, Rykar wanted Ahren to leave. He thought he needed to be alone, to bear his burden on his own. He was about to lash out but decided against it, allowing Ahren to continue.

"They say the stars are the children of the Gapythrad, the grandchildren of the Pythrad. These demigods are there to serve the people and to bring joy to the darkness, except I never quite accepted their origin story. For the Pythrad to create the Gapythrad and the Lopythrad, it had to take part of its ka and give it away. But where did the stars come from? How could there be so many?

"I thought about this for a while. You see, I have always been curious. It took me a long time, but a few heavy losses later and I think I have the answer. They are the hearts of our loved ones. There are so many to remind us to think of them, to keep them alive through our memories of them. They shine brightly and pierce our darkness to show you that in the end, no matter how horrible you might have been to them, if they truly loved you, they forgave you in death. The stars are a memory of the past that are placed there to fix the broken ones who think there is no future."

As he heard this, Rykar felt himself crying. He looked over his shoulder to say something, anything, to Ahren. The man had said something that Rykar needed to hear for a long time. When he turned around, Ahren was gone. Rykar was alone again and sat staring, thinking about how the first words Ahren had said to him were some of the most profound words he had ever heard.

# TIRMEG

*When I first arrived, I thought I had been condemned to Hel. I thought Pythti had stolen my life and my legacy and left nothing in its place. However, the more I learned, the more I realized Gaz was Hel. I had escaped only to find a free, fiery wasteland.*
- *The Demon King*

Ghar was worried. After the initial shock and adrenaline of confirming the existence of something truly mysterious, he realized he didn't know what he was supposed to do. He didn't have the resources to deal with a large group of people, so he needed more information. Somehow, he needed to gather intel on this still-unknown group and use it to make himself appear more interesting to them. He had to pull them out; there was little to no chance they would come to him themselves.

His plans were fine; they just didn't take the gray robes into account. He felt uncomfortable moving forward with them when there was such a large unknown he was being dealt. If he hadn't interacted with them, then the circumstances would be different.

He figured a good way to bring more attention to himself would be to either go to his brother about the issue or reveal their existence to the public. The former felt more appealing as he didn't feel like he had enough evidence to make a significant impact on the public. Contrary to the way most nobles felt, the peasants weren't stupid, just uneducated. There were quite a few clever ones out there.

On the other hand, talking to his brother could give him a lot of leverage as well as extra information. No matter how much Nadren might infuriate him, he was incredibly intelligent and logical. There was a chance he could provide insight into the mystery itself. The problem was that Ghar needed this information to stay within a small circle of people. He needed to be the one who got credit for the discovery or else all of this would go to waste. It worked with the peasants because they couldn't credibly claim they learned it before he did, but Nadren could.

In the end, Ghar decided it would be a good idea to talk to him. At the same time, he realized it might be a good idea to bring Kalia along with him. She had been on her own for far too long and was at risk of becoming a rogue variable, something he simply could not have if he was to be successful.

He wandered around the mansion for some time, looking for her. His worry grew the longer it took him to find her. Ghar did not trust her to go on her own at all, let alone for plans. Eventually, after a decent chunk of the day was spent searching, he found her in the holy room. A ray of light shone through the stained glass windows and made her red hair glow like an eruption of flames. The sight was truly something else.

"Dear Lopythrad," she was saying. Her eyes were closed, and her head was tilted up to be in line with the ray. "Please give me the strength to carry on my family's legacy. My father was a great man. He did his best in raising me, and he would be ashamed of what I have become. All I ask is that you allow me to be accepted by him. Allow me to carry his legacy to our descendants."

Ghar wondered if that was how Tryl Rakdi felt when Drydnar ripped the role of monarch away from the Rakdi family the first time. It was funny how history often repeated itself.

He walked up to Kalia and placed a hand on her shoulder. To a degree, he understood how she felt. Failing to live up to expectations, whether they be from yourself or your father, was incredibly taxing.

At his touch, she flinched. She hadn't heard him enter or even approach her. She opened her eyes and glared at him.

"How long have you been standing there?" she asked, angrily. "How much of that did you hear?"

"Enough to know that our plans must succeed," he answered. "Don't worry. I'm on your side." Ghar said this last part with a scarily straight face as he lied through his teeth. Or *was* he lying? At this point, he wasn't too sure. He wasn't so much opposing her as controlling her, although she would probably see his actions and plans as opposition.

Strangely, she felt the need to hug him again at that moment. He would have been extremely annoyed at this if he weren't quite so invigorated by being in the holy room. Something was very energizing about just standing there. He felt like he was a ship whose sails were overflowing with the power of the winds, ready to blast off toward the horizon.

He pulled away to see that she was crying. People always got so emotional at the weirdest times, and he was getting tired of it. In his mind, the best place to have a mental breakdown was where no one could see so they couldn't witness your weakness.

"You haven't talked to me in a while. Where are you with the plans?" she asked.

For some reason, he felt sort of guilty for ignoring her. His actions were important to his plans, yet a part of him regretted what he did. That just wouldn't do. He quickly banished those thoughts and prepared his mind for an answer to her question.

"Soon, probably tomorrow, we are going to take a trip to Pelto. I think it is time to speak with the king," he said with a smile.

She looked confused, and he felt himself getting irritated. He was hoping he wouldn't have to explain his reasoning to her. It was way easier when she didn't ask unnecessary questions.

"Why are we seeing Nadren?" she annoyingly asked. "Don't we want him to be unaware of our plans?"

"We can speak with him without revealing our plans, young one." He added this last bit about her age to demonstrate his frustration, but she didn't seem to pick up on that. Pity. "We are talking to him to get him to reveal information about himself so we can undermine his regime. I just hope he still loves and trusts me."

"But what could he tell us that is relevant to our plans?" She was still asking questions? Why couldn't she be quiet and let him deal with the gory details? "Rather, what are you planning? It would help me to know."

He took a moment to calm himself. She was seriously infuriating. Her ignorance of social situations was astounding. The fact that she didn't understand how he felt about her annoyed him to no end, but he kept quiet. Better to placate than provoke. In this case, that meant lying.

"I need to get a better understanding of the layout of the palace. If I can map it out and determine how long it takes for him to get between rooms, I can successfully set up a distraction to get him away from the throne room long enough to show you as queen to the people. Is that good enough, or do you want to read my notebook?"

The bit about a notebook was, of course, a bluff. He didn't have one. He was using that detail as a point of emphasis to deter her from asking questions, and, to his excitement, it worked. The plan he had ad-libbed was incredibly flawed, so he was grateful that she didn't pick it apart. It would have been hard to defend.

For example, the best type of distraction would have been one where he sent Nadren out of the palace, ideally quite a ways away. In this case, the time it took him to travel between rooms was trivial. Most of the time was being spent elsewhere.

They walked together out of the room, and he caught her staring at him a few times. Strange. Ghar was almost certain he hadn't changed much about his appearance in quite some time, so there was no reason to stare. Nothing should have stood out. He took note of her suspicious behavior and moved on.

She brushed her hair with her hands and looked him in the eyes. She had darkish green eyes, unlike, again, most of the nobility. Most of them had blue or light-green eyes, but no one had eyes as dark as hers. He had also met her father a few times, but she did not resemble him in any way. She appeared to be about to say something, but he interrupted her. His question was more important anyway.

"Are you a Vyrtra by birth or by honor," he asked in a monotone. He found that fluctuations of pitch and tone could be exhausting, so he had started to make an effort to limit that waste.

Her look changed from one of fascination, possibly even affection, to one of anger in a single tick of a nearby clock. Ghar was confused by this sudden shift of emotions. Luckily, she had also confirmed his suspicions. She was adopted, like a few of his "siblings."

"My father found me in a small fishing town in h'Lu-kanon. I was controlling the waves themselves, pushing away boats I didn't like, and pulling in boats I did. My power was disrupting the local industry. He came up to me and told me that I was divine, blessed by the Lopythrad himself to carry out royal duties. He picked me up and took me home, caring for me as if I were his own. He was, and will always be, my father."

"So you were adopted, then," he said, just to be sure. In her story, she made no note of any biological parents, and her weird speech about him always being her father was confusing. Sentiments like that made objective details seem almost subjective, which annoyed Ghar.

He seemed to have struck a nerve, as she stormed off. She was truly an enigma.

"Join me in the courtyard tomorrow during the rising. That's when we leave for Pelto!" he yelled out.

---

Ghar spent much of the night mentally preparing as well as making an adequate vehicle to take the two of them to the capital. They wouldn't be gone for too long, so supplies were probably unnecessary, but one couldn't be too careful. He packed a little bit of food and water and a lot of extra clothing. You never truly knew what was going to happen.

He then built a vessel out of rocks. He did this by touching the ground with his ka and picking up the nearby loose stones and forming them into a simple, rectangular prism that had the top missing but was hollow on the inside. He then gave his ka an internal command that told the rocks themselves to be tied to the skeleton of the ka, essentially binding them all together as one object. Subsequently, he found the center of mass by lifting it a few times and then tied that to navigation and control. This allowed him to transport the entire ship by only imagining its movement. It needed to be at the center of mass to deter force imbalances. He was pretty sure he was the only person who had ever thought of that and felt quite clever for doing so.

The completed vessel sat before him behind their mansion. Most people passing by on the road in front of the house wouldn't be able to see it, but he didn't mind if they could. No one would be able to guess what it was.

He sat back on a tree stump nearby and decided it was a

good idea to name the vessel. Ghar wasn't exactly fluent in Dok —no one was; the language had died before the ascension of Grax—but for some reason, a Dok name felt right. Its cultural influences still existed over a thousand years after its fall. Sifting through his memories of roots, he ended up picking the name *Tirmeg,* meaning airstone.

The work exhausted him. He felt as if he was going to pass out, but he didn't feel the need to sleep. It was a different kind of fatigue that worried him, as it felt like he was one step away from death. He took a few deep breaths and placed a hand on the ground. For some reason, his Instincts told him to try to draw energy from the planet itself. To his surprise, he felt much better after doing this. He wasn't quite as energized as he was in the holy room, but he did feel like he was back to normal.

Ghar looked up and noticed that the Sun was rising. Any moment now, Kalia would run out of the house and join him on *Tirmeg.* He wasn't sure how ready he was to spend any extended time with her. She was hard to read and hard to understand, but at her core, she was more similar to Ghar than he would have liked to admit. They both sought acceptance through ascension.

Right on cue, he caught her slowly walking out of his home. Again her red hair reacted with the Sunlight, almost making her seem like she was on fire. He thought her appearance was funny considering that her nyxka was to control water and not fire.

"What is that?" she asked as she got closer, most likely about *Tirmeg.* She had a pack slung over her shoulder and was wearing a leather outfit, apparently thinking they would encounter a combat situation.

"This is how we're going to get there," he said. "What did you think we were going to take? Horses? A carriage?"

"I suppose I did," she answered, apparently irritated at his questions.

"Those would take far too long. With this, we can get

there by the time the Sun is at its height." When the Sun was at its height, it was exactly halfway between its rising and its set. "It's called *Tirmeg*."

"Airstone . . ." she whispered, running her hand across the rocky vessel. "How does it work?"

"It's complicated," he said simply. "I fused all of the rocks and placed them on a center of mass that I will control. My nyxka is the movement of rocks with my mind." He usually recited his nyxka as if he were certain of what it was, but not this time. The complexity of his creation compelled him to believe that there was much more to learn about his power and ka in general.

"Alright, sounds good," she replied, satisfied by his response. "When are we leaving?"

"As soon as possible." He hopped into *Tirmeg* and shielded his eyes from the Sun. He felt excitement rising in his chest. Not for the destination, but for the journey. If this worked, then it would be theoretically possible to have entire cities that could fly. The implications of his discovery were cluttering his mind.

He realized right as he stepped onboard that the center of mass would change when he and Kalia got in. A little bit of his excitement faded as he tried to think of a quick and easy solution.

"Wait. What are you doing?" Kalia asked when she saw that Ghar had stopped moving.

"Shush," he whisper-yelled. "I'm thinking." Either he had to give both of them a fixed spot to stand on or he had to be able to tell the system to recalculate the center of mass on its own and constantly update itself. He wasn't sure how he was supposed to go about doing this, so he decided to go with the first option.

Ghar had a few of the rocks raise themselves to stand out. In the end, it looked like an open box with a lump at either end. He figured that he and Kalia could sit on them, although he felt comfortable standing for the whole trip.

"Sit here," he said, motioning to Kalia to put herself on her seat. When she listened, he walked to his area and sat on it. "I need to recalculate the center of mass in order to grab and move the vessel correctly. If I miscalculate this, then imbalances along the outside will cause radial accelerations. It will flip over, and we will fall to our demise."

"Oh," she said under her breath. "Well, I hope you get it right, then."

Her last quip annoyed him. Of course he could get it right. He had done it before; it wasn't hard. He just needed to do it again. Lifting the vessel from the current center of mass, he watched where it tipped toward and moved the center of mass independent of the system to counteract the imbalances. After a moment or two of playing with it, Ghar was confident that the ship was done this time. He would have to account for certain force imbalances himself—people couldn't remain completely motionless—but it seemed like it was going to work how he wanted it to.

Ghar reached down and picked up *Tirmeg* with nothing but his will. Describing his nyxka was nearly impossible; rocks just did what he wanted. It was almost as if they were an extra limb.

The ship rose into the sky with a majesty that could not be explained. People had been able to fly for some time, but it had always been a one-person experience. No one knew how to control such a large object and keep it upright, until now. Ghar was making history.

The wind against his face, the Sun in his eyes: both of them were familiar feelings, but, coupled with the glory of his success, they felt new and incredible. They rose for a few more moments, and Ghar reached out with a strong sense of triumph to touch a cloud.

# END OF PART I

# LOST

L eopold was meditating. This wasn't unusual for him. He spent most of his time training, sleeping, or meditating. Breathe in, breathe out. Focus on finding balance and strength. These were the words he told himself during the hours of the day that he practiced.

*Hours?* he thought. What the Hel was an hour? Why had he thought of that? He wished his memory would improve, that bits and pieces would come to him, but nothing ever changed. His mind was broken, so he focused on improving his body. He would have to be the best at what he could handle.

He wasn't sure what people knew about him. He wasn't fit to command anything, let alone an entire army. Sure, he was physically strong. Leopold had the guts to admit that; he wasn't self-deprecating. He was pretty sure he was one of the strongest creatures in existence. He also wasn't arrogant; he just hadn't seen anything come close to his level of power. Well, that he could remember.

An outsider could look at him during his meditation sessions and assume he experienced a certain degree of inner peace. His calm face, level breathing, and lack of movement for hours supported this. *There it is again. What the Hel?* he thought again, interrupting his other thoughts. Well, all of it indicated he was at peace when—in reality—he was not.

The extended time he spent meditating was more like a

series of huge waves. He would feel great, reminding himself how good it was that he was finding a way to play his part, to live his life. Next would be the feelings that challenged him on why he should be proud of anything about himself. He was mentally unstable, and his condition remained unchanged. He had been this way for as long as he could remember, which was, well, part of the problem.

Reaching down, he felt the scars on his chest. Aervin told him they meant something, that they were remarkable. It made sense; his body was too tough to be scarred or even cut. Whatever caused it was powerful, yet he still couldn't remember what it was.

Within his unstable mind, there was only ever one constant memory. It was one of joy, or so it seemed. In it, he danced with a beautiful woman as a boy and a girl laughed and played among the stars. It was oddly specific, a confusing contrast to the rest of his foggy mind.

He opened his eyes and got up out of the familiar cross-legged position. He felt like he could jump and push his body with enough force to leave the atmosphere of Gaz. In truth, he probably could too. He knew his body all too well. The strength in his legs was a comforting force to the weakness of his mind.

Off to training, then. He wished he could go on missions. Being a commander was taking a toll on him. He never actually did anything with the recruits. Leif was getting to do all of the fun stuff. Leopold never should have been promoted; he wasn't meant for a commanding position.

He got to the training room and felt a wave of relief wash over his body. The smell of sweat, blood, sand, steel . . . These were the smells of glory, victory, and strength. They were like a drug to him, always making him feel better.

The walls were lined with weapons, but he chose none. The tower was full of training partners, but he asked for none of them. His mind creaked, reminding him to ask questions about his lost time, yet he chose to ignore it. He was there to break shit.

*What does that word even mean? Shit?* He was struggling again, unsure of where he had heard that phrase. It just sounded right. Shaking himself from the lack of lucidity, he began feeling out his muscles, his power, his salvation.

Unfortunately, he had to restrain himself or everything would break. At one point, he had been able to spar with the Grathyk, the ultimate weapon of the Warrior Division, and that had been freeing. He remembered the experience better than anything, which wasn't saying much, but it made him finally feel complete. He also broke a lot of stuff, so Aervin had asked him to refrain from doing so again. It made sense; Leopold just wasn't happy about it.

He got into his fighting stance. He knew his left foot was forward and his right foot was back a bit at an angle, but he didn't know what right or left meant. His hands were up at his face as if they were protecting him from some sort of invisible enemy.

Leopold threw a jab. A familiar crack and small rush of air followed. Next a roundhouse kick. The same thing. He did this for a few more minutes, trying to warm up his muscles a little bit. He found that he had better control if he warmed up and could restrain himself more easily. He didn't want to break the entire complex by accident.

After he was ok with his warm-up, he gracefully shifted over to stand in front of a cube of stone. His mind was jumbled with all sorts of numbers and names. At first, the cube looked to him like it was about 1 meter in all directions, except he didn't know what a meter was. He also knew it was a little over 6 rays cubed. The second unit made sense to him, but he wished he remembered the first.

It sat on the floor, almost asking to be split into pieces. Leopold looked down at it and gave it a half-hearted smile. It wouldn't stand a chance, but hopefully it would offer him a little release from his head. Too many thoughts, not enough distractions.

Sure enough, his punch resulted in a nice layer of gravel.

He completely pulverized the stone. A shocking realization came from this. He was getting stronger. The last time he had tried the same task, it had broken into a bunch of pieces for sure, just not quite as easily.

Next, there was a cube made of steel. It was the same size as the last cube and a tiny bit more daunting, but not by much. He knew he would be able to do some serious damage to it. He threw his punch and realized all too late that the target wasn't anchored. His fist sunk into the metal as if it were putty. A thump from the collision echoed throughout the area. The shift of power was too much for the cube to handle. Instead of breaking, it flew through the wall, leaving a gaping hole and a resounding *Crack*. It would probably fly for a few kilometers before finally crashing down, possibly even killing someone.

Some people would probably grow bored with power like his. Hel, he couldn't even use a fraction of it safely. His raw strength was enough to topple countries, even planets, and he was using it to sit around a tower all day.

At some point, Aervin would have to send him on a mission. Leopold needed to feel like he was useful. Maybe his mind would even feel better after something like that. Missions always did a good job of distracting him from his mental issues, if he remembered correctly.

Leopold would probably get in trouble for sending a steel cube at Mach 6 out of the tower. *What the Hel is a Mach?* He felt himself questioning his thoughts and took a moment to reel himself in. He needed to ignore that.

Leaving the training room, he felt even worse than when he had entered. He had made a mess, and not the good kind. It wasn't fun. It felt like he was just going through the motions. He hoped the recruits wouldn't fall into his ruts.

They excited him, especially Rykar. Leopold felt that he had a lot of potential and could be his training partner. That would be a nice change of pace. No one else was strong enough to fight him seriously. Maybe if Aervin hadn't killed Drydnar that would be different.

Thinking about Rykar made his mind hurt. Nyxka, simplicity in life. He wished he could feel like Rykar. Young, unsure of what life could bring, still thinking that nyxka changed anything. Damn, did he wish he had one.

It seemed like he did. He could punch a hole in a planet, run faster than anything he had ever heard of, yet Aervin assured him nothing divine resided in him. Shame. He was still an asset to the Warriors with his mortal power, so Aervin kept him around. Otherwise, he would have been kicked years ago.

Rykar hadn't seen the world as Leopold had. Leopold didn't remember much, but he did know that he had seen it all. He wasn't sure how long he had been alive, definitely longer than a millennium, and they had to have been years of action and adventure. He was sure of it.

He reached out and allowed time to slow. Using his power helped him feel like he was alone. When he needed it, he didn't even have to go to an empty room. He could just activate heightened reflexes, or whatever it was.

In this slow time, he walked down to the beach. The stars shone brightly on the water, and he noticed Rykar and Ahren sitting a few hundred meters down the shore. He decided to avoid them and stayed where he was.

The stars seemed to be waving to him, a sense of familiarity prominent. It was almost as if he had been to the stars in the sky, each one offering a different culture, a different problem, a different family.

He felt no sense of loss when he knew he had forgotten what the stars meant to him. Gaz was his home, Aervin was his friend, the Warriors were his family. The only problem was his mind, which Aervin kept saying he would be able to fix. Leopold refused to get his hopes up.

One day he would either remember everything or forget it all. He was becoming more and more convinced that he couldn't die. The Pythrad had forsaken Leopold's right to a sweet release, and he was stuck in the confines of a shattered mind. How pleasant.

A part of him wanted his mind to just break. Maybe that would be the same thing as his consciousness dying. From what he could tell, no one knew what happened in that scenario. A larger part of him wanted to get better and be able to focus on anything but his shortcomings.

He let himself drift off to sleep on the beach that night. He could still see the Moonlight when he closed his eyes thanks to his heightened senses. He tucked his head to his chin and hugged his legs. He was tired to his core. His fatigue was the kind that couldn't be treated with a sufficient amount of REM or with a break from exercise. He was in a constant internal fight, trying to save himself from himself. He wasn't winning, but he wasn't losing either. This gave him an odd sense of comfort.

Slowly, as a dream rose to the forefront of his mind, a memory followed. It was happiness. It was joy. It was safety and loyalty. It was his first memory. Aervin's voice always made him feel better, but this was different.

*"I look at you, and I see a broken man,"* it whispered to him as it faded from his mind. *"I also see a strength in you that I haven't seen from anyone else. Your situation is astounding, my friend. You may look at yourself and find pity, even hate. You were made of glass, broken too easily. You didn't deserve it. The world didn't care. Stand up, wield your shards of glass, and cut the world across the fucking face. Never cease to fight back, never show weakness, and whatever you do, never let yourself fall forever. Your shards may seem like weakness, but they can be strength."*

A moment later, the memory was almost entirely gone. He knew it was a happy one. He knew it was a safe one. He longed for the next time it would surface in his mind. Feeling himself finally drift off to sleep, he remembered one word that he hoped would stay with him forever. *Friend.*

# START OF PART II

# TO BATTLE

*You ask for forgiveness, but can you ever forgive yourself?*
- *Drydnar Vyrtra to the Freer of Fools*

A new day, another shower. Rykar was growing accustomed to the notion of daily hygiene. He found that cleaning himself not only removed dirt and grime but also improved how he felt, about himself and in general.

He hadn't forgotten Ahren's words. Rykar had even tried to see him a few times after the beach. He wanted to thank the swordsman for the kind words while also getting to know him a bit better. It would help to have friends in this unfamiliar environment. Although he had to admit, it was slowly becoming less and less alien and was beginning to even feel like home. True, it had only been a dozen or so days since his arrival; he just wasn't used to acceptance. He felt as if he were in a family again.

After a few days of training with Leif, Rykar was turned

over to Hjalmir. The large man seemed very enthusiastic about the prospect of training with a recruit, and Leif seemed to have other concerns, so it worked out.

"Hey, kid. You ready to go?" Hjalmir asked, bursting through the door to Rykar's room. The first few times, he had arrived for training before Rykar had awakened, so there had to be some fancy maneuvering for him to be ready by the time Hjalmir got there.

"Yeah. What are your plans for today?" Rykar eagerly inquired. He was excited to see what he could do with his nyxka, and Hjalmir was helping him reach new heights every day. He could now teleport and revert to a saved position along with his normal type of teleportation. It was helpful to work with someone whose power had such an emphasis on memory.

"I'm thinking that you and I will go on a small mission," he responded. This shocked Rykar, and Hjalmir knew it, because he had a wild grin on his face. "It's gonna be fun. I just want you to be prepared for what a real battle is like." Suddenly with no warning, the grin faded. A look of grief replaced it almost immediately. "This guy, Theo, is like Leif in terms of power. The Ruined are no joke. We can't have our squad in a state of disarray when the inevitable fight begins."

Rykar nodded along to this. You couldn't train someone for the adrenaline rush of a hunt by sitting inside all day. Eventually, you had to go out and use your hunting skills in real life. Preparation in a classroom meant very little when compared to experience in the world.

"So, what's the mission, then?"

"There is a group of insurgents in the Lopythtym. They are headed for Pelto, the capital, and I'm sure the new king can handle it. I just think it would be smart for us to intervene. From what I can tell, there are only a few people who have nyxka within their ranks, so this shouldn't be too much of a problem."

Rykar was confused. "Why should we interfere in the politics of the Lopythtym? Will this help further the Research

Division's understanding of political philosophy or something like that? I don't understand the purpose of this mission."

"Again, the purpose of this mission is to shake some of the green off of you," Hjalmir said, chuckling. "The Warrior Division is allowed to go on missions that do more than just help the Researchers."

*Allowed by who?* Rykar thought. There didn't seem to be a book of laws that kept the Warriors in check, nor had he seen a government that presided over the group. Again, he felt himself asking questions and becoming suspicious.

They walked through the maze of halls that lived within their Headquarters, finally arriving at the training room. Rykar grabbed the two knives that he wished to use, and Hjalmir went for two longswords, which he would presumably be wielding one-handed.

Again, they traversed the hallways, except this time their destination was a room Rykar had never been to. This one was extremely long with an opening at the far end. On the sides were metallic objects that Rykar had never seen before. A few almost looked like birds, but the farther they went down, the less they resembled avians.

"What is this?" Rykar asked with fascination in his tone.

"From what I've been told, this is called an airport. These are airplanes, or planes, and they can fly swiftly. The enemy never expects us to dive down from the comforting sky itself, so these are an advantage that we continue to make use of."

*So, the artificial birds are called airplanes. How interesting.* Rykar wandered over to one that had wings above and below it, but as he did this, he noticed that Hjalmir was going in an entirely different direction. "Which one are we taking?" he shouted.

"Those are old, not as reliable," Hjalmir responded. "We are taking one that is much quieter and faster. You'll love flying. It's the closest you can get to the Sun."

Rykar jogged up to Hjalmir and joined him next to a sleek and smooth airplane. It looked a lot less like a bird than the other one he had seen. The wings were almost impossible to see, but they were still there. The design was intriguing to Rykar, and he wished he could stop to learn about it, but there was no time. They had to go before the revolutionaries got to Pelto.

They climbed aboard the plane, which only had two seats, and Rykar sat in the back. Hjalmir seemed confident that he could pilot the vessel, and Rykar took his word for it. He had no reason not to believe him.

"Put on your headset," Hjalmir said over his shoulder right before he put a rounded piece of metal with some foam on the sides over his head. Rykar did the same, and suddenly he could hear Hjalmir's voice right in his ears. It unnerved him so much that he almost threw the headset, but he calmed himself first. "Are you ready for takeoff?" Hjalmir asked in his ear.

"Yessir," Rykar said.

Following his confirmation of readiness, he felt himself being pulled to the back of his seat. The plane was moving forward, and it was gaining speed at the same time. Where he was sitting was also incredibly loud. Rykar imagined it would still be hard to hear Hjalmir, even with the headset right on his ears. The speed increased more still, and the vessel neared the edge of the room. Just as Rykar thought they were going to fall off of the nearing cliff, the plane started picking itself up. The next thing he knew, he was sitting above the clouds with the Sun peeking into his peripheral vision.

---

The flight was nothing if not breathtaking. Rykar thought the peak of Kadmeg had made the world seem small, but this was something else entirely. He wasn't sure how he was even supposed to describe how he felt except for in awe.

They were currently a few minutes away, according to Hjalmir. On the horizon, Rykar thought he could see something. *The Pelrad,* he thought. As they got closer, he realized how massive the plants were. The buildings of the city looked like small pieces of gravel compared to the towering trees. They were grown in a circle, acting as a natural wall for the city, which presumably held the Royal Palace at the center.

Hjalmir landed the plane softly at the base of one of the Pelrad. They were entirely in its shadow, a perfect place to launch an attack during this half of the day and on. Unfortunately, their transportation was very easy to spot. Rykar was about to say something to his senior when he saw him pulling an object out of his bag.

"I know it stands out," Hjalmir said, chuckling to himself. "This lamp can read the memories of the area through the world's natural ka, so it is going to make a bubble of light that remembers the past around the plane. No one will be able to see it while this is active."

"Good. I was worried." Rykar looked around and noticed a distinct lack of insurgents. "What are we doing here right now? I don't see anyone. You're going to have to start telling me stuff, or our squad will be in disarray." He added the last part to verbalize his frustration but felt bad after he said it. Hjalmir was such a nice guy; it was just annoying how nobody thought it was necessary to tell him what was going on.

"Fair. I'm sorry." Hjalmir's face fell, almost like the look of grief from earlier. Quickly, it was replaced by a stern and commanding one. "The most important part of divine combat is preparation. The team that has the greater ka command usually wins. Individual skill rarely plays a huge part in lower-level battles. Once you get up to Leif's power or my own, that changes. For now, you will be spending the next few hours spreading your ka around this field. Get to work." At this, the older man pulled a hat out of his pocket and placed it over his head as he sat down against a tree. He was going to be spending the same time sleeping.

Rykar started wandering around the field. From what Leif had told him, his body would just leak ka. He wished there were a faster way to make it happen, but he didn't know how yet. Now was also not the time for training; he had a battle to prepare for.

After he was satisfied with his work, he sat down next to Hjalmir. He wasn't exhausted or anything; all he had done was walk back and forth for a while. It felt like he had accomplished nothing at all, yet the field was primed and ready for the oncoming battle.

As the Sun went down behind them, an orange glow formed in front of them. Torches. They got a little closer, and it was obvious that there were no more than ten or twenty people, although it was difficult to get an accurate count due to the distance. Based on the intel Hjalmir had given him, these were the insurgents. Their numbers meant they were confident in their plans, expected little to no opposition, and had a few people with nyxka among their ranks.

"They're here," Rykar said, shaking Hjalmir awake. He wasn't sure if the man would have noticed them without him being there to wake him.

"Ah, perfect." Hjalmir didn't look groggy or like he had just taken a nap. He looked pumped and ready for battle. A wide smile spread across his face. "Remember, we are here for combat training. We know they want to overthrow the government. Don't waste your time talking to them. If you convince them to give up, you lose an opportunity. Use this one wisely."

The large man reached down and pulled his twin swords out of their sheaths at his waist. Standing there, wielding two massive swords with a glint in his eye and across his hairless scalp, stood a true Warrior. Not for the first time that day, Rykar was in awe. He was certainly not excited for the battle. He felt his heart beating in his chest, the beautiful precursor to adrenaline. He pulled out his knives and tried to calm his breathing. No need to get energized too early. He would save his hyping up until the battle was a bit closer.

"They're taking too long," Hjalmir said with a sigh. He looked annoyed for the first time since Rykar had met him. "Let's speed this up a bit, shall we?" He searched around and finally returned with a stone and a proud smile. "This should work!" He threw it with a force that didn't seem possible in the direction of the mob. One of the torches dropped a moment later. "Hel, yes! Direct hit!" Hjalmir pumped his swords in celebration.

Rykar looked back at the mob and noticed the torchlight was bouncing. *They're sprinting toward us!* Rykar thought nervously. Suddenly the enemy felt much more real than just a couple of revolutionaries or specks of light in the distance. They were men and women who had hopes and dreams of their own, and he was using them as a training exercise. He knew he should feel bad, but he didn't. He was just worried about getting hurt or dying.

A moment later, they were close enough that Rykar could see human shapes carrying the torches. He felt something, almost like they were touching him, but they weren't; he could barely see them.

"They just stepped in your war zone, kid," Hjalmir whispered. So he hadn't been sleeping and had instead paid attention to Rykar's ka spreading. "Go give 'em Hel. If you get into trouble, come back here. I have your ka on me, so it shouldn't be a problem. Just imagine standing right next to me."

Time slowed. Rykar took a deep breath in and absorbed his surroundings. He imagined himself standing at the edge of his war zone, as Hjalmir had called it, and was suddenly transported there. In front of him stood a group of angry warriors. Frozen, they looked tired and scared. Rykar felt his nerves settle, quickly being replaced by a fire in his chest. They weren't monsters who could immediately kill him, just people.

He sprinted around, slashing the throats of anyone he neared. If anything, it was good practice for fighting normal people. He was so used to fighting Warriors like Leif and Leopold that he forgot what most people were like.

Except one thing felt off. A part of him knew it when he arrived initially, but after he had killed everyone but one person, his suspicions were confirmed. Their leader, a red-haired girl carrying a metal rod, was aware of him. She had barely moved at all, so it was hard to tell, but she had an energy about her. A chill went down his spine as he approached her. He could just tell that she had a nyxka.

He felt weird about attempting to kill or even harm her since she could potentially join the Collective. Couldn't he get in trouble for hurting a member of the nobility? Whatever the case, she certainly wasn't powerful enough to defend herself against him. He turned off his power and approached her as time sped back up. She blinked, surprised at first, and then anger leaped across her face.

"What the Hel just happened?" she demanded while water droplets floated around the end of her steel stick. So that was her nyxka, then—water control. "Who are you?"

"I killed them all," he answered simply. "I am a man who was given a mission, and I am about to complete it. Before I do, tell me this. Who are you, and why are you attacking Pelto?"

"Fine, then. I don't need to know who you are to kill you." It appeared that she was furious. Not what he expected from a noble, if that's what she was; he had heard they were composed, yet she seemed familiar with rage.

With a yell, she threw the water droplets at him at a startling speed. He figured they would feel like rain, but they didn't. They moved much quicker than the natural precipitation. One of the droplets even drew blood on his knuckle.

Rykar sighed. "I was going to let you live. I didn't want to kill you if I didn't have to." For some reason, even though he was inexperienced, he felt calm and in control of the situation. This girl had a nyxka, but she was certainly unpracticed. Someone on Hjalmir's level would have killed him in a moment, not to mention the fact that she couldn't keep up with him when he had slowed down time.

Behind him, he heard Hjalmir sprinting toward them. It took him long enough. Rykar was just about to teleport and finish off the noble girl when Hjalmir approached him and grabbed his arm.

"By Gaz," the large man said when he saw the bloodshed. Every corpse had the same wound on its neck indicating a slit throat. Rykar had wasted no time and was not as new to killing as he was to combat. "How long did this take you?" he asked. It was almost as if he wasn't afraid of Rykar's killing prowess. He seemed interested instead.

"Time was slowed for me, so I'm not sure," Rykar said as he glanced around to make sure the three of them were the only ones left alive. "No more than a moment or two if I had to guess."

"You speak of killing my friends and fellow patriots as if it were trivial! YOU ENDED LIVES! I CANNOT FORGIVE YOU!" the girl roared.

Hjalmir looked at Rykar with a raised eyebrow. "Want me to handle this, or do you have it?"

"I've got it," Rykar said calmly, swallowing all of his doubt because of Hjalmir's support. He wasn't sure if he was doing the right thing, but he wouldn't disrespect the higher-ranking Warrior.

Water was gathering around her again, more this time. Her Instinct was enhanced by her burst of emotion. There was no doubt in his mind that she was more powerful than before, but he didn't know by how much.

He took a deep breath, focusing his Instinct again. Time slowed, and the girl went with it. She was no match for him. He jogged up to her, but just as he was about to slit her throat, he stopped himself. She didn't deserve this. An abrupt ending with no understanding of why she died—he couldn't do that to her. He pushed her to her knees and kneeled as he allowed his mind to process time normally.

"I'm a member of the Warrior Division of the Nyxtad Collective," he whispered into her ear. "This was a training exercise. I don't even know what you're hoping to gain by invading Pelto."

"So you slaughtered my friends for a training exercise, then." She sounded defeated. Suddenly the fire returned to her eyes. "I'LL KILL YOU FOR WHAT YOU DID!" she screamed.

"Believe me, I wish you could," he said under his breath as he slit her throat, ending her life.

# TREASON

*I remember the first time I learned I was in shackles. Yes, I was angry. Yes, I was sad. Even so, most importantly, I was happy, excited even. I learned that I had more to live for. I had a reason to fight. I needed to know what freedom was.*

-       *The Freer of Fools*

Ghar was used to flight. Seeing the world from a top view was certainly not novel. It always felt so small from the sky. People walked around, looking like ants. Forests felt like fields of grass. Rivers and lakes seemed to imitate streams and puddles. Everything felt a little bit different but familiar to him.

Kalia had never flown before. Her face was one of pure awe. She ran her hand through the clouds as they passed and seemed surprised to find moisture on her palms. What did she think clouds were made of? Cotton?

She attempted to make conversation with him as they

soared through the heavens. A few times, she tried to ask about his childhood or his likes and dislikes.

"So, tell me more about you," she would say, apparently under the assumption that their relationship was more than just professional.

"I prefer quiet, meticulous planning to the company of friends," he always responded. Their interactions that morning were more or less like that, with a few deviations. She seemed strangely fascinated with Ghar, and it made him uncomfortable.

Slowly, Pelto came into view, and she grew silent as her jaw dropped. "So that's what it looks like from up here."

"I see why they are called the Pelrad," Ghar called over. He was trying to be polite by saying this, but he was also being sincere. The towering trees were a sight to behold. They tickled the clouds gently while also forming a powerfully defensive wall around the city.

"People say they're symbols for the Lopythrad's creative power," she explained. "I believe it. Nothing else could allow them to grow so big."

Ghar flew over the tops of the trees, and the city came into view. It was much larger than he thought it would be, seeing as it was built at the center of a ring of trees. At the very center of the trees was the Royal Palace: Nadren's new and Kalia's old home. It was beautifully magnificent, made of various stones used to imitate the shades of the Sun. At the top stood a statue of a golden warrior. The first Sun Warrior and King, Grax Rakdi. Even though Drydnar Vyrtra was the most famous Sun King, he apparently couldn't change history.

Ghar landed the vessel in front of the palace. He wanted Nadren to know they were there. He had made quite a scene. Over the walls of the estate, he could hear a crowd forming. People were talking about his arrival.

A woman approached him with a stern look on her face. She was around the same height as Ghar or Kalia but had an air about her that made her seem taller. Her blonde hair was reminiscent of the nobility, and Ghar wondered if she had some connection to the noble houses of Lopythtym or if she was just a servant.

"I'm afraid I am going to have to ask you to leave, sir," she said calmly. She seemed well-practiced at dealing with difficult people.

"Sorry to hear that you're afraid," Ghar said as he avoided the woman's gaze. The line got a giggle out of Kalia. "I'm here to see my brother, so if you would just show me the way to the throne room, then we won't have any problems."

"Apologies, sir, but who exactly are you?" the woman asked in a deep bow.

"I'm Ghar Rakdi, brother of the king. I'd like to speak with him." In the end, Ghar met the servant's gaze and picked up a few stones around him. He wasn't threatening her. He was merely showing that he had more power.

"O-of course, master," the woman stuttered nervously. "Right this way, please." She led them through the entrance of the palace. The inside was just as grand as Ghar had always imagined. Bright, yellow light shone through every possible orifice. It seemed to exude Sunlight. Everything screamed royalty.

They approached the throne room, and Ghar prepared himself for what he was going to say. The speech was perfect; it challenged Nadren's power indirectly while also giving him insight into the gray robe organization. Just as he was sure they were about to turn and enter the room, the servant led them past it.

"Why did we just walk past the throne room?" Ghar asked.

"The king rarely spends any time there. A small portion of his day is used to speak to the common folk in the throne room, but most of it is spent at the training grounds or in the library. Currently, he is in the library."

*Of course he's still studying,* Ghar thought. *Even after he's achieved everything I have ever wanted, he still works hard to be better.* Frustrated at this news, he took a moment to calm himself before he entered the hall of books. Kalia gave him an encouraging look, which, if only for a moment, actually made him feel better.

The woman led them into the room past some book-shelves to where Nadren was sitting. He had a pile of books next to him on the floor and a fire roaring in front of him. He, a king, sat curled in a chair, wrapped in a blanket, with his nose buried in a book. How pathetic.

"Your Light, you have visitors," the servant said, bowing. She turned and left shortly after, leaving Ghar and Kalia alone with Nadren. The king set his book down and stood, allowing the blanket to drop to the ground, revealing his yellow robes.

"How have you been, dear brother?" he asked, voice laced with sincerity. He seemed to care. "And you"—he pointed at Kalia—"must be Kalia Vyrtra. Sorry that I had to evict you from your home, I hope you are doing well." Kalia's encouraging look unsurprisingly changed to one of anger. Just as she was about to erupt, Ghar interrupted her.

"I am well," he responded flatly. "I'm here to discuss something important with you."

"Such as?" Nadren was now approaching him skeptically. This wasn't going to be as easy as Ghar had assumed. He racked his mind, trying to think of something that Nadren would accept. Somehow, he had forgotten how calculating and intelligent the man was. His speech didn't feel like it would work. Instead, he decided to improvise.

"I have reason to believe there are people who wish to challenge your power," Ghar began, getting a glare from Kalia. He hoped she would stay quiet so he could finish his thought. "Kalia, could you leave us please?"

"No, I think I'd like to hear this." Of course. She probably thought he was going to give her up. In all fairness to her, it wasn't a bad idea. It just wasn't what he was doing.

"Ok, you can be here too, I guess. There is a secret organization led by men in gray robes who control the politics of this nation." Nadren looked like he was about to laugh, so Ghar continued. "Remember the men who examined us? I'm not saying they altered the results of the test or anything, but who were they? Do you know? Any information could help."

Nadren took a moment, probably thinking. He looked back and forth between Ghar and Kalia through squinted eyes. This had to work.

"I don't know who they are," he said finally. "They have visited me on several occasions, giving me advice and information. What do you know about them?"

"They have been involved in almost every single ascension since Grax," Ghar began. "I'm not sure what role they have in the kingdom or its politics, but, in my opinion, they shouldn't even have one. No one knows what they do, but I can tell you that they certainly have some sort of influence. Shortly after Drydnar was at the height of his power, he met with a few of them, and they tried to kill him. I did a little bit of digging and found out they are associated with the word *Pythti*."

"How did you find this out?" Nadren asked, nodding along.

"I read through various accounts of pre- and post-Drydnar politics. The one continuity, other than our culture, was the appearance of the gray robes. This means they weren't only a part of the Rakdi dynasty. Then a look through *Lopythtym and Light* revealed that they don't have an explicit role in our politics either. This raised my suspicion, so I dug deeper. The only word I was able to find was *Pythti*. I interrogated a gray robe at our estate, and he reacted in an incriminating manner, confirming my suspicions. They certainly have more motives than the maintenance of our culture and don't want us to know more about *Pythti*."

"I'd like you to continue research on this and report all of your findings to me. This could be a real internal threat. If you can do this, we may have a role for you in the capital. An investigator could be invaluable." With this, the king rewrapped the blanket around him and crawled back into the chair, picking up his book again. He looked up at them over his shoulder. "It was truly good to see you again, brother. You may stay here if you like; you're always welcome. Avyl can show you to your quarters." So that was the name of the servant who had showed them in. "Vyrtra, you may go home. The same servant can show you the way out."

As they left, Kalia leaned over to Ghar. "Good thing he didn't figure out about our plans." Ghar shot her a glare. She needed to be quiet. Involving her was quickly becoming a problem. He was going to have to talk to her after they left.

"What was that?" Nadren called over to them.

*There's no way he could've heard her, unless . . . Oh, Hel. He spread his ka throughout this whole room. He can probably hear everything anyone says,* Ghar thought. When Nadren had picked up the skill, he didn't know, but he was aware of the fact that it was possible. Ghar had heard incredible stories of sensory enhancement through nyxka and ka. This was going to be a problem. *Why couldn't she just stay quiet?*

His brother walked over to them, this time getting close enough to show how much taller he was than they were. One ray was enough to bring Nadren to a little less than one whole head taller than Ghar, and it felt like a lot.

"I'd like to hear about these plans," he said with a smile. "Whatever could you mean, oh kind and regal Vyrtra?" He was enjoying this. It would help him to hurt her public image.

"What plans?" she replied, nervously. If they got out of this, Ghar was going to have to teach her to be a better liar.

"I'm sure you know," Nadren said as he leaned in. "You also know that I can put you both on trial for suspicion of treason. You don't want to make me do that, do you?"

"You truly are a vile king," Kalia said, spitting in his face. "Of course I'm not a traitor. I love this kingdom more than you ever could." Slowly, she realized her mistake. An insult to the king meant going to the dungeon, and spitting would have meant death under her father's rule. Nadren now had solid grounds to severely punish her, not that he couldn't have done it before. He could just unite the people behind his cause now. "Wait. I'm sorry. Please, I didn't mean it. I have problems controlling myself sometimes."

"Yes, you do. That is no excuse for what you've done," he said as he wiped the spittle from his brow. "Avyl, take them to the dungeon, please." The woman came and motioned with her arms as if to ask, *both of them?* "Both of them, if you will. Don't worry, dear brother. I'm sure we can clear this up, and it'll be over in a day or two."

Being sent down the hall by a servant was one of the least dignified moments of Ghar's life. He wished he could condemn Kalia to Hel for her stupidity. He hoped the dungeon wasn't too terrible.

---

Shockingly, the dungeon was like every dungeon Ghar had ever read about. It was a poorly lit, stone tunnel lined with barred cells. Unfortunately, Ghar and Kalia were put in the same cell, even though almost every other cell was empty. Maybe it was because they were "accomplices."

"Why," Ghar said with a sigh, "did you have to say anything at all? We were so close to getting out of here safely. You could have waited until we had walked out the door. But no, you had to reveal THE ONLY THING HE COULDN'T KNOW ABOUT!" He calmed himself when he noticed that he was yelling. "Nice job, truly."

"Well I did, and here we are," she said with a glare. "I messed up. I don't see why we're stuck here, though. Can't you just break the cell with your nyxka?"

This much was true. Since the whole place was made of stone, he could easily manipulate the structure to make his escape. He was worried about causing a collapse, but this wasn't enough to stop him from breaking out. He wouldn't do it because he didn't want to be seen as a fugitive in the eyes of the people. Reputation was everything, and he needed his to be impeccable. With luck, he would be able to successfully defend himself during the trial.

"The tunnel will probably collapse if I try that," he said, purposefully keeping information from her. "I don't know enough about the structure to do it safely, but what about you? Couldn't you use water to break a hole in the walls or the bars?" If she tried to escape and it was shown that he didn't help her, it would make him look better.

"I'm not exactly a prodigy when it comes to my nyxka," she said, appearing ashamed. "Plus, there isn't nearly enough water here to cause any real damage." Ghar knew this last part was false and wondered if she did. A small amount of water shot at a high speed could cut steel. He decided against informing her of this and chose instead to let the issue go.

"Well, then you should probably stop talking to me and try to prepare your defense."

For some reason, this seemed to hurt her. She looked upset when she heard it. He only meant for her to be quiet, but it was also good advice. The trial was incredibly important.

"I thought you cared about me," she said, sniffling. "Now you're abandoning me when I need you."

Ghar's eyes widened as he knit his eyebrows. Was she incapable of understanding the consequences of her actions? He didn't know. She was too self-centered to realize that she had ruined her life all on her own, and he had no reason to help her. It would be easier if she just died. At least then there would be fewer moving pieces in his plans. He refused to respond and engage in conversation with her again. It would look better for him anyway.

"I bet you wish I was dead," she sobbed, apparently crying now. "I cared about you, and you never did anything for me."

Again, silence from his end. Her heartfelt monologue was frustrating, especially since on the surface the plans were all about her. He had told her that he was doing it all to make her the next queen, and she thought he never did anything for her?

"Say something!" she screamed. "You're always so cold." She was almost whispering now. "Why won't you ever let your humanity through? You're a good guy. Smart, handsome, talented, yet you use your gifts to be a cold, heartless monster. Just this once, can you please be there for me?"

Still, he remained silent. He wouldn't let her, a stranger, change his mind. She didn't know him. He looked at her, and she was staring into his eyes. Ghar stood up and looked away, attempting to distance himself from her. She stood and joined him, her face turned toward his again.

"I need you," she said as she reached up to cup his face. Her green eyes shone in the light with a beauty that he wasn't aware even existed. Standing in front of him was someone he could help right now. Should he?

"I don't even know who you are," he finally said. Her face dropped, and she removed her hands.

"After all of this time, you still think of me as a stranger?" she nearly shouted, incredulous. "Who the Hel are you close to? I'm the only person you've had a personal relationship with since your brother ascended. To my Knowledge, you have no other friends than me."

"You're mostly right," he said quietly. "I haven't interacted with very many people recently, but that's because I've been planning for you. You seem to have forgotten that this whole thing was for you. All of it. I've done enough. I refuse to get hurt by your lack of composure. I do have friends, by the way. You just haven't met them."

"You expect me to believe that you did all of this for me? You're too cunning to allow me to take the throne when you could have it yourself. You probably thought you could do this to control me."

So, she wasn't as stupid as she seemed. She gathered information; she just couldn't control herself. Shame. If she were less emotional, they could have made a good team.

"If you knew all of that, then why did you love me?"

he asked after a moment of awkward silence. A shocked look sprang onto her face but was quickly replaced by one of indignance and then one of anger.

"Who said anything about love?"

"You did, or no, it was your body language. You brush your hair when you are around me. You stare when I'm in the same room as you. Hel, even just a few moments ago, you reached in as if you were trying to kiss me. Why do you love me if I'm so terrible?"

"I—" she faltered, not having a readily available answer. "I only ever saw you as a good friend. I thought you were a good guy and were only putting on an act."

"I don't know what to tell you," he said frankly. "This is who I am. If you see it as a ruthless machine of political plans, then that's what you think of me. I can't control it. Don't expect anything from me, though. I can't help you."

"Yes, you can!" she yelled. "You can be good! You don't have to be a cruel, hurt boy who only seeks revenge! You can help people! You can help me! Just tell your brother that I misspoke. He will believe you!"

"I don't want to," he said as he closed his eyes, choosing to ignore her. He had noticed a guard was coming.

The guard opened the cell and escorted them both to the trial. The whole way there, it took a lot of effort for Ghar to ignore the look of betrayal plastered across Kalia's face.

# RECEPTION

*Since the start of time, people have fought for power and success. They slaughter needlessly, thinking they are making a difference when this is just an illusion. They are all the same.*
- *Naria Frektri*

Hjalmir was silent the whole flight home. The lack of conversation worried Rykar. He respected the large man's opinion and wondered if he had made a mistake. He kept telling himself things to make himself feel better. He told you to fight back; death is a part of combat. None of his internal justifications helped. Every passing moment made him feel worse.

Finally, they arrived back at Headquarters, and Hjalmir landed the plane. Even as they climbed out, Hjalmir refused to speak.

"Hey, did I do something wrong?" Rykar finally asked, hoping to break the tension.

Hjalmir turned his head so Rykar could see his face for the first time since the battle had ended. It was wet, presumably from tears. His eyes were red as well. He had been crying.

"With you, our team is stronger," he said, smiling. "A while back, we lost around half of our squad to one of the Ruined." As a tear rolled down his face, he continued. "I don't have to worry about you on the battlefield. Knowing you, basically a member of my family, can take care of yourself makes me happier than many will ever know." He walked up to Rykar and embraced him.

Rykar was unfamiliar with affection. He didn't know how to handle situations like these and felt uncomfortable.

"I'll work hard so I can protect the others too. I know how much they mean to you," he eventually said.

"Thank you. I feel blessed to have you on our squad," Hjalmir replied. Rykar had said the right thing after all. He felt a lot better knowing he wasn't in trouble with a high-ranking Warrior.

They both looked out through the flight exit of the room and saw the full Moon peeking out from the bottom. Rykar felt himself smile when he saw the night sky. There was something peaceful and comforting about nighttime, but he didn't know what it was.

"Shall we inform the rest of the team of your impressive fight today?" Hjalmir asked, back to his normal, cheerful self.

"Sounds good," Rykar said, smiling.

They walked through the maze of hallways again. Still the layout didn't click in Rykar's mind. He had always had a good sense of direction, but this place seemed to transcend that. Strangely, everyone else always seemed to know where they were going.

Hjalmir led them back to the training room, where they found Leif and the rest of the squad waiting. Ahren and Ada were talking to the 4th-class members—he couldn't remember their names—and Karl.

"What's going on?" Rykar whispered to Hjalmir.

"Ada took Ahren, I took you. You both had to get combat experience," he whispered back. "I guess they got back first. They're telling their war stories. This is the best part of being a Warrior."

They joined the rest of the squad in the circle right as Ahren was in the middle of telling his story—with some help from Ada of course.

"One of them even picked up a tree and threw it at me!" Ahren said, getting a big laugh from everyone else. "I dodged it, but they seemed angry for some reason. All we had done was tie up a few of their friends." Again, a few more laughs. "In the end, I tied the end of a rope to my buddy here"—he gestured to his sword—"and he did the rest. It was a simple task, but Ada still found a way to get hurt! "

"Hey, I told you to keep that out of this!" she said, laughing. "One of the branches scraped across my face and scratched me. It's nothing, but sword boy here won't let it go." She finished her part with a punch to Ahren's shoulder. They had bonded over their mission.

The laughter felt welcoming but suspicious. Rykar didn't feel close to anyone in his squad. Sure, they had shown him kindness, but they certainly hadn't done anything to earn his trust or his respect. He wasn't certain if he would ever feel like he belonged in their group, or any group for that matter. He never quite fit in and was fine with that. It was better that his guard was up than down.

He realized a moment later that he had zoned out. It was unusual for him to fall into his subconscious, so he figured he was tired. Leif was calling out to Hjalmir and Rykar, probably asking them how their mission went.

"Ryk! Tell us your war stories!" Yep, Rykar was right.

The looks he got were saddening. He knew he would have to embellish to make the story better. Everyone looked so eager to hear a crazy story when he didn't honestly have one. Hjalmir nodded to him as if giving him the ok to tell the story.

"Well, there wasn't much to it," he began, less than enthusiastically. "Hjalmir hucked a rock and killed someone right before they entered my war zone. When they got in range, I teleported over and killed everyone in a split second. Except I did leave their nyxtad alive. She tried to kill me, but failed, so I told her who I was and killed her."

The rest of the squad didn't clap or laugh or even give him any looks of approval. They stared at him, wide-eyed. He knew it. They would hate him for killing. He would never truly be a part of their group.

"Holy Hel," Leif finally said. "It was that easy?"

"Did you even get hit once?" Mila asked intensely.

"Yeah, my knuckle got scraped a little bit," he replied.

Again, more strange stares. What was going on?

"Is this a bad thing?" he whispered to Hjalmir.

"Everyone, give him a round of applause!" he yelled in response. "This man is strong, stronger than most in his position. Give him your trust, and he will have your back."

The overbearing silence broke into a huge burst of cheering. The entire squad jumped up and gathered around him, forming a group hug.

"We got a good one!" Leif yelled to all of them.

They all picked him up and started tossing him up and down. At that moment, he felt a sliver of acceptance sneak into his heart, but he couldn't quite keep the frustration of ignorance from growing as well.

---

They all left the training room together. It was a tradition to eat as a group most nights, especially after a mission. The banquet hall from his first night felt empty without all of the extra scholars, but he liked it better this way. It was easier to get to the exits and see the entire room.

As it turned out, the tower was being used by people at all times. When some people were asleep, others were awake and researching. It almost seemed to exist outside of day and night cycles. In this case, it meant that cooks were working and could make food even though the Sun was probably at its lowest point.

They sat at the end of one of the long tables in the hall. It probably looked weird, having their whole squad crowd into a small area when they had a lot of space, but they were a group, so it made sense.

Rosa was leaning into one of his sides. He felt safe and relaxed for the first time since . . . since forever. After a moment of thought, he couldn't remember a time when he had felt this good. It would have been before that one night with the bear, if such a time existed.

Her presence was allowing warmth to creep into a place in his body where coldness had only existed before. He was afraid to hug or lean back into her; he didn't want to scare her away. He just didn't want her to leave.

*I'll never forget this night,* he thought as he smiled. All of his problems and fears were still there; they just didn't feel as bad when he was surrounded by these people. He wished the night would last forever.

After what seemed like an eternity later, their food arrived. A steaming platter of various meats came first, and Hjalmir attacked it. Of course, he still shared enough for the others, but he made it clear that he was being gracious. The food was his.

Next came cheese and drinks. The cheese didn't smell that great, and the liquid was fruity and sparkly and various other things Rykar had never seen before. He made an effort to try all of the food, but he didn't want to move too much. Rosa looked too comfortable. He also didn't have much of an appetite after seeing all of the blood on the field.

Next came a platter of fruits and some other plants. He had seen most of them before in the wild. The chefs felt the need to cook some of them and even add seasoning. The squad ate it eagerly, probably because Hjalmir wasn't hogging it as much as the meat. Again, Rykar had very little.

A little bit later, while Rosa was still leaning into him, something called dessert was served. Sweetbread called cakes, cold milk called ice cream, and considerably more were put in front of them. Rykar had a bit of something called chocolate but started to feel sick, so he decided to stop eating entirely. The rest of the team seemed to enjoy it, though.

At this point, he noticed Rosa was falling asleep. He wondered if he should wake her up and tell her that the rest of their squad was leaving after they finished dessert. He thought about it for a moment and decided to wrap his arm around her instead. It just felt right.

The squad left in pairs. Hjalmir and Ada, Karl and Eydis, Mila and Leif. Rykar decided to allow Rosa to sleep as long as possible and just tried to stay relaxed. Maybe he could also fall asleep and finally have a night without nightmares.

Ahren stood up, but instead of leaving, he walked over and sat down in front of Rykar. He had a soft smile on his face. For the first time, Rykar noticed his eye color. The dark-brown eyes felt intense and gentle at the same time. Here, right in front of Rykar, was a man who cared and had no reason to.

"You know, you remind me of my brother," Ahren said after a moment. "He was strong, kind, caring. Most of all, he protected those he cared for. You just have a similar feel, I guess."

"What happened to him?" Rykar inquired.

"Long story or short story?" Ahren said, his smile fading.

"Whatever you feel comfortable telling. You can tell me as much or as little as you want."

"So, he and I used to live by ourselves. I don't know what happened to our parents, I just knew they were out of our lives. My brother was my entire family. We didn't have a physical home, but we were enough for each other. We would wander from town to village, staying with whomever would take us in. Sometimes we built a small tent in the woods because no one accepted us.

"One time, we stayed in a particularly nice town. It was a

small mountain village, but the people saw us and began treating us like family. The group that took us in had kids our age and fed us dinner with them as if we weren't strangers. They put us to bed, probably with plans to keep us in their family. They were genuinely kind.

"In the middle of the night, a huge bang woke us up. It probably killed the rest of them immediately. My brother and I ran out of our room, only to find a haze. There had been a fire. My brother shoved me down so I wouldn't be such a big target, or maybe it was so I wouldn't get knocked down. I'm not sure.

"I sat in the corner, watching blurred figures emerge from the smoke, bringing with them pain and death. Blood pooled up on the ground, and I knew that my brother and I were alone, just like we had been most of our lives. One of the dark silhouettes approached me, sword in hand. At that moment, I knew my death was certain. My breath quickened, but no thoughts or feelings came. I gripped my shirt, preparing for the afterlife.

"My brother rushed into my vision, pushing the evil figure to the side. He faced down one of the most dangerous mercenaries on Gaz to save me. He was only ten.

"I can't remember how the fight went, only that it wasn't long. My brother carried a sword that was two-handed and very heavy. The mercenary cut my dear, older brother like he was slicing steak. I rushed over to him as he lay there, sprawled out on the ground. The last words he said to me were 'I'm sorry.' He died a few moments later.

"Next thing I know, the sword that my brother tried to protect me with is floating an arm's reach away from my waist, and the head of the mercenary is in my hands, his body still in the ashes of my temporary home.

"I may have failed my brother, but I will never fail again." He finished the story as a single tear ran down his cheek. Ahren had poured out his life for Rykar, and he didn't even know how to respond.

"He sounds like he was a great person," he finally said. "I

wish he were here so I could meet him."

Ahren stood up and wiped his eyes. "As do I."

"Remember, he's watching out for you," Rykar said, attempting to console him. "As you said, he's one of the stars. He'll always be there for you, and you'll never forget him."

Hiding his face, Ahren began to leave. "Don't you die on me too."

"I won't," he answered honestly. He was beginning to think he couldn't.

---

He didn't know how long they had been sitting in the cafeteria. Rosa had awakened at one point and said a few things but went right back to sleep. Rykar figured he should try to sleep too, so he had leaned his head against hers and did his best to drift off.

As much as he needed to sleep, he couldn't. His mind was too preoccupied thinking about Ahren and Rosa. What did Ahren see in him? He wasn't like Ahren's brother. He didn't protect those he loved; he hurt them. His sister was proof of that.

Why had Rosa become attached to him? She became glued to him after they left the training room, and he had never even talked to her. Whatever the reason, he felt safer and calmer with her. He felt good, and he never wanted to let that feeling go.

His thoughts wandered from topic to topic as time passed. At a certain point, he figured the Sun was close to rising, so he set Rosa down and walked out of the hall to see. Sure enough, a hint of yellow was peeking out over the horizon. They had a little bit more time before they had to be at the training room, so he went back inside to rejoin Rosa.

When he sat down, he jostled her a little bit, and she woke up. Seeming groggy, she opened her eyes to a squint.

"Thank you for staying with me last night," she said

quietly.

"Of course. Glad you got some sleep."

"I'm going to go take a shower, but I'll see you down at training, right?"

"Yeah, see you at training."

"Hey, Aodal?" *Aodal?* Rykar thought. *Who is that?* "I love you."

With these words, his heart broke. She didn't know who he was.

# THE TRIAL OF KALIA VYRTRA

*You may wonder who you are. Are you defined by your actions, your skills, your thoughts? Or is it something much deeper than that? Don't ask me who you are because I don't know. Hel, even with all of my accolades, I don't know who I am.*

- *Drydnar Vyrtra*

T he courtroom was far less regal than Ghar had expected. Instead of being bright and yellow like much of the rest of the palace, it was brown and wooden. It felt very bland and almost heretical, seeing as it did reside in the center of their most holy city. Couldn't they have at least added yellow dye to the wood?

Kalia sat behind a large wooden table next to a yellow-robed man whom Ghar had never seen before. She was going to be tried first. Ghar was sitting on a bench behind a short wall that Kalia was in front of. Ever since she sat down, she refused to acknowledge him. Her hurt feelings due to a supposed "betrayal" were so obvious, you could practically see them in the air.

The judge also wasn't anyone who Ghar had seen before. She was short, chubby, and had bright-red cheeks that clashed with her white hair. It made him wonder what sort of power this particular tribunal had over the government. Nadren's decisions were absolute, so Ghar's sentence was null and void if he could convince his brother to change it.

"The court brings Kalia Vyrtra to trial with a charge of high treason," the judge began. "Since this accusation comes from our Lord of Light himself, this is mostly just a formality. I would like to remind the defendant that even if I determine she is innocent, she is still not safe. King Rakdi has to agree for the decision to be official. Knowing this, how do you plead?"

"I plead not guilty," Kalia said, unsurprisingly. She would need a miracle to pull this off successfully.

"Who will be representing you in this case?"

"I will be representing myself," she responded, lacking any sort of confidence. Ghar smiled to himself. This could all work out in his favor; he might finally get distanced from her without having to worry about what she might do.

The judge laughed. A shrill cackle echoed through the room, unnerving Ghar to his core. The women exuded diabolical intent. She felt so evil, so wrong, so disturbing. To her credit, self-representation without proper Knowledge was suicide.

A few more things happened, most of them feeling very traditional and unimportant, and then the trial began. The entire time, the judge condescendingly smiled at Kalia. For some reason, this bothered Ghar. He was sure he didn't care about her, so this was an odd and unknown feeling. Not once did Kalia look back at him. She was making sure he knew that she was ignoring him, and he wished she would just know that he didn't care.

"So, explain to us what these plans are that you were heard discussing with Ghar Rakdi, the brother of the king." The judge commanded this with a smirk on her face, knowing that Kalia couldn't provide an honest and non-incriminating answer. The trial was certainly rigged against her, seeing as the judge was acting as the prosecutor.

"We were planning to tell him of our wedding plans," Kalia began. Ghar's eyes shot up, shocked. He figured she would come up with a small, poorly thought-out lie. Not this. This was a problem. "I visited him when the king ascended to form an alliance between our houses. As the daughter of the old king, I felt that I could help the Rakdi family with their new royal duties.

"One thing led to another, and Ghar and I fell in love. He may be cold and calculating, but I would do anything for him because I know he does what he does for me."

Anger rose in his chest. She was going to drag his name through the dirt as she did this. A part of him wanted to object, but he knew it wasn't his place. He needed to show loyalty and adherence to the rules to save himself.

"Well, Ghar Rakdi, what do you say to this?" the judge asked him. "Is she lying?"

"Yes, she is," Ghar said as he bowed to the judge. "She claims we have a romantic attraction when this isn't true. She may be in love with me, and I have reason to believe that she is, but I have never thought of her as anything more than a danger to my brother's power."

He made an effort to tell the whole truth. It made sense that there would be someone in the room, most likely the judge, who had a nyxka associated with determining if someone were lying. He told the truth, but it was extremely selective.

"Your response to this, Vyrtra?"

Kalia stuttered, unable to form complete sentences. She was trapped, and she knew it. All she could do was tell the truth, which proved her guilt.

"Ghar approached me," she began, attempting to calm her newly erratic breathing. "He told me that he could help me win the crown back so the Vyrtra could maintain their legacy. He seemed intent on taking down his brother. I'm not sure why; maybe he's jealous of the king's success. Anyways, in the end, he told me he needed me to practice my nyxka to be able to create a proper Sun Avatar. In the meantime, he would be planning the usurpation of King Rakdi."

"Is this true, Ghar?" the judge asked.

"She is accurately explaining the information that was available to her," he articulated carefully. "However, my intention was always to use this as a cover to reveal her to be a traitor to the kingdom. I had no plans of joining her in this group. I wanted to eventually be like my brother and show my loyalty to Lopythtym and its culture."

The back and forth questioning would have felt amateur and even suspect anywhere else, but it proved to Ghar that someone could tell if they were lying or not. This was most likely a test to reveal information and loyalty. They both had to tell the truth to avoid risking a harsher sentence. Now he just had to figure out how the power worked. If it measured human impulses, then perhaps he could trick it. All he had to do was convince himself he was telling the truth.

"No, you told me that you wanted to take down your brother's claim to the throne," Kalia shouted at him. "Don't lie. You were the mastermind here."

Turning to address the judge, Ghar decided to avoid direct discussion with Kalia. She was acting unpredictable and emotional. It would be hard to control what was said and revealed in discourse with her.

Calming himself, he looked inward. His memories were of betrayal, so if he tried to say anything different while also revealing more information, he would be lying and would probably get caught. All he had to do was trick his mind into thinking that he had different memories. In his head, he fabricated a sequence of information that would show him acting as a spy for his brother to help his family. That would have to do.

"I was acting in favor of my family the whole time," Ghar lied. "I intended to help my brother maintain his position as king. Since the Vyrtra dynasty lasted so long, it would be difficult for our family to cement its role in the capital. I decided it would be best to control her on my terms without telling Nadren, which was certainly a mistake. I apologize."

The lie flowed out of his mouth easily, almost too easily. Kalia stared at him in shock. She probably didn't know what to think anymore. All of her trust in him was gone at this point.

"I appreciate your honesty," the judge said finally, hopefully convinced that he had told the truth. "I will allow the king to pass the final judgment on both of you. Also, since Ghar revealed so much information in this trial, he will not have one of his own. This was an enlightening experience."

"Wait!" Kalia shouted once she realized the judge was done speaking. "What are our sentences?"

"Oh right!" the judge said, hitting her palm to her forehead. Then suddenly she began laughing. "Kalia Vyrtra, I find you guilty of high treason and attempted perjury. Your recommended sentence is death. Ghar Rakdi, I find you not guilty of high treason and recommend you receive a medal for your efforts. Now, all rise for the king. He will pass your final judgment. That is all."

Kalia's head fell, eyes wide. She probably felt betrayed, belittled, and broken. There was nothing she could do to save herself, except maybe beg to Nadren. Knowing his brother, Ghar didn't think he would save Kalia. Maybe Ghar would be proven wrong.

Nadren entered the room slowly. It was as if he wanted everyone to wait for him, and nothing mattered but his presence. While it was annoying, it was certainly regal. He was fitting into his new role well.

"Ghar, brother, I thank you for your service. With further discussion, I tentatively appoint you as the head of espionage for the kingdom," the king finally said. Ghar felt a wave of relief wash over him. All he had to know was the fate of Kalia.

"I will do my best," Ghar said, bowing to his brother.

"I'm sure you will," Nadren said with a smile. Soon after, his smile fell to be replaced with a scowl. "Kalia Vyrtra, I sentence you to death on account of your treasonous activities."

The room went silent. No one had anything to say, anything to add. There was a feeling of intensity that hung in the atmosphere. It was almost as if Nadren were saying, "I have no tolerance for traitors." A moment later, the silence was broken by a bloodcurdling shriek coming directly from Kalia herself.

---

Nadren preferred the library to most other rooms in the palace. Ghar figured he had ascended to some higher plane of existence when he became king, but he was still just Nadren—the boy who preferred solitude and reading to large groups of people and parties. They sat across from each other in front of a fireplace.

"I'm grateful for you, you know that, right?" Nadren explained. "I have had some trouble getting acclimated to my new role as king, and the fact that you chose to help me means a lot. Do you think you could officially become my head of espionage?"

The idea excited Ghar, but it also scared him. It meant that he would be much closer to Nadren, so he could have access to more information. It also meant that it would be easier to catch him and his plans. He thought about it for a moment.

"Yes, I accept. Thank you for this honor," he said after a moment.

"Good. I'm glad," the king said, nodding. "Now, what can you tell me about Kalia Vyrtra? Is she truly a danger?"

This gave Ghar pause. Honestly, she seemed harmless. Unskilled when it came to her nyxka and unpredictable when it came to social interaction. She had a fire inside of her that pushed her to do crazy things, but she wasn't very capable. He frequently found that she couldn't back up what she said she could do. Still, he needed her out of the way.

"I believe that anyone in power, no matter their merit, is a danger to the throne if they don't accept that it is absolute. She may lack physical and divine strength, but her name carries meaning still. I suggest you go through with the execution."

"Yes, I agree. I was never going to pardon her. Once I gave her a sentence, it was a certainty that it would be carried out. I cannot have people see me as weak or forgiving, especially when it comes to traitors. My rule has not been solidified enough yet. I appreciate your help, brother. I'm looking forward to living and working with you again. I've missed you."

The king got up and hugged Ghar. The embrace felt strange but familiar, and for the first time in a long time, Ghar felt sad. He wished he didn't have to do what he had to do, but it was the only way he could find peace and happiness. He had to usurp his brother.

"I have one request, if that's fine," Ghar said as they let go of each other.

"What is it?"

"I'd like to speak to Kalia before the execution," he told his brother. "I believe I could get some valuable information out of her."

"That makes sense," Nadren replied thoughtfully. "Let me know if you learn anything that could benefit us."

"Yes, Your Light," Ghar responded as he bowed. He turned to leave, mentally preparing himself for the coming conversation with Kalia.

"Ghar," Nadren called out before he could exit. "You are truly a kind and loving brother."

With his back turned to him, Ghar felt a frown form on his face. The betrayal was not going to be easy on anyone, especially not himself.

---

The walk down to the dungeon was less stressful this time. The stakes were much lower; all he had to do was talk to Kalia. Except, he did lie to his brother again. He didn't want to learn anything more about her. Strangely, he felt the need to say goodbye.

He approached her cell, expecting her to be cowering in the corner, a shell of her former self. To his surprise, she was standing tall with a defiant look on her face. There was some dirt and grime, but despite that, she looked nobler than ever before.

"What are you doing here?" she spat. He expected this. His testimony and lies had secured her death.

"I wanted to say farewell," he whispered. "I wanted to be honest with you."

"You have no right!" she yelled. "YOU are the reason I'm going to die!"

"You're right," he conceded. "This is my fault. I just wish you would have waited a moment longer before you exposed us. I should have told you to wait, to be quiet, and now you're going to die because of my lack of foresight." He said this with sincerity. He was mad at himself, not because she was going to die, at least he didn't think so, but because he hadn't seen it coming. It wasn't a true spiderweb after all.

To his surprise, she reached through the bars of the cell and grabbed his shirt. He expected her to try to hurt him, but she didn't. She pulled him as close as the confines of the dungeon would allow and rested her head on his chest as she began to cry.

"You were right," she said between sobs. "I did love you. I still love you. I know you care about me too. I just wish we had more time. I'm glad we both didn't have to go. Can you promise me something?" Ghar stopped himself from denying that he cared about her. It felt like it would be poor timing. Plus, he wasn't sure how he felt anymore.

"What can I do for you?"

"Promise me you won't forget about me," she told him.

"I don't know if I can do that," he said honestly.

She gripped his shirt tighter and looked up at him with tears in her eyes. "Please. Just this one thing. Promise me!"

"I swear. I'll remember you," he finally said. Ghar didn't believe he could do it, but if it made her feel better, he would say he could.

"Thank you," she said, letting go of his shirt. "If anyone asks, my last words are 'for Lopythtym.'"

He left her, and this time she did curl up into a ball. The walk out felt much more serious and solemn than the walk in. It finally hit him that she was going to die. He would never be able to see her again. He would never be able to scold her again. It felt like a part of him was missing.

Her loyalty and friendship may have been annoying, but he wasn't ready to be without them. Kalia had started out as a roadblock, but the more Ghar had gotten to know her, the closer they had become. She couldn't die yet, Ghar still wanted her friendship. As he thought about what had happened and what he had done, the smallest sliver of a very unfamiliar feeling formed in his mind. Ghar scowled and banished the guilt from his mind and forced himself to think rationally again.

As he returned to the main level of the palace, an idea formed that could save her life. He wasn't sure if it would work or if he could get away with it, but he had to try. First things first—he had to find a man in a gray robe.

# BROTHERHOOD

*Someone who thinks they are made of steel, hardened, will be cut and broken more thoroughly than someone who accepts their weakness.*

- *Aervin Eroborn*

Rykar took the long route to the training room. He needed time alone to think. Who was Aodal? Why had Rosa sat and stayed with him all night? When he was with her, he found himself asking fewer questions, which was unlike him. It felt good to be thinking logically again, no matter the context.

He probably needed a shower. He hadn't had one since before the mission, which wasn't long ago, but he had worked up a sweat, so he didn't smell great. A part of Rykar didn't even want to go to training. He wanted to stay away from Rosa as he figured things out. Talking to her would only cause drama and problems.

At some point, his long route turned into aimless wandering. Subconsciously, he had confirmed the fact that he wasn't going to go to training. It had also been a while since he had been truly alone. He needed some solitude.

After a lot of walking, he arrived in a courtyard that he was unfamiliar with. It didn't look like there was anyone in it. At the center was a group of trees that had been planted in a tight circle. It seemed like a good place to be alone, so he slipped in between them and sat down in the middle.

It was an almost magical place. Small rays of Sunlight burst through breaks in the branches, illuminating certain shadows. They provided a nice contrast to the natural darkness that enveloped the area.

The light could pierce any shadow, or so it seemed. Its resilience was tremendously satisfying. No matter how desolate and dead a place seemed, Sunlight could revitalize it. Rykar wished he could feel the warmth of the Sun save him from his own personal Hel. He wished it could provide him with love and life as well as light.

He felt the wind, the trees, the warmth, and internalized the feeling. He then imagined his ka attaching itself to these feelings. Controlling his breathing, he told it to leak out faster than it naturally did. He felt emptier once he was done, leading him to believe it worked.

Rykar imagined himself sitting a few strides from where he was. He had never been there, so he was hoping to test this new ability. To his surprise, it worked. He successfully teleported to a place he had never been before by allowing his ka to leak more.

"Hel yeah!" he shouted, feeling a wave of relief and motivation. Maybe if he could prove his worth in combat, he could get more answers.

He tried again, this time with a place outside of the collection of trees. He had never tried teleporting through a solid object and didn't even know if it was possible. Deciding it was a good idea to test, he forced his ka to go even farther out.

He imagined it covering the entire courtyard so he could instantly travel anywhere within those bounds. Imagining himself standing at the entrance, he teleported. It had worked, even through a solid object.

*I need to practice,* he thought. He wanted to be able to beat Leif or even Leopold in a fight. His motivation to get stronger and better was intense, although he wasn't entirely sure where it came from.

He practiced this new way of spreading ka all around their Headquarters. From the courtyard to other rooms adjacent to it, he eventually covered most of the towers that surrounded his current location. It was tiring, but only when he spread his ka. The actual instant shifts were trivial in comparison to how much they took out of him. It almost felt like he could teleport infinitely.

After a while, he was completely exhausted. Not physically, no; it just felt like he couldn't release any more of his ka. He wasn't sure how he could get that to regenerate, but he figured it would do so after he rested or with some time.

"Hey, want a training partner?" someone called out. A man.

Rykar spun on his heels, searching the area around him. Who had said that? Footsteps on the grass. They were quiet, so if they were from a man, he was well trained. A Warrior. Thinking about the voice again, it hit him. Ahren.

"Yeah, where are you?"

Ahren flew down from the sky. Rykar was going to have to get used to looking up when searching. He wasn't watchful for people with the ability to fly.

"Ka or combat training?" Ahren asked.

"Combat. I think I used all of my ka for today," Rykar said as he pulled his knives out of his pocket.

"Good. Glad you got some training."

"Aren't you going to ask why I wasn't with the squad today?" Rykar inquired, mildly confused.

"No, I understand. For now, let's just spar a little bit."

ANNIHILATED

What was there to understand? What did he think he knew? At that moment, it didn't matter. Ahren was standing in a tight, staggered stance with his hands up at his head and his sword floating a few strides away from him. Rykar copied his stance, except he held knives.

He reached in to allow the wind to fill his sails. He wanted to be at his best. Instead of the full gust that usually pushed him, he found a small breeze. It would have to do. Time barely slowed, and Rykar could tell that Ahren had a similar enhancement when he moved with comparable speed and grace.

Rykar rushed in to punch or slash Ahren, but he remembered something at the last second. His peripheral vision confirmed the theoretical danger. The sword was very much in play. It came spinning out of the side of his view, ready to pierce him through the torso. At the last second, Rykar jumped over it and delivered a punch to Ahren's face at the same time.

The other man was well trained. He slipped under the punch and threw his fist into Rykar's chest, right underneath the ribs. Pain shot through his body. It was a good hit.

Rykar backed up, trying to see the sword and Ahren at the same time. Keeping track of both was going to be difficult, but it was the only way he was going to be able to do anything in his current state. Every time he backed up enough to see the sword while also looking at Ahren, the blade would fly behind him. He would have to be able to react to it, because his vision wasn't helping him enough.

A part of him wished he could access his power again. If he could speed up his reflexes and mind like he did when fighting the insurgents, Ahren wouldn't stand a chance. As he thought this, he realized how important it was not to wreck his opponent during training. He needed to build his skills and not just his strength.

His ka was still in the area, so he could use it to teleport and sense the area around him, but that would still make things too easy. He needed something to fall back on in case

159

those powers failed. He needed pure knife training.

He ran at Ahren again, this time to stay close. Range was a problem, and he had to fix it. As he approached, Rykar heard the sword come up behind him. He looked over his shoulder and jumped right as it was about to collide with him. Instead of trying to strike in midair, he landed to plant his feet. When he threw his punch-slash, he was able to react because he wasn't flying uncontrollably.

His current punch was aimed at Ahren's torso, in the same place Rykar had been hit earlier. Ahren dropped his elbow to his hip, blocking the blow. He responded with a knee to the center of Rykar's chest, which hurt like Hel and made distance at the same time.

Instead of retreating like he had last time, Rykar rushed back in to connect with Ahren. If they grappled, the sword would have a harder time targeting him specifically—it might stab Ahren too—thus making the fight easier for him.

He got an underhook, driving his bicep into Ahren's armpit. Unfortunately, his attempt at double underhooks was blocked, and they were both left with one each. Rykar was trying to take the fight to the ground, but Ahren was making it incredibly difficult.

With his overhook, Rykar elbowed Ahren in the teeth. The blow didn't seem to damage the strong man, but it dazed him. In that moment of confusion, Rykar wove his upper arm underneath Ahren's other armpit and forced his forehead into the man's chest. He didn't want to get hit, plus the force imbalance would push Ahren to the ground.

It worked just as he had planned. Rykar ended up on top of Ahren, straddling his body with his legs. He kept forgetting he had knives in his hands and found himself throwing punches to his face instead. The idea that you shouldn't kick a man when he was down wasn't applicable in hunting, so Rykar didn't follow it. Plus, he was punching, so it wasn't the same.

Blood leaked out of Ahren's split eyebrow. He tried to hit back once or twice, so Rykar pinned his biceps with his knees.

Rykar made sure he kept his head and chest low on Ahren so he wouldn't get knocked off. It also helped him from getting struck by the sword. The closer he was to Ahren, the harder it would be to hit him.

Another punch, this one dazing Ahren too much, caused Ahren's body to go limp for a second. An elbow, drawing more blood. He was finished. Rykar knew it. Ahren probably wasn't lucid enough to know it, but he was. A final punch to the temple, and he went out for good.

---

Rykar wished there were a place he could relax at HQ. The cafeteria was a place of fun memories but also of sad ones. The training room felt alien. Every single room was strange or uncomfortable. He felt the safest when he was in his room, so that's where he took Ahren after the sparring session.

Of course, the swordsman hadn't been unconscious the whole way back. He had awoken a few moments after Rykar started carrying him. He held Ahren the same way he carried his sister and the man he took to Gyl right before he left home. He wondered if he should feel bad for leaving all of a sudden. Should he try to contact Gyl? Probably not. His mentor only cared about hunting. If anything, he missed Rykar's stories of the hunt.

A bed welcomed Ahren's pained body into its comforting sheets. As he set him down, Rykar silently panicked for a moment. Where was Ahren's sword? Would he have to go back for it? Before he ran through the door to go searching for it, it glided through the threshold, entering the room.

"Well, that's handy," Rykar whispered to himself. Ahren heard this, because he perked up as Rykar said it.

"Kyrx is always there for me," Ahren explained, almost slurring. His eyes were closed. It was likely that he was mildly concussed.

"Who is Kyrx?" he asked as he pulled up a chair next to

the bed.

"My protector. He's always there for me."

That didn't clear things up for Rykar, but he assumed Ahren was talking about the sword.

"What was that way you carried me?" Ahren asked slowly. "My head hurts, but it didn't jostle me around too much."

Rykar thought for a moment, not sure how to answer. Should he tell him the truth? About how he used it to make himself feel better for the way he treated his sister? How some superstitious part of him believed that doing it would revive his sister or allow her to forgive him? No, this was not the time for that.

"That's redemption for something I broke. I'll teach it to you sometime." He didn't want to close himself off completely from Ahren, so that answer would have to suffice.

"No, don't," Ahren whispered as he looked like he was going to fall asleep. "Your redemption is your own. I can help, but I cannot carry your burdens . . ." The last part faded into silence and then shifted into snoring. He would benefit from some sleep.

---

There was a medical group at HQ. They had restorative nyxtad who knew how to heal people efficiently. This information annoyed and astounded Rykar. It annoyed him because no one had told him, and it astounded him because he didn't think it was possible to nearly heal someone in an instant. They showed up at Rykar's room without any notice and used their nyxka to heal Ahren.

The second time Ahren woke up, he was much more lucid. He didn't seem irritated or upset that Rykar hadn't taken him to a medical professional after the knockout. He didn't seem irritated at all, not even for the brutal beating Rykar gave him.

"Sorry for knocking you out," Rykar apologized as Ahren sat up in his bed. Rykar had spent a sleepless night under the stars on the beach.

"Well, now I know how strong you are," Ahren said with a smile, sitting up in bed. "So long as you're loyal, I value that strength. If you prove to be a problem, then I fear it."

"From what I can tell, I don't think we'll be enemies any time soon," Rykar replied. This seemed to satisfy Ahren.

The swordsman got up out of bed, steadying himself with Kyrx. Rykar reached over to give it some support but only earned a mild glare from Ahren.

"Please, never touch him," Ahren said in response, the smile fading. "He's very precious to me."

*He?* was all Rykar thought, but he decided to keep quiet. Everyone had their oddities, and Ahren's weren't anything dangerous that Rykar knew of.

"Sorry, I won't. Thank you for telling me about that," Rykar said as Ahren looked to the door to leave the room.

Suddenly Ahren turned on his heels. His eyes wide, he looked like he either had an intense revelation or had remembered something important.

"Wait."

"What's up?"

"You fought me when your power was completely exhausted, didn't you?"

Rykar wasn't sure how he was supposed to answer. In front of him stood a proud Warrior, a man who had been beaten down, broken, and fought back anyway. His mental and physical fortitude was crazy, yet even so, Rykar beat him easily when he was weak.

"I had spent most of the morning learning how to control the spread of my ka, and by the time you arrived, I had none left." He hoped this was a respectful way to answer. He didn't want to anger Ahren; in fact, he wanted to befriend the man.

To his surprise, this was met with another smile from

Ahren.

"I knew you were special when I saw you fight Leopold. I'm excited to see what you can do."

"You'll see when we take down Theo," Rykar said, attempting to smile back. He had trouble showing emotion, especially when he felt uncomfortable, but he felt like he was doing his best. It wasn't that he didn't understand social cues, he just felt weird being disingenuous.

"Or we could go on a mission of our own. Fifth class only." Ahren said this with a glint of mischief in his eye. At that moment, he seemed like a much deeper person than the square rule-follower that he appeared to be when Rykar had first seen him.

"What are you thinking?" Rykar asked, essentially confirming that he was interested. It could be a good experience. He needed more combat proficiency.

"I have friends all over the rise side of the continent in the Moon Kingdom. We could visit to see if any of them have anything for us."

"Could we go to my old home, if we're headed that way?" Rykar had some unfinished business he needed to tend to.

"Sure. Just let me know where it is." Ahren stretched out a bit and walked out of the room. Leaning his head back in, he said, "We'll meet in the airport when the Moon is rising. No one needs to know about this, so we'll do it in a single night." Then he tucked his head out and was gone.

# KNOWLEDGE IS POWER

*When the storm comes, you're the one who decides to make it through or not. Your friends may provide you with resources to survive, but only you can use them. Only you can choose to make it through the darkness to find the light again.*

- *The Freer of Fools*

G har expected his search to be both long and arduous. The men in gray robes seemed to be ignoring or even avoiding him, which would have made things difficult. Luckily, they were the ones to approach him this time. While he was walking down the hallway, he saw a line of them traveling toward him. When he ran to catch them before they disappeared, he was pleasantly surprised that they rushed forward as well.

"Ghar Rakdi, we have some questions for you," the one in

the middle said. They all had white hair and eyes and wore gray robes, but there were some clear differences between them. The one in the middle was tall, perhaps 11 and a half rays, while most of the rest were closer to 10 and a half or 11. He also had a striking, pointy nose. He didn't look aged, maybe thirty years old. There were very few wrinkles on his face. Finally, it stood out that he had a black cuff on one hand and a white one on the other.

"I have a request for you," Ghar said to the tall one.

"You do not," he commanded. A bright-white light flashed in between them, momentarily blinding Ghar. All of his muscles tensed at once, then they were all relaxed, numb. It took him a moment to realize that his sense of hearing had been attacked too. He couldn't hear anything, see anything, and his sense of touch was shot to Hel. All that was left was his smell, taste, and ka.

He attempted to use his ka to attach to anything in the area. Before the flash, he had noticed various rocks in the structure of the palace. They would have to suffice. When he reached out to carry them, they were gone. Nothing. No rocks were anywhere near him. Somehow, they were in an entirely new location. He tried to connect to any parts of his ka, but to no avail. His ka barely spread out a ray around him.

"Where the Hel am I?" he thought he said. He wasn't too sure, though. It was surprising how much of a part his hearing played in his speech.

His sight was returning, his hearing not far behind. He was in a chair in an entirely white room. At first, he wasn't sure where his arms had gone. Lacking lucidity and feeling, he couldn't seem to locate them. A moment later, he realized they were tied behind the chair.

The man he talked to before sat in a chair across from him. He seemed to understand that Ghar wasn't able to process information, because he wasn't doing anything. He sat motionless, presumably waiting for Ghar's mind to begin its normal processes.

"You made my life difficult," the man finally said. Ghar's hearing was working again. "Figuring out about our organization. No one has ever done that without some help from us." He went silent again, probably to think.

"We can help each other," Ghar said, grasping at straws. He didn't want to be on this guy's bad side. He seemed incredibly dangerous.

"We cannot. There is nothing you can do for me except tell me how you found out about me."

Ghar's mind went into overdrive. He needed to pick up every little detail that he possibly could. If he was going to be tested, he needed to make sure he knew what was going on.

The cuffs. One white, one black. They probably symbolized creation and destruction, so the man was the balance. The other people were gone. The man felt more comfortable passing through with them, so they had strength in numbers on the outside. That was their credibility. The fact that he was alone with Ghar also meant that he didn't need his lackeys to help him; he was strong enough on his own. All of that, plus Ghar's sudden urge to be a dramatic fool, led to an incredibly satisfying reveal for him.

"Oh, so you're Pythti."

"Yes, I'm Pythti. How did you find out about us?" Pythti asked flatly. Any sense of patience was absent from his tone.

"You really ought to stay a little bit more secret. I'm curious as to how no one found out about you earlier. Helping with the king's ascension? Really? Could you have picked a more obvious role with a less plausible excuse? It would take an idiot to believe that mess of a cover story."

Pythti's face remained still. He didn't react to this at all. Ghar was beginning to like him. His no-nonsense attitude, his power, all of it showed a side that most people lacked. It showed a man who commanded people on Instinct alone. Ghar wished he could learn from him.

"Or perhaps you have a mind fit to join us," Pythti finally said with a sigh. "Would you be willing to take a test to see if you could join our scholars?" His face looked inquisitive. He seemed genuine. Ghar didn't exactly trust him, but this was a way to get more information.

"I will if you break Kalia Vyrtra out of the dungeon and give her a safe place to stay," Ghar said confidently. Perhaps this could work out for him.

"You can do that yourself if you prove that you're an asset to us," Pythti said with a smirk as he waved his hand at Ghar. All feeling and other senses rushed back to him. His wrists were beginning to hurt from the restraints, but luckily they fell away, and he could move his arms again. A door appeared to the otherwise-blank room, and Pythti got up and walked out, motioning for Ghar to follow.

Ghar felt his legs before he stood up. They were a little shaky but feeling better by the moment. When he was satisfied with their strength, he strode through the door after Pythti.

It led to a grassy area with a huge tower in front of it. Pythti made a slight nod to the door, and it closed, disappearing. In front of them was a series of islands with towers on them. Waves crashed at the base of the islands, causing water to spray high into the air.

"Where are we?" Ghar asked, incredulous. He was familiar with the geography of most of Hakiro, and this didn't fit in either country within the continent.

"This is the Nyxtad Archipelago, my home. If you pass the test, it will be yours too." Pythti looked across the area with a proud look of admiration and joy. He was very emotionally attached to it.

"Ok, who exactly are you, then? Also, what kind of test would I be taking?" Ghar didn't want to waste any time cutting to the chase. The clock was ticking. He had to be quick if he wanted to save Kalia.

Ghar didn't understand where his motivation to save her came from. Sure, she was kind and somewhat beautiful, but she was also infuriating at times. Even so, she had never left him. She always believed in him. Whether it be for companionship or for someone to exert his power over, he was somewhat connected to Kalia, and he wasn't ready to let that go.

Pythti looked at Ghar with a raised eyebrow. Thinking back, Ghar might have been rude or disrespectful in asking questions, but he didn't care. He had to know.

"Knowledge is more important to me than hierarchies that exist to put me in a position of submission." Ghar hoped to defend himself with the explanation. "I'm sure you can understand," he added quickly, trying to connect to him.

Luckily, this got a laugh out of Pythti. "As somewhat of an expert on Knowledge, I think I can." He took a moment of silence, probably considering whether or not he should answer. "I don't know how to describe my role, in all honesty. I collect information from all over the universe to benefit my group, which is called the Nyxtad Collective."

Finally, Ghar was getting answers. The gray robes were a group called the Nyxtad Collective. They gathered information, but what kind of information? What did they deem worthy of research? He would have to dig deeper once he was among their ranks.

"The test will just be a quick mission to acquire Knowledge," Pythti continued. "We don't care about your current Knowledge, but we do want our members to be able to get it quickly. The level of information you bring will determine your rank."

Ghar was intrigued and curious as to what he could bring.

"How do you define the quality of information? To someone who doesn't know about the Collective, its existence would be groundbreaking, but to you, it wouldn't. What scale should I aim for?" Ghar was genuinely curious, but a small part of him wanted to find some sort of loophole.

"It has to be something most people don't know yet," Pythti revealed. "If you give me something like the name of a villager on some random planet, you will probably not be accepted. If you discover a new culture of people or a new galaxy or a new Radka, then I'll consider giving you the role of Regional Scholar—the second-highest role in the Research Division of the Collective.

"Does that help?" he finished, seemingly genuinely curious to see if he had answered Ghar's question. He was too transparent for what appeared to be the leader of a secret organization.

"Yes, it does. When do I need to get the information to you?" He felt dumb for asking the question after he asked it. He would have to move fast to acquire the Collective's resources and influence to save Kalia.

"There isn't a specific time limit, but I will consider how long it took when giving you your rank."

"Alright, can I start right now?"

"You may begin. I wish you the best of luck," Pythti said with a smile.

A flash of light blinded Ghar. This one was much less intense than the first one; it didn't deafen him or make him go numb. That was nice. When his vision returned, Pythti was gone, and Ghar was still in the Nyxtad Archipelago, ready to begin his test.

---

Ghar spent an embarrassingly long time searching for the library. If they collected a lot of information, then their library was probably a massive database of Knowledge. He figured there would be a lot of people coming in and out of the library if it was a center of learning, but no such thing happened.

Eventually, he decided to just start walking into rooms. To his surprise, the first room he walked into was full of books. So was the second, so was the third, the fourth, the fifth, and so on. Every single room was filled to the brim with Knowledge.

After a moment of awe, he found a Researcher and decided to ask him about it.

"Every room that isn't used for medicine, transportation, living, training, or hygiene is used for learning. The towers each have their topic and are organized further based on rise- or set-side and level. I think Pythti is the only one who truly understands the book sorting." After his long-winded answer, the man kept walking in the direction he had come from. Ghar could get used to receiving answers like that.

Not sure where to start or where to go, he jumped into the nearest room, overflowing with excitement. There were no clear indicators as to what was in it, but he didn't care. He figured he could just read until he found something interesting or move on.

The first book he opened was about the art of engineering that he had read about before. He didn't fully understand what it said—things like resistors and electrical circuits were beyond him—but he swore he would learn. He picked up every book about engineering and electricity that he could find.

Learning was slow. Most of the books seemed to be for people who were already familiar with the topics that they were written about. Fortunately, he was a quick learner. After a few days of sleepless research, which involved defining words based on context and referring back to certain books over and over again, he thought he finally understood electricity at a basic level.

Another thing he had to learn was a more advanced form of mathematics. He wasn't too new to this, which was a blessing. Not entirely blind, he dove into math books as well to supplement his understanding of electrical principles.

Ideas like algebra and capacitance were becoming less huge and abstract. He knew why they worked and how to use them in real life. Circuitry, magnetism, resistance—all of it was no longer alien to him.

Perhaps he was in a research fervor. Maybe he was going crazy. All he knew was that he wanted to try to create an electrical circuit with his ka, even though it wasn't his nyxka. It wasn't exactly a new concept, to be fair to his possible insanity. Every person with a nyxka could manifest a Sun Avatar, so maybe there were other things like that.

He figured that in the same way he picked up rocks by tricking them into thinking they had a different location, he could trick the particles touching his ka into having a different charge. Nothing crazy, right?

He began by taking a glass filled with water and attaching one line of ka into the water so that it curved into a sort of horseshoe shape. The source of power, or the battery as the books called it, would come from the ka itself. Ghar just had to trick that part into thinking it stored electrical energy.

The idea was that he would know it was working if the water bubbled. The glass, full of seawater, was supposed to revert to a gaseous state when electrically charged.

Just as he was about to begin, he realized that he had no idea how to visualize electrically charging something. When he picked up rocks, he imagined them moving, and they moved to where they needed to go. In this case, he didn't even know what electricity felt like. It was a completely foreign and abstract idea to him still, even though he knew so much about it. He needed to know what it *felt* like to recreate it.

Luckily, he knew how to create it artificially. The books talked about something called a solenoid, which used electromagnetism to push something. It could also generate electricity if the something—a magnet—that it was pushing was instead being pushed by an outside force.

Doing some fancy engineering, as his books would say, he rigged up a device made out of rocks that, when spun at a high speed, would generate electricity. He figured his ka would be able to carry the electricity since it could carry his nyxka. To feel the electricity and the effects it had on his body, he made himself a part of the circuit and spun it.

The sensation was certainly not what he expected. It felt like every muscle in his body was being contracted at once. Even though it was extremely painful, he did it a few times to make sure he remembered it well. In his mind, he would have to recreate that feeling on his ka to create it without the use of his device. Luckily, the device also proved something to him. Conversion of ka to electricity was not only feasible and possible, but also easy. They worked well together.

He went back to the cup of seawater, hoping he had enough Knowledge and information to make it work. This time, he imagined his ka experiencing the sensation that he felt as part of the circuit. At first, he tried to have the whole thing do it at once, but it didn't feel right. Plus, in all of the diagrams, they showed batteries as a small portion of the circuit, so he shifted his mindset. He only made one part of his ka feel it, while all of the others were simply meant to be conduits like when he made electricity earlier.

Bubbles! It worked! His research was amounting to something. He needed a basis for his future research—a goal, or maybe just a direction he wanted to take it in. A theory felt like the best way to truly highlight what he wanted to do.

His theory was this: everyone who had a nyxka seemed to have a specific one that was somewhat unique to them. This ability was Instinctual. With enough understanding or Knowledge of a foreign nyxka, it seemed that replication was possible. In short, with enough Knowledge, he would be able to do almost anything.

For example, if he learned enough about fluid mechanics, he could probably move water like Kalia. If she learned more about geology and classical physics, she would be able to pick up rocks as well.

Reminded of Kalia, the moment became bittersweet. He wished he could work faster to save her, but he couldn't. He was already working inhumanly fast. He hadn't slept in days and was still making breakthroughs. Trying to focus on his success, he got back to work.

---

Kalia Vyrtra, the pride of h'Lukanon, daughter of the

dead king, sat in a cage awaiting her death. Her friend had abandoned her, but she hadn't abandoned hope. She would never give up—that was the one thing that she knew about herself.

From the moment Ghar left her, she began planning her escape. She wasn't a brilliant tactician or strategist like he was, but she still had a nyxka. There was probably enough moisture in the air and in her body to make a piece of water that could be shot through the bars, cutting them. It would just take some practice. Her other option was to erode the stone walls of the dungeon, but that seemed like it would take longer, and she didn't know anything about its structural integrity.

She took all of the excess water in the area and formed it in a ball in front of her face. This included the moisture on her skin and in her mouth, and she felt its effects immediately. It looked delicious—she was parched—but she knew she had to try to cut the bars with it.

The first shot did nothing. It splashed helplessly against the metal. Again. She would have to go until she got it or she would die, and she wasn't planning on dying. A few more times. The same result. More attempts, more failures. She put her head down and repeated the steps over and over again, each time giving it a little bit more speed.

When her eyes felt like they were drooping from fatigue, she used her hands to keep them open. When her back hurt from sitting in the same position, she imagined she was doing a back exercise, and it was supposed to feel that way. Every now and then, she stood up and walked around to get her blood flowing. She wouldn't rest until she progressed a little bit.

Finally, the perfect strike hit the bar. A piece of metal shot out. There was a small but visible slit in the bar—one that she had created. Feeling triumphant but lacking the energy to show it, she collapsed on the floor of her cell and immediately fell asleep.

# FATHERHOOD

*What is my purpose, you ask? Why do I fight so hard, never ceasing? Well, I have perhaps the most important task that anyone has ever been given. I must save humanity from itself.*
- *Naria Frektri*

R ykar met Ahren in the airport later that night. It was chilly; a gust of wind ran through the opening to the outside, brushing against the airplanes and inhabitants inside. Ahren stood stoically next to one of the faster-looking jets with his sword floating close to his side. His black cloak flowed beside him. The cold didn't seem to bother his muscular frame.

Rykar wore a similar black cloak, which was filled to the brim with knives. A bit of leather protection underneath, and he felt safe. For the most part. Anything more and he would lose too much mobility.

"Where to?" Ahren asked as Rykar arrived.

"Gidura," Rykar answered. The old fishing and hunting village he lived in with Gyl wasn't his true home—he didn't have one—but he felt like he needed to talk to his old mentor before he fully committed himself to this new life.

Ahren only responded with a knowing nod, and they both proceeded to climb into the jet-black airplane they stood next to. It was thin and pointy, looking a lot like a falcon. It was very similar to the one Rykar had ridden in with Hjalmir, except it could supposedly do something called "vertical takeoff and landing." This meant that it didn't need to pick up speed so much like the other plane; it could just go straight up into the air.

Ahren sat in the pilot's seat, but Rykar wasn't sure if he even knew how to fly it. Rykar didn't, so the lack of Knowledge would certainly deter them from leaving that way. Luckily, he flipped switches and pushed buttons deliberately. If they got in a crash, it would be a confident one.

"You know how to fly this thing?" Rykar yelled as he put his headset on.

"Sort of," Ahren replied as he did the same. "It can mostly fly itself, and Ada trained me a bit."

The takeoff was rocky, not nearly as nice as Hjalmir's, but it ended up working. The familiar sensation of being pulled to the back of his chair comforted Rykar. He was building good memories with the acceleration.

Once they got high enough, Ahren seemed to be able to gain more control. The ride became calm. The stars smiled down on them as they soared above the clouds. The Moon was just peeking above the horizon, rising higher into the sky in front of their fascinated faces. Even though the two of them exchanged no words, Rykar knew their connection would be strengthened by the experience. It was pure bliss, peace, and beauty.

They sat in silence the whole ride. Even though they had headsets on and were ready to converse, they chose not to use them. Rykar wasn't sure why; it just felt right to him. Maybe talking would break their focus or ruin the moment? Whatever the reason, they both subscribed to the silence wholly.

Gidura, the location of his old residence, approached. Rykar felt dread rising in his chest. He didn't know why he wanted to talk to Gyl. He didn't know what he was supposed to say. Most of all, he didn't know what to expect. He hadn't known Gyl too well when he got whisked away by the Collective, even though he had lived with him for almost half of his life.

There was no visible place to land. They couldn't slow down enough in the area constrained by a forest. Or this would have been true if they didn't have vertical takeoff and landing, or VTOL. It allowed them to lower themselves vertically while maintaining control, enabling them to land in almost any level environment.

A flat rock not too far from the town center worked. Ahren landed on it, still lacking an excessive amount of skill, but it worked. They had arrived in one piece. At that moment, Rykar considered something that he hadn't before. What was Ahren going to do while he was reuniting with Gyl?

Probably noticing his concern, Ahren gave him a reassuring look and broke the prevailing silence.

"I can stay or I can come with you," he said, almost as if he were able to read Rykar's mind. "I don't mind staying here for a while. Just don't take too long."

Rykar thought for a moment. Should he allow Ahren into a personal part of his life? He remembered the night with Rosa and all that the swordsman had revealed. He trusted Rykar enough to share with him, so he should probably try to reciprocate that trust.

"You can come with me," Rykar responded. "Although, I have no idea how this will go. Be prepared for almost anything to happen."

Ahren gave him a slow, understanding nod. He seemed to have experience with similar situations. They started walking toward Rykar's old house while the Moon and starlight shone on them, a memory of both of their failures.

---

Every day, Gyl sat on his porch waiting for Rykar to return. The younger man was cold, dark, probably partially broken, but he had patched a hole in Gyl. The moments that he taught Rykar about the nuances of hunting and how to survive were the moments when he felt happy and alive. Few things had brought him joy quite like that had.

He didn't know what happened to Rykar. They were talking about an event that had confused Rykar, something called the Warrior Division, and when he recited a phrase, he vanished. With him went a piece of Gyl's spirit.

Gyl had never had kids. Yorimal had never wanted them. She claimed they were too loud, but she was probably just worried that they would ruin their dynamic as a couple. So much for that. The fact that she wasn't with him any longer made him question what loyalty meant. He knew it wasn't her fault that she had to leave him. He just wished she could have stayed.

Left alone at a young age, Gyl turned to the forest. Humanity didn't interest him if he couldn't experience it with Yori. She had made everything fun, in her own way, and he felt weird experiencing life without her.

It turned out, the wilderness wasn't nearly as fun and full of adventure as people seemed to think. Every day, creatures fought to survive. They killed, they fought, and they were good at it. Gyl wanted to learn how to survive and thrive as they did. His goal was to be a part of their wild community, avoiding any reminders of Yori.

Learning was slow. He didn't have many weapons or tools to help him. The only thing he had was his inexperienced mind. Various wild herbs and plants were his only source of sustenance for his first few days in the forest.

Soon, he had enough food to eat some and use the rest to

build traps. This allowed him to catch animals, like rabbits. He finally had a source of meat. Once he learned the basics of trapping, he wanted to learn more. Experimenting with all sorts of strange designs, he eventually learned how to do it efficiently. Gyl's hunger subsided as he became more accustomed to his new reality.

One day, everything changed. He stumbled across a child. The kid had brownish-black hair, striking blue eyes, and looked particularly funny when he hung from his ankles. Gyl's traps had become good enough to catch humans. Or maybe this human was dumb enough to fall into a trap. At the time, he wasn't sure.

He took the newcomer to his small hut, feeding and clothing him appropriately. They sat in silence around a fire, watching meat cook. The child, who revealed that he did have a name—Rykar—was starved. He took the first offering of venison and ate it in the blink of an eye. Gyl smiled, glad he could help someone even if it weren't himself. Even if he needed the help.

The following morning, Rykar made it clear that he wanted to leave again. For some reason, perhaps it was his feeling of fulfillment from the night before, Gyl convinced him to stay. He taught Rykar to trap. He taught him which plants were safe and which ones the animals avoided. Gyl seemed to have a passion for hunting, but the truth was he only had a passion for teaching Rykar to live his life.

One day, a few days after they had met, Rykar disappeared. Gyl felt a hole in his heart open up. Panicking, he began searching the forest. He had no idea where to look; he just knew that he had to. Rykar barely knew how to stay safe in the wild.

The Moon began to rise, and Gyl headed back to their camp. Keeping back tears, he felt empty again. About to feel sorry for himself, he noticed a glow coming from their home. A fire? As he got closer, he saw Rykar cooking a mountain lion over the flames.

The only words he remembered from the event were the only words that mattered to him. "What took you so long?" was all he got from the child.

Days turned into years, and Gyl learned to trust Rykar's understanding of the wilderness. His was much more intuitive than Gyl's. He could think like a wild animal, and whether that was a good or bad thing, Gyl didn't know. He just knew that the ability had saved Rykar's life multiple times.

Their lives continuously changed. Gyl realized he had to take Rykar to human society. Rykar didn't deserve solitude just because Gyl couldn't handle the death of his wife. They went to a small village called Gidura and advertised themselves as professional hunters.

People would come in from all over the town asking for help. At first, they mostly dealt with small rodents and pests. Nothing difficult at all, and, if anything, it was quite annoying.

Even though they lived in a village, Rykar still felt a strong connection to the wild. He would disappear for days at a time, probably to go experience the forest. One important thing, to Gyl, was that he always came back. No matter how long he was gone, he always returned.

Gyl wanted to use Rykar's talents. He felt that the young man had a knack for hunting, so he told others that Rykar was a Master Hunter. This got their attention, and they began receiving more and more difficult requests.

No matter how impossible the mission seemed, Rykar always came back. Injured or unharmed, at night or during the day, successful or—on the rarest of occasions—unsuccessful, he always returned.

This time, he didn't. Nothing. He was gone. Gyl stared up at the stars, certain that his protégé had died. He always thought that they had too much of a bond for Rykar to abandon him.

Tears filling his eyes, he ran through his last moments with his student. Carrying an injured man, Rykar came inside and set the man on a bed. The man had recovered from his wounds and moved out. Gyl took note to tell Rykar that when he saw him next.

Next, they talked about the Warrior Division, and Rykar vanished. Gyl wasn't sure what the Warrior Division even was. All of his efforts to learn more from his last moments with Rykar were for naught. He wasn't smart enough, and Rykar had probably paid the price for it.

Swallowing his sobs, he closed his eyes and tried to make the best mental image of Rykar that he could. His blue eyes, his average frame—not too tall, not too short, kind of muscular—his dark hair, all of it was important to Gyl. He wished as much as he could that he was safe and happy. Perhaps selfishly, he wished that his son would come home.

Opening his eyes, he expected to see an empty street like every other night since Rykar's disappearance. To his surprise, there Rykar stood. He and a man next to him wore black robes, but Gyl didn't pay too much attention to their appearances. No longer able to contain himself, he sprinted to Rykar. He held his son in an embrace and couldn't hold the sobs back any longer.

---

Rykar held Gyl in a hug and felt something he hadn't felt in a long time. He felt loved. He felt cared for. He felt accepted. Never realizing how Gyl felt, he always assumed his mentor didn't care about him. He was wrong.

Gyl took them inside and told Rykar about how the man he had saved had healed and left safely. For the first time since Rykar had known him, he didn't seem interested in talking about hunting. He wanted to know what happened to Rykar and if he was safe.

Rykar felt a little guilty about the fact that he thought Gyl didn't care for him. He also wondered if he should have contacted his mentor sooner. Rykar's return seemed like it was important to Gyl.

"I was put on an island and told I could join a group of Warriors," Rykar explained. "This is Ahren. He joined at the same time as I did. He has helped me adjust to life in the Collective. I'm doing well."

"What even is the Warrior Division?" Gyl asked, fascinated.

"We fight for those we care about and for the Research Division, which mostly does research," Ahren said, stepping in.

Gyl took a moment to himself. He had a sad smile on his face, eyes still red from crying. Rykar had no idea how Gyl felt; he just hoped he felt happy.

"I'm glad you're doing well."

"I am. The Warriors almost feel like a family."

Something barely noticeable changed when Rykar said this. Someone who didn't know Gyl wouldn't have been able to spot it, but Rykar could. A slight twitch, a forced smile, and Rykar knew that Gyl felt uncomfortable with this news. He wasn't sure why; he just knew it was the truth.

They only spoke a little longer, and during that short time, Gyl took the liberty of telling Ahren embarrassing stories about Rykar as a child. They got some laughs, but they weren't anything special.

Eventually, Rykar stood up. They had to leave if they were to get a practice mission in before the Sun rose.

"It was good to see you, Gyl," Rykar said as they left.

"You too." Rykar turned to leave when Gyl's voice cut through the night again. "Hey, Rykar?"

"Yeah?"

"I'm proud of you. Keep fighting for the people you love."

---

Gyl was happy to see Rykar again. He was also glad to see that he had made friends his own age. Other people probably thought it was weird that Rykar hung around Gyl, an older adult, so much.

Ahren seemed like a good friend. He jumped in when Rykar wasn't sure how to answer and laughed with them. He even enjoyed the heartwarming stories of Rykar as a kid. Thinking of those times always made Gyl smile. They were truly special memories.

Watching Rykar go on another mission, this time to be prepared to protect those he loved, caused Gyl to swell with pride. He may not have been his son biologically, but Gyl didn't care. He would be there for Rykar in any form necessary. Whether he be a father figure or a friend, it didn't matter to Gyl.

---

Rykar always thought of Gyl as a stranger, obsessed with hunting and lacking the ability to connect with other humans. He seemed like a wild man who couldn't be contained—someone who belonged in the woods.

Surprisingly, that one encounter had changed Rykar's mind. Gyl cared in his way. Rykar knew he would have to visit Gyl every once in a while. They had a strange bond, but they still had a connection.

Rykar had never learned why Gyl had gone into the wild for the first time. Gyl's past was a mystery to him. In the same way, Rykar's was a mystery to Gyl. They avoided personal stuff as much as they could, but they still knew each other. Even though they didn't know specific details about themselves, they could still read each other.

Climbing back into the plane, Rykar smiled. He realized that Gyl had raised him. Gyl had strengthened him, cared for him. Gyl had made him into the man that he was.

# A GREAT ESCAPE

*Few things are certain. The Sun and Moon will rise and set, death will become every mortal's final fight, and the power of humanity will fail.*

- *Pythti*

Unlike his political research from before, Ghar spent a lot of time outside, testing new theories and abilities. Hands-on work allowed him to feel new abilities. This gave him a deeper understanding than he would have received from just reading about them.

The Sun was in the process of setting; a sliver of orange peeked over the horizon to the set. Waves crashed around him, his golden robe and hair whipping against his body as he was buffeted by the wind. He was only just now getting used to the pervasive smell of salt.

His Knowledge of electricity was increasing drastically. Each day, he felt like he was discovering new and important information for his research. After he learned about electrical arcs, he realized that he could replicate a lightning bolt by creating hundreds of tiny arcs and making it appear like they were connected. To manipulate electricity, one simply needed to change different levels of voltage or various other electrical concepts.

To practice with his new power, he waited for it to storm. He wanted to see how well he could emulate a lightning bolt. In his mind, he would have properly mastered the electricity when his own was indiscernible from nature's.

A thunderstorm was rolling in from the rise. It seemed to be materializing into existence with the night sky. The Moon was most likely hidden by the thick, anvil-shaped clouds. Every now and then, a small flash of light would form inside the clouds—a special type of lightning sometimes called sheet lightning.

Ghar felt himself getting nervous. He was anxious to get enough of a basis for his research to save Kalia, but what if he wasn't done with electricity yet? He couldn't afford to fall short. Every moment had to be one of excellence if he wanted to succeed.

The clouds came closer, and rain started to pelt against Ghar's face. The cold splatter was soothing, and he felt himself relax, if only a little. The wind rushed harder now, causing the waves to grow. A true tempest stood before him, and he wanted to prove that he could imitate it. Feeling its power before him, Ghar felt foolish.

He flew into the clouds, being carried by rocks he had gathered around him. As he rose, he dropped his ka in a specific shape—one that he hoped would allow the electricity to recreate a bolt of lightning.

A huge crack sounded around him as he ascended. Natural lightning struck the island he had been standing on. Its majesty was astounding. Before he had done his research, Ghar knew lightning was powerful. Now he could feel it.

When he was satisfied with how high he had flown, he

stopped and closed his eyes. He needed to feel the storm, to absorb its power and its sensations. Everything needed to click with him or it wouldn't work.

He imagined sending a pure bolt of lightning through his fingertips, into and through his ka, then into the ground. He imagined it would feel like all of his muscles tensing for a moment and then releasing all the pent-up energy.

Opening his eyes, he did exactly that.

*CRACK*

To his surprise, two lightning bolts had protruded from him, one from each arm. They were almost completely indistinguishable from natural lightning bolts, and Ghar felt relief wash over his body. He had flown into the clouds, nearly certain he would be, once again, acquainted with defeat and failure. He was wrong. Instead, he met success and power. A smile formed on his face as he realized how limitless his possibilities were becoming.

He was growing more and more unsure of whether or not he could save Kalia before her execution, but, then again, should he? Ghar had the power of gods at his fingertips. What need did he have for companionship?

---

Kalia kept cutting diligently. With her new technique, she had been able to cut into a few bars. She was trying to get a hole big enough for her to fit through.

With each blast, she felt a little bit more satisfied. She kept proving to herself that she wasn't done, that she wasn't useless. She still had a role to play on Gaz. She wasn't done yet. Nadren Rakdi would not have her head unless she was the one giving it to him.

Working with her nyxka was exhausting in a different way than she was used to. A lack of sleep made her eyes droop, and she lost control of her emotions. Physical exhaustion made her want to lie down and never move again. This kind of work just made her feel . . . empty. After working with her power for too long, she felt incapable, incompetent, and weak. It was demoralizing, but she didn't care. The progress and proof of her power sat in front of her in the form of cut steel.

Finally, after what must have been days of work, she cut through a bar. Quickly, she reached out and caught it before it hit the ground. She was worried that the noise would alert a guard. She kept working, except this time she didn't cut through the rest of the bars. With her new bar, she would be able to pry them off once they were thin enough.

Suddenly a thought occurred to her. The guards patrolled the corridors of the dungeon every once in a while. If they saw the cut in the bars, they would likely hasten her execution. She wasn't sure how long she had before a guard came, but she did know that it would be soon. Time was of the essence, so she needed to move faster.

Feeling frantic, she switched from her precision, ka technique to using physical brute force. Slamming her body against the bars, she wasn't sure what she expected to happen. She couldn't move solid steel. She was too weak. Trapped, not only in the cage but also in the consequences of her actions, she hung her head. About to give up, she remembered her father. He never gave up, even when the sickness took his legs. Even when it took his voice. He always looked at her with joy, with pride. Ever since then, she decided she would never give up either.

"Why did you care?" she whispered to herself. "I'm not even your daughter." She felt tears in her eyes and forced them back. She knew he was watching from the sky with the Pythrad. She wouldn't let him see her weakness; he needed to know that he had done enough to prepare her for life without him. She needed him to know that, even if she would have never been ready for that life.

Fueled by emotions, she took a deep breath—not to relax but to prepare. She glared at the bars to her cage and charged at them as she imagined her ka powering her motions. To her surprise, this worked. The bars broke off the rock and slammed into the other side of the hallway, cracking the wall.

Her cutting work wasn't for naught, however. She picked up the cut piece of steel and realized it could be a good weapon for the future. If she ran into any guards, she was pretty sure she would be able to fight some of them. Her nyxka was helpful for some things. Unfortunately, she wasn't trained in combat. All she had was passion, a steel rod, and an intimate understanding of Pelto.

Smiling, she realized she was on her home turf. Regardless of whether or not she lived there, Pelto was her home. She *needed* to retake her home from the Rakdi dynasty. Suddenly seeing a clarity that she thought she would never see again, Kalia began to plan her revolution as she fled her childhood home.

---

Ghar was making a lot of progress with his research. First he had conquered his Instinct, although that had been years ago. Now he was working on expanding his power by furthering his Knowledge.

These were the words he was using for each aspect of the power: Instinct for the powers one is born with and Knowledge for the powers one learns. Ghar felt lucky that he was more intelligent than most, so his Knowledge limit could be higher than almost everyone else. That, coupled with the fact that no one else knew about Knowledge—that he knew of—meant that Ghar could become the strongest. His father wouldn't look down on him anymore. He would praise Ghar for the first time.

After he had created lightning, he remembered that a lot of forest fires were caused by lightning strikes. Since he could turn divine power into electricity and electricity could start fires, that meant that he could probably start fires with Knowledge. He knew this was a possibility; the reasoning just strengthened his theory.

Standing on the beach of a towerless island in the archipelago, Ghar let the night sky envelop him. He found that it was important to mentally become one with Gaz before he did anything with ka. Ghar spread his ka in a bubble around him; its radius was about as tall as he was: 10 rays. In his mind's eye, he imagined a fireball erupting around him. He felt the heat, saw the orange-red color, and smelled the smoke. He also imagined pain, so he added a protective shell of ka around himself.

Opening his eyes, he willed the area to combust. It wasn't as strong of a sensation as electricity had been; his muscles didn't tense as they had with that. He just needed to *feel* it. Listening to his command, the air combusted into a fireball. Even with his heat shield, its power could be felt. Glass formed beside his feet. There was less smoke than he had envisioned, but a few wisps floated up and faded into the starry sky.

"HEL YEAH!" he yelled into the sky.

The trial was a success. Ghar now had access to his Instinct skill, as well as electricity manipulation and fire manipulation. He figured he was probably one of the strongest nyxtad ever, simply because he had discovered Knowledge.

Satisfied with his work, he decided it was time to report his research to Pythti. He imagined this discovery would forever change the world. Maybe everyone could use Knowledge and not everyone could use Instinct? If that was the case, they could change the world. The advancements would be monumental, allowing people—like the farming family he had met earlier—to avoid poverty and starvation.

Ghar realized he didn't know how to contact Pythti. He hadn't explained how to turn the research in once it was completed. Pythti seemed Knowledgeable enough that he would be looking out for extraordinary events.

So that's what Ghar would give him. Smiling, he imagined his ka being shaped into the words "I'm done." It took a lot longer to form than when he allowed his ka to form a bubble or a line. He had to concentrate to make the shape stay true. He figured some error wouldn't matter too much, but enough would reduce the magnificence.

Once it traced the correct phrase, Ghar imagined heat, smoke, and exhalation. This time he didn't feel the need to close his eyes, so he could witness the explosion of flame across the correct zone. The words were hard to read from the side, so he started to fly up to see them from the top, but he was stopped by a hand on the shoulder.

"Show me your Knowledge," Pythti said in a calm but stern tone.

---

Escaping the palace was the easy part. Even though there were guards stationed throughout the house, most of them stayed in the dungeon. Once she got out of the dungeon safely, there was no real threat to her in the castle except, of course, the king himself.

Most of the staff was familiar with her, so she figured if she was caught by them, she could talk her way out of it. Luckily, no one saw her, a thin, red-haired girl in rags from a dungeon with a steel pole in hand, running through the house. It was simply too big for there to be someone in all parts of it at once. Plus, she remembered the habits of a lot of their servants enough to avoid them. She hadn't moved away too long ago.

Escaping the city was going to be a struggle, but she needed to get out. When Nadren had ascended, most of her father's friends and supporters had fled the city. They were afraid of being condemned for showing a connection to the Vyrtra line. In their absence, a sycophant power vacuum opened, bringing with it a group of people extremely loyal to Nadren Rakdi. He was surprisingly influential and powerful as the king. Kalia thought only the Vyrtra could be great royals, but she saw now that she had been wrong.

Even so, she needed to take the throne. Having another

Rakdi dynasty just wouldn't do. Drydnar's legacy would be besmirched as would the legacy of her father. She needed to prove herself to her line and her country. Doing that required getting out of the city and regrouping with the supporters of her father. If anyone had her back, they did. Houses Pikna, Tyrno, and Wafla had always been supporters of House Vyrtra.

She was worried about getting out of the city because of the Pelrad. Without a team of people, the king, or someone with the gift of flight, getting in and out of Pelto was difficult. The large trees formed a natural wall reaching into the clouds. Kalia had access to none of these ways. Instead of thinking about this roadblock, she pushed forward. She sprinted through the streets of her once-home, feeling like there was a power behind each step. It couldn't have been her nyxka, right?

A while later, she approached the Pelrad. She forgot how huge Pelto was. It was fitting, seeing as the trees that formed the grove it was built in were huge as well. She looked up, attempting to see the tops of the trees but couldn't. A low rain-cloud hung in the sky, cutting off the trunks of the trees at— what she assumed to be—the midsection.

That boded well for her. Rain meant water and, for Kalia, water meant power. A smile formed on her face as it began to sprinkle, little drops of moisture landing around her and fading as they struck. The Lopythrad had smiled on her by making it rain right when she needed it.

With rain washing the dirt and grime from her dungeon-ridden body, she realized it was time to consider how she would get through the wall that was formed by the Pelrad. Their majesty did serve a purpose in defense, so they made passing in and out of the city difficult.

There were, of course, gaps between the trunks of the huge trees. These were highly regulated by Nadren, though. The bottoms of each of them had gates that required proper forms and often taxes. It was said that the gatekeepers were corrupt and easy to bribe, but she didn't want to test her luck.

Another way out was through secret tunnels carved into

the trees themselves. These were blasphemous. The Pelrad were the purest form of creation from the Lopythrad, and they had been defaced by humanity. Kalia shook her head with sadness when she remembered them. Even if she were willing to abandon her faith to leave, she would have needed ties in the underworld of Pelto to get through them. Only criminals used the tunnels.

Her final option was to get over the gates. At first, she hadn't considered this to be a real option, but her mind had changed with the weather. She began gathering up all of the water around her, forming it into a bubble at her feet.

When she was satisfied with the size of it, she took a deep breath, trying to calm herself. This wasn't going to be easy. Plus, she wasn't very practiced with her nyxka and didn't even know if it was a good way to go about getting out of the city. She assumed she would find out after she succeeded or she failed.

Feeling power rush into her legs, she jumped into the sky as she shot the bubble up toward herself at the same angle. It was the same technique as before—the one from the dungeon —but on a much larger scale.

Air rushed into her eyes immediately, causing them to shut. She forced them open so that she would be able to see where she was going. Tears streamed from them, blurring her vision, but, to her surprise, she was going the right way. The Pelrad were on either side of her, so they passed by as she flew through the air instead of colliding with her.

Reaching the apex of her launch, she felt her stomach rise. For a moment, she felt weightless, peaceful. Pelto behind her, symbolizing the life she left behind, the rest of the kingdom in front of her, showing her the possibilities for the rest of her life.

Then the world started rushing up to meet her. She realized that she hadn't thought of how she would land and began to panic. Her arms and legs flailed wildly for a moment before she calmed herself. She still had control over the water that she had used to assist her jump. All she had to do was figure out how to use it to cushion her fall. Easy peasy.

Focusing on the water, she imagined it forming a protective shell around her legs. The water flew back in and created the bubble, just as she imagined. Accelerating, she felt the wind hit her in the eyes again. She needed her vision to time the landing, but she would have no such luck.

Faster.

Faster.

If she mistimed this, that would mean death for her. Failure for her family. No. Failure was not an option. She *would* succeed. Hel, who needed their eyes? She would fight the Rakdi dynasty even if she were deaf, blind, and missing her arms and legs.

On Instinct, she blasted the water bubble up toward herself again. If she had been able to see, she would have noticed that she was the perfect height for the acceleration to slow her down just enough for the fall to be safe. It was the best anyone could have possibly done with that exact scenario. Landing awkwardly on the ground, she realized that her Instincts had saved her.

She stood up and smiled. Seeing the Pelrad at the base from behind them—or was it in front of them?—was weird. She was used to seeing the other side. Satisfied, she turned her back on her home. She had to spend some time away from it to win it back, but to do that, she needed some help.

---

For a moment, Ghar panicked. Knowledge? How did Pythti know his terminology? Silently calming himself, he figured it must have been the general usage of the word, not the one Ghar used in his research and theory.

"You discovered Knowledge and Instinct," Pythti continued, "isn't that right?"

Shock spread across Ghar's face. How did he know?

What was going on?

"Yes, I did," said Ghar, narrowing his eyes. "How did you know?"

"You're not the only person to have learned about this distinction, you know. I am beginning to think I was the first, and a few people learned about it after me." Ghar felt something crack inside of him. He thought he was special. He thought he was changing the world, but he wasn't. Someone had already done everything he had done.

"So what happens, then? Do I fail?" Ghar asked nervously. He wasn't ready to give up the Knowledge available to him in the library of the Nyxtad Collective.

To his surprise, Pythti started laughing. Ghar glared at him, not seeing what was so funny. Anger began rising in his chest. One of his hands crackled with lightning, the other burst into flames. Rocks flew around his body, protecting and attacking. It was an emotional response. He didn't mean to do it, but it still felt right. Pythti raised an eyebrow and made a dramatic show of blowing on all of the power. Just like that, all of the strength Ghar had felt faded. He felt calm, relaxed. What had just happened?

"The test was rigged the whole time," Pythti explained as he sat down on the sand. He clutched his knees to his chest with one arm and motioned for Ghar to sit with the other. Ghar followed his command, and Pythti continued. "If there was some monumental piece of information I didn't know about, you wouldn't have been able to find it."

"What do you mean?" Ghar wasn't sure what he meant.

"Who do you think gathered the Knowledge that resides in these towers?" the older man asked as he motioned to the rest of the archipelago. "I've probably contributed around ninety-nine percent of the books."

Ghar's jaw dropped. The towers went on forever in all directions, and every single one of them held hundreds of times more books than his home library. Suddenly Pythti's insane power made sense.

"I wanted to see how you could expand your understanding of the world. You did phenomenally. Truly. Meet me at the largest tower during the rise tomorrow. You will be reborn as a member of our Research Division."

Ghar silently cheered. He was relieved, excited, and happy. All of his dreams of power were coming true. Maybe he didn't need the role of king to be powerful. With Knowledge, he could *rule* kings.

"Oh, and Ghar?"

Ghar looked up to see Pythti standing, looking like he was ready to leave.

"I'd prefer if you kept your Knowledge secret. I don't want it to fall into problematic hands. You and I are the only ones in the Collective who know about it."

"Wait"—something occurred to Ghar—"what about the others? Who are they?"

Pythti's face darkened. It seemed like he was recalling a bad memory. One of pain, of struggle.

"Problems," he answered as he vanished into a pillar of light.

# BANDITS

*Does a warrior bend to expectations? Does a warrior submit to an uncomfortable or painful scenario? No. Warriors stand their ground. Warriors may lose, but they do so while they fight.*
-    *Theodar Vyrtra*

A hren landed the plane in an area he was familiar with —or so he told Rykar. Rykar didn't think to question him. His companion had been to most of the Gapythtym before his entry into the Warrior Division.

They were quite a ways from Gidura, and it was much hotter where they were, even under the veil of the night sky. Rykar wasn't sure why, but he figured it had to do with the position of the Sun.

Smoke rose over the forest, and an orange glow fed its way through the trees. Suddenly it occurred to Rykar that the heat could be coming from something else. There was a fire in the village where they landed. He wasn't sure how he hadn't seen it from the sky, but then he remembered his habit of staring at the stars and Moon as they flew.

Ahren leaped out of the plane and began to sprint toward the town. It was hard to see, but there was a determined set in his jaw as he passed by Rykar. Rykar had to follow suit to keep up. Whatever was happening in the village was seriously bothering Ahren.

A thought struck Rykar. Ahren told him that his brother was killed by some bandits and described how they had burned down a village in the process. The scene before them seemed eerily similar. Worried, he made sure to keep his comrade in view. He didn't want the man to do something he would regret.

As they broke through the leafy covering of the forest, the situation became a lot clearer. The fire burned harshly, destroying a little over half of the buildings in the community. The rest of them weren't unmarked, however. Men in leather coverings were sweeping through, killing, sacking, and raping.

Rykar caught up to Ahren and saw a tear run down his cheek. It probably reminded him of the night his brother died. Rykar placed a hand on his shoulder in consolation.

"How did you know about this?" Rykar asked quietly.

Ahren turned to face him, and Rykar saw panic in his eyes.

"This group raids areas like this all the time. I saw smoke and guessed that it was their work."

"I've got your back, man," was all Rykar could articulate. He had no idea what to say. All he knew was that when he needed it, on the beach, Ahren had been there for him. When Rosa hurt him, Ahren had been there for him. When he was uncertain about his meeting with Gyl, Ahren had been there for him. The least he could do was return the favor.

"Thank you," Ahren said as he moved to join the fray. With Kyrx floating beside him, he looked ready to kill.

Rykar pulled on his shoulder, stopping him. "What are we doing here? Fill me in on the details."

"These bandits sack and kill. They've been doing it for some time. They're evil men, and we need to stop them to save the people who will be subjected to the same torture that I experienced." The look in his eyes was not one of anger or hatred. It was of sadness and purpose. Ahren realized what he needed to do but was sad that men like the bandits even existed.

This time, when Ahren moved to join the chaos, Rykar didn't stop him. He could practically feel the fear in the air. The sounds of screaming women, crying children, and dying men all made Rykar angry. He wanted it to stop. He *needed* to save these people. He needed to take a step to show that he was in control of his power.

Rykar pulled two wickedly curved knives from his cloak and began to spread his ka in a bubble. To be as efficient as possible, his war zone needed to cover the entire village. As he did it, he looked to Ahren. The swordsman had wasted no time. He was fighting one man hand-to-hand while his sword slashed through other enemies, killing multiple foes in a mere moment.

A little bit later, with his war zone complete, Rykar began to fight as well. He didn't want to teleport too much; it felt like a last resort, an escape if he needed it. He felt comfortable just using the physical increase from his nyxka, so he took a deep breath and allowed the wind to fill his sails.

The familiar feeling of time slowing met him. Kyrx slowly soared toward the back of a bandit's head. Ahren was throwing an enhanced kick to another bandit's face. He could probably handle most of them on his own, but he didn't need to. He had Rykar, and Rykar had something else to assist him: power.

He walked up to a bandit and stood there long enough to make sure he saw Rykar's face. Rykar wanted to be the last thing the bandit saw before he died. When he was satisfied his enemy had seen him, he jammed a knife into the bottom of his chin. It had enough force to break his skull, but the knife itself was driven into the man's brain, killing him.

He moved on to another. The bandit was assaulting a naked woman and was much larger than the man Rykar had just killed. The bandit seemed to enjoy it. Somehow, he was enjoying harming the woman so much. Rykar didn't understand how that was possible. He saw killing as a quick technique. He never dragged it out. He never made his prey suffer. He couldn't disrespect something that much. Or so he thought until he saw the way the bandit was treating the woman.

Rykar shoved the man off of her, feeling the bandit's ribs crack beneath his enhanced fingers. He sped up time for a moment.

"You shouldn't have done that," Rykar said as the man gasped for breath. "You shouldn't have done any of this. You should have left them alone."

The man was too hurt to talk. His lungs were probably punctured, so his death was inevitable. No matter how much Rykar hated him for raping the woman, he couldn't allow himself to torture the man. There would be no exceptions to his rules if he was to save himself from the darkness within.

Begrudgingly, Rykar began planning his next cut. He was going to carve up his neck, leaving him for dead, but instead decided to mangle the man's manhood first. He moved to cut his neck so quickly that the man would barely even register the cuts to his genitals. If he did, however, he would know that he had made a mistake by taking the woman. If he somehow survived Rykar's cuts, he would never be able to do such horrid deeds again. Luckily, Rykar's precise slashes hit their mark, and the man dropped down to the ground in slow motion, dead.

At this point, Rykar's nonchalant walking turned into jogging and slashing and then sprinting. As much as he hated the situation, he needed to train. Plus, finishing the attack would help the villagers a lot more than letting it drag on for dramatic effect.

Bodies dropped like flies. Even in slowed time, he had a hard time having his mind keep up with his body. Most of the bandits were dead. They hadn't been there long enough for the group of attackers to even register the threat to flee. Good. They shouldn't be allowed to live. They chose to make other people live in Hel.

Suddenly Rykar remembered Ahren. He hadn't seen his comrade in some time. He figured it was because of Ahren's inability to keep up with his speed, but then he returned to where he and Ahren had entered the town. Ahren was eerily absent, and Rykar felt dread rise in his chest.

---

Ahren had no idea how *efficient* Rykar was. Ahren had expected him to move quickly but not imperceptibly so. He vanished and appeared in front of a bandit for a moment, then vanished again. Each person he moved in front of dropped dead a few moments later. It didn't even seem like he was teleporting yet, because he didn't arrive instantaneously. There was some delay between positions.

He had to pull his focus away from Rykar's killing. He had his own enemies to deal with. Kyrx was being as helpful as usual, killing anyone he told him to. Ahren focused his attention on another bandit and began to fight him hand-to-hand.

It wasn't difficult. He threw an elbow to the temple. He grabbed the back of the man's neck and forced his temple into his upward knee. The man's temple was not having a good night. When Ahren was satisfied that he was unconscious, he reached down and snapped his neck. Enhanced speed and strength made fights a whole lot easier.

Kyrx kept slashing through all of the bandits he could see, so Ahren moved on to his next opponent. The man closest to him was incredibly large, almost as big as Hjalmir. He was muscular and seemed powerful. Ahren prepared himself for the fight, and just as he was about to run to confront him, the man noticed Ahren.

Before Ahren could react, the enemy closed the distance between them and picked Ahren up. Ahren's assessment was correct: he was strong. A moment later, Ahren felt his opponent's powerful arms cock back as he moved to throw Ahren into a nearby building.

Surprisingly, crashing through the walls wasn't that painful. The wood itself didn't give that much resistance; it was too thin to cause any damage. Unfortunately, the impact of the landing still dazed him. His head swam for a moment as he tried to compose himself. The attacker was coming to kill him, so he needed to recover as soon as possible.

The man appeared in the hole that Ahren had just made. His huge figure was just a silhouette with the fire lit behind his back. Ahren had been in this place before. Last time, his brother had died. He clenched his jaw and prepared for the coming fight. The huge man pulled a sword from the scabbard on his waist. He raised it above his head, preparing to butcher Ahren.

Ahren calmed himself, and time slowed dramatically. It slowed more than ever before. The sword inched toward his body, ready to slash through him and kill him.

Out of nowhere, Rykar teleported into the room for a brief moment. Smoke clouded around him, and his eyes were exuding a faint, red light. For a second, he looked like a monster, a creature meant only to kill.

It was almost as if he were checking to make sure Ahren was ok, and satisfied that Ahren was, he left. Strangely, this motivated Ahren. He knew that Rykar was there for him. He wouldn't give up. He needed to win this fight and save the village from bandits.

Calling Kyrx to his hand, he rose. No one would die this time. No one would hurt because of his weakness, and he was going to prove it. His brief experience with super-slow time ran out, and he was back to his normal enhanced speed.

He dove toward the huge man, getting inside of the overhead strike, no elbows or knees this time. For some reason, he wanted to be a little dramatic. Driving the heel of his hand into the man's throat, he felt it crush beneath his blow. As he did this, Kyrx arrived from the other side, impaling the man's neck from behind. It would be hard to tell for an outside observer, but Kyrx's stab stopped just short of cutting Ahren. The tip of the sword was touching his palm. Ahren backed away, and Kyrx did just what he wanted by spinning and beheading the enemy.

---

Rykar searched his war zone for any sign of Ahren. Unfortunately, he wasn't able to look for the presence of nyxka within it just yet. He was constrained in that he could only feel size and shape.

Luckily, this did give him some results. Three people seemed like they were around the right size to be Ahren, and only one of them was anywhere close to where Rykar had seen him fight.

This felt like the right time to use his teleportation. If not now, then there was no good time. He imagined standing next to Ahren, or the person he figured was Ahren, and found himself inside a room.

Smoke flowed upward through a hole in the wall. A huge man stood in front of it, in the middle of the smoke cloud, holding a sword above his head. He looked ready to slash, to kill Ahren.

Rykar felt the need to step in. He couldn't let his friend die. Just as he was about to move in and stop the attacker, he looked at Ahren. The look on his face surprised Rykar. Ahren didn't look scared. He looked angry. He was ready to get up and kill the man standing before him.

Realizing his mistake, Rykar teleported out of the room. This was Ahren's fight. That specific scenario was exactly how he imagined the death of Ahren's brother had looked, except this time Ahren didn't have someone to protect him. He needed to protect himself. This was an important step for Rykar's comrade.

Kyrx flew through the sky, and, for a moment, Rykar was worried that it was rushing to save its owner from certain death. Then a head rolled out of the building. Dusting himself off, Ahren stepped through the hole in the wall.

Rykar sprinted toward him, understanding how monumental that moment was for Ahren. He had overcome his fear and taken a step toward healing his internal wounds. Rykar didn't know what to say, so he just clapped him on the back.

"How many are left?" Ahren asked, looking exhausted.

"None of the bandits in my war zone survived," Rykar answered quickly. He didn't want to take the glory from Ahren. That fight was more important than any of the others.

Ahren's tired face changed to one of relief, one of joy. "What the Hel!? We did it!" He started pumping his fists into the air. "You hear that Kyrx!? I'm not weak anymore! I'd kick your ass in a fight now! You'd better watch your back up there!"

Rykar couldn't help but laugh as he saw his friend scream into the stars. It had been far too long since he had done that: laughed. Ahren's weakness was turning into strength. His insecurity and guilt had taken a hit. Rykar was jealous but glad it felt so good.

"What now?" Rykar asked. Part of him wanted to leave, but he knew that they should help the people after the attack. There was more to recovering from a crisis than just dealing with the crisis itself. What came after was arguably just as important.

"I'll help them, you can stay here until I'm done," Ahren said as he went to aid a man who had been cut. Rykar wanted to follow his friend, but he knew that it was important to Ahren to help them himself. It was all a part of his healing.

After a while, Ahren came back to where Rykar was waiting. He had helped the villagers put out a fire, performed first aid, and assisted in cleaning up the debris. Rykar was impressed with his work.

The walk back to the plane was a triumphant one. Every now and then, Ahren would jump into a little dance or yell into the sky. It was probably just the adrenaline rush, but Rykar was still happy to see his friend in such a good mood. Rykar didn't feel the rush of adrenaline in the same way, so he just felt a little emptier after having used some of his nyxka.

The plane sat in the same place they had left it, completely open for the world to see. Rykar hadn't thought anything of it when they landed, because they were rushing. Now, he understood his mistake. They could get in serious trouble if someone found them.

"Hello?"

Rykar's ears perked up, unsure of whether or not he had heard that correctly. It sounded like a girl speaking.

"Is anyone there?" the noise said.

Rykar and Ahren searched around the plane until Rykar found a small ball of fabric sitting beside one of the wheels. She had brown hair and dark-blue eyes that were full of fear. Freckles were scattered across her face. Rykar felt his heart fall. She looked like Nyral.

"Who are you?" Rykar asked softly as he reached out to help her. The fear in her eyes diminished when she took it.

"I'm Syla," she responded as she stood up. She couldn't have been more than ten or eleven years old. She was very small, only reaching up to Rykar's waist, and he wasn't even that tall.

"What happened to you?" Ahren asked gently, taking a knee beside her.

Tears filled her eyes, and she began to cry. Her parents had probably been killed by the bandits.

"M-my parents . . . d-died," she said in between sobs.

"Did the bandits kill them?" Ahren asked, seriousness returning to his voice.

Suddenly Syla's tears stopped. Her soft, fearful face hardened into one of anger and hatred. Rykar felt himself dreading her answer, sure that he had killed them.

"No, you did," Syla snarled.

Rykar resigned from the conversation, appalled that he

had made the same mistake twice. It didn't help that Syla was the spitting image of Nyral either. All the guilt that he had fought back over all of the years resurfaced.

"We didn't kill any villagers," Ahren explained, unsure of what she meant.

"We just wanted food," she whispered. "We never have enough. The people of this village are always well-fed, so Papa came to ask them for anything they could spare." As she said this, she started to cry. "They were taking a long time, so I came to see what was happening. And then I saw you cut his *head* off," she hissed. "GET AWAY FROM ME!" she screamed as she turned and sprinted away.

Ahren moved to catch her, but Rykar stopped him. Ahren looked at him, sorrow in his eyes. He could relate to Syla, Rykar realized. Being without parents, on her own, he had lived life in a very similar way.

"We can't help her after what we've done," Rykar said as he shook his head. "To her, we're demons."

---

The trip back to HQ was silent, just like the flight out. The Moon and stars were as glorious as before. They made it back just in time. The Sun peeked out over the horizon to the rise. While they hadn't slept that night, they weren't tired. It was time to train.

Walking through the hallway, Rykar felt broken. Syla reminded him too much of Nyral: his failure. Ahren looked like he was becoming whole again, like he probably had been before his brother died.

Rykar looked to his companion and realized that he was the closest friend Rykar had ever had. Ahren had shared his past, and his fight to get better, with Rykar. He knew that Ahren leaned on him, and as the guilt grew unbearable in his chest, Rykar knew it was time to get help.

He understood that Ahren couldn't solve his problems.

He knew he had to be the one to deal the final blow as Ahren had done with the man from before. Rykar just wanted someone to help him to the finish line so he could finally bring an end to the pain and cross it.

# THE TRUTH

*Success, failure: all outcomes are subjective. One fisherman could feel satisfied with filling one net with fish while another might never be satisfied with his catch. Those who are never satisfied are the ones who rise to be great. Those who still think they will find satisfaction are the ones who break worlds.*
- *Naria Frektri*

Yellow light shone through a stained glass window in a banquet hall. The Sun was rising, yet the room was still empty. Ghar was unsure of whether or not he was in the right place. Pythti had said the largest tower, right? Also, every other room served a purpose, so that left the empty room he was currently standing in.

Just as Ghar was about to leave, he spread his ka out in a bubble. Maybe he could feel where other people were? Sure enough, a bunch of shapes were nearing him down the hallway. Realizing what was happening, Ghar relaxed. Pythti probably made sure he was late to show how people waited for him. It was a show of power.

A moment later, the group of people broke through the doors and entered the room. For a second, Ghar forgot that he was there to join them and felt animosity toward the mass of gray robes.

Scanning the crowd, Ghar realized that Pythti was still absent. He figured the rest of the Collective knew this as well, but they didn't show any worry or curiosity on their faces. They just shuffled in and sat at the long table in the center of the room, watching Ghar as he stood on the stage in front of the stained glass wall.

Almost as if he understood the awkward silence forming, Pythti appeared on the stage a moment later in a blinding flash of light. Respectful applause broke out from the crowd. These were not people of intense emotion or passion; they were Researchers. Calm, collected, analytical machines, yet Ghar had discovered a secret none of them knew.

"I have brought you here today for the acceptance ceremony of the nine hundred fifty-first Collective Compatibility Assessment," Pythti began. The introduction led Ghar to believe that the speech would not be brief. "The applicants this year were all picked because of their critical thinking skills and intellect. Of over four hundred applicants, only one passed." This revelation brought about a hushed silence. Ghar paused to try to figure out why but stopped himself. Now was his moment; analysis would come later. Even with this suppression of thought, he still put a little effort into trying to solve every puzzle he could find.

"This man that you see before you is astounding. He found the source of nyxka and figured out how to determine one's ability from birth." A moment of confusion later and Ghar realized why Pythti was lying. The rest of the Collective would probably wonder what his project was, and Knowledge was a well-kept secret.

"His work has earned him the rank of Regional Scholar,"

Pythti continued. The crowd didn't seem too happy with this, but it kept its calm, for the most part. One scholar huffed in annoyance, and another even stood up and left. No one said anything. Pythti ignored the crowd and kept speaking.

"I can't grant you another nyxka, so you will just be reborn in the eyes of the Pythrad. Your new name will be Hadrian. Congratulations. You are now the Regional Scholar of this solar system and a few other areas that I will show you." Then, turning to the crowd with a stern look, Pythti gave a command. "Applaud."

The entire room broke out into huge applause, apparently now ecstatic by his acceptance and promotion. Ghar took a mental note to keep Pythti's influence in mind when thinking about the Collective.

Pythti waved his hand, and he and Ghar were transported to another location. His ability to teleport was unsettling, but Ghar was becoming more and more accustomed to it as time went on.

They were on top of the main tower, the Sun rising in front of them. The clear sky allowed the rise to reflect off the ocean, leaving a yellow streak. The wind blew harder at their height, and Ghar had to stabilize himself so he didn't fall off. Pythti did no such thing, apparently unaffected by the powerful gusts.

"I took you up here to answer any questions you have about this world," Pythti explained as he gazed out on the horizon. Ghar looked to Pythti and noticed, not for the first time, how much taller the older man was compared to himself.

"What are the limits of Knowledge?" Ghar asked after a brief moment of contemplation.

Pythti gave a sly smile and took a moment to respond as well. It felt like he was hiding, but Ghar kept quiet. "Knowledge is limited by the charged parts of your ka," he explained. "Ka is the force that powers nyxka. If you use all of the charge in your ka, you run out of both Instinct and Knowledge."

"Is Kalia dead yet?" Ghar asked reluctantly. He felt the

need to know, but he assured himself that he didn't care for her.

"I think she'll surprise you," Pythti said with a chuckle.

Ghar refused to think or even ask about her more, so he shoved her out of his mind. Now was the time for incredible secrets to be revealed, not information about silly noblewomen. Kalia wasn't important enough to discuss.

"Why does the Collective interfere in the politics of Lopythtym?" Ghar inquired. He had planned to use them as a common enemy for the kingdom as a way of gaining power and only just now realized how much his plans had changed.

"Now that is an interesting question," Pythti said as he let out a sigh. "It's complicated too." Ghar slumped over, thinking he wouldn't get an answer, but was surprised to hear him continue. "A long time ago, there was a man named Drydnar Vyrtra. I'm sure you know of him. He's probably one of the most well-known people on this continent.

"Back in those days, there were naturally occurring Golems that roamed the world. They are a race of powerful, humanlike creatures. They could access the power of Gaz at a startlingly efficient rate. Some were even said to have the ability to recharge uncharged ka, an ability reserved for the planet we are standing on.

"Drydnar soon realized that the power of the Golems was tied to the strength of magic fields. The stronger the field, the stronger the Golem. He began experimenting with this by tearing chunks out of Gapythtym. He was going to upset the balance of the world for an experiment.

"As he went on, he discovered Knowledge because of the attributes of the Golems. His nyxka, coupled with Knowledge, made him the most powerful nyxtad ever, if you exclude me.

"I had to step in to return peace and order to the continent. I killed all of the Golems and confronted Drydnar. We fought. Hard. Luckily, in the end I bested him, and that was the end of his rule. We intervene in Lopythtym politics to prevent anyone like Drydnar from rising to power. The Collective maintains balance throughout the universe, and this cell does it on this continent.

"To prevent anyone from rising to the same level as Drydnar, I have kept most of the information that humanity used to have for myself. Without education, the likelihood that Knowledge becomes a problem is small. This is why you'll find extremely advanced technology and books here while the outside world is still quite primitive."

Ghar stared at him, wide-eyed. Everything made sense. People must have inflated his ascension numbers to have him fit in with their idea of who he was as a conqueror. The Collective's intervention was also becoming clear.

"How can I increase my Knowledge so I can become more like you?" Ghar asked after he had processed what Pythti had just told him.

"Are you aware that everything with ka also has a memory?" asked Pythti. Ghar gave him a confused look in response, so he continued. "With the proper Knowledge, you can access the memory of almost anything you touch. It's not perfect, but it can make us seem omniscient when we aren't actually."

"How do I do that?"

"Here, try on me. I'll walk you through the process," Pythti said, encouragingly. "First, you need to touch some of my ka. It should be floating around me right now, but I'll just send some to you. Next, grab it with your mind. Imagine it's a book and you're trying to read it."

Ghar did this and got a glimpse of Pythti sitting alone in a dirty room. It felt off. After a moment of analysis, he realized Pythti had black hair in the image.

"I saw an image of you with darker hair!" Ghar exclaimed. Pythti didn't react to this news and continued explaining.

"The more you practice, the more literate you will become in ka reading. Remember, this is not mind reading. It is just a way to peer into the past. The ka stores information, and you are accessing it."

"Alright, thanks," Ghar said, excited to practice. "I noticed that the rest of the Research Division didn't look like it was trained for combat." He was referring to the fact that they looked mostly out of shape or extremely skinny. "Why is that? How can you maintain balance and control without proper combat power?"

"The Research Division is only half of our organization. The other half is our Warrior Division. They have a similar structure to the Research Division. I'm still their leader, but they are more reminiscent of a military. Their equivalent to the Regional Scholars are the Pactri. The Pactri are a group of powerful fighters. One or two of them could probably even go toe-to-toe with Drydnar. Leopold is the Pactri of our region, although he really should be promoted to Pythkav. The lower-level nyxtad are organized into groups defined by a number. These are called classes. The lower the number, the better."

"What makes Leopold so powerful?" Ghar asked. "Does he have an incredible nyxka?"

"No, he doesn't have one," Pythti said, nonchalantly.

"What!?" Ghar was sure he had misheard the older man.

"He has no nyxka, he can't use Knowledge due to amnesia, yet he is still the strongest combat nyxtad alive."

Ghar paled. He was stronger than *Pythti*? How?

"What is his power? Where does it come from?"

"He is physically stronger, faster, more durable, and more agile than anyone. From what I can tell, he got it by Compounding. Don't ask me about that. I'm still unsure of how it works, but my research has been promising. Some other time."

"Wait," Ghar remembered, "you mentioned that we were on a continent, and you also referred to a larger universe. How much do I not know?"

"So much," Pythti chuckled. "We live on a sphere that orbits around the Sun. There is another planet that also revolves around the Sun in our system. Outside of our system are countless others. Some have life, some don't. These systems combine to make galaxies, and there are countless galaxies.

These galaxies and the empty space of the universe combine to make the rest of the universe. At the center is something that no one understands. It is said that you can become a god if you make it there, but no one knows. I hope to find out one day."

"Why can't you go there?" asked Ghar.

"No one knows where it is."

"How far does the Collective's power and influence spread?" Ghar asked, fascinated with the idea of a huge universe.

"Far," was the only answer Pythti would give.

"Oh. You mentioned becoming a god. Are there any real gods?" Ghar was curious to see if his culture was formed on truth or just blind belief.

"Yes, there are some. The powerful ones are called Radka. They control Instinct, and it is even rumored that they gave humanity the power of ka in the first place."

"And the not-as-powerful ones?"

"Some are men who call themselves gods. Others are Golems with incredible levels of sentience and power."

"Wait, so Golems can have lower levels of sentience?" Ghar was intrigued by the concept of another race of powerful beings. "Could you remove their consciousness altogether, then?"

"The Collective did it with one of the most powerful ones. It's called the Grathyk. At first, we kept it to show our power, but then Leopold showed up, and we didn't need it for the outside anymore. Right now, its purpose is to keep Leopold in check if he loses his mind."

Leopold losing his mind? "You make it sound like that's likely. Why is that? Also, if the Grathyk can go toe-to-toe with Leopold, why didn't you use him against Drydnar?"

"Compounding seems to harm the mind. Each day, it's as if less of him is there." Pythti said this with a sad look in his eyes. He didn't enjoy the prospect of killing Leopold; it seemed as if they were even friends. "As for the Grathyk, we sacrificed its choice for total control over it. Basically, it can *only* fight

Leopold as it is right now."

That made sense. When Ghar created things, they could only do exactly what he asked them to do. The Grathyk must have been the same way. Although Leopold was still a mystery that Ghar wanted some answers to.

"Tell me about Leopold?"

"He was stuck in an eternal Hel when I found him. I'm not sure what happened, to be honest, but it seems like he was there of his own free will. I saved him from it, and we've been friends ever since."

"Is he from Lopythtym or Gapythtym?" It felt good to get answers to his questions, so Ghar shifted to asking more specific and less important questions.

Pythti laughed. "Neither. You're not thinking big enough."

"Where then?"

"I found him in the Land of Wishes, but I think he's from a place called Earth." Pythti seemed oddly unsure about his answer.

"Do you not know?"

"Not with certainty. His Hel was very far from Earth, but his genetic makeup suggests terrestrial origin."

"What is the other life in the universe like?" Ghar asked, imagining strange people living on different planets. "Is it like life on Gaz?"

"Only a few are like Gaz. Earth is one, and there are a few others. Most of the others would seem incredibly foreign to you. There are worlds with more magic than you can imagine, making the world completely inhospitable to human life. Most of the life in the universe is extremely primitive, barely even able to think or function. The worlds that have intelligent life are mostly space faring at this point, meaning they can travel between planets, at a minimum."

"How do people travel between planets?"

"Everyone has their own method, but the most effective for large masses of people seems to be via spaceship. These are enclosed capsules that blast something out behind them to gain speed. Some of the most advanced ships in the universe can warp spacetime and appear to exceed the speed of light."

"Light doesn't travel instantaneously?" Ghar had never really thought about how fast light could travel; it always just seemed like it could teleport everywhere.

"Not nearly, no. It was the fastest thing until technology progressed far enough to bend the known laws of physics."

Question after question, Ghar began to break out of his trance of curiosity. His skeptical mind returned, and he began to have questions about the current situation rather than the world. Pythti was starting to make Ghar uncomfortable with his transparency. The whole thing felt off to Ghar.

"Why are you answering my questions like this?" Ghar asked. "Don't you want to keep some things to yourself?"

"In truth, Knowledge brings solitude and loneliness," Pythti said. He sounded genuine, but Ghar didn't know him well enough to know if he could lie or not. "I needed someone who I could trust to share my Knowledge with, and since you're the newest Regional Scholar, I figured you would be a good choice."

"Ok, if you're so transparent, tell me this, then," Ghar said, eyes turning to slits. Pythti seemed to sense the incoming question. His face went blank, no longer one of enjoyment or comedy. "Who are you, really?"

# END OF PART II

# THE BEGINNING

**1,500 Years Ago**

Aervin Eroborn was unashamedly in love with the queen. Ever since he met her, Naria Frektri had held a special place in his heart. She was beautiful. She was kind and powerful. She knew who she was, and Aervin envied that.

He was useless. Without a nyxka, his position in a minor house of Gapythtym was meaningless. Maybe if he were born blessed, he could change something about his life. Maybe if he could marry the Gapythlyk, he could become more than just a chubby man wandering to his death. Maybe he would be more.

He changed his name from an old, Dok-derived name to something newer. He hoped the identity change would help him become something. It didn't, and he lost all reason to change it back. No matter what he called himself, Aervin was a waste.

The other nobles mocked him, and why shouldn't they? All of them had the power of the gods. They could perform miracles. Naria's Moon Avatar could stand above the trees, showing off her grace and destructive power. He was good at reading and was smarter than most of them, but that didn't mean anything. They could kill him without a second thought.

At a certain point, around the age of twenty-five, Aervin started living with the peasants instead. He didn't want to be ridiculed. He wanted to feel happy. Every time he saw the peasants working when he was entrenched in the culture of the higher class, they seemed happy, even in their toils. He figured he should join them and find what they had.

A few years among the peasantry, and he didn't feel anything but emptiness. He missed seeing Naria. No matter how much he wished he would stop getting picked on, some of the nobles felt like his friends. He was starting to romanticize the bad parts of his life. There was nostalgia around things he hated.

One day, the village he lived in experienced a life-changing event. A farmer had lit a lamp thousands of times, but that day it lit itself. There was no fuel required, and the lamp was even entirely out of oil. Something was powering it, and Aervin had an urge to find out what.

That night, he stole the lamp and fled into the wilderness. He had no plan; he knew he wasn't good enough to have one. He figured he would spend enough time with the lamp to figure out how it worked or find someone else who could.

The lamp fluctuated in size and brightness based on where he went. When he got close to the capital of the Gapythtym, Megto, it got so bright that he thought he would go blind. When he was in the middle of the woods, it would barely provide enough light to be useful. It seemed like the lamp had a nyxka. How else would it stay lit without fuel and have different levels of strength?

Sitting on the forest floor, surrounded by cold and darkness, Aervin wished the lamp would finally just go out. If it did indeed have a nyxka, then it proved that he had less use than a lamp. He imagined his life without the little warmth and light that the lamp provided. He held the lamp in his arms and wished, more than anything, that it would stop mocking him.

And suddenly it did. He had seemingly controlled the nyxka of an inanimate object.

The darkness of night wasn't as all-encompassing as he thought it was. Without lamplight, his eyes were forced to adjust to the ambient light coming from the Moon. It seemed even more beautiful than daytime.

Just to make sure he wasn't hallucinating, he willed it to reignite. This time, he held the lamp in his arms and imagined the warmth and light returning to him.

Same as before, it listened to his internal commands. A small flame formed in the center as if he had just lit a candle. Still, there was no fuel. He figured some sort of nyxka must be powering it, but he didn't know how or why it worked.

His travels continued, the same as before, except now he took time each day to practice turning the lamp on and off. As he got better and more efficient, he realized he could control the size and shape of the flame as well. In places where it wanted to be bright, he could turn it down, and in places where it wanted to die out, he could vitalize it.

At a certain point, Aervin began to wonder if he could create flames *outside* of the lamp. It seemed possible, but his lack of a nyxka disagreed. He decided to throw out all of his past notions of himself and see what would happen if he tried to light a tree on fire.

Moonlight lit the area, providing a striking silhouette of a tree as a target for Aervin. He brushed his dark hair out of his eyes and calmed his breathing. He needed to have a lot of control to get this right.

He willed the tree to light on fire, but nothing happened. Again, this time imagining more heat and light, he tried, but to no avail. Nothing happened. Aervin thought back to what he did every time he caused a combustion inside of the lamp and realized that he had always been touching it. This annoyed him. Standing far away from the tree was a safety measure. If he got any closer, he might catch on fire and get severely burned or even die.

Throwing caution to the wind, he walked to the tree and placed his hands on its rough bark. For the third time, he imagined heat and light but, this time, only where his hands were.

His palms began to smoke and burn. Quickly, he pulled them away from the surface of the tree and saw what had happened beneath his skin, where his eyes couldn't see. Scorch marks in the shape of hands were burned into the tree.

Aervin felt his excitement growing. He was strong; he just hadn't realized it before. He tried to light the tree again, but this time he stepped away from it. In his mind's eye, the light and heat appeared again. In front of him, in real life, the midsection of the tree—near where his hands touched it— burst into flames.

Excitement turned into curiosity. How was he able to manipulate flames without a nyxka? Maybe his power had always been fire control and he hadn't realized it yet? Aervin tabled the question but made a note not to drop it. He needed answers, and the origin of his powers was important.

Each day after, he tried to catch different things on fire. Moving targets were harder—but not impossible—to hit. He soon found that he could ignite any place he had personally been to. Anywhere else was immune to his will of combustion.

It took him a few years of travel and adventure to learn about ka. He knew that something was connecting his location to the location of the fire, but he didn't know what. That is, until he imagined expanding himself to the area around him. He imagined a bubble that represented *him* and allowed it to expand. After he did that, he could ignite places and things he had never touched.

Feeling truly powerful, Aervin decided to visit the home and life he had abandoned all those years prior. As he walked the road that led to Megto, he wondered what returning would be like. He imagined the nobility receiving him with scorn and having that change to awe when he demonstrated his power. Maybe Naria would even fall for him? Hope was on his mind as he strode through the borders of their capital.

No one recognized him. It had been many years, so he wasn't surprised by this. Peasants treated him like their equal, and the nobility ignored him, just as they had done before. Aervin wasn't sure if they ignored him because of a lack of recognition or because they knew exactly who he was, so he decided to make himself known.

The palace wasn't well defended. It sat in a powerful field, as indicated by the lamp Aervin still carried, but other than the queen's power, there were no visible defenses. Confidently, he walked into the majestic building and threw open the doors to the throne room.

Naria Frektri sat on the throne. Her beauty had aged. Black curls were turning gray. Wrinkles were forming on her previously smooth face. Her piercing, blue eyes were more intense than ever. The position of queen was wearing her down.

"Guards!" she yelled as she summoned her Moon Avatar. The Avatar was large, but Aervin knew that it was more for show than anything. The guards approached, about to throw Aervin out or into a dungeon, but Aervin stopped them by expanding his war zone and creating a wall of fire.

"Naria," he said as he approached the throne, "don't you recognize me?" His face was much harder than it had been before he left. Aervin felt himself smiling. Traveling the kingdom had cut away the level of fat that had felt at home around his waist. He bore scars from burns and wild animals. The old him had died on his journeys, replaced by a man with power and Knowledge. She probably didn't know what to think.

Her eyes widened as he got closer, a sense of familiarity creeping onto her strangely wrinkled face. "Ae-ervin?" she stuttered. "How is this possible?"

"How is what possible?" he asked with a smirk.

"How are you alive? How do you have a nyxka?"

"If you understand something, and I mean truly understand something, that thing can become yours to control," Aervin explained. "I spent the last few years studying power, and I have acquired it." As he said this, he made the wall of flames grow as high as the ceiling and then shrink back into the floor with the rise and fall of his hand. The look of awe never left Naria's face.

Aervin left her dumbfounded on the throne. His little trip to visit his old life had two purposes. He wanted to let them know who he was now. Mockery and ridicule couldn't touch him anymore. He also wanted to know if he made the right decision by leaving, and the look on Naria's beautiful face proved that it was. Aervin knew he wasn't worthless anymore.

He wanted to see what he could do with his Knowledge. He began to experiment with plant growth and his regeneration, and he learned that agelessness and immortality weren't hard to achieve either.

Soon, he knew enough to be certain that he was the strongest person in the Gapythtym. Even Naria and her awesome power couldn't stand up to his own. However, he loved her too much to usurp her. She was the true queen of the Moon, and he would do nothing to change that. So, in an attempt to save her from himself and his ambition, he fled to the set. Once he hit the ocean, he went farther, flying above the water.

He flew day in and day out, hoping to get far enough away from the Gapythtym that he wouldn't be able to hurt it. The Wildlands were to the set, but Aervin hoped there was something in between them that he could live on.

To his luck, he discovered an archipelago in the middle of the Sigpyth—the sea that connected Wildlands and Gapythtym. Hoping to create a new kingdom entirely, he set up camp and made plans to explore the island system that he was going to call his home.

The archipelago was sparsely populated by a group of fishermen. They didn't appear to be native to Hakiro, as they didn't speak the same language or even understand Dok-derived words at all.

Aervin figured he could start a kingdom by ruling these people and expanding from there. He had all the time in the world; he couldn't age and could regenerate from almost any wound. Before landing to meet them, he changed his appearance such that he had white hair and eyes so that he would appear foreign.

As he developed his island nation, Aervin frequently made trips to the Wildlands. They were on the other side of Hakiro, the broken half of the grand continent. It seemed like it could become something more, so Aervin sought out someone he could put in a position of power.

After some searching, Aervin found Grax Rakdi and decided to grant him the role of Lopythlok. Aervin then told Rakdi about the structure of Gapythtym and told him to mirror it in order to create balance on Hakiro. Rakdi gladly obliged due to the two-sided religion and culture of Hakiro.

Moving on from the mainland, Aervin began to acquaint himself with the fishermen. At first, he learned their language and taught some of his own. This was particularly difficult seeing as they had little in common and were without a translator. A few years passed, and to Aervin's delight, communication became possible.

He learned a great deal from the fishermen, mostly about their culture and opinions, but a lot, nonetheless. The archipelago was called h'Lukakos in their language. According to some shoddy translation, it meant "The World's End." They didn't know much about science and history, but they understood the natural world far better than he did. Their poor grasp of science and magic led them to believe that Aervin was a god. His power wasn't anything they had ever seen before.

When the time for Aervin's introduction came, he decided that his old name wasn't the name of a god. If they were in the Sigpyth—loosely meaning Sea of the Sky—then he could call himself the Lord of the Sky. Aervin introduced himself as Pythti and dove into the role of god.

He frequently appeared to the people of Old h'Lukakos—as he called it—and performed miracles by utilizing his Knowledge. He made fire appear, he healed their children, he moved the winds, and he controlled the storms.

Soon, their acknowledgment of him as a god turned into worship. He had successfully built up his reputation as a divine being and was rewarded with the people of Old h'Lukakos.

With their conversion, he rewarded them by renaming the land the Nyxtad Archipelago.

To gain more power, Pythti had to learn more. He had to acquire more Knowledge and find a place to keep it. Most of the noble houses held a collection of books known as a library. Pythti knew he wanted to put the nobility to shame, so he decided that he would make a library system that would dwarf the collections of both Gapythtym and Lopythtym.

As he began to collect Knowledge, he realized something important. If the fishermen learned the truth about the world, then they might come to know that Pythti was not, in fact, a god. He maintained his power by creating a Knowledge differential between himself and those that he ruled.

The more he thought about it, the more he realized how important Knowledge and ignorance were for his style of ruling and government. Too much Knowledge from those he ruled could lead to mutinies and coups, neither of which were particularly desirable.

Every now and then, Pythti would find someone curious and allow them to join his ruling class, which he called the Nyxtad Collective. Their military was called the Warrior Division. They had to take a test, known as the Collective Compatibility Assessment, to see if they would fit in.

Most people failed. He went years without finding anyone who fit what he was looking for. It was common for a curious person to have an excessive amount of ambition, as was the case with Drydnar. Other than his intense lust for power, he would have been perfect for the Collective.

Later, Pythti realized how much potential his system of government had and began to expand. The continents around him refused to change their ways and culture easily. A grand conversion didn't seem likely, so he decided to change strategies. Controlling the flow of Knowledge, he knew he could control the rulers of the kingdoms that he wished to rule himself.

His influence wasn't limited to Gaz. Once Pythti learned

more about the universe, he began to expand to other planets and galaxies, with similar results. People didn't like being told what to believe, so he controlled what information they had, forcing them to fall into his rule.

Some may call it malicious. Those people could never be great. Some may call it selfish. Those people could never lead. Pythti knew that he was sacrificing his humanity to bear the burdens of all of life itself. If ignorance was bliss, then he was the most damned person in the universe.

# START OF PART III

# CAPTURE THE KNIFE

*Why do you want power? Do you want to save someone? Do you want to find happiness? Because I promise you, power will bring you nothing but pain and fatigue. You'll see soon enough.*
- *Naria Frektri*

R osa seemed to be ignoring Rykar during training. He was ok with this; he even preferred that she did so. It was easier to act like nothing happened than to relive that embarrassing chapter in his life.

Part of him was annoyed by the fact that she had said the wrong name. He wished she had been lucid, that she would have known who he was. Rykar didn't know what happened to her to make her think that he was someone else, but he didn't think it mattered. She wasn't interested in him; she had feelings for that "Aodal" guy, whoever he was.

It was hard not to feel angry at Rosa. She had led him on by cuddling with him. She should have known what she was doing. He hadn't been around girls enough to know what they were truly like; he just knew that he liked them.

A larger part of him was angry at himself for being so vulnerable. Why did he care about Rosa? He knew better than to get attached to people at all, let alone those he barely even knew. For some reason, he felt comfortable around Ahren, like he could tell the swordsman anything, but worried that his trust in Ahren would someday betray him.

A few days had passed since their secret mission together, and their bond seemed to be strengthening over time. They spent most of their free time together, except for when they had time before bed. There was an unspoken rule that the dead of night was far too personal to be shared.

Rykar was enjoying Ahren's company. It was strange to say, but he was beginning to think they were even friends. He figured Ahren felt the same way, but he was frightened that his asking would scare the other man away.

The rest of the squad was still treating him normally, luckily. Hjalmir continued to joke around with everyone, Leif didn't cease to give out quiet wisdom, and Ada existed as a foil to Hjalmir. The three of them did a good job making sure training was going well.

After their secret mission, Rykar noticed that he wasn't receiving nearly as much attention as he had before his first mission with Hjalmir. Rykar enjoyed the freedom, but at first it confused him. He was used to being scooped up by a senior squad member for sparring or specific training. Since the change, he had turned to sparring with Ahren almost every day. To switch things up, Leif would sometimes volunteer to spar with one or the other, but it wasn't often. He seemed content with watching their growth from a distance.

Rykar wasn't sure what Leopold was doing throughout all of this. The commander's strength seemed valuable to the Warriors, so he didn't know why they weren't using it. Rykar's best guess was that he had other, more important things to attend to, but he couldn't guess what.

He went back to his room after a long day of training. It wasn't particularly easy, but it was becoming more and more normal. Rykar was getting used to sparring and felt himself falling into a habit. Comforted by this, he drifted off to sleep without taking the time to gaze upon the stars by himself.

---

Rykar was getting used to the darkness. The pain wasn't fading, but it wasn't as much of a problem as it used to be. He remembered the days when it was debilitating but was sure it was just his attitude that had changed, not the pain itself.

He trudged through the cold, dark wasteland, still hoping to find some sort of border. The more he traveled, the farther he found he was able to walk; it just took a lot of effort. Strangely, his body wasn't tired from walking. His mind was. He frequently felt his emotional state slipping. Sleep became an ever-present need, residing slightly behind his eyes.

Faster than he would have liked to admit, he lost track of time. He could've been in the dark Hel for years or mere moments, and he wouldn't know which. All he knew was that life was a dull ache, and all he wanted to do was move forward with the hope that someday it might stop.

Now and then, the pressure behind his eyes would fade, and the cold would be washed away by warmth. He wasn't sure why it happened or how he could recreate it, so he savored every minute of the release. It seemed as if those moments were indicators of what life would be like back in the light.

One day, when the release came, he decided to pay attention to where it was coming from. He looked everywhere, hoping to see another person made of light like before. Unfortunately, he was still alone. About to feel sorry for himself because no one was coming for him, he noticed that there was a small, yellow light emanating from his chest. It was faint but there.

A wild smile on his face grew even bigger. The light

began spreading throughout his entire body, and the pain that the darkness brought with it faded a little bit as well. At that moment, he had a realization. He already knew the strength to save himself would come from within, but he never would have guessed that it was already there.

---

That morning, Rykar was strangely vitalized. He felt motivated by something other than fear for the first time in a long time. He wanted to get stronger because it felt good. Not because he was afraid of letting the people he loved down. Maybe it was because he knew that his friends could protect themselves, or maybe it was something else. Whatever the reason, he was ready to train.

He rushed through his shower but was still careful not to get any of the soaps in his eyes. With practice, showering was becoming more and more relaxing, even while he cleaned himself.

Not caring what anyone else thought of him, he sprinted to training. He passed a few members of the Research Division as he ran and was met with expressions of shock. Rykar didn't understand why the Researchers were so stuck up, but then again, he didn't care. He was a killer; scholarly efforts were not his problem.

As he ran, Rykar realized that he knew exactly where he was going. The walls that used to seem foreign were becoming familiar to him. He passed an intersection and knew that turning down one of the hallways would take him to the cafeteria and going the other way would take him out of the building. Continuing straight would take him to the training room, so he kept on his current trajectory.

Finally, after what felt like far too long, Rykar arrived in time for training. Ahren and Leif were the only ones there so far. They seemed to be discussing something, so Rykar took a seat on the floor, symbolizing that he was ready for the day to begin. Slowly, people began filtering in. Karl and Eydis came first, followed by Hjalmir and Ada, then finally Rosa and Mila. For some reason, they always seemed to come in pairs. Ahren, Rykar, and Leif were the exceptions to the rule of two that everyone else subscribed to.

"Welcome, everyone," Leif began. "Today we're going to be running training a little bit differently." Rykar felt his heart sink a little. He was beginning to like the habit he was falling into, and change was certainly not something that he was thinking about. "Instead of splitting you up for sparring, we are going to run some larger group exercises."

"Why are we suddenly changing everything?" Rykar asked, hoping not to sound too rude. He did, however, wish to express his annoyance with the turn of events. "Breaking habits will most likely lead to worse performances." He continued to neglect to say "sir" after he was done speaking, much to Ahren's dismay. Rykar felt like using that word made him seem inferior to Leif, and that status was not something he believed. No one was better than him in the same way that he was not better than anyone else.

"It has come to my attention that a few members of our squad are worried about lacking teamwork skills and actual combat experience. These are real concerns that could bring about another failure like the one we experienced a few months before you showed up. I swear this is for your good. I would hate to fail again."

Before Rykar could think of a retort, he noticed that Rosa had started crying. Maybe Aodal was one of the squad members who died on their failed mission? It was just a guess, but, for some reason, Rykar felt confident that it was at least partially true.

"Alright, then. What's the exercise?" Rykar asked, hoping to show that he did not mean any disrespect.

"I will split you up into two teams of four, and we will play a simple game," Leif explained. "Each team will have an item that represents them. If the opposing team gains possession of your team's item, you will have lost. You will be given only a small amount of time to prepare to simulate an actual battle. Try not to hurt your teammates, because of obvious reasons. Work together as best as you can to ensure victory."

"What are the teams?" Ahren asked, slightly startling Rykar. He hadn't expected the swordsman to talk.

"Hjalmir, Ahren, Rykar, and Ada will be a team. Karl, Eydis, Rosa, and Mila will be the other. The idea is that we want to have balanced teams based on rank. Plus, you should have some experience working with your other squad members already."

"When can we pick our items, and when does the challenge start?" Karl asked, yawning. He didn't seem particularly interested in the game. Rykar felt a similar amount of disinterest, but he figured he could use his opponents' lack of motivation against them. Just because he didn't want to play did not mean he didn't want to win.

"You can pick your items when I finish speaking. The game begins when I decide, and it ends when the other item is stolen or when I wish for it to be done. I don't want this to drag on longer than it needs to."

Once Leif was done, they broke off into their groups and started strategizing. Competition was rising in the air, and Rykar loved it. The tension, the racing heartbeats, the atmosphere itself left an uneasiness in his stomach that he thought he loved. It was hard to tell.

"Some people think big items are good for this game," Hjalmir began. "They think that if you can't move them, then you can't take them. I think smaller is better, hoping they won't even be able to find it." Hjalmir's introduction and experience naturally pushed him into the role of team leader. "Ahren and Rykar can try to steal the opponent's object, mostly due to Rykar's nyxka. Ada and I will defend."

On the other side of the room, the opposing team was talking. It looked like Eydis had taken the lead. A part of Rykar felt bad for them. Even though they were "balanced" based on rank, he knew that he was far stronger than at least Rosa. Rank didn't mean a whole lot outside of demanding a certain level of respect.

"Are we going to be playing this in the training room?" Rykar asked. The small confines of the inside felt suffocating. He was hoping they could expand the boundaries into the outside, where he was far more comfortable.

Hjalmir gave him a shrug in response, so they motioned to Leif and asked him their question.

"There are no boundaries."

A smile formed across Rykar's face. As he watched Leif relay that information to the other team, he began to strategize. To his Knowledge, his war zone still existed in the courtyard where he had first learned zone expansion. If he could lure the other attackers into that area, then he could fight and incapacitate them. This was going to be fun.

"What's our item going to be, then?" Ahren asked.

At this, Ada ripped a sleeve off of her robe and clenched it in her fist. "I think this should do just fine," she said roughly.

"HA! Yes! I must agree!" Hjalmir boomed, laughing.

For the next few moments, they prepared for the game to start. To maintain an air of secrecy, they wouldn't be revealing who had the item or who had what role. They wanted to make the opposing team struggle when looking for the sleeve.

Hjalmir was a defender, but since he didn't have the sleeve itself, he had to stay close to Ada to defend her. Rykar and Ahren had the role of searching for the other team's item, but to deter suspicion from falling upon Hjalmir and Ada, they would have to stick close together as well.

"After I finish this next speech, each team will present their items. Once I have approved them, the game will begin," Leif started. "I would like to remind you to have fun. We are, after all, a team of friends. I also encourage you to take this seriously to an extent. This could save your life. Alright, then. Enough of that. Bring your items forward."

Ada brought forth the sleeve, and Eydis presented a

knife. It wasn't anything special—just a normal, single-edged blade. Rykar looked to the rest of her team and noticed that they all carried identical weapons, most likely to confuse his team.

"Hjalmir and Ada's team will be defending this sleeve!" Leif announced. "Karl and Eydis's team will be protecting this blade! Now then, return to your teams." He took a moment to pause as Ada and Eydis returned to their starting positions. When Ada got back, she made a show of turning her back to the other team and looking like she handed it to another person. It would be hard for them to guess who had the sleeve. "Let the games begin," Leif said, releasing the building tension from the room.

Time slowed for Rykar, and he sprinted out of the room down a familiar hallway. A few moments after he started running, he remembered Ahren and turned to check on him. The swordsman was a few strides behind him, so Rykar allowed time to quicken so that he wouldn't have to wait on Ahren as much. Luckily, Ahren wasn't the only one behind him. Karl and Rosa were on their trail, most likely not able to keep up with the pace because of Rosa.

To his surprise, they had no trouble at all with keeping up. Rykar was sure that they weren't as good at physical nyxka enhancement as he and Ahren were. Rosa could have been pushing them with her wind, but Rykar wasn't sure. Ultimately, it wasn't too important to him, as he was leading them through the hallways of the tower to the courtyard containing his ka. He hoped it hadn't faded, but he would just have to wait and see.

A light at the end of the pathway grew, and suddenly they burst out of the building. Rykar reached out, trying to see if his power was still there, and, to his relief, it was. He had the advantage of preparation, even if it was unplanned.

He took a moment to slow down time as much as possible. He needed to analyze the information in front of him. Karl and Rosa were approaching them, meaning they decided to balance their team even further based on rank. Karl's nyxka was also pretty good for stealing—he could stop time on objects—so it was likely that he did not have the right knife. Plus, he didn't seem interested in the event, so it was even less probable that he carried their item. Rosa's lack of experience made it unlikely that she would have it either. That left Eydis and Mila. Since Eydis could fly, it was likely she had it.

Time sped back up, and Karl and Rosa rushed forward. Ahren whipped around and threw Kyrx at them right as he saw Rykar stop. Ahren knew that Karl was the stronger of the two, so he, along with Rykar, decided to target him. Kyrx spun through the air, preparing to slice through Karl. Rykar knew that Ahren wouldn't *actually* kill Karl, but it still looked extremely lethal. Right as Kyrx was about to impale him, Karl poked the edge of the blade with his finger. Instead of slicing, or even cutting, Kyrx stopped in midair. Ahren's quiet curses probably meant that Kyrx couldn't be moved at all. Karl had used his nyxka well.

Luckily for Rykar's team, it didn't appear that Rosa knew how to use *her* nyxka particularly well. As Kyrx sat frozen in time, she tried to push them around with a few minor gusts of wind. None of them were even strong enough to move Rykar without him giving up all of his resistance and base. If anything, they felt kind of soothing and were a relaxing, cool pressure against his skin.

Kyrx broke off from Karl's control, and relief washed over Ahren's face. The relief suddenly switched to a darker look, maybe even one of anger. It was hard to tell, but it seemed like Ahren wanted to hurt Karl for doing that. He stretched his hand out as he broke into a sprint. Kyrx flew into his hand, and Rykar saw something that he had never seen before. Ahren was fighting with the sword in his hand.

Not only that, but he was good at it too. He ran at Karl, faking a huge, overhead swing. At the last moment, he diverted the slash away from Karl's outstretched hand, which was probably going to try to stop it in time, and he kicked Karl in the side of the ribs with his shin. While Karl was doubled over, he aimed Kyrx at his neck and was about to slash. Rykar looked deeper and saw something he didn't like: murder. Ahren intended to kill Karl.

Rykar slowed down time as much as possible and teleported in between them. As he looked closer at his teammates, he saw what they each wanted to do in the fight. Karl wanted to waste time. His indifference was due to boredom, and he didn't truly care about the exercise. Ahren wanted to kill. He wanted to hack Karl apart, presumably for affecting Kyrx like that. His nose was wrinkled, and his eyes could practically cut Karl on their own.

Knowing he had to do something, Rykar grabbed Karl and pulled him out of the way of the blow. He had to do it gently, otherwise he might break some of Karl's bones. He also took Ahren's robe and tied him up in it. Finally, to finish it off, he moved Rosa, slowly again, to make it seem like she had done it all with her nyxka. Rykar liked his friendship with Ahren and wasn't going to jeopardize it, even if it meant saving his teammate's life.

Allowing time to speed back up, Rykar watched it all unfold. Ahren's frustration was still pointed at a dazed Karl, but the more he struggled in his coat, the more it became directed at his garments. After deciding his efforts wouldn't amount to anything, Ahren allowed Kyrx to fly around, cutting the coat off of his body instead of taking the time to untangle it. Rykar looked at Rosa, who seemed just as dazed as Karl, probably because she was wondering what she had done.

Realizing he had to stop the fighting once and for all, he slowed time again and teleported to Karl to steal his knife. He searched for a moment, found it, and did the same to Rosa. A few moments later, he was standing in his original position from just before he slowed time, with two new knives in hand.

"Ahren, I got the knives!" Rykar yelled, hoping to shake the swordsman from his rage. He blinked a few times, and then he looked over to Rykar, perhaps realizing what was going on.

"Good job. Should we keep fighting these two?" Ahren asked, possibly hoping to fight Karl more.

"Nah, let's get out of here. We gotta help Hjalmir and Ada," Rykar said as he started to run to the entrance of the courtyard. Hjalmir and Ada had agreed to stay close to the training room, so if they backtracked, they should be able to find them easily.

Sure enough, the closer they got to the starting location, the louder the sounds of fighting became. Karl and Rosa were still following them, much to Rykar's annoyance, so he pushed his physical enhancement further. He wanted to see what Hjalmir and Ada could do in combat; he had never seen their true skills before.

He rounded the last corner before the starting location and found the action. Hjalmir and Ada seemed completely and utterly in control of the situation. Eydis was flying above the two of them, presumably the one with the item. Mila was attempting to fend Hjalmir off with her plants, but he just easily hacked them away with his large swords.

"How are you guys planning on taking this from me?" Eydis yelled down as she casually spun her knife in her fingers. Maybe it was a bluff, but there was no way to be sure. Plus, it was certainly logical for her to be the one holding the object.

Suddenly, in a blur, Ada pulled out the former sleeve of her jacket—Rykar's team's item. Almost faster than he could follow, she rubbed her hand across the length of the fabric, and it seemed to turn into a knife itself. Her nyxka, which allowed her to change the properties of objects she touched, was extremely useful. Next, she threw it upward with incredible precision and ripped a hole in Eydis's hand, causing her to drop her knife. Ada sauntered over to where it fell and picked it up.

"We win," she said.

Eydis fell to the floor and started to scream when she saw her injured hand.

A look of annoyance formed across Ada's face. "Oh be quiet. One of the healing nyxtad can fix you up. You're fine."

Hjalmir started to cheer and ran in to hug Ada. She didn't seem upset by the hug, but she didn't accept it like Rykar figured a significant other would. Maybe they weren't dating? He was having a hard time understanding the team dynamic.

Ahren walked up behind him, panting. "We won, then?"

"Yeah, we won. Nice job," Rykar said, giving Ahren a quick hug.

Karl and Rosa filtered in a few moments later, but neither of them seemed to care about the outcome. Rosa seemed distant, like she wasn't together mentally. Karl probably just didn't care. From Rykar's perspective, he was cool enough. Rykar just didn't know him that well yet.

"Congratulations, Hjalmir, Ada, Rykar, and Ahren," Leif said as he joined the rest of the squad in the room just outside of training. "You have proven yourselves to be a good team. I'm excited to see what you can do against Theo. We leave five days from now. Be prepared, all of you. You have earned your rest. Dismissed."

"How do they know that Theo will be in a specific location in five days?" Rykar asked Ahren.

"I've been doing some looking around, and I think Theo is staying in one place," Ahren whispered. "It sounds like they waited this long to prepare us as a team. Realistically, we could have left whenever, but they wanted to make sure we were ready." Rykar nodded in understanding.

With that, everyone went their separate ways. Hjalmir and Ada went together, so maybe they were a couple? Rykar's mind hurt thinking about all of the different relationships that could exist in the squad. All he knew was that he was going to go to the cafeteria with Ahren.

---

"So what was that with Karl earlier today?" Rykar asked before he took a bite of chicken on a skewer.

"What do you mean?" Ahren replied, mouth full of pork.

People who chewed with their mouths open disgusted Rykar, but he didn't say anything. Not yet at least.

"You looked like you wanted to kill him," Rykar explained, but only *after* he had swallowed the meat.

Ahren's attention turned to his plate. Head slouched, he almost looked ashamed of his brutality during the game. "He controlled Kyrx," Ahren finally said after a moment.

"Only you can do that?" Rykar inquired, confused.

"Nobody can. He's a free spirit just like you or me," Ahren practically spat.

Rykar took a moment to think. He didn't understand. Not one bit. The sword meant everything to Ahren. Rykar was pretty sure Ahren would willingly give up his life for the safety of the blade, and Rykar didn't even know why.

Kyrx had been there for Ahren since the death of his brother. Kyrx had saved him from the bandit during their secret mission. With a newfound realization, Rykar found his voice.

"Why did killing the bandit mean so much to you?"

Ahren looked up again, tears in his eyes and a slight smile on his face. "Karl tried to take Kyrx from me, tried to destroy him. It was wrong. I was happy to see Kyrx kill the bandit because he finally succeeded. He doesn't need to be sorry anymore.

"Kyrx died thinking he failed me, but he didn't. He's saved me countless times, and he means more to me than my own life."

Rykar finished his meal in silence, for he now understood Ahren more profoundly. To Ahren, Kyrx *was* his brother.

# THE OVERWHELMING POWER OF FEAR

*I am not afraid of those who know pain. They could be Knowledgeable about how to inflict it or even have a difficult past, full of suffering. Those who scare me are the few, unfortunate souls who not only know pain but are friends with it.*
-   *Drydnar Vyrtra*

G har spent the next few days trying to read the memory of almost every object he saw. He figured if he could do that well, then his Knowledge would increase incredibly quickly. The secrets and nuances of the universe would become much less unfamiliar to him.

He had started in the library, only to find out that most

of the books present were stolen from other planets by Pythti or his followers. A lot of them were built in massive, metal fortresses that glowed and whirred. They felt entirely unnatural, most likely operated by a high understanding of electricity.

The more he dug, the more Ghar realized how much information was available to him. Each stone, each bed, each piece of wood had its own personal history. At first, this seemed interesting to Ghar. Maybe he could learn something important from one of these. However, the more he read their memories, the more he learned about filtration. Certain things simply *weren't* special or worth his time. He had to find things that taught him enough for the ability to read memories to be valuable.

After he learned that most of the objects didn't have interesting pasts, he moved on to people. He wasn't under any illusions that some nyxtad may have a groundbreaking secret—logically, Pythti would have found it by then—he just wanted the practice. Being able to read people's pasts and their memories seemed like it could be an extremely useful skill, especially for manipulation.

A few days of practice later, and he was becoming exceptionally good at it. Trauma, secrets—all became readily available to him. It was remarkable to Ghar how easily he could reveal the true nature of somebody, simply by feeling the memory of their ka. He was taught from an early age—especially for the games of the nobility—that people were complex, confusing creatures. For a time, he agreed with this, but with his newfound power, he knew something much different. People were simple. Most of them wanted love, happiness, acceptance, or forgiveness for something.

The more he walked among them, the harder it was to relate to them. His power was beginning to reach higher than they could imagine. How could they think that they even had a purpose? What motivated them to stay alive? He desperately wanted to know, but a search into the past could only reveal so much information. Personal bias and expression in the form of self-preservation were often hard to read in ka. It was much easier to see the objective truth and interpret how they may feel, simply because he saw image sequences and didn't feel their emotions.

On some very rare occasions, he was able to read someone's own bias. Through further observation, he determined that they were deeply, emotionally connected to their nyxka. Their ka was not only a sliver of power being used as a tool, but also a part of them. The people who truly knew how to use their nyxka could have their minds read, or so his theory went.

---

A few days later, Pythti announced that the Warriors were having an acceptance ceremony. Some of the recruits had stood out and taken part in the CCA—the Collective Compatibility Assessment—offsite, which was quite rare. It meant they were rare—probably good with their divine nyxka—so Ghar wanted to test his ka reading out on them.

The induction ceremony was in the banquet hall. Most of the nyxtad at HQ attended, but Ghar still didn't know many of their names. He didn't care much about friendship or company. He was mostly interested in success.

On stage stood Leopold and two unfamiliar men. One carried a sword. He was taller than the other but a bit shorter than Leopold. His dark eyes felt hardened by the burdens of war. He was a good fit for the Warrior Division. The other was a different story. His blue eyes were intense. They were filled with anger and suspicion. Just looking at him gave Ghar goosebumps.

"Standing before you are the next members of your Warrior Division, our family. These men know horrors most have only imagined. They have gone through Hel to get here, and the future doesn't look much brighter. Their faces have been marred by blood and sweat, and they have kept moving, even when death was certain.

"They have proven their strength in carrying their own lives. Now allow them to carry yours. With men like these on our side, you can feel safe unraveling the secrets of the universe, all for the sake of humanity.

"Now, you two," he said, turning to face them. "Do you accept the risk and reward that comes with this job? It won't be easy. You may even die. Your reward, however, is priceless. You will feel like you are making a difference. You will be able to protect those you love. Most of all, you will be changing the world for the good."

"So, what do you say?" he asked finally.

"I accept the risk, sir!" one of them practically screamed. Ghar thought he noticed a streak of moisture on his cheek, but he was sure that he was mistaken. This man was far too tough to cry at a time like this.

"As do I," the other said, dripping with reluctance. It didn't seem that he wanted to be there. "Sir," he added quickly at the end.

The darker-eyed one jumped on his sword and flew out of the room. He didn't appear to care for the idea of a party in his name. The other, however, did seem to care for the reception, though he looked unused to the attention. It was almost as if he had never been in a situation where people felt honored to be in the same room as him. He was being swarmed by most of the rest of the Collective, much to his apparent discomfort.

By principle, Ghar refused to partake in events that involved going with the general behavior of a crowd. It felt strange, being associated with human stupidity. For this reason, he stood off to the side of the room, away from the group of fools surrounding the newer Warriors. Unsurprisingly, the man was drawn to him. He began to wade through the sea of bodies and reached for Ghar's hand when he met him.

By Instinct, Ghar began to search through his ka's memories. A sea of information swarmed into his mind, and Ghar sorted through it with extreme care and finesse. Strangely, he saw the man surrounded by a dark cloud.

Next, he *felt* the intense despair that the man felt. The guilt, the anger, the pain—all of it erupted into Ghar. For a second, he thought he might die, so he moved into a different part of his memory. He saw a girl—the boy called her Nyral—a bear, protecting its cubs, and then . . .

Ghar gaped as he saw the next scene. A bear assaulted by the power of what Ghar could only describe as truly divine. A child, the man he was talking to now, killing—no, obliterating—a full-grown bear.

Next, he only saw death and destruction. Fear. Escape. Afraid of what else he may see, Ghar switched to simply finding out what his name was. Then he saw a campfire, an older man, and some food.

"What is your name?" the old man had asked.

"Rykar," the then-child answered.

Ghar knew that the Collective renamed its members after the CCA. This was done to set the members of the Collective above the normal populations of the universe; having different names was a good way to differentiate between people. To find Rykar's new name, Ghar searched into his more recent memory. To his luck, he retrieved Rykar's divine name quite easily.

Satisfied with what he had found, Ghar began to converse with him.

"Your name is Rykar. Or wait, no. Is it Frederick?" he began. "This whole renaming thing is confusing. Either way, I know you but you don't know me. So allow ME to introduce myself. My name is Hadrian. I'm one of the Regional Scholars. I'm the same rank as Leopold, except I'm with the Researchers, not the Warriors."

Rykar's eyes turned to slits. "How do you know my name?" he asked.

"Oh, you know. My position revolves around the fact that I know things. When you deal with people like me, you should be asking what I don't know."

"What don't you know, then?" he responded.

Ghar sighed, dropping his chin to his chest. "Isn't that the million ray question."

Rykar shook his head, probably confused. Ghar understood the feeling of powerlessness and ignorance, and upon seeing that head shake, he swore that he would never feel that way again.

"Well anyways," Ghar said, kicking off the wall to walk away. "If you have any questions, just ask for me, and I'll do my best to answer them. Although, I'll probably know when you need my help." He said this last bit as he walked away, waving with the back of his hand. It wasn't entirely true, of course. He just needed to make Rykar feel like he was omniscient. It was important for the maintenance of the secret of his Knowledge.

Leaving the banquet hall, he reflected on the encounter. He tried, really tried, to think about it logically. To his dismay, he couldn't keep his emotions out of it. The sheer power, the instability, the *destruction*. It made his blood run cold. Retreating to his room for the first time since he had arrived, Ghar took a moment to analyze what he was feeling. Upon further introspection, he realized he only felt one thing from learning about Rykar's power. The fact that a man without any Knowledge, only Instinct, was more powerful than him only made Ghar feel one thing: *fear.*

---

As hard as it was to admit, Ghar wasn't used to being scared. Hel, that was debilitating. For days, he did nothing but cower in his room, imagining the pure destructive power that could be unleashed on the world at any time. Scarier than that, he felt powerless even with his Knowledge. Even with all of his strength, he still wasn't strong enough to defeat someone with talent, just like his brother.

After a few days of feeling sorry for himself, Ghar's fear turned into anger and motivation. He knew that he had to do something to protect the world from Rykar. So, he got to doing what he was used to. Plotting, scheming, and—most of all—preparing for every possible outcome of every situation. He needed a true spiderweb this time, and not just for himself but for the safety of the world.

First, he needed a reason to meet up with Rykar again. Ghar needed more information if he was to brew a successful plot to defeat Rykar. Second, he needed to determine how to stop Rykar without excessive force, as he was nearly certain that he would lose a fight against the Warrior. Third, he needed a way to make sure that Rykar didn't come back after the second part was complete. The more he thought about it, the more he saw similarities between his conflict with Rykar and Pythti's with Drydnar. Strange how history found ways to repeat itself.

Ghar was sure that the first part of his plan would go smoothly. Rykar seemed like a curious person, and the Warrior Division was often overly secretive. He wanted answers, and Ghar had made it clear that he could provide them. Ghar was glad that he had mentioned his eagerness to answer any questions. It allowed him to keep a tab on Rykar, just like what he had done with Kalia.

Being reminded of Kalia, Ghar began to wonder how she was doing. He hoped she hadn't been executed by Nadren yet. As much as he didn't like to admit it, he cared for Kalia, if only a little. Her death would upset him, but it wouldn't be the worst thing ever, right? Never mind that; he had work to do.

Ghar needed to wait for Rykar to approach him. He didn't want to seem like he had an interest in Rykar, as that might arouse suspicion. From what Ghar had seen, Rykar was clever and paranoid. He needed the Warrior to seek him out instead. This meant that he had to do some waiting. In the meantime, Ghar decided to practice ka reading. So far, the skill had been quite an asset. It couldn't hurt to develop it a little bit more.

He wandered through the tower for an unknown period.

Honestly, he couldn't tell someone how long it had been. He knew the Sun had risen and set a few times, but he was pre-occupied. He was still unable to get over his fear of Rykar, and the Warrior never really left his mind. The longer he walked through the hallways, the more Ghar wished Rykar would just ask him for help. Dread built in his chest with each step, creating mental tension as well. The strain of the scenario was almost too much for him. Almost.

At some point, he grew tired of walking and chose to fly by picking himself up with a bunch of small rocks. It was one fewer thing to think about. Muscle movement was strangely mentally exhausting but using his nyxka wasn't—not at HQ, at least.

Suddenly an ear-piercing scream cut through the air and brought relief with it.

"HADRIAN! I NEED YOUR HELP!" Rykar had finally decided to reach out to him to ask questions. Ghar was beginning to worry that he may never get another chance to read him and was about to start devising a new path to Rykar's defeat.

"Hey, Ryk. How can I help you?" he said, feigning enthusiasm as he reached out to shake Rykar's hand. In truth, he felt nothing but anxiety and nervousness, but Rykar couldn't know that. Luckily, Rykar returned the gesture.

Reaching back into Rykar's ka's memories, Ghar began to search for a way to defeat him. He needed something strong enough to beat him, something debilitating. Further and further he went, remembering the despair and fear that Rykar had felt in the past, with hopes of reigniting those feelings. At some point, he started to track the strength of those feelings. As if he were a blind man searching for something with his cane, he found his way to the epicenter of the guilt and hatred. Rykar's sister, Nyral. The person he had broken because of his passion. Smiling to himself, Ghar came back to the present conversation. All he had to do was successfully finish the conversation without arousing suspicion, and then he could move on to the next steps of his true spiderweb.

"I need some answers," Rykar explained. "I have no idea what we do here, why we do it, why I should help, or anything at all. Leif told me he would explain and then didn't, so I figured you could give me some insight."

"Ah, yes. Most people feel that way when they first arrive here. The Nyxtad Collective is secretive by nature, so we often forget that there are people we must share our Knowledge with. I can help you, though, don't worry. Strangely, most people neglect to ask as you did and just spend their time trying to figure it all out on their own.

"The Research Division was founded a few centuries ago by Pythti. Its purpose is simply to gather Knowledge by any means necessary. There isn't much more about the Research Division itself; we're just a school.

"The Warrior Division has a bit of a shorter history. When Pythti realized that some people from faraway lands didn't wish to share their secrets, he formed a group of elite combat nyxtad to steal them. These people became the very first squad of the Warrior Division. Now the Warriors are used whenever the Researchers need protection when trying to learn more. After the formation of the Warrior Division, Pythti decided to rename the organization to the Nyxtad Collective, as we are a collection of all kinds of nyxtad."

Ghar stopped for a moment, wondering if he could turn Rykar to his side. It was unsettling, seeing this kind of power standing in front of you, asking to be molded into a weapon of mass destruction for your benefit. Upset, and sure it was showing, Ghar silently decided to end Rykar so that no one could ever exploit his power. That and Ghar didn't trust anyone's power but his own.

"As to what you, specifically, are doing here," Ghar continued, "I don't entirely know. I know your next mission is to apprehend a member of the Ruined. They are a terrorist cell that is essentially the largest opposition to the Warrior Division right now. Leopold is Hel-bent on taking them down."

"Can you tell me about Leopold?" Rykar asked.

"He has been a member of the Warrior Division for at least a century," Ghar said, nonchalantly. He wanted to completely alter Rykar's worldview so that he thought of Ghar as a power above and beyond him. He needed to act like a peerless god to remain safe from the stronger, 5th-class Warrior.

"Although, even with all that information, we still don't know much about his history," he continued. "He could be thousands of years old. No one knows, except for maybe Pythti. Some people think Pythti could be a God of Knowledge."

"Wait. Sorry, I didn't hear some of what you said," Rykar admitted. "Could you repeat what you said before you mentioned how little we know and possibly tell me about Leopold's nyxka?"

"Well, that works out, I guess," Ghar said, chuckling. "You know just as much as I do at this point. According to our records, Leopold is without a nyxka. Even so, it is theorized that he is the strongest combat nyxtad ever."

With that, he left Rykar to ponder what he had just said. He was sure that he had shocked Rykar. With any luck, he had enough information to stop him. As Ghar began forming the next steps of his plan, he felt an old, unwelcome friend creep into his mind. Was he strong enough or smart enough to succeed? He didn't know. Insecurity and uncertainty never ceased to plague him at the most inopportune times.

---

Kalia tried to calm herself as she approached the front door to House Tyrno. If she failed, she would have to journey far just to speak with the heads of House Pikna and House Wafla. There was no guarantee for success with them, and the distance made the journey almost too hard for her to want to attempt. Without a horse, it took forever to get anywhere.

Unlike her attempts at the other noble houses, the Tyrno let her inside their home. A butler received her, but Kalia thought it was still a good sign, hopeful that they would aid her in her endeavor. She wanted to meet with Hyrax Tyrno, the patriarch of the house. He was one of her father's closest friends, so she figured he would help her as well.

The servant led her through the house, and unlike her visit to Pelto, he led her to the main room of the house. In a non-royal house, it must have been the equivalent of a throne room. In the center of the room, speaking to a group of servants, stood the proud Hyrax Tyrno. Tall, with dirty-blond-and-now-gray hair, he looked the same as he did the day her father had died. It was easy to forget that it hadn't been that long since Nadren had ascended to the throne. Kalia felt herself breathe out a sigh of relief when she saw him. He would know what to do, how to help. She could have direction again.

"Lord Tyrno," the butler said, bowing, "Kalia Vyrtra to see you."

Hyrax turned, and, to her displeasure, he frowned when he saw her.

"What are you doing here?" he asked critically. "I thought you were to be executed in Pelto."

"I escaped to save my own life," she replied, doing her best to hide all emotion. The noble rules of conversation always irritated her, but now she felt strangely nostalgic abiding by them again.

"Yes, of course. But why are you at my house, specifically?" he said, almost sounding irritated. This was not the Hyrax she remembered. Her memory of him was one of laughter and joy. He had practically been her uncle.

"I would like to seek help from House Tyrno as the head of House Vyrtra," she explained as she bowed down on one knee. Hopefully, showing respect would help her. "The throne is my birthright, and I hope you have not forgotten the loyalty and love that you showed my father during his time as Lopythlok."

"I was a fool!" he shouted, then took a breath, probably to calm himself. "A sycophant, hoping my proximity to the throne would benefit me. I was wrong. My loyalty was to the throne, my love to your father. He was like a brother to me. I know neither when I see you." Kalia felt her heart sink as she heard the words. She began to wonder if all of the nobility were as disingenuous as he, or if she had only been exposed to the worst of them. No, not all were liars and power-hungry madmen. Ghar wasn't. He was honest, to a fault. Most would call him brutal, but she called him charming. She just wished she could say it to his face.

"Speak to one of my children about helping you further," he finally added with a sigh. Perhaps he did care for her, if only a little. "I won't be responsible for what happens next, but they may still wish to aid you."

"Thank you," Kalia said, unemotionally. He couldn't know the effects of his words. She wouldn't allow him to know how deep they cut. To know that he, one of the kindest men she thought she knew, would betray her was almost too much to bear.

The butler led her through the house again, this time to what she assumed to be the quarters of Hyrax's children. The rooms were eerily similar to the room that she first met Ghar in, and she felt an empty pit open in her heart. As much as she was upset that he had betrayed her, she still missed him. Shaking her head, she tried not to think of that. Currently, she had to focus on gaining the favor of one of the Tyrno children.

"This is the room of Hilan Tyrno," the butler explained as he gave the door a firm knock.

The door opened, and Kalia briefly saw the back of Hilan, who moved to sit in a chair a few rays from the entrance. She looked a lot like her father, except that she was shorter than he was. Plus, she didn't have the speckles of gray in her hair.

Hilan waved for Kalia to sit down in the chair across from her, presumably unaware of why Kalia was there. Kalia wasn't particularly close with Hilan, but they had been friends as children. She probably thought Kalia was there to reminisce, not to revolt.

Doing her best to ignore the room and its apparent connection to her first meeting with Ghar, Kalia tried to form the words that would ask for help.

"Kalia Vyrtra," Hilan began, with the same smirk she always wore as a child, "how would you like to win your throne back?"

Kalia was dumbstruck, how did she know?

"Do you think I'm foolish?" Hilan chuckled. "I know how much you wanted to ascend when you first moved in as King Vyrtra's daughter. Why else would you be here if not to plan a revolution? You were never one to make friends, so the only reason you would come to me would be to ask for help. Am I wrong?"

"No," Kalia said, with an exasperated sigh. "You're exactly right. So, will you help?"

"Of course," she said as she stood up and stretched her hand out. "Are you ready to return the kingdom to its former glory?"

Kalia couldn't help but smile as she shook Hilan's hand, ready to tear Nadren from *her* throne.

# RUINED

*A man can conquer a kingdom and gain riches. A woman can conquer the world and acquire power. When they conquer their demons, however, is when they find freedom.*
- *Theodar Vyrtra*

The morning before they left for the mission to apprehend Theo was pure chaos. Rykar wasn't sure how best to prepare for the mission, so he just picked up a bunch of knives and loaded them into his coat as he had done with his secret trip with Ahren. Most of them were pretty small, standard knives, but he did have two larger, curved blades as well. The smaller ones would be thrown while the curved semi-swords would be used for close combat.

For some reason, the rest of the squad seemed just as confused as he had been when Leif announced when they were leaving. Everyone thought the mission would still be a few days out since Leif had told them they had five days to prepare only three days prior. Worse yet, they only had one night's notice. The day before, as the Sun was setting, Leif had told the squad that they were going to leave the next day. Hjalmir laughed and cheered, trying to hype everyone up, but the general mood was anxiety and fear. Most of them didn't feel ready for the battle, and Rykar worried for Mila and Rosa. He wasn't sure they would survive.

They had met in the training room while the Sun was rising. People packed their bags with weapons and armor, preparing for the mission. They still didn't know Theo's power, just that he was doubtless extremely destructive like the other members of the Ruined.

After Leif was satisfied that they were prepared, the squad moved to the airport and began to board the largest plane Rykar had ever seen. It had multiple propellers along each wing, unlike the other jets he had ridden in that didn't appear to have any. It was also taller and rounder than the other sharper vehicles.

Once they had boarded the plane, they each sat in chairs that were facing sideways, across from one another. For a second, Rykar wondered who would be flying the plane, but then a person outside of their squad, probably a Researcher, joined them and took her place in the pilot's chair.

The familiar sensation of takeoff pushed itself into Rykar's side this time. The entire situation felt off. Everything was happening too fast. Just a few days ago, he was joking around with Ahren and Hjalmir. Now he was risking his life for a cause, but he still didn't know if he wanted to. Why was *he* doing what he was doing? Having a hard time dealing with the present, Rykar's mind slipped into the past, trying to think of familiar, good times. Disconnected from his body, his consciousness felt oddly free. After all, pain and discomfort were constructs of the mind, so why should he not be able to control their flow?

Some time passed, yet Rykar remained in his head. He had no idea what to do. On one hand, these people were his closest allies, but on another, he had never had any trouble cutting ties with people. Safety and survival had always been his priority.

"Everyone, listen up!" Leif shouted, pulling Rykar back to reality. The plane wasn't nearly as loud as any of the other jets he had been on. Maybe the pilot was doing something to dampen the sound of the propellers? "We are about to enter a battle. Normal people see these and cower behind shields and walls provided by their government. We, the brave souls of the universe, see battle and view it as an opportunity to protect, grow, and prove ourselves. You and I do not see battle and shake from fear. No. We see battle and smile, for we know that our victory is assured. Our enemies, the villains that they may be, will march to their doom. When these doors open"—he motioned toward the back of the plane—"we will rain Hel upon the Ruined. THEY will be the ones mourning their losses. THEY will be the ones licking their wounds, hoping to someday recover. THEY will lose! WE WILL PREVAIL! WE WILL DECIMATE THEM! We will avenge those who they have taken from us . . . Trust your Instincts, and you will be a Warrior as fearsome as the commander himself."

Next, Leif moved to speak to each of the squad one at a time.

"Hjalmir, you are practically unkillable. I admire your passion, your strength. I'm proud of the man you've become and glad that you're here to guard your fellow squad members." At this, Hjalmir gave an oddly serious nod in response, entirely unlike his normal, cheery self.

"The day I meet a woman with more finesse than you, Ada, is the day I go crazy. Your unparalleled skill should deter all of our opposition, yet there are still people foolish enough to fight you."

He went around to the rest of the team, attempting to encourage them, but his words didn't seem to be helping that much. Those who were already prepared didn't need an extra hype-up, and the ones who were ridden with anxiety could not be consoled by a few words. Rykar wasn't sure which one he was.

Finally, Leif got to Rykar. Kneeling, Leif whispered one short phrase into Rykar's ear. "They should be scared of you."

Rykar felt a shiver run down his spine as he realized one simple truth about himself. He was nervous, but not for the battle. He wasn't afraid of death or the death of anyone except for maybe Ahren. Even still, he was scared. Deathly. He was terrified of himself, of his power. Shaking, he held his head in his hands. What would happen if he became the villain again? How would he recover? At that moment, he knew that he wasn't prepared for the horrors he was about to commit. Everything was so much easier when he didn't care about anyone.

"When we dive into chaos hoping to defeat a demon, we will be the ones striking fear. Think not about your failures and insecurity. All that matters is your survival and success. When we win, I will make sure every one of you is given an honor fit for a hero. Show me what you're worth. Show me your power. Show me the head of Theo, and I will give you my eternal respect and protection."

With that, Hjalmir let out a roar and began to rhythmically thump his chest as he stood up. Ahren joined in, then Eydis, then Mila. Soon, everyone was roaring and beating as Leif hit the button to open the rear door. The hatch lowered, creating a ramp.

"TO BATTLE!" Leif screamed as they all sprinted and dove out of the plane toward the chaos of combat.

---

As Rykar fell, he realized that he had no way of slowing himself, nor did the rest of the squad. The height they were falling from wasn't trivial either. The ground was rising to meet them, and it was going to hurt when it did. Analyzing the geography of the area, Rykar saw that they were most likely in Gapythtym again, near where he had grown up. An immediate unsettledness grew in his chest. He wasn't prepared to revisit his past, especially not on a life-and-death mission. Wind rushed into his face, and they were low enough to see individual trees. Almost certain that he would die on impact, he prepared to teleport himself back into the airplane. But just as he was about to do so, he felt an updraft of warm air against his body. Leif was creating a strong source of heat to slow the fall of most of the squad, except for Hjalmir. He kept hurtling toward the ground, making a deafening impact on arrival. The rest of the team landed hard as well, but not enough to kill anyone.

Rykar would have been lying if he had said he was comfortable with the situation. For one, he didn't know anything about the minute details of the mission. He just knew that they were a kill squad, assigned to take out an extremely powerful opponent of the Collective. Unaware of why they were in a forest, where they were going, or if Hjalmir was even alive, Rykar turned to his Instincts for answers. He would have to find solace in deduction and intuition, as he had a hunch that no one else would feel the need to provide him with answers.

Not for the first time, Rykar found that he was incredibly frustrated with the vague nature of the Collective as a whole. For some reason, that attitude of secrecy seemed to have found a place in the Warrior Division as well. No matter how much people claimed they knew how he was feeling—scared, confused—they did nothing to change those feelings.

"HEL, YEAH!" A massive, familiar scream broke through Rykar's silent anger. Hjalmir. Brushing himself off, he stepped through the trees nearby. Not only did he seem completely intact, but the large Warrior also looked hyped-up and ready for battle. That must have been a result of his nyxka, which nearly made him immortal.

Rykar looked around to see how everyone else was feeling. Aside from some excessive nausea coming from Rosa, they all seemed fine. Grateful for Leif, Rykar moved toward Ahren.

He felt comfortable working with the swordsman. Ahren seemed relieved by the movement, dropping his shoulders just slightly, showing signs of released tension. The mission ahead was not going to be easy, and everyone knew it.

The rest of the squad formed up into groups of two as well. Strangely, they all looked as if they were the most comfortable with those of the same rank. Karl and Eydis, Hjalmir and Ada, and Rosa and Mila all sorted naturally into their pairs based on class. Ignoring the sorting, Leif started to slowly and quietly make his way through the thick underbrush of the forest. Rykar and Ahren followed him, with Rosa and Mila behind them. Then came Karl and Eydis, and pulling up the rear were Hjalmir and Ada. Even though they were all on the same team, supposed to be peers, they felt the need to protect those who seemed weaker. Rykar did not think Rosa and Mila should have come.

They walked for some time, and Rykar's annoyance only grew. Only a few of them knew how to move quietly through the wilderness. The squad was loud, both in sound and smell, basically asking to be found. Anyone who knew what to look for would have been able to find them. Not only that, but someone's bag was making an unpredictable clicking noise. Rykar couldn't for the life of him tell who or where it was coming from, but it needed to stop soon. He felt like he was going crazy. He tried to predict when it would come, maybe even make a song out of it, but he *always* missed the next click. It was completely random, or so it seemed.

To make matters worse, Rykar still didn't know where they were going, where Theo was, or what they planned to do to him when they found him. If it hadn't been for Ahren and maybe Hjalmir, he would have teleported away a little after they landed. Leif needed to come up with something soon or those two wouldn't be enough to keep him there.

Suddenly Leif stopped.

"We'll lay the traps here," Leif whispered to the group as they gathered around him. "According to intel, Theo is going to pass through here. If we're lucky, we'll have a few days before he arrives. Set up war zones first, camp second, and don't go far. We need all of the power we have and need to be prepared for anything."

Rykar wasn't sure what "intel" they were using and wasn't sure that he even trusted it. If Theo was as strong as people claimed, there was a good chance he already knew the squad was there. If he didn't yet, he would when he saw the fires and heard the noises that accompanied a group of uneducated campers.

Spending some time expanding his war zone, Rykar decided to scout the area as well. At one point, Ahren joined him. As much as Rykar loved the presence of his friend, complete solitude was becoming rarer as days passed. He couldn't say so to Ahren, but the feeling that everything was off persisted, especially in the campsite. Something was wrong; he just didn't know what. Hopefully, it was just paranoia, but he would rather survive because of a false alarm than die due to carelessness.

Strangely, the clicking persisted. To his Knowledge, everyone had set their gear down at this point. What could be the source of it? He had checked himself multiple times, worried that he may be getting frustrated due to his own stupidity.

"Hey, Ahren," he whispered after some contemplation.

"What's up?"

"Do you hear that random clicking?"

"Yeah, what about it?"

"Any idea what it is?" Rykar asked, part of him hoping that this whole thing was nothing to worry about. Another, surprisingly large, part of him *wanted* it to be a problem. That part wanted a fight, wanted to prove himself by releasing all of his pent-up rage. He desperately needed a release.

"No, it's kind of annoying, though," Ahren said, wincing as another *Click* permeated through the woods. "I wish it would stop."

"I'll say. It's been following us since we landed." Rykar

was relieved that he wasn't the only one who was irritated. Ahren seemed to have a talent at consoling him. "Any idea how Leif knows where Theo is going to go?"

"I have a guess," Ahren said, casually twirling Kyrx in front of them. He didn't need to spread his ka, because he only manipulated Kyrx, nothing else. He could essentially relax while Rykar prepared for the fight. "When I got bored at the tower, I would follow and spy on random nyxtad. There are these things called ka zones that are pretty important," Ahren continued, with a surprisingly thorough answer. "With enough understanding of them, someone can detect all of the information passing through one. The only people who can do this are people like Hadrian and Pythti. With this, they track Theo's position across the continent and try to formulate trends. I'm guessing they've been gathering information for a month or two now. They needed enough data to have an accurate trend. I'm guessing they liked the strategic value of this location, which also happened to be on Theo's path."

For some reason, Rykar hadn't thought that Ahren was as educated as his answer indicated. He didn't seem particularly smart, but then again, Rykar was beginning to compare all people of intellect with Hadrian, and that was just unfair. That was probably like comparing an extremely athletic, unenhanced male to Leopold. It wasn't even a contest. Hadrian and Leopold were like gods among their respective specialties.

*Click*

"There! It was closer this time!" Rykar whisper-shouted, falling into his stalking stance. He *needed* to find the source of the noise.

*Click*

The sounds were becoming more and more predictable, coming closer together. Even more strangely, it seemed to be moving around them in a circle. Rykar looked to Ahren, who was beginning to panic. Frantically spinning on his heels, searching for all signs of the noise, Ahren was losing his cool. Rykar, however, knew better. He quieted his mind, focusing on the scene around him. His Instincts were strong enough to tell him that the clicks weren't just noise, they were a problem. Somehow, he knew that they meant doom.

He trusted his gut, for if not it then who? Traveling back to the center of the camp, Rykar prepared to announce his beliefs and findings. Maybe if the squad worked together, they could stay safe and find the noise before it tore his mind apart from the inside.

Just as he was about to get there, every muscle in his body told him to stop, to *run*. To get the Hel out of there. Confused and scared, Rykar turned and started to sprint right as an explosion destroyed everything he was about to get to. Ahren was slower, getting caught in more of the force than Rykar. He hoped his friend was ok.

Knocked to the ground, he thought he could make out someone whispering. "Oh, you're a strong one."

---

Immediately, Ahren got to his feet. A shockwave had knocked him down, its origins unknown. He took a moment to think. He had fallen on his butt, backward, meaning that it had come from in front of him. Using that, he reoriented himself and started to look for Rykar or anyone else close by.

He stumbled around, suddenly noticing a ringing in his ears. What was that about? His head hurt a lot, but it wasn't enough to keep him down. Luckily, he could still feel Kyrx. The connection hadn't been severed or anything, so that was good. Ahren didn't know if it could be, but he wasn't planning on finding out.

The clicking was gone. Or wait. All sounds were replaced by an intense ringing, and he realized that his balance was terrible. Each step seemed to miss where he aimed for his feet to go. The ground flowed into walls and slopes as his vision swam.

His senses regained most of their clarity after some

time, but Rykar was still nowhere to be found. Forcing himself not to panic, he moved to search for anyone else in the squad. Being alone after a crisis was dangerous. People often didn't handle adrenaline well, and the crash destroyed their sensibility even more. Any of the senior members would know what to do, so he just had to find one of them.

A moment later, he found Hjalmir kneeling by a tree. Relieved, he wanted to yell out to the large man, but his hurt lungs and throat wouldn't allow him. That was a good thing, too, as he realized that yelling, after something that may have been an attack on the squad, may not be a good idea. Instead, he just walked over with as much care as he could muster, but in his state, he must have been a dizzy, wild mess.

Hjalmir turned as he heard Ahren coming. His face looked red, perhaps from the heat? It was hard to tell. Speaking of heat, why hadn't a fire formed after the explosion? It was certainly hot enough to start one. Shaking his head, he decided not to focus on that. He had to talk to Hjalmir. Just as Ahren was about to say something, Hjalmir turned back to the tree and put his head in his hands.

"How could this happen . . ." Hjalmir sobbed as Ahren walked closer to hear him more clearly. "W-we were so prepared. H-how . . ." Confused, Ahren took a look at the tree. Horror-struck, he knew why Hjalmir was reacting the way he was.

A shadow fell over his hope. At a certain point, he started to think that everyone on the team was invincible. With people like Leif and Rykar present, how could anyone die? But still, there, in many bloody and broken pieces, was Rosa.

# A DANCE WITH DEATH

*I looked to the horizon and saw death. I looked behind me and saw horrors. I searched within myself and found nothing but despair.*
-     *The Freer of Fools*

Planning the destruction of Rykar was quick and easy. Or maybe it was just easy. Ghar wasn't good at keeping track of time when he was engrossed in his work. Not for the first time, one or one hundred days could have passed, and he wouldn't have been able to tell which. It wasn't even that he didn't have an internal clock either. He did, and he even thought it was a pretty good one. No, it was the fact that to him, his plans and his work often overshadowed the need for an understanding of time. He didn't stress deadlines because that wasted time and energy. He worked quietly, efficiently, and privately, and he saw results.

Ghar's current plans were much less complex than his initial attempt at a perfect spiderweb. He had learned from his mistakes. He now knew that simplicity often gave plans a higher chance of success than complexity. Too many moving parts allowed there to be excessive uncertainty, therefore making the outcome somewhat random.

After some time, Ghar knew what he must do to completely and utterly defeat Rykar in a confrontation. In single combat, he would surely lose, but if he could catch him off guard or put him in a trap, then Ghar may be able to win. The problem came after the fight. Ghar wasn't sure he could contain him or even kill him as an alternative to imprisonment. People with that amount of raw power were not meant or made to be incarcerated.

Frustrated, Ghar decided to avoid focusing on that part quite yet. He knew that a solution would present itself at some point; he just didn't know when. Unfortunately, the more he tried not to think about the final stages of the plan, the more they bothered him. They were arguably the most important, so if he couldn't get them right, then the whole operation would have been for nothing. Suddenly an idea occurred to him. Something that he seldom considered now seemed like a good option. He was going to ask for help.

Pythti had experienced similar things with Drydnar Vyrtra a few centuries prior, so all Ghar had to do was copy the loose outline of Pythti's plans, and he would be fine. Plus, it would allow him to focus on the parts that were unique to his conflict with Rykar. Ghar wanted to avoid reinventing the wheel as much as possible for the sake of efficiency. Again, he wrote in flames to get Pythti's attention, except this time he reluctantly wrote the words "I need help."

This time, the flash of light that signified Pythti's arrival was not only tolerable but didn't cause Ghar any discomfort at all. Maybe Ghar was getting stronger?

"How can I help?" Pythti asked, yawning. If Ghar didn't know any better, he would have thought that Pythti was tired.

In Ghar's mind, Pythti was an infallible, indefatigable immortal—a god of a man. It was strange to see anything but strength plastered across his face.

"Can you tell me how you killed Drydnar?" Ghar replied. As he asked this, the look on Pythti's face switched from irritation and fatigue to concern. Even now, it seemed like Drydnar still scared Pythti.

"Why . . . ?" Pythti's voice faded as he answered with a question of his own. Ghar's concern grew at this. Pythti was hiding something. Something extremely important at that.

"I found a threat that needs my attention," Ghar answered quickly, not wanting to reveal anything if he could avoid it. He wasn't sure why he was hiding information, but his Instincts told him to.

"Would you say this 'threat' is on a similar level to Drydnar, then?" Pythti asked, eyes widening. Fear was not a good look on the leader of the Nyxtad Collective.

Ghar didn't know how to respond. He had never met Drydnar or even seen his power. All the stories of him were ones of incredible strength, though, so he figured it was safe to compare Rykar's raw, insane power to Drydnar's. If not, then Drydnar was even more of a nightmare for Pythti to deal with than Ghar had ever imagined.

"I would say so. The scariest part is he has no Knowledge skill, just Instinct. His raw power is what scares me. What if he gains Knowledge?" Ghar was getting irritated with the length of the conversation. It shouldn't take this long to get an answer as simple as the one he sought. "So, how did you defeat him, then?"

Pythti dropped his head in his hands and began to groan. Ghar was almost certain something was wrong at this point.

"Who do you think were the 'problems' I mentioned earlier?" Pythti asked, a sort of craze behind his words. This was *not* the quiet yet powerful Pythti that Ghar knew. This was a weak man, someone who had let fear consume him. Then, with a wild look in his eyes, Pythti looked up and stared at

Ghar. "He's not fucking dead!"

---

Hilan was eager and had good intentions, but she wasn't exactly helpful. The more Kalia worked with her, the more she realized how much of her persona was crafted to make her seem noble and intelligent. Not that she wasn't intelligent. She was good at reading people on a personal level. It was one of her hobbies to analyze people around the mansion. Servants and nobility alike were subjected to her scrutiny.

The problem came when they started planning, and Kalia realized that, unlike Ghar, Hilan had little to no understanding of politics. Kalia knew this because she had a larger wealth of Knowledge on the topic than Hilan did, and she felt like she knew nothing at all. Everything had been so much easier when she was collaborating with Ghar. Finally, after many days of planning with no clear direction, Kalia felt the need to have an honest talk with her partner.

"What were you thinking when you said that you could help me get on the throne?" Kalia asked, perhaps more aggressively than necessary. "It feels insincere to say you'll help me when you can't do anything to help." If her words hurt Hilan, she didn't show it. Her poise and elegance were extremely impressive.

"I have resources, I figured you had the intelligence and Knowledge. I was unaware of the fact that we are both completely ignorant to the politics of our nation," Hilan said simply, unresponsive to the apparent animosity coming from Kalia.

"You didn't think to bring this up earlier?" Kalia was beginning to relate to Ghar and his irritation that came from working with herself. Incompetency was awful. "All of this time has essentially been wasted."

"No use dwelling on the past," Hilan said, stifling a yawn. At that moment, Kalia only wanted one thing and that was to punch her in the face. How could she just dismiss her failings that easily? It was infuriating.

"I think there is. If someone killed another person, would you stop dwelling on the past simply because it's inconvenient to accept?" Hilan opened her mouth to answer, but Kalia cut her off and continued. "No, understanding the past helps us understand the consequences of our actions. In the courthouse, it allows you to determine a sentence. With history, it can help people avoid making the same mistakes over and over again. You have to explain yourself."

"Uh, I—uh—just . . . sorry, can I get some fresh air?" Hilan was trying to avoid the confrontation again. Kalia was growing to hate her more and more with each passing moment. Just as she was about to hurt Hilan, she took a few deep breaths to calm herself. Murdering your benefactor was generally not a good idea.

"What resources do you have?" Kalia asked through clenched teeth. She hoped she could still benefit from their partnership.

"I have a small guard of about one hundred men and women. I can offer you thirty of them," Hilan answered, composed again.

Kalia was incredulous. "How are thirty people going to help me overthrow an entire nation? That's almost nothing!" She was about to continue yelling, scolding Hilan for her ineptitude, when she realized that those thirty soldiers were all she had. Ghar had abandoned her. Hyrax refused to think about helping. Hilan and her small force would have to do. Stopping her rant, Kalia changed tactics. "Wait, sorry. Now that I think about it, that's incredible!" she forced herself to say. "Is there any chance I could have closer to fifty, though?"

"No," Hilan said, unwavering. It was probably impossible to negotiate with her when she had her mind made up about something; she seemed extremely stubborn. Thirty people plus herself would have to be enough, then. Enough to usurp an incredibly strong king. Enough to change the politics of a nation that had been forged by thousands of years of stability. Enough to allow her to live up to the legacy and expectations of her father.

---

Ghar wasn't sure what "fucking" meant, but he was pretty sure it was being used as a curse. Just the way that Pythti spat it at him was enough to make it unpleasant, but Pythti's facial expression gave an even more significant effect.

On top of that, the realization that Drydnar was alive was almost enough to make Ghar want to disconnect his mind from his body. How could he be? Pythti was strong enough to kill him, right? If he was alive, where had he been since his fight with Pythti? Ghar had so many questions. Just as he turned to Pythti to ask them, he noticed something almost as unnerving as the news. Pythti was in tears, sobbing like a child who had just skinned their knee on some stones. Drydnar had given him some severe trauma.

Strangely, he wasn't upset with Pythti for having lied to him. Maybe it was because he knew that the older man wasn't incompetent? Whatever the reason, where he usually found irritation, he now found curiosity.

"What happened?"

"I couldn't kill him, no matter how hard I tried. He evaded every attack at first, but his confidence grew, and he started to meet me on the battlefield." His voice grew shaky as he continued. "He became less and less scared of me. By the end, I doubt he even saw me as a threat. People like him are unkillable."

"How do you beat someone immortal?"

"If you can't beat them on the battlefield, you remove them from it by any means necessary."

"What do you mean?"

"I banished him. Sent him to Hel. He's probably still there today."

"So what, is Hel like a penal colony, then?" Everything was extremely hard to process, but Ghar was doing his best to stay calm. The best planning came from relaxation and composure. Losing his cool would just derail the mission.

"The most dangerously powerful people in this system have been exiled to Hel," Pythti whispered, clearly ashamed of this fact. With a sharp inhale, Ghar realized why Pythti was so scared, so full of guilt.

"Wait!"

Ghar's exclamation of surprise and anger was met with a low groan from Pythti.

"YOU PUT THE MOST DANGEROUS PEOPLE TOGETHER, UNSUPERVISED, WITH ONE OF THE STRONGEST MEN EVER?!" Ghar couldn't believe what he was hearing. The lack of foresight was astounding.

At this outburst, the real Pythti was back. The strong, confident man replaced the weak, broken one. He stood up straight and stared down into Ghar's eyes, almost as if to say, *I'm better than you.*

"I have plans to deal with them. It is also important to note that Hel is not hospitable to anyone except for a few, resilient people. Some areas are so primal and dangerous that they could even kill Leopold. So, if you would like to help me, you may." At this, his confident tone changed to stern. "You may *not*, however, talk to me like that ever again. You are my subordinate, and you need to remember that."

Ghar wanted to punch him in the face. He wasn't taking responsibility for his actions. Even if he sent them to one of the most dangerous places in the universe, some people were bound to have survived the transfer. Drydnar most likely did, due to his power, but Ghar was less sure that others could. Pythti was the one who had just been crying like a child. He was the one who had failed all those years ago, so why was he Ghar's superior? What made him any better than Ghar? At that moment, Ghar decided to stop listening to Pythti almost completely. No need to subject himself to idiotic leadership.

Unfortunately, Pythti's endorsement was still important. The Collective had a lot of resources, resources that Ghar needed if he was going to get more powerful.

Instead of giving him the satisfaction of responding, Ghar just gave Pythti a dismissive wave and flew away in a whirlwind of rock, fire, and lightning. He wanted Pythti to see exactly how strong he was. The farther he flew away from him, the more Ghar realized that he felt free without people "leading" him. Everything felt so much better when it was under his control.

When he got back to the particular area he had been working in, Ghar went over his encounter with Pythti again to see if he could use any of the information for his confrontation with Rykar. After he had sorted through the details a few times, he determined that the only helpful thing was the revelation that only certain parts of Hel were hospitable. Sending him to Hel was not a great idea. Worst case, Rykar would survive and join forces with Drydnar. Best case, he would die directly after the transfer. Ghar wasn't willing to take that chance.

With that, Ghar took to studying. If he was going to come up with a new way to defeat Rykar, he needed to increase his Knowledge. He searched for some time, and, again, he couldn't tell how long. Not that it mattered either. He didn't need sleep to survive. Some areas of the archipelago left him feeling emptier than others, but ultimately, he only seemed to need to breathe to survive. He was too engrossed in his work to worry about that. Too worried about how to keep the horrors of Rykar from the rest of Gaz to care.

---

As Kalia and what she referred to as her Queensguard approached, the tops of the Pelrad of Pelto slowly came into view on the horizon. Their beauty was breathtaking, even from such a distance. She heard some of the soldiers gasp as they saw the city, probably for the first time.

The closer they got, the more Kalia realized that she had no idea what she was going to do. The warriors only followed her because Hilan told them to. For that, Kalia was grateful, but she didn't think the mission would be successful. What, they were going to simply march into the capital of Lopythtym, kill the Lopythlok, and peacefully take over? Well yeah, that was the only option that Kalia saw. Nothing else would work since Ghar wasn't helping anymore.

The Sun was setting, so it was becoming hard to see. About half of her entourage lit torches to help. They only had half of them carry lights in case they were seen; if someone were to count the lights, they would assume there were fewer people than she had with her.

She was still carrying the steel rod from her cell in the royal dungeon. For some reason, she felt attached to it. It made her feel stronger, like she could do anything. Ever since Ghar left, her motivation had been low, so she kept anything that would help her feel better.

As she took another step closer to Pelto, everything felt wrong. An awful power seemed to overwhelm her, suffocating her nyxka. She summoned all of the water around her, but only a few droplets responded to her call. Confused, she looked down at her hands while she tried again and got the same result.

Looking up, she noticed something horrifying. Everyone she had been walking with had just been ripped apart. Blood flowed from their throats, and their lives leaked out onto the grass. Something had slaughtered them in a matter of moments, and she hadn't even seen it happen. She was out of her league with this enemy. She blinked, and a man in black robes stood in front of her. He wasn't very tall, but he exuded enough confidence and power to make himself seem like a large man.

"What the Hel just happened?" she demanded, while water droplets floated around the end of her steel stick. "Who are you?"

"I killed them all," he answered simply. "I am a man who was given a mission, and I am about to complete it." The way he spoke sent a chill down Kalia's spine. His voice was low, almost gravelly, but it still spoke with enough power to make him seem dangerous. "Before I do, tell me this. Who are you, and why are you attacking Pelto?"

"Fine, then. I don't need to know who you are to kill you." She was angry and had no intention of calming herself. Rage had always been a good source of strength for her in combat. Her opponent might be stronger than she was, but she was almost certainly more passionate. Her will to live would protect her.

With a yell, she threw the water droplets in the same way that she cut the steel bars to her prison. Some of them missed while others dug into his skin, drawing blood.

The man sighed. "I was going to let you live. I didn't want to kill if I didn't have to." He seemed incredibly experienced with combat. Her attack hadn't even fazed him. Doubts formed in her mind, telling her that she was going to die. With effort, Kalia forced them out. She needed to believe in herself if she was going to win.

Behind him, a huge, bald man sprinted toward them. The smaller man seemed familiar with him, so Kalia figured they were teammates. Perfect. Just what she needed. She was already going to have trouble with the first one, so why shouldn't he have reinforcements.

"By Gaz," the large man said when he saw the bloodshed. This surprised Kalia. It appeared as if he was afraid of the killing potential of the smaller man in the black robes. This made her question the nature of their relationship. "How long did this take you?"

"Time was slowed for me, so I'm not sure," the other man replied as he glanced around. "No more than a moment or two if I had to guess."

This was too much for Kalia. "You speak of killing my friends and fellow patriots as if it were trivial! YOU ENDED

LIVES! I CANNOT FORGIVE YOU!" she screamed, outraged at the casual nature of their conversation. Sure, she hadn't known the men and women who were tasked with following her very well, but they didn't deserve to die.

The bald man raised an eyebrow. "Want me to handle this, or do you have it?"

"I've got it," the other said calmly. Kalia, on the other hand, was anything but calm. She was full of rage and regret, and she was going to use it to her advantage. This time, when she summoned water, it responded the way she wanted it to. Something had changed, and she was able to break through the barrier that had been stopping her before.

Just as she was about to attack, he became a blur. Kalia didn't know what to think. How was someone this strong? Who was he? Another nobleman? Maybe he was working for Nadren, but if he was this powerful, then why was he not the king? Nothing made sense as she was forced to her knees. He materialized next to her and kneeled, probably to address her. Everything about him unsettled her, and she realized that she had never been more uncomfortable than she was at that moment.

"I'm a member of the Warrior Division of the Nyxtad Collective," he whispered into her ear. "This was a training exercise. I don't even know what you're hoping to gain by invading Pelto."

"So you slaughtered my friends for a training exercise, then." She felt defeated. Suddenly her fire returned. "I'LL KILL YOU FOR WHAT YOU DID!" she screamed. Looking at him, she realized that her threats were empty. This wasn't a man. This was an agent of death. No, this was death itself. Well, at least she had gone out fighting.

"Believe me, I wish you could," he said under his breath as he slit her throat, ending her life.

# PAIN

*Honesty may not take you as far as manipulation can, but it will leave you without regret. Live a genuine life, and you can die knowing you were true to yourself.*
- *Grax Rakdi*

"What is this?" a deep, gravelly voice inquired. Rykar searched through the darkness, hoping to identify where the voice had come from, but he had no luck. It was far too dark to see anything.

"Who are you?" Rykar called out. His body still hurt from all of the walking. He looked down at his chest to confirm that the light was still there, and, to his relief, it was. He wasn't broken yet.

"Strange, I didn't know someone who only has Instinct could be so strong."

"What's happening?" Rykar yelled, hyperventilating as his confusion turned into frustration.

"Did you create a world . . . in your mind?"

"What do you want?!"

"No, this isn't a world . . ."

"WHO THE HEL ARE YOU!?"

"Is this power?"

A mist began to flow around Rykar, and at the center stood a man. He was muscular and tall, and the closer he got the more Rykar could see just how scarred, old, and gray he was. Except, unlike Rykar, his scars weren't signs of weakness or fear. They felt more like strength and experience, signs that it was possible to survive even the toughest trials.

"Ah, I see. This is pain."

Seeing the man turned Rykar's anger back into confusion. Rykar almost thought he recognized the man from somewhere. *Wait,* he thought. *Is this the guy I saved right before I was teleported to the Nyxtad Archipelago?* A better look, and Rykar realized that was the truth. Who was he? Just as he was about to ask, he noticed a sad look forming across the man's face.

"Oh, you poor child . . . This pain, this guilt, what you must have experienced to feel this." With this, the man reached forward and pulled Rykar into an embrace. Rykar felt himself begin to cry. He didn't know he even needed to. The light in his chest grew with each passing moment, and Rykar continued to let his emotions flow with his tears.

"Your strength and endurance are impressive. You never gave up, always pushing forward. Know this, however. Life doesn't have to be full of pain. You can walk without feeling the weight of your past on your shoulders. The light can come back. You don't deserve what you're putting yourself through."

Squeezing tighter, Rykar's soft crying turned into loud sobs. His chest heaved up and down as he collapsed into the stranger's chest. How could he know? Rykar's mask had always been so strong, but having someone pierce through it so easily was almost liberating.

"I'm Theodar, by the way," the man said as he pulled away. "Theodar Vyrtra." With that, he stretched out his hand to Rykar.

Wiping his eyes with one hand, Rykar shook Theodar's hand with the other. Theodar's grip was strong but reassuring. For some odd reason, Rykar felt that he could trust this man.

"What's going on?" Rykar asked after taking a moment to calm himself.

"In your head or the real world?"

"The real world. This stuff, this pain, is insignificant compared to what's happening."

"It isn't insignificant. That's why you can't move past it. If you can't accept your pain, then you'll never be free of it."

Rykar took a moment to think about what Theodar was saying. He wasn't sure that he agreed with the older man. Pain was a construct of the mind, so being able to turn off his mind was the simple solution to his problems. Or so he had thought. When Theodar had hugged him, he felt vulnerable but safe. Freer than he had ever been, but still trapped. Maybe he was wrong about pain?

"Your squad is being attacked," Theodar explained. "I don't know by who, or for what reason. I just know that they're in great danger. They need you."

"Why . . . ?"

"Why what?"

"Why would they need me?"

This question seemed to make Theodar stop and think. His face shifted, creating a sad, confused smile.

"Have you seen how strong you are?" Theodar asked finally. "I've never seen talent or power on par with yours. Honestly. And I've seen a lot of horrific shit. Enough to break some of the strongest men."

"Then you know that strength isn't the problem!" Rykar didn't mean to yell, but he couldn't help himself when he was this emotional. "Control is. I don't want to add to the horrors you've seen. I don't want to be scared of myself anymore."

"What happened wasn't your fault. You did your best but couldn't help the people who needed it. I understand that, truly. Failure can be debilitating. Just think about right now. What do these people mean to you? Can you save them? Can you lose so much again?"

The way Theodar spoke about failure was strange. It was almost as if he knew about Rykar's past, the way he had killed his entire family because he couldn't control his power. How could he know?

"You can save them. If these people mean anything to you, then I know it is within your power to keep them safe. Just go out there and show me what you can do." Just as Rykar was about to go, Theodar pulled him back, giving him a knowing and apologetic look. "Make this a first, and do it for yourself."

---

Rykar shook his head, feeling dazed and confused. Who was Theodar? What had just happened? He expected to feel off, but to his surprise, he found that he now had a motivation to do good, to help his family. Brushing himself off from the fall, he got up and got to searching for the rest of his squad. They needed his help.

---

Rosa had never been the same since Aodal died. When they were dating, she had always been bright and happy. Even before that, she couldn't remember a time when she was unhappy for more than a day or two. Then, when he came into her life, he changed it forever. He was confident, supportive, helpful, and, best of all, he loved Rosa more than anything. She thought they would be together forever, that he would be able to laugh and joke and lend her a shoulder to lean on until their final days together. It broke her heart that she was wrong.

Aodal was strong, stronger than most. He knew how to fight, when to fight, and who to fight for. When Leif mentioned that they would need a few of the members in the squad to go and take out a member of the Ruined, he volunteered immediately. Rosa was proud, and a little scared. In the end, she knew he would be ok; after all, he was always so careful and strong.

So when the group of volunteers came back and Aodal was missing, she couldn't believe it. She couldn't remember feeling anything except shock. At first, she froze, went numb. A few moments later, she knew it wasn't true. They had just forgotten him. He was fine, of course, just like he had always been. A few days passed, and she realized that he was dead. All she remembered after that was intense guilt, regret, and anger. Why the Hel did she have to let him go? It was all her fault that he was dead. She should have cared more for him, and now, since she was too stupid to be a better girlfriend, Aodal, her soulmate, was gone forever.

For a time, she didn't know how long, she didn't want to do anything. She stayed in bed a lot, wishing she could just sleep forever, or maybe even magically cease to exist at one point. It wasn't that she wanted to kill herself; it would just have been easier if she wasn't there to waste so much time doing nothing. Everyone else would have probably had it easier without her.

One day, she was forced to get up, to do something. She couldn't remember who made her get out of bed. She didn't remember what she did, how she did it, or whether or not her will to live had returned at all. All she knew was that their squad was accepting two new members. Two more people to lose. Two more people to force herself not to love, not to care about, because of the possibility that she would one day wake up and see one of their corpses.

Frederick—although he went by Rykar—and Ahren. They both seemed so hopeful. So whole, not broken or beaten down by the realities of life. She remembered when she had their naivety. When she was happy. When she knew how to feel anything but empty.

Her memory wasn't great. Certain things didn't exactly stick. They just sort of blurred together, making it difficult to pick through the information they stored. One of her only clear and distinct memories after the arrival of the newbies was a dinner. Rosa had mistaken Rykar for Aodal. Looking back, she wasn't exactly sure why. Rykar was shorter, stronger, and generally darker than Aodal. Whatever her reasoning was, she ended up cuddling with him and telling him—thinking he was Aodal—that she loved him.

This was when her mind snapped. She started trying to kill herself, but nothing ever actually happened. One night, when she was feeling particularly awful, she climbed to the top of one of the towers with plans to jump. As she got to the top, she got a glimpse of the Moon and stopped. It wasn't even like she wanted to stop; it was just so beautiful that it took her mind off of everything for a second. For the first time in a long time, she let her mind and her emotions wander. She ended up thinking about how much Aodal would have loved the scene. The night sky had always been his favorite. He had once told Rosa that nighttime was too personal to share with anyone, that it was the time for solitude and self-care. Then, one night, he brought her out under the stars and kissed her.

Thinking of that memory nearly broke her. She fell to her knees and began to cry, remembering what it was like to know in her heart that Aodal would always be there for her. At that moment, the death of her soulmate attacked her all over again. She swore she wouldn't let anyone else see her pain. They couldn't be allowed into the only thing she still shared with Aodal.

A few days later, they left for their mission. She didn't know much about the purpose of the operation, just that she didn't care what it was. She didn't care about anything but her memories of Aodal and being alone. That was why when the explosion hit her, ripped into her flesh, tearing her limb from limb, she didn't care. It was doing her a favor. It had made a decision that she never could—the decision to just die. With luck, she would see Aodal playing among the stars.

---

Another explosion shook the forest. Rykar tried not to focus on where it came from, instead trying to listen for the rest of his squad. That was the second explosion that he was aware of. The fact that there had been multiple attacks implied there would be more, so Rykar kept his guard up. Listening as intently as possible, he thought he heard crying, so he turned and ran toward it. Unwilling to slow down time because of the way it affected sound, he pushed his body to the limit without his nyxka. Luckily, he was extremely athletic and in shape from all of his years as a hunter, so navigating the forest quickly wasn't a problem.

As he ran, he thought back on his encounter with Theodar. How had he been able to cut so deeply into Rykar's psyche? Who was Theodar? Just as he was about to leap over a fallen log, he realized something. Theodar, Theo, that couldn't be a coincidence. They had to be the same person. *Why would the enemy help me?* Rykar couldn't understand, but he forced himself to refocus on his reason for running in the first place. He had to get to the rest of the squad to make sure they were safe.

He sprinted for a moment longer, feeling fatigue slip into his body. His throat was growing dry from the heavy breathing, and his legs were feeling heavier with each step. He just had to keep going, to keep searching. He had to show himself that he was good enough to save those he cared about.

Streams, fallen logs, Moonlight shining through the tops of trees—all of it was there, but none of it registered in his mind. Rykar was Hel-bent on finding his team. Finally, after what felt like an eternity, the crying grew louder. The sound of the crunching leaves below his feet no longer felt so lonely.

Hjalmir and Ahren came into view, and Rykar slowed down to a walk. He couldn't tell what was wrong yet, but with the help of his sight, Rykar could tell that Hjalmir was the one crying. His head in his hands, Hjalmir sobbed, his massive shoulders shaking as he kneeled in front of a red splatter.

Ahren wasn't doing anything. He was just frozen in place, eyes wide as he stared down at the smear.

"What's going o—" Rykar asked as he took a step closer, only to realize why they were upset. It was hard to tell, but he was pretty sure they were looking at the remains of Rosa. A few bones and smaller parts of her body were intact, but all in all, she had been destroyed by the blast.

Rykar searched within himself for the right words, but he couldn't find any. He didn't have a moment of clarity like he did with Fryd. Here, lying in a pile of broken bones and blood, was a girl he had never truly known. She was never genuine, never truly herself. Rykar was only sad to have missed the opportunity to meet her.

"I—" Hjalmir began, choking up halfway through his sentence. "I hope you find your love again." With that, he bowed his head and muttered a prayer. Rykar wasn't sure what to do or how he could be of use in the scenario, so he just silently stood next to Ahren.

"The night sky just gained another star," Ahren said softly.

Rykar wasn't about to admit it aloud, but he felt extremely uncomfortable. He didn't know Rosa. He had no attachment to her, no true reason to be sad besides basic human decency. Sure, she seemed all right, but his only real connection to her was that one night where she thought he was some guy named Aodal and the fact that they were on the same squad. Apart from that, she was just another person who came into his life and left quickly after.

Another explosion rocked through the forest. Rykar felt the shockwave in his chest. It almost felt like he were a drum being played by the hands of some cruel, divine creature. Smoke filled his vision as a fire burst through the underbrush. The entire forest was going up in flames, and the whole squad was going to be caught in it.

Slowing down time by speeding up the pace of his thoughts, Rykar began to analyze the situation. Was it the work of Leif? He did have temperature control for his nyxka, so it was possible. The only problem with that train of thought was that there was no reason for Leif to surround the three of them in a fire. No, it was someone else, someone who was not on their side.

Theo, then? No, probably not. He seemed like he cared too much about Rykar to do something so aggressive. It was someone new, someone dangerous. Not only that, but it was likely that there were multiple people. The existence of the unnaturally spreading fire and the explosions led Rykar to believe there were multiple nyxka at play. It was either that or one extremely strong nyxka. Knowing he didn't have enough information to continue down that path, he allowed his mind to slow back down to confer with his teammates.

"What do you guys think is going on?" Rykar asked innocently. He wasn't about to reveal the fact that he was pretty sure he just had a therapy session with the enemy; that wouldn't help anything.

Hjalmir stood up and wiped his eyes, most likely only then coming to terms with what was happening. Ahren seemed like he had been analyzing like Rykar, though, because he was staring intently into the forest.

"There's someone there," Ahren said, pointing to where he was looking.

The wall of flames opened up, and two people appeared as silhouettes in the smoke. So Rykar was right, then: multiple people for multiple nyxka. One of them was able to blow things up, and the other probably had a similar skill to Leif. Now all he had to do was figure out who was who and determine which person was more dangerous.

Just as he was about to travel down that mental road, the figures came into view. At the sight of them, Rykar wasn't sure if he was relieved or breaking. Why here? Why now? Why them?

"Brother, please don't cause any more death and destruction than necessary," Nyral, his dear sister, pleaded from her wheelchair as she rolled toward him, accompanied by none other than Hadrian, the Regional Scholar.

# RAGE AND RESOLVE

*The person who lives a full life is the one who passes on happy with what they've done and where they've gone. Length has nothing to do with it; experience does.*
- *Aervin Eroborn*

According to what Ghar had seen, the Warriors who were staying at HQ at the moment didn't go on very many missions. They had official tasks given to them twice per year, but other than that, they didn't have any real obligations. Most of them didn't do much, spending most of their time lying around, waiting for the next mission. Rykar, however, wasn't like most of his peers. He trained every day, only making Ghar fear him more.

Rykar was slowly getting stronger. The more he practiced, the easier using his nyxka came to him. Unfortunately, his years spent as a hunter had paid off, as his Instincts were incredibly honed. He seemed to have a sixth sense when it came to what he needed to do to survive.

Then, one day, Ghar learned what the Warriors did between missions besides training and lounging. They had enough freedom that they could choose to go on missions for themselves and not for the good of the Collective. This meant that if a Warrior wanted to simply go out and kill someone, no one would stop them.

Ghar knew this because he had decided to take a break from his Knowledge research to better understand Rykar. He had read somewhere that it was wise to know your enemy if you wished to defeat them, so Ghar figured he might as well try to understand Rykar a little bit better. With this in mind, he trailed the hunter for some time. He made sure he didn't get close enough to make him suspicious; that would've ruined everything. No, he stayed just far enough away that he could get glimpses of him, hoping to gain any sort of beneficial information.

He seemed to have a routine, showering in the morning, training during the day with meals mixed in, then stargazing each night. It was almost as if he were dividing his life into the three most important parts: hygiene, fitness, and whatever the night sky meant to him. For some reason, Ghar had a feeling that he had to truly decode the secrets of the night sky to better understand how to defeat Rykar. He had to know his enemy.

Unfortunately, the unassigned missions weren't stored in any database anywhere. This meant that Ghar might have missed something important about Rykar in the time that he was initially planning the Warrior's destruction.

As the thought occurred to him, it began to eat away at Ghar's mind. The idea that he had missed something due to his intense focus was terrifying. He needed to find out what Rykar had done between his arrival and then; everything had to be known before Ghar was satisfied.

Luck was on his side, as the information did exist regardless of whether or not it was manually stored anywhere. Ka storage was truly an amazing thing. The only hurdle he had to overcome was where to read. Once he could get a hold of where Rykar was, he could determine what he had done.

He started in the training area after dark. No one, except for Leopold, used the room after the Sun had set, so he could spend some time reading the data available to him. He found a few things on some of the members. A large, bald guy had secretly made love to a sort of cold, smaller woman. They seemed happy.

For some reason, that reminded him of Kalia. *Why here? Why now?* He couldn't comprehend why he was still thinking of her. She was an inconvenience, and he had gotten rid of her as soon as possible. There was no reason to continue thinking of her. She was probably dead by now. He was almost certain that Nadren had executed her for treason.

Trying to think of anything else, Ghar continued his search for significant places to find out information about Rykar. The other places he frequented were the showers, the beach, his room, and the cafeteria.

The showers didn't reveal much either. When he read the ka in the room, all he got was a lot of naked people and an interesting scene of Rykar getting soap in his eyes, repeatedly. While it was incredibly funny, Ghar didn't think it was going to help him defeat the hunter, so he moved on to some of the other rooms.

He searched throughout the rest of the rooms on his checklist—the beach, the cafeteria, Rykar's quarters—but none of them revealed anything helpful. Fortunately, Ghar was too careful to allow himself to feel satisfied just yet, so he went to one last place.

If Rykar were to have gone on a mission, there was a good chance he would have left from the airport. Just as Ghar realized this, he kicked himself for being so stupid. Why did he waste so much time checking boring places when he should have searched in the place most associated with going on missions? The only problem with the airport was that if he wanted to get any sort of real information, he would have to check each plane until he found something. So, slowly but surely, he got to work.

It became tedious at some point, but Ghar didn't find it boring at all. A lot of ka reading was like any other form of research: you just had to sort through a huge mess of data, hoping to find something useful.

He learned a few things by doing this. The Warriors never had the same squad for more than a year. It was almost inevitable that one of them would die during a mission or by freak accident. Ghar also discovered that there were *a lot* of squads in the Warrior Division. He couldn't figure out exactly how many, just that there were probably well over thirty of them who had used the planes he was reading. Only one squad was allowed to call HQ home at a time.

After a lot of looking, Ghar found what he was searching for. A black jet that almost looked like a crow carried memories of Rykar and the larger man from the training room. As Ghar dug through the information it had, he nearly froze. Why had they gone to Pelto? What was going on?

The more he saw, the less he believed. Rykar had gone to the capital of Lopythtym to stop a rebellion. The very same rebellion Ghar had planned on leading had been stopped by a man who didn't even know he was Ghar's enemy. The irony was hard to ignore. If Ghar believed in him, he would have thought that the Pythrad was trying to tell Rykar something.

It was difficult to see how Rykar handled the rebellion; the plane's ka didn't get a view of what happened after they landed. Having a feeling that he needed to know what had transpired, Ghar took off in a whirlwind of rock and lightning. If he was going to get any more information, he would have to go to Pelto. Perhaps his brother would have some insight.

---

Nadren still didn't quite feel like he was a king—not truly at least. He wasn't sure that he ever would. Ever since he was a small child, he had associated royalty with the name Vyrtra. After all, Drydnar Vyrtra had been a symbol of strength and power. He was essentially the Lopythrad himself, so it felt like all of his ancestors had divine blood as well.

The worst part was that, according to most people, his politics and orders were incredible, yet he still didn't seem like a king in the eyes of the people. They saw him as a substitute. A stand-in for the real king, one of the Vyrtra bloodline. Most people probably didn't even realize that a Vyrtra wasn't in charge anymore. When Nadren ascended, he was astounded to find how little education each of his citizens had.

To remedy this, he made an effort to walk through the streets of the Pelto at least twice a day. He wanted the people to see him—not only as a king but as one of them. Too often, the king was seen as above the rest of the country he ruled. Nadren wanted to prove that he was just another person. The only difference between him and everyone else was that he had the title of King.

As much as he wanted to seem like another in a long line of kings, Nadren knew that he was different from his predecessors. Aside from the lack of genetic connection, he knew that he was much more empathetic than they were. He truly cared about each citizen of Lopythtym, whereas it didn't feel like any of the past monarchs did in the same way. They had set an unfortunate precedent where the king was much more disconnected than Nadren wanted to be.

That day, during his walk, his mind was on the people he grew up around. Most of the other nobles he knew as a child were cold and callous, much like his brother, Ghar. However, that wasn't to say Ghar was like the rest of the nobility, because he wasn't. Ghar didn't concern himself with understanding fickle things like the politics of conversation. He was known to just be flat-out rude and aggressive, making it unsurprising that few people liked him.

On top of that, he was almost scarily ambitious. Nadren always knew that Ghar wanted power; he just wasn't sure how the boy was going to get it. Ghar never showed any interest in his work. All of his life, he had been lazy, relying on whatever raw talent he carried with him. Nadren knew it wasn't going to be enough, that Ghar was going to be crushed by his ambition; he was just surprised to see it happen so soon.

As much as Nadren was sad to see his brother fail, he was also happy that Ghar was not the successor to King Frakt Vyrtra. His intentions for the throne had always been ambiguous, but knowing Ghar, they were less than pure. Nadren knew he had his own biases, but he was still far more comfortable with the throne in his own hands than in the hands of his brother. At least Nadren knew that he wanted power to help rather than to hurt.

Strangely enough, as he walked along, thinking about his dear brother, none other than Ghar Rakdi flew down from the sky. Except this time he wasn't just surrounded by rocks. It looked like lightning bolts were protruding from his body while he was surrounded by a thin veil of flame and stone. What was going on? When had he been able to do something like that?

"Brother," Ghar greeted Nadren as he shook his hand. As Nadren looked down on his younger sibling, he knew that any of the monarchs during the Vyrtra dynasty would have corrected his "brother" to "Your Light," which was why Nadren was not going to do that.

"Ghar, how are things?" Nadren asked, doing his best to mask his confusion.

"I was wondering if you had any information on a recent incident just outside of Pelto."

Nadren took a deep breath. He had forgotten how different it was talking to Ghar than anyone else of noble blood. He was far blunter than Nadren was used to.

"Do you have any more information than that? That's not a lot to go on."

"Nothing is for certain, but I believe it was a small rebellion that was stopped by a few people."

"Oh, yep. I heard about that. I was going to use you for the investigation, but you disappeared, and I had no way of contacting you."

"What can you tell me about it?"

"It was a massacre . . ." Nadren was struggling to talk about it. Hearing about the amount of death had made him incredibly sad. Perhaps he cared too much about the people he governed. "Not a single person survived. Everyone had the same cause of death too. Slit throat. There was blood everywhere."

"Did you identify anyone who was killed?"

"It was mostly the personal guard for someone of House Tyrno, if I remember correctly."

"Why would they want to attack the capital?"

"Now do you see why it would have been convenient for you to have been an investigator for me?" Nadren sighed. "You were always better than me at deduction when you applied yourself. I could have used your skills, and you would have all of your answers. Wait. Where the Hel did you even go?" His usual annoyance with his little brother was slowly returning, and Nadren found that he didn't care if he kept up his composure.

"You know how I've always been searching for power?" The look in his eyes unsettled Nadren. It wasn't necessarily one of passion or love; no, it felt more like a craze. His obsession with power had certainly not been destroyed yet. "Well, I found it. I'm stronger than you, stronger than everyone except for a few people."

"Which people . . . ?"

"The kind of people who massacre a group of guards outside of Pelto," Ghar answered simply as if he had been planning on saying that.

"Where, specifically, did you go?" Nadren asked, more forcefully this time. Ghar was his brother, but saying that he was stronger than the king was still heavily frowned upon in their culture. "And why did you come to me, asking about this event?"

"I can't tell you where I went, but I can tell you this. The man who killed those people, he's as strong as, if not stronger than, Drydnar."

Nadren felt a chill run down his spine. That was almost like saying this mysterious person was a god. Drydnar's myth had been told so often, inflated so much, that many people probably thought he was a god himself.

"How do you know this?"

"It's just a guess," Ghar said, clearly lying. He had always been a terrible liar. It was obvious that he was hiding something, something important, but Nadren wasn't sure what it was.

"You know we didn't execute Kalia, right?" Nadren asked, trying to see if he could show Ghar that they were on the same side. "A few days after you left, she broke out of prison and wasn't seen or heard from for a while."

As Nadren said this, he saw relief wash over Ghar's face. So he *did* care about something other than power.

"Do you know where she is right now?" Ghar asked, trying to hide his eagerness.

Nadren put a hand on his brother's shoulder and gave him the most sincerely apologetic look he could muster.

"I'm sorry, dear brother, but she's dead."

"You just said you didn't kill her!"

"I didn't. She escaped, as I said. The demon man that you told me about killed her."

Ghar's eyes widened with anger, and rocks began to fly around him. Just as Nadren thought that someone was about to get severely injured, Ghar calmed himself back down with a deep breath. It felt too cold, too unnatural, to be sincere. Except, however, Ghar had been able to successfully control the way his emotions impacted his nyxka. As weird as it was to admit, Nadren was impressed with his brother's control.

"May I see the body, to confirm?" Ghar asked, completely absent of any emotion in his tone.

"It's been too long; the body is decomposing. I'm sorry. You'll just have to trust my word."

It didn't seem like Ghar was able to truly accept this, and his face showed it. It practically screamed disapproval. With that, without any warning, Ghar exploded into a ball of rocks, lightning, and fire, and he flew away, leaving just as abruptly as he had arrived.

---

As Ghar flew away, he reflected on his encounter with Nadren. Unfortunately, Nadren hadn't changed much. Even as a king, he was still obtuse and difficult to work with. He seemed more focused on protecting those he cared about than he did about himself, and that was something Ghar could never understand. Nadren was simply too naive for Ghar to relate to anymore.

Not only that, but he was incredibly upset that Kalia had died. If Ghar wanted Kalia dead, fine, but that wasn't Nadren's decision, nor was it Rykar's. She had been loyal to Ghar, not Nadren. Why had Nadren spent most of the conversation acting as if nothing had happened? HE SHOULD HAVE SAID SOMETHING. He *should* have said something. He should have said something . . .

Ghar felt a tear fall down his cheek. He wished it were because of the way the wind blew into his eyes, but deep down, he knew that the tear was for Kalia. As much as he didn't want to admit it, he cared for her. She may have been irritating, emotional, and stubborn, but at least she had been loyal; she had been there. She had been his friend.

Why would Rykar kill her? He couldn't understand what Kalia could have done to make him take her life within a few moments of their meeting. Was Rykar truly that evil? That scarily powerful that anything he didn't like would be subjected to his power and be destroyed? Not on Ghar's watch. As HQ came into view, Ghar realized that to defeat Rykar he couldn't just hurt him physically. He had to take something from him to break his spirit too. Smiling, Ghar understood what he needed to do to win. He was going to take someone from Rykar, the same way Rykar had taken Kalia from him.

# REUNITED

*This world, our only world, is plagued by sickness and fear. Those who suffer from it, who need help, are often told that their suffering is false, creating more struggle. Almost nothing is worse than invalidation. Those who are strong, who can help the weak, choose to push them down instead of picking them up. My only hope is that the strong may one day cure the weak, allowing them to live free lives.*
*-   Naria Frektri*

Rykar was having trouble processing what was before him. Why was Hadrian there? How was Nyral even alive? Nothing made sense, and Rykar felt himself disconnecting from reality more and more as the moments passed.

Nyral rolled toward him, with Hadrian not too far behind. Besides her paralysis, she looked well. She had grown up to be a woman. Rykar had always thought of her as a young girl, so seeing her when she was fifteen was almost surreal. He didn't know what to think. On one hand, he was proud to see who she was, but on another, he hated himself because he knew that he was the one who took her legs.

"Where have you been?" she asked as she stopped herself. "Why did you leave me broken and alone?"

"I couldn't bear to see you when you were in pain," Rykar found himself saying, unable to look her in the eyes.

"I was a child!"

"I know."

"YOU LEFT ME ALONE WITH OUR DEAD PARENTS!"

"I know . . ."

"I can't even walk because of you!"

"Nyral, I know," Rykar said, with tears in his eyes as he found the strength to look at her. "I haven't stopped hating myself for what I did, for everything I failed to do. It's all my fault."

With this, Nyral started to cry. "Why did you do it? Why did you have to hit me?"

Rykar couldn't bring himself to answer her question. There was so much that he wished he could explain to her, but in truth, none of it mattered. All of his reasoning felt empty, like he was searching for an excuse to forgive himself when he didn't deserve forgiveness.

"That day changed everything about me. I remember every detail, every reality-shattering moment as it happened," she spat at him. "I woke up a normal girl, hoping to go exploring with my friends and my big brother. I passed out disabled, holding Mom's hand, wishing she would just open her eyes and kiss me, making all of the pain go away." The look of hatred shifted into sadness as she continued. "How could you put that on me? Do you even know how long I was there, lying with the rotting corpses of Mom and Dad?"

Again, Rykar couldn't find his voice. It was hard to hear what she had to say, but in a way, he was grateful. He often wondered what had happened to Nyral, but he figured she had just died soon after he left. Never would he have guessed that she was strong enough to survive.

"I stayed there for two days . . . Two days in Hel, thinking Mom and Dad would wake up any moment, telling me that I was ok. Do you know the kind of impact that has on a person, let alone someone who is only eight years old? It kills you, it does. My innocence died that day. I buried it when I buried Mom and Dad."

"How did you survive?" Rykar finally asked.

"Is that really what you're asking me right now? It makes it sound like you wish I had died, like that was your intention the whole time. Do you realize that you haven't even said you're sorry? Why did you do that?" The look on her face hurt. Rykar realized that while she was angry, she still had hope that her older brother wasn't a coldhearted killer. She needed to know that her anger had been misplaced the whole time. She wanted her family back, but that was a lie, and Rykar knew it. He couldn't tell Nyral anything but the truth.

"When I lost control, I did it because I was scared that I would lose you. I don't remember anything but pure rage and power when I saw the bear run toward you. And I am sorry, I want you to know that. Truly. I don't know how much my words mean to you, but I have to tell you the truth.

"So, in all honesty, it felt good to let go, to let myself be taken by my rage. Killing the bear was one of the most satisfying things I've ever done. It felt so *good*. Wanna know why? Because I had the power to destroy something that threatened my happiness.

"And then, without realizing it, I hit you. I still remember how it felt." Rykar closed his eyes, feeling the tears flow down his cheeks as he recalled the event. "A snap. I know it broke you, literally, but the instant I felt it, it broke me too. I knew then and still know now that there's nothing I can do to fix it. I hope you can join me in hating me," he finished, whispering the words he had wished he could say for all of those years.

When he opened his eyes, he saw something that turned

his self-loathing into hatred. Hadrian was *smiling*? What the Hel . . . ? What was going on? Pulled back to reality, Rykar was reminded of what was going on. Why were Hadrian and Nyral even there? Had they caused the explosions? Did Nyral help Hadrian kill Rosa?

"Hadrian, why are you here?" Rykar asked, trying to ignore the fact that he was interrupting Nyral's response.

"I wanted to reunite you with your sister," he said, a smile plastered across his face. "Aren't you happy to see her? Isn't it amazing to know that she isn't dead?"

Rykar didn't know how Hadrian had found Nyral, but it certainly didn't feel good. Seeing Nyral had opened a deep cut, one that he wished would just heal. He wanted the pain to go away, and for that to happen, he needed time away from the problem. As much as he hated himself for it, a part of Rykar wished that Nyral had died that day. Everything would have been much simpler.

Suddenly Rykar felt a hand touch his shoulder, and everything stopped. The fire itself was sitting still as if frozen in time. Rykar turned to see who had touched him, and to his surprise, there stood Theodar. Somehow, he had frozen time in a specific radius around them, allowing them to temporarily live in a time between time.

"I know," he said, giving Rykar a sad look. "I know how much it hurts. The first step is the hardest. I hope you see that you had to confront your past at some point. It's good that she's here, able to talk to you. Now you can get closure."

"How can you be sure? How do you know so much?"

"You're not the first person I've seen struggle with something."

"What am I supposed to say, then? She has every right to hate me. Why would I want to make her feel any more pain than she needs to feel?"

"Have you ever considered that she may want to build a relationship with you? That one mistake—which wasn't entirely your fault, might I add—can be forgiven? She is your sister, after all. Don't you want to have a bond again?"

Rykar wasn't sure how to respond. He missed and loved his sister, but she deserved to decide whether or not she wanted him back in her life.

"It's her choice, not mine."

"Do you know what *is* your choice, though?"

"What?"

"The choice to move past your sins. I know it may not seem connected, but rebuilding your relationship with your sister will make you feel better. You have other options besides reconciling your past with Nyral, though."

"I want to overcome this. I don't know if she wants me to, though. What other options do I have?"

Theodar took his hand off of Rykar's shoulder and turned to walk away. Time outside of their bubble was beginning to speed back up. "If all of this goes wrong, come find me. We'll help you control your power."

"We?"

"You'll see."

With that, the normal flow of time returned.

"So, are you happy to see Nyral, then?" Hadrian asked, innocently. For some reason, Rykar felt like the scholar was doing this to hurt him. He was far too Knowledgeable to think that Rykar would have received his sister well.

Just as Rykar was about to respond, he felt himself freeze. It was almost like the opposite of his experience with Theodar. He tried to talk, to move his body, to do *anything*, but literally could not.

"Say something!" Nyral screamed. "Anything! I need to know that you aren't the person who broke me! I want to joke around with you again! Please! Please. Please . . ." Her voice faded away as she began to softly cry.

A second later, the rest of the world froze as well. Or so Rykar had thought. Hadrian walked toward Rykar's immobile body, a wide smirk plastered across his face.

"You live your life assuming that power allows you to

take things. You're mistaken. I'm here to prove to you that your power has limits. It can't change the past." Hadrian stared at Rykar with a crazed look in his eyes. "You took something from me, and now you're going to watch me take something from you."

Hadrian returned to his spot next to Nyral and sped time back up.

"Why won't you answer your sister?" Hadrian asked, maintaining a mask of curiosity.

"Rykar, I'm begging you! Say something! Anything!" Nyral pleaded.

Her crying broke Rykar's heart. He wished he could reply to her, but Hadrian wouldn't let her. The worst part was that he knew he could break out of being frozen in time by using his nyxka enough. He didn't know how he knew he could do it; he just knew. Even if he were to use his nyxka, it would just prove to Nyral that he was still a monster, and she would hate him even more. There was nothing Rykar could do.

"I don't think he's going to say anything, Nyral. I'm sorry."

"No, I don't think he will either," Nyral said as her face hardened. Rykar couldn't deal with the fact that he had failed his sister again and attempted to just completely shut down. It was too much to watch. "Can we go?" Rykar thought he heard his sister ask.

"Yes, I'm sorry that you had to see this. Let's go see what we can do for your legs."

A bright light filled the area, and they were gone.

Rykar fell to the ground and let out a scream.

"No. No. Please come back," Rykar whispered to himself as he beat his fists on the ground. All of his worst nightmares had just come true, and he felt the light inside himself fading.

"What just happened?" Rykar heard behind him. Trying to feel calm, Rykar took a few deep breaths and turned to see who had just spoken. It was only Ahren, who happened to be standing next to Hjalmir. Thank the Pythrad.

"Ahren, you stay here with Ryk. I'm going to try to find the rest of the squad. Don't move." Hjalmir ran into the flames, and Rykar was secretly grateful to be alone with Ahren. Hjalmir was great, but he wasn't Rykar's friend.

"That was my sister," Rykar explained to Ahren.

"Your sister? What's the deal with that?"

"I paralyzed her while I was trying to save her from a bear. As a result, my parents died, so now she hates me."

Instead of looking shocked or angry, Ahren looked sad to hear this.

"I'm sorry, man."

"Do you ever wish that you could change the past?" Rykar asked, with tears in his eyes. He couldn't tell if it was from emotion or the smoke.

"Every day of my life."

"Are you afraid of making more mistakes?"

"Of course, but you can't let fear control you. Just try to listen to your Instincts and do the right thing whenever possible. But why are you asking me this? Didn't your sister just abandon you?"

Strangely, Rykar wasn't thinking about Nyral at that moment. Maybe he was crazy, but it hadn't registered with him that any of that had even happened.

"Well, I think working for the Collective may be a mistake." At this, Ahren gave Rykar a skeptical, worrisome look. "Hear me out. Ever since I arrived, I've had a really weird feeling about this organization. I figured it was just paranoia, but think about it. They never tell anyone anything. A group of people who are supposed to be finding the truth seems comfortable with keeping secrets."

"How does that make us working for them a mistake, though?"

"What are we fighting for? What gives us the right to silence the voices of the people we are told to kill?"

"I—" Ahren paused and thought for a moment. "I don't know."

"We have to stop and question what's happening to us. Is the Nyxtad Collective truly a benevolent organization? Are we fighting the Ruined for the good of the world or on behalf of a small few who wish for vengeance? Because I'm not even sure if they're the bad guys."

"How can you say that? You saw what they did to Rosa! They killed her boyfriend too! These people aren't just your squad members, you know. They're our family."

"Theodar didn't do that. I'm pretty sure Hadrian did."

"Theodar?"

"Theo, whatever, they're the same person. He spoke to me, and he's far too kind and gentle to be the kind of person that just goes out of his way to blow people up."

"How do you know? People can wear masks. You and I should know that better than anyone!"

"Hadrian also arrived just as a ring of fire appeared around us," Rykar explained, doing his best to appear confident. "I have a really bad feeling about him."

"Ok, let's assume you're right. What do you want me to do?"

This gave Rykar pause. In his heart of hearts, he knew he had been deceived. He knew the Collective wasn't an organization founded on good principles. He didn't, however, know exactly what he was going to do with that information.

"Do you want us to go with Theo? To join the Ruined? How do we know they're any better?"

"I don't know. Maybe. We'll have to see. Are you with me, though?"

"Can we talk to the rest of the squad before we make a decision like this? I want them to be here to defend themselves. It's easier to hurl accusations when the person you're accusing isn't even there."

Before Rykar could protest this action, as if on cue, Hjalmir and Leif arrived, accompanied by the rest of the team. Mila, Karl, and Eydis looked worn, the soot covering their faces amplifying the effects of their facial expressions. Hjalmir and

Leif looked tired, but like they were trying to remain stoic and calm in the face of the crisis that had just befallen the team. Ada looked . . . the same as she always did—cold and calculating.

"How is everyone?" Leif asked as they arrived. Nobody responded to his query, making it clear that they were all either ok or too shocked by the battle to be able to answer.

"Ryk has some pretty serious things he would like to talk to you all about," Ahren blurted out. This annoyed Rykar. He wished Ahren would believe him, but it was good that the swordsman wasn't naive enough to trust just anything he heard.

"Why do you all fight for the Collective?" Rykar asked. "Do you even know?" He looked around the group only to find a few looks of uncertainty. Others remained unresponsive, as if they hadn't even heard him ask the question.

"I've started to ask myself that question," he explained. "I think critical thinking is important for a soldier. A moral compass is as well. If we follow evil orders, does that make us evil? How do we know that we're even fighting a good fight?"

"We fight for each other," Leif said finally. "Isn't that enough proof for you? Aren't we enough for you? Has your time with us meant nothing?"

"I'm sorry, but it's not. You guys are great, but I need to know why I'm being asked to kill someone before I feel comfortable doing it. At least from now on. I think Hadrian was the one who killed Rosa, not the Ruined. I've made mistakes in the past, killed people who probably didn't deserve it, but that's going to change."

"How?" Rykar was surprised to hear Ahren asking him this question. It looked like Rykar had captured his interest again.

"I met with Theo, or Theodar, and he helped save me from myself. I can tell when someone is going to be a problem, and I don't believe that he is going to be. I think we're the evil ones, and he's the warrior for justice."

"So what, you want us to defect and join the Ruined with you?" Hjalmir asked. His disappointment was hard for Rykar to handle. He didn't realize how much he respected the older man. His disapproval was painful, but Rykar needed to do this.

"If they'll have us, then maybe." The looks he got for saying this were extremely cold. They didn't believe him when he claimed Hadrian was the killer. Turning away from their looks of betrayal, Rykar called out. "Theodar, take me with you!"

A flash of light filled Rykar's vision, bringing Theodar with it.

"So, you've decided to join me?"

Rykar nodded, trying to avoid the gaze of the rest of his team.

"Go with him, then," Leif said, looking at his feet. "I can't stop you. I won't even try. This is my last favor to you as one of my friends. I hope we don't see each other again, because if we do, know that it will be as enemies." Leif's speech made Rykar sad. His allegiance seemed so flawed, and Leif didn't even know it.

"Anyone else?" Theodar asked.

Seemingly reluctantly, Ahren stepped forward. "I'm coming too, Rykar. I go where you go. I may disagree with your decision, but I need to make sure you don't die, brother." He reached forward and hugged Rykar as he said this. Rykar couldn't tell if he did so because he cared or if he was trying to avoid the gaze of the rest of the team, but for whatever reason, the hug made him feel more cared for than anything he had experienced in a long time.

Theodar reached his long arms around the two of them as they hugged, chuckling to himself. "Are you two ready?" Ahren and Rykar nodded in response, nervous for what was to come. "No need to be nervous," he said, almost as if he could read their minds. "You'll love Hel." Rykar's eyes widened, and suddenly Theodar exploded into a fireball, taking Ahren and Rykar with him.

# CONFRONTATION

*The scariest thing to consider when going into battle is the fact that almost everyone assumes that their actions are morally justified. The evilest, most villainous people see themselves as good. Who is right? Who is wrong? I don't think I'll ever know.*
- *Ahren*

G har could feel everything coming together. It was so satisfying, being able to see his hard work begin to pay off. He knew exactly what he needed to do to beat Rykar; now all he had to do was execute his plans. Then, with another agent of death destroyed, everything would be ok, and he could move on with his life.

Remembering his dive into Rykar's past, Ghar knew that he needed to use one of the people he had seen there. The only person who could still be alive was Nyral, his younger sister. Rykar's parents had died, but Nyral had only suffered from a broken back. Without proper medical treatment or a nyxka, she would have died, but Ghar figured she was something special, like her brother. There was a good chance that she was still alive.

The only problem was finding her. The only thing he knew about her whereabouts was that she and Rykar had grown up on the rise side of Gapythtym. The wildlife in Rykar's memories gave Ghar some more clues, but not enough to give him an exact location. Finding her was going to take time.

As he flew across Gapythtym from set to rise, Ghar thought about how he was going to find her within each village he searched. Clouds raced past his face, relaxing him. He found that it was much easier to think while he was flying, especially under the stars. As his mind analyzed the data, he almost felt himself being pulled toward a specific destination on the horizon.

Nyral would most likely be paralyzed; people didn't walk away from back breaks like that. He was also unaware of naming customs in Gapythtym, but he had never heard of anyone going by the name Nyral before. All he had to do was call out her name and wait to see if anyone without the use of her legs responded.

A village came into view on the horizon, just to the rise of Ghar. He didn't have an exact idea of where to go, so he had just flown to the rise, planning to stop once he had reached the ocean. Luckily, it worked out, and he could even see a few other villages as he got closer to the one he had his eye on.

Landing in a flash of lightning and flames, he saw that practically every citizen of the humble town had their eyes on him. They had probably never seen an educated nyxtad, let alone someone as powerful as Ghar. *This is the closest they'll ever get to seeing a god.*

"Does anyone know a girl by the name of Nyral?" he called out in his most noble-sounding voice. No one responded. They were probably shocked to hear him speak, grateful that he had graced them with his presence. "From what I remember, she shouldn't be able to use her legs," he continued. This got their attention. A few of them perked up, looking like they wanted to respond.

"Oh 'er? Yeah, she comes through every now and again, handin' out medicine an' such," an older man explained. "I din't know 'er name was Nyral, though."

"Does anyone know where she lives?" Ghar asked, hoping to latch on to this lead. The fact that she couldn't walk led him to believe that she lived nearby. He had heard of chairs with wheels being used for older people, but none of the designs that he knew of could travel long distances.

He got no response except for a few head shakes.

"When was the last time she was here, and which direction did she go?"

"She always comes from rise to set," a young woman answered. "You just missed her. Must've came through just before the Sun set."

"Thank you, good people of the Moon. Your service is appreciated. May you be blessed with full stomachs and happy hearts."

The villagers smiled and nodded, showing their appreciation. Each time Ghar visited a group of peasants, he always felt a little bit happier. For some reason, their simple lives and relaxed attitudes always made Ghar feel better about the stresses of his own life. They would never know what real pain and struggle were.

Trying to show off a little bit for the villagers, Ghar covered himself in rocks, lightning, and fire, and took off into the night sky. He was lucky to have found a connection to Nyral so early on in his search. He hoped his good fortune hadn't stopped there and began to search along the road that traveled from set to rise.

Parts of it were covered by a layer of trees, so he wasn't going to be able to scan the whole thing. He hoped he would still be able to see her. After a moment of flying and searching, he realized how lucky he was that it was nighttime. Sure, everything was darker, but that meant that sources of light would stand out. Nyral probably had a lamp of some sort lighting the way. Ghar just had to search for orange-yellow glows on the trail.

"What the Hel . . ." Ghar whispered to himself as he saw one come into view. Why was everything going his way? It was uncomfortable. He wasn't used to having anything handed to him. It shouldn't have been this easy to find her.

He aimed at the light and flew toward it. As he landed, he noticed that something was wrong. A cart was moving, but there was no one moving it. It seemed as if it were being pulled by an invisible horse. Ghar was almost certain that self-driving vehicles hadn't been invented yet, so what was this?

"Is there anyone named Nyral here?" Ghar shouted, hoping that she was somehow connected to the movement of the cart.

As he asked, the vehicle came to a stop. A door opened in the back, and a girl in a wheelchair rolled out. *Click* Her chair seemed to click as she moved, but it didn't seem to bother her at all. It didn't seem to inhibit her movement at all either, as she moved with impressive dexterity for someone in a wheelchair. She had a slightly freckled face, the most beautiful dark hair and blue eyes that Ghar had ever seen, and a look of annoyance that would make any nobleman fall for her instantly.

"That's me," Nyral said. "Why do you ask?"

Ghar was astounded by his luck. Plans never went so well for him. There were times when things felt like they were going exactly as planned, but inevitably something always seemed to go wrong.

"I'm a noble, and I heard of your medicine," Ghar began, improvising his lies as he went. "I was curious if you had anything that could cure chronic fatigue or back pain? Fatigue for my dad, back pain for me," he said as he chuckled.

"Yeah, I can treat that, but you don't need medicine for your injury," she said, reaching for his back. On Instinct, Ghar flinched away from her touch.

"What are you doing?" he asked nervously while still

trying to maintain his cheerful persona.

"I can heal you if you let me touch you," she explained.

So, she had a nyxka, then. Her survival made sense, and Ghar was happy to have had his suspicions confirmed. Except, this time, both of his theories seemed to have been confirmed. With her ability to heal, and her boosted stamina and strength from having a nyxka, she had probably survived the wound easily. His only question was why she hadn't given herself the ability to walk again. Otherwise, everything else added up.

"Ok, that would be great. Thank you," he said, curious to see how it would feel.

She placed her hand on his back, and Ghar felt her energy, her warmth flow through his body. It wasn't exactly like he was getting healed, since he didn't have any injuries. No, it felt more like a revitalization.

"Whoa . . ." Nyral whispered under her breath.

"What?!" Ghar asked, trying to hide his panic. What had she found?

"Are you even human?"

"Yes, I'm a human."

"Ha, well ok. You just don't feel like any other human I've ever treated."

Ghar wasn't sure whether to take that as a compliment or an insult, so he just tried to laugh it off. Regardless of whether or not he felt human, she had made him feel way better. He felt *full* for the first time in a long time, like he could do anything. Satisfied, he began to stargaze for a second. He wanted to relax for a moment before he took Nyral back to HQ with him. Working on his plans was exhausting, so a short break would go a long way.

A shadow moved across the sky. *No!* Ghar thought. Was today the day of their mission? Feeling himself panic, he stared at the plane, hoping it would simply pass over them. He needed more time; he wasn't ready.

Squinting, Ghar thought he could see a few more shadows. Were they jumping out of the plane? *Why here? Why now?* He knew his luck had been too good. He had to adapt, or he wasn't going to get another chance.

"Nyral, listen to me," he said, talking as fast as possible while still retaining clarity. "We're about to be surrounded by some dangerous people. This could get ugly, but just do as I say, and everything will be alright." He was counting on his ability to improvise to save them. It hadn't let him down yet. "Can you do that?"

"I'll listen to you, but how do you know?"

Ghar just pointed up as a loud *THUD* and a "HEL YEAH" broke through the forest.

"Aaaand there they are," Ghar said, smiling sarcastically. Why the Hel did they have to show up then? "Come on, we need to move," he said, walking quickly as he kept an eye on her. To his relief, she was able to move well with her wheelchair. The forest they were in also had little to no roots obstructing her movement. The only problem with it was that it kept clicking.

"Is there any way you can get your wheelchair to be a little quieter?" Ghar whispered to Nyral.

"Don't worry, this is a tactic I've developed for situations like these," she whispered back. "My wheelchair clicks by design, so when people follow me, they follow the clicking. I use these"—she pulled out a bag of beads—"to throw people off. When I throw them, they make an identical sound, causing people to track them instead of me."

Ghar was dumbfounded. That was a really smart plan.

"Did you come up with that all on your own?"

"Yeah. What do you think?"

"You're a genius," was all Ghar could think to say.

"Why, thank you!" Nyral whisper-yelled, beaming as she threw a bead.

They walked for some time, and Nyral periodically threw beads as they went.

Eventually, one of the members of Rykar's squad—Ghar couldn't tell who—started trying to figure out where the clicks were coming from. Ghar could hear their whispering, and he was pretty sure that Nyral could as well.

"That voice, it sounds familiar," Nyral said. "Who are these people?"

"I only know a few of them," Ghar replied, turning his head away from her so she couldn't see his smile. "That man you hear is named Rykar. He is the most dangerous person on this team, which is a kill squad for an unknown organization."

"Wait wait wait . . . Hold on, what was his name again?"

"Rykar. Why? Do you recognize it?"

"Yeah . . ." she said as she threw another bead. *Good, she's having trouble processing this.* "He's my brother."

Ghar had to separate the squad. Enhancing his senses through a large-scale ka reading, he could tell that they were all closely packed together. *Perfect,* he thought. Rykar and Ahren, who had just been talking near him and Nyral, were rushing back toward the rest of the group. As they arrived, Ghar launched his newfound plan into action and caused an explosion where they were standing.

By reading the nearby ka, he could tell that it had killed one of the members of their squad—a smaller female who Ghar had never heard of. The large man that Ghar had seen in his training room vision was kneeling to pay his respects. Ahren walked over as well, standing close to him, but none of that was important. Ghar had to find Rykar and keep tabs on where he was at all times if his plan was going to work.

"What's happening?" Nyral asked. She had finally come to terms with the fact that her brother was there.

"I'm trying to cause a distraction to keep them away from us. Is that ok?" Ghar explained innocently. He wanted to gauge their relationship, although from what he had seen from Rykar, it was likely they didn't have one anymore.

"Yes, that's good."

Ghar turned his attention back to the chaos, only to find Rykar sprinting toward Ahren. In a half-hearted attempt to stop him from reuniting with his peers, Ghar let out another explosion in the opposite direction. He hoped it would disorient Rykar and cause him to turn around, but it had no such effect.

The group took a moment to mourn their fallen friend, so Ghar decided to stop watching them, if only briefly. He wasn't so obsessed with destroying Rykar that he would disrespect the dead. Almost everyone deserved a heartfelt eulogy, and this was hers.

When he was satisfied that enough time had passed, Ghar decided he should make his entrance. Nyral had to confront Rykar for Ghar to get his desired outcome, and this was as good a time as any. He surrounded the group of three men in a wall of fire to build tension in the situation. As Ghar approached, a hole formed in the wall, allowing him and Nyral to pass through. Rykar turned to look at Ghar and only stared with wide eyes.

Rykar was having trouble processing what was before him. He was probably wondering why Ghar, or Hadrian as he knew him to be, was there. He was probably confused as to how his sister was alive. Rykar's incredulity was just so fun to see.

Ghar just had to let Nyral take charge. If his suspicions were correct, she wouldn't be happy to see Rykar; she was probably going to get angry. Ghar followed closely behind her as she rolled forward to confront her older brother.

"Where have you been?" she asked as she stopped herself. "Why did you leave me broken and alone?"

"I couldn't bear to see you when you were in pain," Rykar muttered as he shuffled his feet.

"I was a child!"

"I know."

"YOU LEFT ME ALONE WITH OUR DEAD PARENTS!"

"I know . . ."

"I can't even walk because of you!"

"Nyral, I know," Rykar said, finally looking at his sister. "I haven't stopped hating myself for what I did, for everything I failed to do. It's all my fault."

For some reason, Nyral started to cry. "Why did you do it? Why did you have to hit me? That day changed everything about me. I remember every detail, every reality-shattering moment as it happened," she spat at him. "I woke up a normal girl, hoping to go exploring with my friends and my big brother. I passed out disabled, holding Mom's hand, wishing she would just open her eyes and kiss me, making all of the pain go away." The look of hatred shifted into cold, retired anger as she continued. "How could you put that on me? Do you even know how long I was there, lying with the rotting corpses of Mom and Dad?"

Again, Rykar wouldn't respond.

"I stayed there for two days . . . Two days in Hel, thinking Mom and Dad would wake up any moment, telling me that I was ok. Do you know the kind of impact that has on a person, let alone someone who is only eight years old? It kills you, it does. My innocence died that day. I buried it when I buried Mom and Dad."

"How did you survive?" Rykar replied, finally able to say something, anything to his sister. Ghar couldn't believe anyone liked him. What he was hearing from the man's sister was pure hatred, yet he thought he deserved love? He really was a fool.

"Is that really what you're asking me right now? It makes it sound like you wish I had died; like that was your intention the whole time. Do you realize that you haven't even said you're sorry? Why did you do that?"

"When I lost control, I did it because I was scared that I would lose you. I don't remember anything but pure rage and power when I saw the bear run toward you. And I am sorry, I want you to know that. Truly. I don't know how much my words mean to you, but I have to tell you the truth.

"So, in all honesty, it felt good to let go, to let myself be taken by my rage. Killing the bear was one of the most satisfying things I've ever done. It felt so *good*. Wanna know why? Because I had the power to destroy something that threatened my happiness.

"And then, without realizing it, I hit you. I still remember how it felt. A snap. I know it broke you, literally, but the instant I felt it, it broke me too. I knew then and still know now that there's nothing I can do to fix it. I hope you can join me in hating me," he finished, whispering the words instead of approaching his problems confidently.

It was hard to listen to their conversation, to hear how much Nyral had been wronged by Rykar, but Ghar knew he needed to hear it. It was good to have his plans and ideas validated.

"Hadrian, why are you here?" Rykar asked, satisfyingly ignorant of who Ghar was.

"I wanted to reunite you with your sister. Aren't you happy to see her? Isn't it amazing to know that she isn't dead?" Instead of saying anything, Ghar noticed Rykar shift positions suddenly. One moment one of his hands was on his head, the next it was back at his side. It was almost as if he had completely moved independently of the normal flow of time. Thinking about that gave Ghar an idea.

"So, are you happy to see Nyral, then?" Ghar asked again.

Ghar noticed that Rykar was about to respond, probably with something just as incriminating as his last speeches, but Ghar decided to freeze his body in time. All he had to do was think about his body as a type of math equation—a parametric, to be specific—and just keep the time value constant. It was quite easy. He had to make sure the brain, eyes, and ears worked, however. Rykar had to witness what was happening if Ghar was to be successful.

"Say something!" Nyral screamed. "Anything! I need to know that you aren't the person who broke me! I want to joke around with you again! Please! Please. Please . . ." Her voice faded away as she began to softly cry.

Ghar realized that he had a lot of things he needed to say to Rykar as well. He had been hurt by the man too; Nyral wasn't the only one. The only problem was he didn't want Nyral to know that he had any connection to Rykar. She couldn't know that Ghar hated her brother, or she might end up hating him too. He had to keep his secrets a secret, so he decided to see if he could stop time for everyone and everything his ka was touching. He did the same thing that he did to Rykar, but throughout his entire ka, and was surprised to find that it had the exact effect that he wanted. *Good,* he thought as he walked toward Rykar, happy that he was going to have the opportunity to say the things he wanted to say.

"You live your life assuming that power allows you to take things. You're mistaken. I'm here to prove to you that your power has limits. It can't change the past," Ghar said with a sad smile on his face. "You took something from me, and now you're going to watch me take something from you."

Ghar returned to his spot next to Nyral and allowed time to revert to normal for everything except Rykar. He would just have to remain a spectator for a little while longer.

"Why won't you answer your sister?" Ghar asked, trying to seem genuinely curious and caring.

"Rykar, I'm begging you! Say something! Anything!" Nyral begged, in tears.

"I don't think he's going to say anything, Nyral. I'm sorry," Ghar explained with a sad tone to his voice.

"No, I don't think he will either," Nyral said as her face hardened. "Can we go?"

"Yes, I'm sorry that you had to see this. Let's go see what we can do for your legs."

Ghar teleported them away in a flash of light, unsatisfied with the way that had ended. Sure, he had beaten Rykar, but it wasn't permanent, and he knew it. The hunter was still powerful, if only a little bit more broken now. Curious to see how the confrontation had impacted him, Ghar watched the event via ka reading. Maybe Rykar was too broken to fight anymore. Who knew?

Strangely, from what Ghar could tell, Rykar hadn't been affected at all by what his sister had said. The things he was

314

saying had nothing to do with her, so Ghar gave him some time. An inability to truly process a traumatic event wasn't uncommon. Rykar's brain probably wasn't letting him accept that any of that had even happened, the same way it numbed an arm or a leg after it had been broken.

Then Rykar called out. Ghar didn't have a good enough connection to know exactly what he said, but it sounded something like "Theodar." *Theodar? Theodar Vyrtra? No!* Ghar couldn't believe what he was hearing. Rykar could never be allowed to connect with the Vyrtra. It was just far too dangerous.

A man appeared, probably Theodar, and Ahren went to join them. They all embraced in a hug and looked like they were talking, but Ghar couldn't make out any of it. It was just too quiet.

Panicking, Ghar teleported back to hear what they were saying. He *needed* to know what was going on. All he heard was "You'll love Hel" before his dreams were shattered, and he watched the most dangerous person on Gaz go to team up with the most dangerous person in the universe.

# THE GATES OF KITYM

*When someone has had everything stripped from them, their pride, their loved ones, their belongings, and their freedom, it should not be a surprise when they prioritize self-preservation over all else.*

- *The Freer of Fools*

R ykar blinked, trying to let his eyes adjust to the flash of light. Theodar's teleportation felt much different from his own, almost as if they were slingshot instead of transported immediately. As his eyes readjusted to normal levels, some of the disorientation faded, and Rykar could see where he was.

It looked like he was in a dome, surrounded by a bunch of broken and decrepit people lying on the ground. The more his vision adjusted, the better Rykar could see that the dome was made of stone with archways holding it up while also acting as entrances and exits to an outside world.

"Where are we?" Rykar heard from behind him. He turned to see who it was, relieved to find Ahren in the alien environment.

"I'm not sure," Rykar said, giving the area another scan. "Maybe we can ask someone?"

"I don't know about that," Ahren leaned in to whisper. "They seem like they might not be much help."

As unfortunate as it was, Ahren had a point. The only discernible noises were various groans and snores. No one was talking or moving at all. It was almost as if they were simply awaiting their deaths.

"Let's go see what's outside," Rykar said, louder this time. "We might get some answers from the geology. How good is your geography?" As he proposed the idea, he could've sworn that an old man nearby snickered. It was probably just his imagination.

"It's not great, but let's check anyway. Some information is better than none."

They navigated through the mess of bodies—no, people—to get to the edge of the dome. Strangely, it looked like they were teleported to the exact center of the area, which had an apparent lack of people. It was the only place in the whole dome where people weren't lying.

As they got to the edge of the covering, Rykar got a view of the outside world. The landscape was covered in fire and some liquid that almost looked like a weird combination of flames and water. The rocks were bright-red and black, and the sky was an orange-red hue.

"Why don't you guys just leave?" Rykar asked to no one in particular as he stepped out of the dome and immediately erupted into flames.

Panicking, he dove back under the dome and rolled around to put the fire out. Luckily it worked, and as his adrenaline rush faded, he thought he could hear something coming from the broken people. Wait, was that . . . was that laughter?

"Every time!" one of the women yelled. "It gets funnier

every time!"

"What does?" Rykar asked indignantly.

"Each time Pythti sends another person to us, they always think they can be the first to just leave," a man explained. "It's pretty fuckin' funny."

"It's almost like a rite of passage at this point," the original woman added.

"Pythti didn't send us. He sent you?" Ahren asked. "Where even are we?"

This got a few gasps of shock. No one seemed to be able to comprehend the fact that they had been sent by Theodar instead of Pythti. It was extremely abnormal. That reminded Rykar, where was Theodar? He had teleported with them, so why wasn't he in the dome as well? Everything was so confusing, and all Rykar wanted was the whole picture.

"We're in Hel!" one of them screamed, laughing hysterically.

"This place will break you. It's a matter of when, not if," the woman who had been answering added. "Most choose to live out their last days in silent memory of their loved ones and their lives. When your mind goes, we will throw you into the wasteland to burn away with the rocks that cover this damned planet."

"Wait, we can't die otherwise?" Rykar asked.

"Something about this place will keep you alive with ka alone. Too much strenuous activity can cause you to go hungry or die of thirst, but if you just sit still, you can't die. It's surprising how easily the mind breaks when the body cannot," the woman explained, becoming incredibly helpful.

"You can't win, can't go back to the way things were," she continued, standing up to face them. Her dirty-blonde hair, green eyes, and partially freckled face were all embarrassingly attractive to Rykar. The way she spoke, she sounded as if she were much older, but didn't look a day over twenty. "I know that look. You think you'll be different, think you'll be able to make it halfway across the planet to the blessed city of Sigto, but you can't."

Rykar stood tall, smiling through the deeply rooted pain of all that had just happened. "For too long, I've struggled with who I am and what I'm meant to be," he announced for everyone to hear. "I have lost so much, hurt so many, only to find myself here, hopefully for a reason. I swear to you, to all of you, that I will bring you to this city that you speak of."

# END OF PART III

# EPILOGUE

"How has Sigto been?" Theodar asked his father. They were sitting on a balcony that overlooked the grand city of water. Theodar had been to many places across the universe, and none made him feel the way Sigto did.

"I spoke to the Radka," Drydnar responded as he stared blankly to the horizon, not acknowledging Theodar's question. "They're either angry or indifferent. Hard to tell with them."

This was a shock to Theodar. "What did you talk to them about?" he asked while trying to remain calm.

"I wanted to know if they would support me upon my return to Gaz." The way Drydnar spoke so casually about talking to actual gods was unnerving. It was almost as if he thought of himself as their equal. Theodar wouldn't have been surprised to find that that was the case.

"And they won't?"

"No one seemed to have a problem until that piece of shit cat said something," Drydnar growled. He was probably referring to Klidar, the Lion Radka. The cat hated Drydnar and his ambitions. Only Drydnar would argue with one of the Radka and then proceed to insult it.

"Have you retrieved the Hrithak? We need to attack soon," Drydnar asked, probably trying to shift the subject of conversation. "Aervin has been in power for too long."

"The Hrithak is still on Gaz. I apologize. My mission did not go as planned. I believe he has discovered Knowledge and has chosen to side with Aervin."

Drydnar turned and stared into Theodar's eyes. The way one of his looks could pierce a soul was incredible and scary at the same time. Theodar knew he was being picked apart by his father but had become accustomed to the feeling a long time ago.

"What have you brought me then, if not the Hrithak?"

"A boy, broken and alone, waiting to be molded into a man. His power is extraordinary. I believe he could easily kill the Hrithak if he needed to."

"Where is he?"

"He just passed into the Gates of Kitym."

"Why was he not transported directly to Sigto?"

"I needed to see something first."

"If he was as strong as you thought?"

"Yes."

"Well, he needs to arrive quickly, if he is. With the Ruined, I have some decent lieutenants, but my plans require more power. The Hrithak was supposed to fill that role, but he is no longer reliable, as you've said."

"I hope he arrives soon, Father."

Suddenly the look on Drydnar's face shifted from ponderous to serious, almost scared.

"Without the help of the Radka, this battle is not even. We have me, the Ruined, this new kid, and whatever is left of the Dead Army. Aervin has the Hrithak, the Grathyk, the Pactri, and the entirety of the Warrior Division at his disposal. There are even rumors that one of the Pactri is stronger than I am. We must be careful. As we fight for the freedom of not only our people but the people of Gaz, we must remember to practice caution. If the Radka or the Tirtan interfere with us, then we won't just fail, Theodar." His eyes burned with a fear and a passion that Theodar had never seen before. Its intensity was enough to make him want to follow his father to the end, even if death was inevitable. "We'll be *annihilated*."